The
Fae King's
Prize

JAMIE SCHLOSSER

THE FAE KING'S PRIZE

Copyright © 2021 Jamie Schlosser
All rights reserved.

This novel is for your enjoyment only and may not be reproduced, distributed, or transmitted without permission from the author except for brief quotations in a book review. Please do not participate in or encourage piracy of copyrighted materials in violation of the author's rights. Purchase only authorized editions.

This novel is a work of fiction. All names, characters, places, and events are a product of the author's imagination. Any resemblance to actual people, living or dead, or to locations or incidents are coincidental.

Due to language and sexual content, this book is intended for readers 18 and older.

Cover design: Book Cover Kingdom
Photographer: Golden Czermak at FuriousFotog
Model: Joey Berry
Formatting: Champagne Book Design
Editing: Amy Q Editing
Proofreading: Deaton Author Services

To Stacey, who makes the inside of my books beautiful.

PROLOGUE

Seven Years Old
Zander

"Stop. Please," I whisper through dry, cracked lips, but the effort it takes to beg only makes the pain worse.

I'm burning. It feels like my whole body is on fire. Heat spreads through me with every breath I take, and I think I'm ready to die. I just can't stand this any longer.

Another flame shoots up my spine, and I jerk on the hard marble floor.

Hoping the cool tiles will at least lend relief to my burning face, I press my cheek to the smooth surface.

It's useless. Nothing helps.

Unbelievable pressure builds in my forearm until it snaps in two. It hurts so bad I can't help crying out, and I don't get time to catch my breath before more bones are breaking.

My. Bones. Are. Breaking.

Every single one of them.

Surely, the end is near. I welcome it, but instead of peace, I experience fury. Rage for how unfair life is. Anguish over leaving my mother behind.

I can hear her weeping in the far corner of the room. She's

been chained there ever since she tried to stop my father from letting the wizard do a spell on me. I didn't understand all the words the magical fae man said as he sprinkled dust over every inch of my naked body. I've been slacking on my Old Fae language studies, however, I did catch *strength*, *pain*, and *king*.

I don't know how long ago that was. Minutes? Days?

At first, I thought my father was trying to restore my sight. Because of a war between the Day and Night realms, a coven of powerful witches cast a blindness curse on all the firstborn children of the royals last year. The only way I'll ever break the curse is if I find my fated mate.

But I'm dying, so that'll never happen.

Will it be dark after I die?

I'm scared of the dark. I had always felt so lucky to be born in a realm where the suns shine all the time, but then everything went black just before my sixth birthday, and I haven't seen a speck of light since.

Not being able to see makes everything feel like so much *more*. Including pain.

A surge of heat whips through my skull, and I scream. Loud.

My skull splits, the trembling plates separating.

I try to crawl forward, but I can't get my fingers to grasp anything. Slapping the floor, I realize I have no control over my hand. It keeps slipping as if my arm is made of jelly.

"Por favor," my mother begs.

There's a crack and a yelp. Father hit her again.

"I told you to stop using that language," he tells her sternly. "You live here now. You'll speak as we do."

"P-please," she tries again, her Portuguese accent thicker than usual because she's upset.

"The wizard said the first transformation is the worst," Father mutters, irritated. "It's not uncommon for it to take a couple days."

"It's been three days," she cries. "It's killing him. You're killing our son."

"I'm making him stronger."

"He's fine the way he is."

"He's blind, and he has no power!" Father roars. "No one in the royal line has ever lacked fae ability. Until now. Because of you."

"I gave you a child," Mother says with defiance. "Is that not enough?"

"No, it's not." His voice is calm now, but I'm not fooled. His temper is still boiling, just like the blood in my veins. "He's too… human. But I'm fixing it. Zander will be the pride of the kingdom soon."

"If we're not good enough for you, then send us back."

Don't, Mother.

I want to tell her not to say such things. It makes Father so mad. He might hurt her again.

He can't stand to hear her talk about her home—the place she was taken from. She tells me in secret. At night, when it's just the two of us, she speaks of a place called Brazil. She describes the cattle farm she grew up on and something called a jungle. It sounds magical.

I'm sad I'll never get to see it.

Father's footsteps march toward her, and even though I can barely move, I do what I always do when he goes after her—distract him.

I yell, but a sound I don't recognize comes from my throat. It's a squawk and a screech.

Silence falls.

Father's boots stop their stomping. Mother's chains no longer clink and jingle.

It's too quiet.

Suddenly, there's light. I blink as blurry objects appear. Within seconds, the room sharpens.

I see the marble columns decorating the tall walls of my bedroom. The yellow comforter on my bed. Mother's tear-streaked face and her bloodied wrists from the iron shackles.

My father did it. He brought my sight back.

Was it worth it? I'm not sure yet.

The pain and fire have lessened, becoming a dull ache all over my body. Hot blood pumps from my heart, but it's not unpleasant to feel the rush of heat through my veins.

Rolling to my back, I try to sit up. I still don't have very good control of my arms. My hand slips against the floor again, and I end up sprawled out on my side.

"What did you do to him?" Mother questions, horrified. "What did you do to my baby?"

"The wizard said he would be powerful." Father sounds just as stunned. "*Strike* it all. That bastard tricked me."

I wince as the cursed word zaps my mother's hand, and I wait for the shock to come to me, too. But it doesn't.

Mother is sobbing now. "Will he change back?"

Change back? Change back from what?

"I… don't know."

Something I know about the Day king—he doesn't like to admit he's made a mistake and he never says he's sorry. So the uncertainty I catch in his voice isn't reassuring.

Flailing, I finally get up onto all fours, bracing myself on my hands and knees.

Only, something isn't right. My arms are out at my sides, so what's holding me up?

When I look down, I see long talons on deformed feet. Then I lower my head to look behind me and realize I have the legs of an animal. My feet are furry paws. To my side, there are large black feathered wings spanning out where my arms should be. They're like the wings I usually have, only much bigger.

That's why I couldn't use my hands. Why they kept slipping.

They're just feathers now.

Waddling, I make my way over to the oval standing mirror, and another squawk escapes from my throat when I see my reflection.

I don't recognize the creature looking back at me.

I have a beak instead of a face. A white feathered head changes to smooth brown fur on my body. A tail whips behind me, the brown tuft on the end restlessly hitting the floor.

The only part of me that's the same is my eyes. They glow back at me like two gold coins reflecting candlelight.

I'm terrifying.

"Strike you!" Mother shouts forcefully at my father. "*Strike you to the depths of hell!*"

A pop ignites against my father's cheek and another quickly follows. Again, I wait for the cursed word to spark against me, but it doesn't. Maybe it can't get to me when I'm in this form.

I could change back. Somehow, I know this to be true. But I also think it will hurt, and I'm not ready to go through the pain again.

I'll stay like this for a while.

Once Father has recovered from the electric shocks Mother gave him, he turns his anger to her and raises his fist. Before he can punch her, I'm skidding across the floor, my talons and claws leaving deep grooves in the marble as I slide between them.

As soon as I'm shielding Mother, I snap my teeth at my father's hand.

No, not my teeth—my beak.

He rears back, fear flashing in his golden eyes as he cradles his arm to his chest. He almost lost a finger just then. I'm sorry I missed. I wouldn't mind feeling the crunch of his bone and tasting his coppery blood—payback for the way he's mistreated my mother and me.

My movements feel unnatural as I crouch down, staring at my father while I make myself comfortable as Mother's guardian. Even though I'm sitting, I'm as tall as him. Strength flows through my big body, and now that I can see, I recognize the expression on his face.

Regret.

Not because he feels bad about what he did to me, but because I'm dangerous. He's scared of me.

"By the suns, what has become of you?" His tone is full of disgust.

And I know the answer to his question.

A monster. He turned me into a monster.

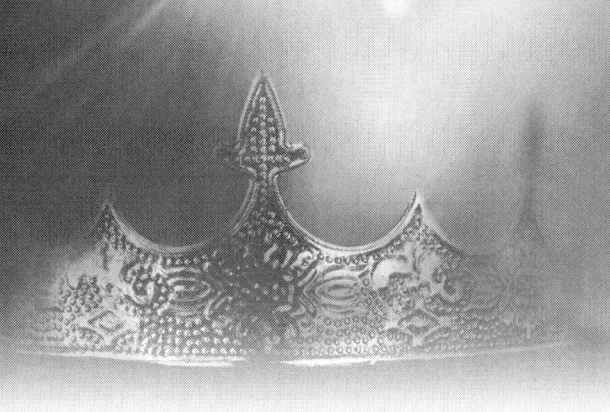

CHAPTER 1

Present Day
Maelyn

THE COVERED WAGON STOPS WITH A JOLT, AND whimpers and cries sound all around me. I can't seem to make a peep. Fear has left me frozen and mute.

The girl to my left starts sobbing again, and someone else starts praying in Spanish.

I want to cry and pray, too, but even silent tears would make me all snotty, and I already feel like I'm suffocating with this burlap sack against my face. The scratchy fabric is full of tiny holes for breathability, but it's still unbelievably hot and it stinks in here. I'm not sure if it's the bag over my head that smells or the wagon itself.

My cell phone and purse are missing. Even though my wrists are bound in front of me, limiting my range of motion, I've done my best to search my pockets and the area where I'm seated. I have nothing.

Worst of all, my glasses are gone. They must've fallen off in the scuffle.

As I rack my foggy brain for the last thing I remember, all my parents' warnings about walking to my car alone in dark parking lots come back to haunt me.

I recall the flickering streetlamp, the stillness of early morning before sunrise, and the quiet crunch of my sneakers on the gravel with each step. Out of nowhere, there was an arm around my neck, a body pressed against my back, and a cloth shoved over my nose and mouth.

Then, just darkness.

I'd been visiting my roommate at her work. Paige is always hungry halfway through her shift, and since I'm an early riser, I do what any good best friend does—I occasionally bring her breakfast. Paige dances at a strip club. Although it's in a bad area of town, they have good bouncers. One of the guys usually escorts the girls to their cars when they leave, and even though I don't work there, they do the same for me.

Except for last night. They were short staffed, and I just wanted to get back to my apartment. So, instead of waiting, I told them not to worry about it.

Big mistake.

Next thing I knew, I woke up here.

Since then, I estimate we've been riding for about an hour. At least, I think we have. The journey has been bumpy and slow, and time passes differently when you're fairly positive you're going to die.

Suddenly, someone opens the back doors, and bright light replaces the darkness I've gotten used to.

Time's up.

As the sunlight filters through the burlap sack, I try to see through the meshy material. There's an outline of a man—a bulky shadow—but that's all I can tell.

Chains rattle, and there are more frightened cries as the man starts ushering girls out. Or dragging, in some cases. A couple of the girls are fighting him. It seems like a good idea until I hear a dull slap and a thud.

"Get up," the man snarls. "We can do this the easy way or the hard way."

Easy. I'll choose that any day.

Some might call me a coward, but I've never been hit before, and I don't want to find out what it feels like.

I'm not tough. No part of me has ever been broken. Not a bone. Not my heart. Never even had a cavity.

I've lived a good life, and while I appreciate that, it didn't prepare me for harsh conditions.

I have zero tolerance for pain.

To sum it up, I'm a wimp.

Considering my occupation, I feel like I should have a better backbone. I should be stronger. Because what kind of person counsels abused women, convincing them that leaving their violent partners was the right move, when all along I know I might not be so brave?

I'd always suspected if there were a contest for the best kidnapping victim, I'd lose. Or maybe I'd win. I guess it depends on what the end goal is—escaping at all costs, or just being compliant and doing whatever it takes to *not* piss the captor off.

Whenever I've seen news stories about missing women found years after their disappearance, and no one can understand why they didn't try to get away sooner… I get it. I do. Same goes for women trapped in bad relationships. I can't blame them. The promise of pain would keep me in line, too. I can barely watch TV shows with torture scenes. If it were me in that situation, I'd cave and blubber and beg at the first threat of torment.

My parents used to say I was the perfect kid. I was obedient to a fault. I never had a rebellious streak, even during adolescence. Instead of making my own mistakes, I learned from others. I've lived my life carefully, too scared to let personal experience be my teacher.

Until last night.

One bad judgement call, and here I am.

Abducted.

Since all the captives are tied together like preschoolers on a walk to the park, the rope around my wrists cuts into my skin when the person ahead of me is jerked forward.

The chafing is almost too much. My fingers tingle from lack of circulation. Sweat trickles down my temple, sliding down the side of my flushed face as I shuffle toward the light. Even though I'm cooperating, the man roughly yanks at my rope, causing it to tighten further.

A whine finally escapes as I fall to my knees. The wooden boards of the wagon are unforgiving, leaving bruises on my legs.

As the pain radiates through my body, I crawl forward the rest of the way, until my hands find the ledge. I don't want to tumble out headfirst, so I gingerly swing my legs over and make sure my tennis shoes land on the ground before I slide my butt off the wagon.

And speaking of that. Who uses wagons and horses for travel these days?

Once I get a few feet away from the guy, I finally find my voice and whisper to a fellow captee in front of me, "Hey, do you know what's going on?"

"I have an idea," she replies, her voice accented. Irish or English? "I'm Sasha."

"Maelyn."

"Are you human?"

Huh? "I'm sorry, what did you just ask me?"

"No talking," a gravelly voice barks. "Everyone out."

The last few women do as he says. In total, I've counted ten of us. I think.

With these numbers, this has to be some sort of sex trafficking thing. Or a sex cult. Why else would someone round up a bunch of girls and throw bags over our heads so we can't see where we're going?

And isn't that just a kick in the teeth? I've spent a good part of my life guarding my virginity as though it's something special. The couple guys I've dated had a reputation of sleeping around, and I refused to be another notch on their bedposts. Sure, they'd sweet talked their way into a couple of dates, but my suspicions about what they really wanted from me were confirmed when they broke up with me for not putting out.

I even avoided partying and drinking in the past, because I was too afraid I'd be less picky if I was intoxicated.

Now I might end up being raped.

Bile rises in my throat, but I swallow it down. Being trapped inside this sack with vomit all over my face is the last thing I need.

"Single file line," our kidnapper orders, walking from person to person.

From his jerky motions, it seems like he's checking our bindings.

When he gets to Sasha, she hisses with pain.

"You don't have to be rough about it," I say, keeping my voice soft and placating. "We're doing what you want. There's no point in hurting her."

The man just chuckles. I flinch as he moves on to me, anticipating his fist. Instead, his hands go to my wrists. If I thought the knots were tight before, I was mistaken. He tugs, and I swear I feel my blood soaking the rope as the fibers cut into my skin.

Once we're all secured, someone new pulls us from the front, forcing us to walk.

Being in the sun makes me impossibly hotter. I thought it would be better out in the open, but there's barely any breeze, and the sun beats down relentlessly. Maybe that heatwave we're supposed to get came a couple days early.

At least I'm wearing a tank top. When I make out fuzzy outlines of the other girls, I see a couple of them wearing long dresses, including Sasha. They've got to be burning up.

As I put one foot in front of the other, panic and resignation war with each other. I don't know what to do.

Scream or stay quiet? Fight or go along with everything?

Not like I have much of a choice.

If I yell, I'll probably just end up getting punched. And even if I could get away, I wouldn't make it very far with my hands tied up. Not to mention, I don't know where we are.

We can't be far from Dallas. If we were moseying along in a freaking horse and buggy the whole time, we couldn't have gotten out of Texas.

Obviously, we're in the middle of nowhere. But are we north or south of my home?

I tune into my other senses. Overgrown grass is soft under my feet. There's a lack of sound. I hear the far-off rustling of leaves and some birds twittering, but there are no cars driving by. I don't smell anything from the city—no asphalt or exhaust.

It feels like we walk for hours before I hear anything different, and when I realize what it is, hope erupts in my chest.

Talking. The murmur of a crowd. A big one.

Up ahead, I make out a dark blob against the expanse of green. There's movement, like people are milling about.

Oh, thank God.

They'll see us, and someone will call the police.

Noise from the gathering grows louder as we get closer. I keep waiting for someone to shout at these men. To tell them to let us go.

Then I see the shape of something large, rectangular, and about six feet high looming in front of us. A stage? When we come to a stop right next to it, my hope withers.

There are no calls for help. In fact, it's the opposite. Instead of sounding alarmed, the people all chatter in excited tones.

A sinking feeling weighs in my gut. My heartrate picks up.

"All right, ladies," our leader greets us jovially, as if we're here of our own free will. "Up the stairs. Careful now. If you bust your face, we're going to have issues. Speaking of that, Tarik, you're going to pay for the merchandise you damaged."

"It was a tap," he defends.

"If her face is bleeding or bruised, you'll pay. Those are the rules."

They grumble at each other a little more, but I don't hear the words because my thoughts are stuck on one word in particular.

Merchandise.

Motherfucking shit bags, I was right. We are so fucked. I rarely cuss—I usually keep it pretty PG, even in my mind. Early on, I adopted my dad's habit of using silly exclamations instead of swear words. But dagnabbit and geeminy criminy aren't going to cut it under the current circumstances.

So, so fucked.

Fear kicks into overdrive, and I start envisioning ways to get out of this: Bide my time. Lull my captor into a false sense of security by being docile and compliant. Allow my body to be abused but always keep my mind protected.

I might be traumatized if I get away but surviving with some damage is better than living in a literal hell.

Maybe I was wrong about myself. You never know how you're going to react to a life-threatening situation until you're in it, and maybe I do have it in me to fight. Because I can't be someone's sex toy for the rest of my life.

There's collective trembling from all of us as the first girl in line moves up. I feel it vibrating through the rope. When I get to the stairs, my eyes start to sting as I place my foot on the first step. I don't think I can hold back the tears much longer.

I'm almost to the top of the platform when the toe of my tennis shoe catches on a ledge. I fall, and pain explodes along my right shin.

Damn my uneven feet. About sixty percent of people have different sized feet, though for most it's usually not extreme enough to be noticeable. My right foot is a full size smaller than my left, and it causes me to be clumsy.

Murmurs and gasps come from the onlookers, and for a second, I think about staying down. I could pretend to pass out. No one would have much use for an unconscious girl. Or, on second thought, would they?

I really might throw up.

Someone starts tugging me up from the elbow, and the touch is gentle.

"Come on," Sasha encourages. "Look strong. It's better that way."

Her kindness gives me the encouragement I need to stand. My leg throbs, but I try not to limp as we all move along until a man tells us to stop.

"Thank you," I whisper to my right.

"You're welcome." Her quiet response is almost lost in the rumble of the crowd, but she sways closer. "I need you to listen to me. We're at an auction. It's important that you make yourself seem as appealing as possible. Show that you're smart, but not too smart. If you have a talent or special skills, make it known."

A shuddering breath leaves me. "Why? What does it matter?"

"Best case scenario is for someone to choose you as a companion. At least you'll have a chance at being treated well. Make eye contact with the single men. Do not look at the married couples. It may seem disarming when a woman is with them, but it's not a situation you want. They're looking for someone to breed."

"Breed?" I'm woozy, my head spinning. "Like *The Handmaid's Tale?*"

"The what?" Sasha sounds confused, but I'm too busy blinking away the dizziness to explain.

Before I can pass out, the sack is pulled off my head.

I blink against the harsh sudden brightness.

My eyesight isn't terrible without my glasses, but I silently mourn the loss of my new trendy pink frames as I squint at the unkempt field of overgrown weeds beyond the stage. With a slow sweep, I estimate there are at least fifty people out there.

And I quickly come to the realization that this crowd isn't what you'd see on a Saturday at the farmers market. Or in this case, a human market.

These people look like Viking barbarians. Most of the men

have mohawks, many aren't wearing shirts, and there are swords strapped to every single belt. Some have thick black liner painted around their eyes, and others have dark streaks swiped across their upper cheeks.

If this were a movie, I'd probably find them attractive, but the leering stares are enough to make my skin crawl. I spot a few women in old-fashioned dresses. Empire waists. Cap sleeves. Material so thin, I can make out the silhouette of their legs in their skirts. One is wearing a bonnet, and the others have parasols to shade themselves.

I do as Sasha said and avoid eye contact with them.

I turn my head toward my new friend, and I'm caught off-guard by how pretty she is. Even with dirt on her face and hay stuck in her side braid, she's still one of the most beautiful people I've ever seen.

She's taller than me. Not surprising or hard to achieve, considering I barely clear five feet. But in addition to our height difference, we're opposites in other ways. Me, with blond hair and hazel eyes, and her with long raven locks and eyes such an intense gray, they almost appear silver. She's willowy, while I'm not. I work hard to stay in shape, but no matter how skinny I get, my butt and breasts never seem to get any smaller.

The blue dress Sasha wears has long sleeves. There's a dark rust color around the cuffs at her wrists, and it's the same along the swooping neckline. At first, I think the color variation is part of the dress's design, but then I lean forward a little to get a better look at her. I suck in a gasp as I follow the red streaks on her chest up to her neck.

Blood.

Horrified, my jaw drops. The metal collar around her neck and the shackles on her wrists are making her bleed.

"Iron," she clarifies. "It burns me."

Face wrinkling with confusion, I open my mouth to question her about what that means, but she gives me a subtle shake of her head.

My teeth snap shut. I don't want to make things worse for her, so I stay silent.

"Good morning," the man at the front of the line says to the crowd before doing a graceful, over-the-top bow. With his posh-sounding accent and pleasant tone, it's almost hard to believe he's a total psycho. "I'm Byris, and I'm going to make sure that at least ten of you walk away very happy today. No multiples—that's a rule. One female per male or couple. Bidding starts at fifty gold coins."

Not wasting any time, he begins making the girls introduce themselves. The first three are crying too hard to say more than five words. One of them is the girl who was praying in the wagon, and she continues to do so now. Her black hair is pulled into a ponytail, and she's wearing pajama pants with pink hearts on them. She looks like she could be in high school, and the pain of this situation becomes too much for me to bear.

Numbness sets in as I gaze ahead. Scanning the horizon with blurry vision, I search for tall buildings, powerlines, or landmarks. Anything to tell me where I am.

Nothing.

It's just trees and more fields as far as I can see.

As I search the sea of people, I wonder who will bid on me. A few men aren't taking their eyes off my body, and I wish I were more covered. My jeans are skintight and my top dips low, showing some cleavage.

A figure in the middle stands out to me. He's wearing a short tan cloak. While he's not the only one with a hood up to shadow his face from the bright sun, his eyes hold me captive. They're golden and glittering, almost as if they're glowing.

Even without crystal clear vision, I can tell the set of his mouth is unhappy. His sharp jaw, dusted with dark facial hair, is clenched as if he's grinding his teeth. A thick brown leather strap is slung across his chest, and the hilt of a large sword sticks out from behind his back.

There's an air of danger about him. An intensity that can't be denied.

He just looks so mean.

I shiver, suddenly feeling chilled, despite the heat.

"Number seven." The ringleader points at Sasha.

She steps forward, her chin held high. "I'm a full-blooded fae, I'm fifty-seven years old, and I'm from the Night Realm. I weave blankets and tapestries."

I do a double take as I look at her again. Most of what she said doesn't make sense at all, especially her age. There's no way she's that old. She can't be more than twenty-five. She tucks some hair behind her ear, and I almost make a noise of surprise. It's pointy.

Fae.

She asked me if I'm human.

Because she's not.

Where in the ever-loving hell am I?

I don't have time to think about it, because the man gestures at me impatiently. "Eight, you're up."

This is it—my opportunity to get these people to view me as something other than merchandise. To make them see me as a living, breathing human being. A person with feelings and a family.

It's a simple strategy that, unfortunately, women have to learn in life. Same goes for not wearing your hair in a ponytail so an attacker can't grab it. Or keeping your keys poised between your fingers like Wolverine in case you need to defend yourself.

I failed at both, and now I'm paying the price.

With clammy palms and a dry tongue, I square my shoulders and inch forward as much as the rope will allow. Some of my hair has come loose from my ponytail, and the strands stick to the sweat on my face. I probably look like crap, but I suppose that's not a bad thing. Maybe I'll be undesirable.

"My name is Maelyn Moore." My voice wavers. I swallow hard and take a slow inhale. "I tend to ramble when I'm nervous, so buckle up and get ready for an epic overshare." There's no reaction from anyone. Not even a twitch of a smile. "I'm twenty-one years old, and my favorite color is pink. I grew up in a small town an hour outside of Dallas called Bliss. My parents—Artie and June—got divorced a few years ago, but they still get along really well. Seriously, they take peaceful co-parenting to a whole new level. I started volunteering at a women's shelter when I was eighteen, and I found my passion—helping people. So I finished college a year early, and I just got a job working as a domestic violence counselor—"

"What's that?" a blond man shouts in front, moving closer to the stage. He has a long mohawk that's been French braided to his scalp. His narrowed blue eyes wander from the tennis shoes on my feet up to my breasts. They stop there, as if they're glued to my chest.

"Uh, basically, I talk to people who've suffered through abusive relationships. Or rather, they talk to me. Sometimes I help them find resources for protection, temporary housing, food, or jobs—anything they need to get back on their feet." I'm proud of myself for holding eye contact with him, even if he does look utterly confused by my job description.

"Can you cook?"

"Not really," I admit, wondering if I should lie.

"Can you sew?"

"No, but I can sing. I did musical theater in high school and I'm in a local singing group called the Belting Belles. We perform once a month. Usually at churches or schools. We're a non-profit organization, and all of our ticket money goes to food banks. I know it doesn't sound like a lot, but last month we had fifty-six people show up to listen to—"

"Lullabies?" a woman asks, and I quickly shake my head when I remember Sasha's words about breeding.

"No. Musical theater numbers, mostly."

All that earns me is a few blank stares.

"That's enough questions," Byris interjects, announcing number nine next.

But the man who first started grilling me cuts in, "Nah. I'm not done with this one yet. If I'm going to pay full price, I want to know what she can do." He pats a small black velvet bag hanging from his belt, and I hear the jingling of coins. "Sing for us, pretty bird."

"All right," Byris relents. "One song."

He points at me, and I gulp.

He expects me to perform. Right now. A Capella.

Maybe this is my chance to appeal to their compassion. Music has a way of evoking emotions. It can move someone to tears. Bring people together.

My throat is dry from fear, nervousness, and dehydration, but somehow, I find the will to start the first line of "Amazing Grace." I don't have the kind of voice that would ever take me to Broadway, but I'm confident in my ability to carry a tune. The notes come out clear, smooth, and on-pitch.

As I start the second verse, there's movement in the crowd.

People are shifting closer, drawn in by the song. The interest I've sparked with these perverts is obvious. I wouldn't be surprised if some of them started drooling, and I begin to wonder if I shouldn't have taken Sasha's advice.

It feels dirty, *selling* myself like this.

In a way, I'm reminded of all the beauty pageants I was in when I was little. Around the age of three, my mom thought it would be a good idea to enter me into the local county fair Little Miss Bliss contest. I lost. Or rather, I didn't place first. And my losing streak continued, even though Mom entered me in several contests per year until I was ten. Guess I didn't have the sparkle the judges were looking for. Or coordination. Didn't help that whenever it was time for me to talk about myself, I rambled on and on. I've always hated being the center of attention, and when I'm uncomfortable, I'm either silent or talking a mile a minute. There's no in-between with me.

Mom finally threw in the towel when I admitted I hated it. I'd broken down after a particularly bad tripping-over-my-own-feet incident where I fell off the stage, and my mom had been blindsided by my confession. She thought pageants were *our thing*. A special bonding experience we did together. And for years, I didn't have the heart to tell her I wanted to stop.

That's the length I'll go for someone I love. I'll be their real-life doll, dressing and acting the part, just so I won't hurt their feelings. The worst part is, my mom had felt terrible because she'd thought I was having fun the whole time. She never would've forced me into anything if she thought I didn't want to do it.

God, I miss her. I just saw her last night for our weekly dinner, but I'd give anything to be with her now.

The guy who'd asked all the questions is smiling. It's not a reassuring, kind smile. I can read cruel tendencies behind his grin.

My stomach roils, and my nausea increases when I notice the cloaked guy again. He's meandering through the hordes of people, and he's heading straight for me, those glowing eyes fixed in my direction.

No.

Not him. Anyone but him.

My breath catches in my throat, and my voice falters, but I continue singing as I return my attention the blond man who showed so much interest before. Aesthetically, he's good looking. Obviously, he's total garbage because he's here, but he just might be the lesser of two evils.

"All right, that's enough." The kidnapper cuts me off before the end. "I'd like to get this place cleared out before the suns merge. It's already hot enough as it is."

Suns, as in, plural?

Craning my head, I look to the sky. On the left, the sun is bright and, judging by its distance from the horizon, I'd say it's about eight in the morning. But then I swivel to the right, and an identical orb is hovering in a similar way, just opposite of the first. I glance back and forth between the two, unable to believe what I'm seeing.

Two suns.

What?

As the next girl in line steps up, I realize the terrifying cloaked guy is just feet away from the stage now. His face seems even more hidden in the shadows up close, but his irises still burn under his hood.

My eyes go back to Mr. Garbage #1, and through a haze of tears, I silently plead with him to buy me. It won't matter in the long run. As soon as I get a chance to escape, I'm taking it. Here and now, I'm making myself that promise.

I'll be a good girl—the most obedient captive ever.

I'll gain his trust and figure out how to get home.

Then when his guard is down, I'll run.

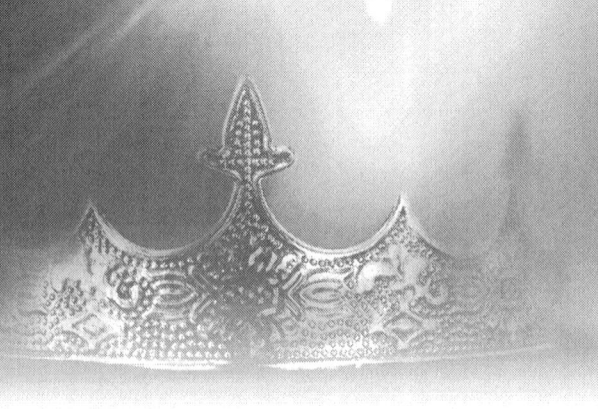

CHAPTER 2

Zander

Because of the plague that decimated the female population in the Day Realm, the demand for women here is high. The price people are willing to pay is even higher and, apparently, Byris is willing to take on the risk for the reward.

He'll get his punishment. I've heard his name more than once from my spies. He's made a name for himself as a heavy seller, and I'll enjoy personally carrying out his execution.

Every single time I take down one of these organized rings, I get a euphoric rush. I've busted a lot of auctions since gaining control of this kingdom five years go. I've executed many men and a few women who dared to defy the law.

I'm a monster who snuffs out other monsters.

Some—however few—would call me a hero. My men know my intentions are good and the women we've saved will never forget what I've done for them.

Bottom line—selling women is wrong.

My own mother was a victim of kidnapping and forced breeding, and I'll be damned if I let that happen under my rule.

But I'd be lying if I said I didn't have ulterior motives.

I always suspected I might find my mate at one of these cesspools.

You'll know her by her voice. She won't be with you by choice.

The clues of my curse repeat in my head over and over as I near the stage.

As soon as Maelyn said her name, I felt it in my bones. An electric zing ran up my spine. The hairs on the back of my neck stood on end. A shiver racked my body.

But when she started singing? Fire ignited inside of my soul.

The ever-present darkness clouding my vision keeps me from seeing her, but the sweet melody coming from her mouth fills me with a longing so strong I have trouble staying on my feet. Fighting against my weak knees, I keep moving on trembling legs, nearing the one who will claim my heart forever.

The one who will break my curse.

The one who will be my queen.

Using my shoulders, I push through the bodies in my way. A few annoyed grunts and gasps get lost behind me, and I resist the urge to crush their throats.

The time for violence will come.

Maelyn's all that matters now.

As I get closer to her, my emotions become a whirlwind.

I'm overwhelmed with elation because I finally found her, but I'm also battling with rage because she's been mistreated. Along with her sweet smell in the breeze, I can detect the scent of her blood.

They hurt her, and I can feel her pain. My wrists itch and sting, and there's an ache in my leg.

Every instinct inside me is screaming to rush the stage and take her. I could easily release her from her bindings and fly her somewhere far away. My soldiers would take care of the mayhem left in my wake, but I'd be blowing the entire plan and putting the other females in danger.

Six of my best warriors are posing as buyers in the audience, and I've got an entire army stationed in the forest behind us. Our operation will be the same as always—capture the criminals. Kill them if necessary. Free the females.

All I have to do is give the signal.

As soon as I lower my hood and reveal my crown, they'll swarm the crowd and end this debauchery. I could do it now, but we usually wait until the auction is halfway done before we intercede.

Besides, the sadistic side of me wants to know who will bid on Maelyn.

Who wants to buy her, to defile her, to own her?

They'll be the ones receiving the harshest punishments once we get them back to Hailene. The execution courtyard will be bathed with their blood.

I sidle up next to the man who peppered my mate with questions. He dared to look at her, to speak to her, to imagine himself with her.

He'll pay dearly for that mistake.

Suddenly, the auctioneer rudely interrupts my mate's singing, and I jolt from the loss of her sweet voice.

I want to rip his head off.

I just might do that.

After all, he deserves it for the crimes he's committed.

The snatchers are all the same. Greedy. Merciless.

Only someone with a truly blackened heart could uproot young women from their homes and thrust them into the waiting arms of someone who wants to use their bodies for their own pleasure.

After the last two girls on the stage go through introductions and questions, the bidding begins.

As I wait, my anger simmers, a low boil of rage rippling under the surface of my calm façade. Anticipation is thick in the air as the people around me jingle the gold stashed away in their pockets.

The first five women are bought by my own men. One sobs as she leaves the stage, but the others scream and fight as they're dragged off, not realizing they're being saved.

An eager couple in the crowd out-bids my last soldier for the sixth female. I hate executing women—especially since females are so treasured here—but the wives at the auctions are just as bad as the men who brought them along. They want children so badly, they don't care if they have to highjack someone else's womb to get a baby.

The seventh woman gets bought by a lone man.

I'm not worried—some of my warriors will be following them as they leave.

As the seconds stretch on, I can feel the questioning stares from my men. They're wondering why I haven't given the signal yet.

They don't realize everything is about to change. For me. For the kingdom.

"Number eight, the morning bird," the auctioneer announces, giving her a special nickname to up the price. "Bidding for this one starts at one hundred gold coins."

The man next to me raises his hand.

Another behind me calls, "One hundred and twenty."

"One fifty."

"Two hundred."

Bids come from all around me, fast and without hesitation.

Perverted desire pushes Maelyn's price up into the thousands. They sense her sweetness. Her innocence. And I can tell she's smaller than the others. Many men like the petite ones because they can be overpowered more easily.

I clench my jaw so hard I'm afraid my teeth will break.

Enough of this shit.

"Ten thousand gold coins." My outrageous bid causes a hush over the crowd.

No one has ever paid that much.

Byris' breath hitches with excitement. "Ten thousand going once, going twice—"

"Eleven," the first man—the one filled with questions—says.

Although I can't see him, I send a glare at him from under my hood. "Twelve."

"Thirteen."

"Fourteen."

"Fif—"

"We could stand here for the rest of the day and bid," I interrupt him. "But all we're doing is lining someone else's pockets. So I have a proposition for you."

"Yes?"

"A game."

"A game?" he repeats, his tone taunting as if he thinks I'm joking.

Nonchalant, I shrug. "I like a good bet."

"What's in it for me?"

"If I win, I get the girl. But if I lose…" I tilt my head from left to right as if I'm considering a huge decision. "You can have the girl and my gold. I'll basically be buying her for you."

The man sucks on his teeth, and I know I've got him. No one could refuse such an attractive wager.

"Do you play poker?" I ask, producing a deck from my satchel.

It's an old set of cards. Each one has an imperfection that makes them unique and easy for me to recognize, despite my blindness. A scratch. A frayed corner. A carefully placed crease.

I've memorized every single one.

I hear the man shake his head. "You might cheat. Your cards could be enchanted."

A slow smirk lifts my lips because I'd been hoping he'd say that. "Chess, then? If you can see the board the entire time, you'll know I'm playing fair."

Grumbling, my opponent begrudgingly agrees, and the auctioneer mutters a few curses. He could refuse us. He could tell us that bidding is the only way to win here.

But he won't. Entertainment is a commodity.

In our long, long lives, it can be difficult to come across new and thrilling experiences. Watching two desperate men gamble over a human girl will be something people talk about for ages, even if we'll be out here sweating our asses off when the suns merge at dawn.

Reaching into my bag, I take out my chess set. The leather board is flexible, and before I can unroll it, someone brings over a barrel of ale for me to set it on.

As Byris skips over Maelyn and auctions off the last two, my surroundings fall away while I place the wooden pieces where they belong.

It's calming and familiar. This game of strategy is as much a part of my life as breathing.

If my opponent were smarter, he might realize he has no chance of winning against someone who carries around their own chess set. But I'm also challenging his pride. He could've declined, but it would've made him look weak.

That's the downfall of Day Realm men. We're just too damn proud, myself included.

"What's your name?" I ask him, keeping up the appearance of a friendly exchange.

"Gideon. And yours?"

"Rey." It's a half-lie—Rey is my mother's maiden name—and I feel the squeeze in my stomach from the dishonesty. The painful side effect is something I've gotten used to. It adds more shadows to my already darkened soul, but what does it matter?

I live in darkness. I've thrived in it for so long, a little more isn't going to make a difference.

"Well, Rey, I hope you're not a sore loser," Gideon drawls, and I picture the smug look he surely has on his face.

I say nothing. Sometimes silence is a better intimidator than words.

Finishing up with the white pawns, I listen as each one makes a distinct noise when they get moved. Gideon was right to worry about enchanted games, but not for the reason he thinks. The bottoms of these wooden pieces are coated with a magical paint. When they slide or get placed down, they emit a musical sound only I can hear. I wouldn't call it cheating, though. It doesn't help me win. It's simply necessary so I can recognize what moves are being made by my opponent.

Maelyn's labored breathing breaks through my concentration, and I realize she's the only one left on the stage, except for the auctioneer.

Soon, she'll be all mine.

"Byris." Turning toward the stage, I toss a silver coin at him. "Would you do the honors? Gideon, suns or stars?"

"Suns," Gideon says confidently.

The *whoosh whoosh whoosh* of the circular metal flipping through the air follows, along with a soft slap on skin.

"Suns," Byris announces. "First turn goes to Gideon."

Nodding cordially, I walk around to the other side of the board to play the black team and wait for Gideon's first move.

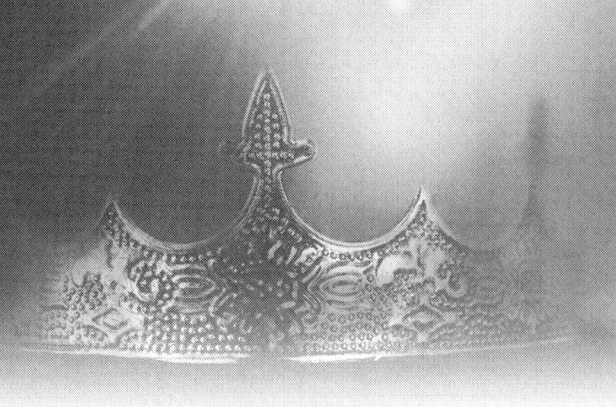

CHAPTER 3

Maelyn

Mr. Garbage #1—Gideon—is playing white. This is good. He'll have an advantage from the start. When he opens with pawn to E4, a little tension leaves my body.

He knows what he's doing. Good.

Rey—Mr. Garbage #2, AKA, the terrifying cloaked man—moves his pawn to E5.

Gideon brings out his knight. So does Rey.

The next move is the white bishop. Black does the same.

I swallow hard, my throat painfully dry, as I watch the basic chess opening. It's a scenario I've played out with my dad many times. What Gideon does next could be pivotal to his win.

My heart is thundering in my chest as I stand next to Byris. His meaty hand is wrapped around my upper arm. Although it isn't a bruising grip, I get the sense that if I even breathe wrong, I'm going to feel it tighten.

At least the people aren't looking at me anymore. Now they're ensnared by the game, just as I am. Gideon has already castled, further protecting his king. Both of Rey's bishops are out, and he's just lost a knight.

Instead of playing the bishop, Rey nudges his pawn one space over. It's an unexpected move, because that means sacrificing his bishop.

My stomach drops as I get a bad feeling. An experienced player wouldn't do that without a reason.

Studying the board, I try to see what he does. I'm certainly not a genius when it comes to chess, but I did win a few tournaments in high school. I've always been good at predicting the next few moves the players might make.

Gideon wears a victorious grin, even though he hasn't won yet. He thinks he's got this in the bag, but he's probably falling into a trap and he doesn't realize it. His knight captures another black pawn.

Oh, no.

No.

I see it then.

After the black knight takes a white pawn, it will leave a clear path for Rey to move his queen. There will be nothing Gideon can do to prevent it.

Closing my eyes, I let myself sink into the disappointment and dread.

The very last person I wanted to end up with is going to win me.

Merchandise. I hate that word almost as much as the next one uttered by Rey.

"Checkmate." Very matter of fact. No gloating.

When I open my eyes, Gideon is slack jawed, staring down at the game like he can't believe what just happened.

He got conned. That's what happened. And in less than five minutes, too. I'm actually embarrassed for him.

"You cheated," he grits out, his hand slowly inching toward a giant knife on his belt.

"I did not." Rey calmly gestures to the board. "There were no tricks here. Just strategy."

Byris lets go of my arm because the rising tension requires his full attention. "Gentlemen. Come on, now." His tone is placating as he starts down the steps on the opposite side of the stage. "We all watched, Gideon. It was a fair win."

"You promised me a woman!" Gideon roars.

"What about the others you have at home? There's always next time."

My gaze darts between the two.

They know each other. Gideon's a returning customer.

Others. At home.

Oh, God.

No matter who won the game, I was always going to end up in a fate worse than I can imagine.

I glance at the cloaked man, expecting a salacious leer as he inspects his new prize—me. Only, he's not looking in my direction.

Calmly collecting the pieces on his board, he seems undisturbed by Gideon and Byris' arguing as he puts his game away.

Soon, he'll come up here. He'll drag me away.

Tears spring to my eyes, and one escapes, trailing down my cheek. Another follows on the other side, and I don't wipe them away. There'd be no point when they'd just be replaced with more. Pressure rises in my throat. A sob builds to the point of painful, but somehow, I manage to swallow it down. I don't want to draw more attention to myself.

I jump when Gideon's voice elevates to a shout, his finger pointed accusingly at Byris.

Then something wonderful happens.

Byris throws a punch. Blood sprays from Gideon's mouth, splattering the chest and face of a nearby woman. She screams. The man she's with goes after the fighting men, but Gideon's already got his knife out. Spinning, he swings it at Rey.

Hopping back, Rey quickly removes the sword strapped to his back and blocks.

Within seconds, the others in the crowd are joining in with aggressive shouts and weapons. As the scuffle grows, there's a loud sound—like bedsheets on a clothesline whipping in a strong wind—and then large wings explode from several people's backs.

Honest to God wings.

They just came out of nowhere.

Startled, I fall to my butt. Pain shoots up my tailbone because I'm not able to break my fall with my hands tied, but I'm too shocked to let it register.

Humans don't have wings. Any semblance of hope that I'm still anywhere near my home vanishes, and the hard reality finally sets in.

I've been kidnapped. By beings who aren't even human. In a world with two suns. A world where riots are accompanied by lots and lots of sharp objects.

Roars and battle cries come from the forest behind the crowd, and about two dozen more men charge this way.

The rioting gets worse when they join in the fight, wielding axes, daggers, and spears. Gideon gets hit in the mouth with the hilt of Rey's sword, and a tooth flies up to the stage. The white piece is coated with blood as it clatters and rolls across the wood a few feet away from me.

Wide-eyed, I catch a glimpse of Gideon and Rey on the ground in a wrestling match. It's a blur of fists landing on jaws, mouths, and eyes.

With the mayhem and chaos, everyone seems to have forgotten about me. I scoot toward the stairs, waiting for someone to notice and stop me.

No one does.

This is my opportunity to escape.

Looking in the distance, I assess my options. There's a wide grassy expanse leading away from this place, but I'm pretty sure that's where we came in from. Then there's the woods.

Woods it is.

I'd rather take my chances in an unknown world alone than stay and wait for the hell coming my way with these men.

I have some basic wilderness survival skills. My dad and I used to go camping every summer.

Hands still bound tightly in front of me, I get up and run. My sneakers pound down the steps, and I half-expect someone to come after me. To tackle me to the ground.

But they don't, and I keep running, refusing to look back.

My lungs and leg muscles burn as I put every drop of energy I have into sprinting to safety. The trees are almost within reach. Once I get there, my chances of escape will be much better.

The shouts and metal clanking against metal have faded far behind me, and I'm panting hard as I make it to the leafy bushes. The trees above are blooming with millions of tiny white flowers, and the petals fall to the ground, floating around me like snow.

If I wasn't terrified out of my mind, I might be able to appreciate the beauty of it.

However, I'm driven by one goal—going as fast as I can without falling. I stomp over sticks, leaves, fallen branches, and all the other obstacles you find in the untamed wilderness.

I'm going to get lost. That's a certainty.

I don't care. I'll just keep traveling deeper into the woods. I can go for a couple of hours until I find fresh water. Without a filter or tools, I'll have to take my chances with bacteria.

Then there's my wrists. I could try to cut the rope with a sharp rock, but I'd rather try to unknot it with my teeth and keep the length whole. A rope is a commodity in the wild.

I haven't gotten very far when I hear the snap of a twig.

My entire body tenses and my heart leaps, but I don't stop moving. I can't tell where the sound came from. It could've been an animal, but just in case it wasn't, I need to go faster.

Trying to keep my huffing and puffing to a minimum, I increase the speed of my hike. In fact, I've gained so much momentum that when someone steps out from behind a tree right in front of me, I can't stop in time.

I run straight into him. He doesn't even flinch, as if he's a brick wall. Glancing up, I see everything I'm trying to avoid—a blond mohawk styled into several bubble ponytails over the curve of his scalp. Black paint lined around his eyes. A sword strapped to his belt.

I don't recognize him from the auction, but that doesn't mean he isn't one of them.

When his hand clamps around my forearm, I'm frozen with fear. Paralyzed, not even able to scream.

He lifts my bound wrists above my head and raises a dagger from his pocket.

My middle is wide open. Totally vulnerable to attack.

Cowering, I slam my eyes shut as I wait for the sharp blade to pierce my gut. Or my neck. Maybe he'll make it quick and plunge it straight into my heart.

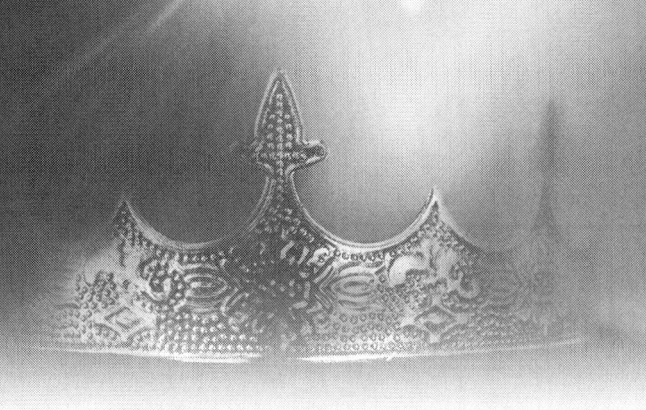

CHAPTER 4

Maelyn

NO PAIN COMES. WHEN I FEEL THE BACK-AND-FORTH sawing of the rope, I peek through one eye. He's cutting me free.

Gaping, I stand perfectly still as he expertly slices the fibers digging into my wrists. And he manages to do it without hurting me further.

The rope falls to the ground in pieces.

"My name is Thayne, and you're safe," the man says, putting the weapon back in his pants with one hand while his other stays firmly wrapped around my arm.

"Thayne." I deliberately use his name to try to form a connection, and I nod my head toward the depths of the forest. "I'm headed that way, thank you very much."

"I can't let you do that."

"Why not?"

"It's too dangerous out there."

I bark out a hysterical-sounding cackle.

"After the day I've had, I'm willing to take my chances." I try to jerk away, but his hold on me won't loosen. "Get away from me." Panicked, I search the woods for anyone who might be hunting me down. "Listen, I'm running away from some really bad people."

"I know."

Ice infuses my veins as I lock onto his coal-lined eyes. "Are you with them?"

"Not the bad ones."

He's implying there are good ones. Even so, I want nothing to do with this man. "If you're a good guy, then let me go. I just want to go home."

"That's what I'm trying to do," he says, his tone flat, almost as if he's bored.

I stop struggling. "You're rescuing me?"

It's too much to hope. He could be lying to get me to calm down, but when he nods, I let the hope take over. Maybe it's wishful thinking or the ridiculously irrational optimism I've been accused of having in the past, but I want to believe him.

"So you're, like, the police?"

Thayne shrugs. "Something like that."

"Get your hands off her."

I startle at the voice coming from my left, and somehow, I know who it belongs to without even looking.

Swallowing thickly, I turn to the guy with glowing eyes. They don't appear as radiant with his hood off, but they're still unsettlingly bright, glinting like the golden crown on his head. The luxurious band is about two inches wide, with seven points. The whole thing is decorated with jewels and pearls. Light streams through the branches overhead, and it sparkles in the mashup of warm colors—white, peach, and orange.

With his cloak pushed back, broad shoulders, muscular pecs, and defined abs are revealed. His khaki pants ride low on his hips, and I spy V muscles and a dark happy trail disappearing into the waistband.

Forcing my eyes up to a more proper place, I lock onto his frowning face.

"Your majesty." Thayne gives a slight bow with his head. "I found one of the humans trying to run."

"You'll give her to me now." The command isn't loud, but it's sharp and dark, like a whip.

Frightened, I shrink away from him when he comes close. His head tilts, he furrows his brows, and his eyes narrow.

Like he's... confused?

I don't read anger or malicious intent on Rey's face when Thayne passes me off, so I reluctantly go to him.

His hand gently cups my elbow, and as soon as he touches me, he hisses out a breath.

I blink, unsure of what to say or do. If Thayne was telling the truth and these two are part of the same group, then maybe he's not as bad as I thought.

"Th—Thayne said you're going to take me h-home," I stutter out.

"Did he?" Another inquisitive head tilt.

"Yes."

Instead of confirming, he slips his hand into mine in a greeting-like hold and bows down. When he straightens, instead of stepping back, he sways even closer. "I'm Zander."

I'm so short I have to lean my head all the way back just to see his stoic face. "I heard you say your name is Rey."

"It's not."

"Zander," I repeat, and he closes his eyes like I just whispered the sweetest compliment.

"*King* Zander," Thayne interjects, correcting me as he emphasizes the title.

Zander aims his frown at his friend. "Just Zander for her. My queen will bow to no one."

Bewilderment falls over Thayne's features for a moment. Then his eyes widen as he looks at me with a new expression I can't interpret. "Yes, your majesties."

Queen? Majesties?

"Well, okay then," I cough out. "I'm Maelyn. I thank you in advance for returning me to Dallas. You don't even have to bring me to my apartment. Just get me near the city and I'll find my way back."

At my rambling, Zander's lips quirk up on one side. It's not quite a smile, but I get the feeling he's amused. Maybe he's not so scary after all.

He holds out his elbow, offering his arm like a gentleman would. "Let's rejoin my men and the other females. They should be safe by now."

Thankful, I slide my hand around his forearm. The heat from his skin is surprising but not unpleasant. While I was in flight mode, all my blood rushed to my head and organs, leaving my fingers icy cold.

Thayne takes the lead, using a large ax to hack away at the overgrown bushes and sticks in our path. While being careful not to trip, I sneak side-glances at Zander and study his features.

Now that I'm not terrified of him, I take a second to appreciate how good-looking he is.

Like the other men, he has a mohawk-like strip of hair, but his isn't blond or long enough to braid. The messy four-inch strands are as black as can be.

It's a little jarring to see the pointy ear against the shaved side of his head, but he has a sharp jaw, high cheekbones, and a straight nose. The crown fits his head in an odd way—too tight—like it was made for someone else. His inky bangs are spilling over it, but he doesn't seem bothered by having hair in his eyes.

Speaking of his eyes, he doesn't wear the makeup everyone else does, but his lashes are dark and thick, giving him the appearance of eyeliner. My focus lands on his lips. They're unbelievably full. Pouty. Pretty. Pink.

I start to wonder if they're swollen from the fight. From what I saw, he took a few good hits to the face, but I don't see any evidence of it now.

He protected me. He fought for me.

His head starts to shift my way, and I blush violently as I jerk my gaze to the flowering trees around us.

I hope he didn't catch me checking him out. "Did you arrest the people who kidnapped me?"

"They've been captured, yes." His voice is deep, but there's a certain gentleness when he speaks to me, unlike the way he talked to Thayne. "They'll be punished for what they did to you."

"Good. I hope they rot in prison."

He grunts, and I'm not sure if it's an agreement or just a noise of disgruntlement for how crappy today has been. I wait for him to fill the quiet journey with conversation, but he doesn't.

Ah, the strong and silent type.

I've never been okay with awkward pauses. It's not comfortable for me. I don't like not knowing what someone else is thinking, especially in times of turmoil.

"Want to explain what happened earlier?" I toss out the opening for him to start talking.

"No."

Several seconds pass after his refusal, and we're getting near the exit of the forest.

"Why not?" I press, and when he doesn't answer right away, I push on, "Obviously, they were selling people. And, from what one of the other women said, I can conclude it was for, ah, sexual reasons. I just want to know why I was brought here. Where is here? Why me?"

Zander stops abruptly, just a few feet from the bright light of the grassy field. His movement is so sudden, I get yanked back because I'm still holding onto his arm.

When I see the fury on his face, I remove my hand as if I got burned and back up a couple paces. I don't get the feeling his anger is directed at me, but it's still scary all the same.

His eyebrows knit tighter and his snarl produces a peek of straight, white teeth. "You want me to tell you what they intended to do with you? I can't. I can't even think about it."

He's shaking with rage. His fingers tremble at his sides and his chest rises and falls with quick breaths. Glowing gold flashes from his eyes, and I swear I see his irises take on a different shape. They elongate, turning into dark slits for a second.

"Your majesty," Thayne barks from a few feet away, and the term of respect has lost the reverence I heard earlier. Now, it sounds like a concerned warning. "Calm yourself."

The anger drops from Zander's face. Taking a few slow breaths, the stoic mask comes back up.

He holds his hand out to me like he didn't just almost go all Hulk-mode a second ago.

I've gone back to being wary. Obviously, this guy's got a temper.

I'm grateful he's here; he intervened for us women, but I'm so ready to leave this place.

Ignoring his offered hand, I forge ahead, skirting around Thayne to go out into the sunlight. Heat beats down on my shoulders as I look ahead. A few men are dismantling the stage with their axes and using the wood for a bonfire. Flames hiss and crackle when they add the lumber to the pile.

To the right of that, there's a large group, and I recognize some of them from the auction.

Zander wasn't kidding about them being punished.

Along with Byris, a bunch of the potential buyers are chained together. They don't look excited now. The creepy leering is gone. Shackled and beaten down, they're kneeling. Blood runs from where the chains are wrapped around their necks and wrists.

An army of shirtless, winged warriors circle them with spears in hand, and they're so close to the fire their skin is pink and glistening with sweat. Some of the women are crying, leaning on their partners in crime.

I don't know what will become of them, but evil lost today.

I'm so relieved I could cry.

Looking to the far end of the field, I find Sasha. Without my glasses, her form is fuzzy, but I can see her comforting another woman. I scan the huddled group and count nine heads. A breath

I didn't realize I was holding whooshes from my lungs, and my chest feels lighter.

Thayne and Zander really did rescue them all.

I quickly glance over my shoulder and see Zander taking strides toward me. I want to put as much distance between me and this whole experience as possible, so I run to the group of my fellow captives.

Sasha welcomes me with open arms and hugs me. "It'll be okay now. You're all right. You're all right, dear."

The motherly tone in her voice finally makes me crack.

A loud sob spasms in my chest. The first is followed by an avalanche of others, and I'm slightly aware that I sound like a dying seal while totally losing it.

I'm not a quiet crier. Never have been. I don't do it often, so when it does happen, it's like my body lets out a bunch of bottled up breakdowns all at once. Tears coat my cheeks and snot runs from my nose. Short wails and whines burst from my throat.

There's a soft touch on my back, and at first I think it's one of the other girls, but when I glance behind me, it's him.

Zander.

"You'll give her to me now," he says to Sasha. His demand is missing the dark edge it had when he said the same thing to Thayne earlier, but it's still firm and unyielding.

I cling tighter to Sasha, and she spins us in a protective move. "It seems she doesn't want to go with you, Day king."

Thayne approaches and whispers something in her ear. They're both so much taller than me that I don't catch what he says. But whatever it is, it's enough to convince her to do what Zander asks.

Gazing down at me, she gives me a reassuring smile with happiness sparkling in her eyes. "You're a lucky one."

"What?" Confused, I hiccup and wipe my face as she steps away from me.

I hold onto her hand, trying to be careful of the wounds on

her wrist, but when I take a good look at the area, I see perfect skin.

I stare, wondering if I imagined her injuries. Her neck is better, too. The only evidence she was hurt is the rust-color still staining parts of her dress. How could she go from bleeding to not even having a scratch?

"Is she hurt, your majesty?" A new guy comes over, his hands reaching toward me.

Pure instinct makes me recoil. Dropping Sasha's hand, I end up backing up into Zander.

"It's okay," Zander says softly, rubbing his thumbs over the skin on my upper arms. "This is Marek, and he's going to take away your pain."

I don't even know what that means.

The man still has his hands out. Just like most of the other guys, his head is shaved on the sides, but the white-blond hair of his mohawk is shorter like Zander's. A few frosty strands cling to the sweat on his forehead. Matching eyebrows knit together with emotion I can't identify. Concern? Frustration that I'm not cooperating?

I feel a stab of betrayal. I thought the time for cooperation was over. I'm supposed to be free now.

Squirming, I press against Zander harder. "I don't want you to touch me. I'm fine with my pain. Really."

"Well, I'm not fine with it," Zander states. "Do it, Marek."

I tense when Marek's palm stops an inch away from my upper chest, but to his credit, he doesn't actually touch me. For a few seconds, he hovers there. A cold sensation emanates from him, and I shiver, even though it's gotten hotter out here.

"Do you need my guidance, Marek?" Another guy steps forward. Although he doesn't look a day over thirty, he has wrinkles around his eyes and mouth. They deepen as he frowns.

And suddenly, I'm distracted by his rough appearance. His face and arms are badly scarred. Long, jagged, flesh-colored streaks disappear into his sleeveless shirt, and I'd be willing to bet his torso is covered with them, too.

Of course, I'd never judge someone for being disfigured. In fact, it's the opposite. Despite his scowl, I get slammed with sympathy for this man, and I can't help wondering where all the marks came from.

I'm so lost in my thoughts that I barely notice the subtle differences in my own body. The stinging around my wrists eases up and the throbbing on my shin fades.

I raise my hands.

Just like Sasha, the red ligature marks are gone. If I rolled up my pants leg, I'd be willing to bet I'd see no bruises.

"No need, Kai," Marek says to the scarred man, grinning over his shoulder. "Got it handled."

"How did you do that?" I ask, baffled as I rub the perfect skin around my wrists.

When I glance up at Marek, I'm startled by the sudden clarity in my vision. The leaves of the trees in the distance are no longer blurry. The clouds are distinct instead of just looking like fluffy blobs. Everything is sharp and clear.

Out of habit, I move my hand toward my face to adjust my glasses. But I just end up poking myself on the temple because they're not there.

"My eyes," I exclaim breathlessly as I blink.

Zander's grip on my shoulders tightens. "What about your eyes? Are you damaged? Marek, what did you do?"

His thunderous voice has me scrambling to defend the man who fixed me. "Nothing's wrong. I can see really well. I—I don't need glasses anymore."

I can't believe it. I've always wanted Lasik, but for someone who can't even wear contacts because I can't stand the thought of putting a finger in my eye, a laser was out of the question.

This Marek guy not only healed my injuries, but he fixed my nearsightedness. "Thank you, Marek. How did you do it?"

Marek doesn't reply. He just gives me a respectful incline of his head and turns to leave.

A gentle prodding of my shoulders gets me to turn around, and I'm met by Zander's tender expression. "You'll get all the answers you seek, Mae."

"It's Maelyn," I correct him.

"I like Mae."

"I don't."

He doesn't know me. If he did, he definitely wouldn't call me that. Aside from the fact that it speaks of a familiarity we don't have, I hate the nickname. I feel like it makes me sound like a country bumpkin, which is a persona I've spent a good part of my adult life trying to shed. Growing up in the small town of Bliss, I had three guarantees during my childhood: church on Sundays, big hair at pageants, and home-cooked meals on the table every night at exactly six p.m.

The city is faster, busier, more complicated. More sophisticated. My permanent move to Dallas was a deliberate attempt to be those things.

Before I can assert my deeper opinion on the subject, Zander wraps an arm around my waist, presses me to his side, and faces all the women.

"If you're fae, step over here." He motions to the left where some of his warriors stand at attention, and three women break away from the group to join them. "These men will escort you back to your homes, however far it may be. You'll be compensated for your troubles and you'll receive a formal written apology from the Day kingdom."

All traces of Sasha's earlier skepticism about Zander have vanished. She and the other girls beam at him, and I don't think it's my imagination when I see one of them peruse Zander from head to toe in a very appreciative way.

It's more than hero worship. It's attraction. They're looking at him the same way I did in the woods.

For a second, jealousy flares through me.

I mentally shake it off. I have no business feeling that way. There's only one goal here—get back home.

Whoever Zander is—king or whatever—I'll thank him and wish him a good life before I go.

CHAPTER 5

Zander

I LISTEN TO MY MEN LEADING THE FAE FEMALES AWAY. THEY know the drill. Once they get into the forest and out of sight, they'll spread their wings and fly. I suppose they could do it here, but I know from past experience humans don't react well to that. They've already seen enough today, and I don't want to frighten them more.

Grateful sighs and relaxed chatter comes from the retreating group as they step through some bushes. By tonight, the three women should be back where they belong in the Night Realm.

Now for the others. You could cut the silent tension in the air with a knife. The six humans before me are exhausted, untrusting, and likely traumatized.

This part of the rescue operation is always the same. Getting the girls to believe everything I say will be difficult.

"Hello. I'm King Zander, ruler of the Day Realm. As you might have concluded by now, you're not on Earth. This is a world called Valora. You were brought through a portal."

Murmurs of relief and disbelief break out among the girls as they cling to each other.

And I add, "No, I'm not teasing you. I'm not lying. You were taken for nefarious purposes, but you've been rescued."

"What does nefarious mean?" one of the girls asks.

"Evil. However, what they had planned for you won't be your fate. You have options. If you'd like to return to where you came from, I can make that happen."

Maelyn stiffens next to me as a burst of excitement comes from her.

I pause, not understanding the emotions traveling through the bond. First, she was frightened by me. Now, it seems as though the thought of leaving makes her happy.

That simply can't be. We're mates. She should be drawn to me. She's supposed to feel safe, calm, and content in my presence. Being separated from me should feel wrong on every level.

Dismissing my concern, I continue, "Or you can stay here. It's a known fact that the snatchers like to take females who come from hard lives, and I suspect today isn't the worst event you've been through. Maybe you're orphans or you live in poverty. Maybe there's no one at home to miss you. But there's a place for you here, if you want it."

"What kind of place?" someone speaks up, apprehensive. "I don't understand what you're offering."

"A place where you'll have possibilities," I answer. "You'll be given housing."

"Nothing is free," another chimes in skeptically.

"You're right," I tell her. "There are many jobs to choose from. Good jobs, with honest work that'll allow you to be independent. Some require training, but we would provide your education at no cost."

"I already have an apartment and a job," the first voice retorts. "How's it different here?"

"Well, some of the biggest incentives are that you would turn fae within a decade, and when that happens, your aging slows to almost a standstill. Aches and pains won't ail you. We don't have natural viruses here, so you'll never get sick. If you grow wings, you might be able to fly eventually. Best of all, you could live for up to thirty thousand years."

Gasps ring out all around me, including a small one from my mate.

Yes, that last fact is usually very convincing. Human lifespan is tragically short.

"The way you ended up here is unfortunate," I say, "but it doesn't have to be that way going forward. You could be happy."

"Are you sure this isn't a joke?" A girl who hasn't spoken until now pipes up meekly. "Or a trick? Or a dream?"

"It's real."

"You'll have to excuse me for calling bullshit."

"Does it feel like you're dreaming?"

There's no answer, but the group nervously shifts around as they contemplate all I've told them.

Letting reality soak in, I patiently say, "I'm going to give you a few minutes to process this."

Their skepticism is warranted. Until today, they might've believed in ghosts or aliens, but their world hardly acknowledges faerie folklore anymore.

The giant bonfire behind us crackles, and I catch the scent of burning flesh. Quite a bit of it, in fact. I'm guessing about six or seven criminals lost their heads during the fight, and now their bodies are being disposed of, turning to ash. Good riddance.

One female starts crying again. It doesn't sound like the relieved or happy kind.

"Don't be scared or upset," I say the words gently in her direction. "Whatever you decide will be respected."

My reassurance only makes her sob louder.

"I don't think she speaks English," Maelyn murmurs quietly. She's so small, her breath caresses my ribs beneath my pectoral when she turns her head toward me. "I can translate to Spanish for her."

"Truly?" I ask, and she nods.

Pride surges through me. My mate is smart and considerate.

"I appreciate the offer, but there's no need."

During my many years of exile at the palace, I studied subjects of all kinds. I'm fluent in several common Earth languages, and it comes in handy for times like this.

The snatchers usually try to stick to countries where the prominent language is English because that's what we speak here. Buyers want their commands carried out swiftly by their new slaves, without having to repeat themselves. Trying to bark orders at someone who can't understand the words is frustrating for them. But sometimes the kidnappers grab someone without consideration to that fact.

I start speaking to the girl in Spanish. I find out her name is Lupe and she's from Mexico. Once I explain the situation, she thanks me profusely and passionately before quieting down.

Admiration and awe emanate from Maelyn.

That's more like it.

She's impressed with me, just as I am with her. Though I don't sense any intense love through the tether, mutual respect is a good place to start.

"People go missing in your world sometimes, right?" I ask the group, to which they quietly confirm. "Not all of them are gone—they've simply traveled to a different world. Many humans have settled here, and they've found success they never got close to in their old life. However, if the promise of security and magic aren't enough to entice you to stay, you can return to Earth." I motion to Thayne, who holds the portals. "Step over here if you want to leave, but know that you can never talk about this place or what happened…"

I trail off because Maelyn is shrugging my arm away. Wrapping her little hand around mine, she peels my fingers off her waist. Then, along with one other human, she trudges over to Thayne.

And I'm too stunned to react.

I wasn't speaking to her. She wasn't included in those options, but she just made herself very clear.

Maelyn truly wants to leave me, and she just demonstrated her opinion in front of all my men. I'm sure by now many of them suspect she's my fated mate. I never personally handle any of the victims we save. I don't comfort them, don't touch them. I just give them a choice and send them on their merry way.

Yet I won't let Maelyn go. I refuse. I can't.

But the fact that she doesn't feel the same cuts me deep. It hurts.

Rejection.

There's never been a case of mate rejection before. The bond is too demanding.

As I rub my aching chest, the elation I felt earlier is muddied with sadness, anger, and disappointment. In the short time Maelyn and I have known each other, she's already found me unworthy.

For a second, I question myself. Was I wrong about her? Was I mistaken about our connection?

I still feel the tingling along my side where our previous contact had been. My fingers burn with her absence. Just the thought of being away from her hurts my soul more than it would if I'd told a lie.

If there's one thing I'm certain of, it's that Maelyn is mine.

Perhaps she's too scared to realize it. Earlier in the forest, her fear was so strong I felt physically ill.

It's understandable if she needs time to adjust. Besides, the more we're together, the more the bond will push her to me.

Slowly stalking toward my mate, I aim a translated version at Lupe, and she joins the other human wanting to leave.

I anchor Maelyn to me once more as I declare, "You can never speak of what happened to you today. Time passes differently here. A year in Valora is a day on Earth. Where you're from, mere seconds have gone by since you've been missing, and it's unlikely anyone will believe you if you try to tell them about this ordeal."

"I understand," Maelyn intones seriously, while the other girl firmly says, "My mouth is zipped."

After explaining the rest to Lupe, I speak at the other woman. "What's your name?"

"Jackie."

"Jackie, we can give you safety. Shelter, food, and clothes."

"I don't need a handout. My life isn't much to brag about, but it's mine. I made it for myself and I want to go back."

I nod. "Fair enough."

This happens sometimes. The allure of Valora isn't enough for some people to give up what they've built for themselves, even if their environment is full of struggle and strife.

Maelyn clears her throat and looks to the girls wanting to stay. "I'm sorry if you've had a hard time before all this," she says with genuine sympathy. "If you want to come back with me, I can help you. I know of a great shelter that could take you in."

"Can you make me live for thirty thousand years?" one of them asks, her tone friendly and teasing.

Huffing out a laugh, Maelyn shakes her head. "Nope. And I can't blame you for wanting that." She turns to me. "I like my life the way it is. I'm happy. I appreciate your willingness to take me in, but it's not necessary."

Tilting my head, I give her a disbelieving look. Is she lying to me? Being human, dishonesty won't affect her the same way it would a faerie, so there's no way for me to tell.

Ignoring her, I gently tug her away by the elbow and nod from Thayne to Jackie and Lupe. "Go ahead."

My warrior lifts the lid of his wooden box, and I'm immediately hit with the portal smell. It's like the air after a big rain. I enjoy the scent. We don't get storms often in the Day Realm, but I've learned to like them. They used to frighten me as a child, but I stopped fearing thunder the day I turned into a griffin shifter.

I stopped being scared of a lot of things that day.

Thayne places the tiny portal in Jackie's palm and instructs, "Don't let it fall yet. When you're ready, think of where you want to go. Picture it in your mind as if you're already there. Then let the portal drop to the ground. You should see your destination on the other side. Walk through, and you'll be where you want to be." He pauses before giving her one last chance to change her mind. "This is a one-way deal. Once you've gone through, the doorway will vanish, and you can't come back."

"Fine with me."

"All right." He steps away.

I hear Jackie's head shift to look back at the remaining humans. "Y'all sure about this?"

"I don't have much to go back to," someone replies, while another adds, "I was living on the street. If I don't have to spend another night sleeping behind a dumpster, I won't."

"Okay," Jackie sighs. "Bye, ladies. Good luck."

Then she drops the portal.

The burst of magic is palpable, and several of the girls make noises of shock, including Maelyn. My mate sways away from me, toward the opening to her world. I pull her back.

As she turns her eyes to my face, I can feel her scrutinizing me. Questioning me.

Soon, she'll understand why I can't let her go.

A sound of dismay resounds in her throat when the portal closes.

Then Lupe's going, and yet again, Maelyn seems as if she wants to jump in after the woman.

"It's my turn now, right?" The hope in her voice is obvious, shredding my pride to ribbons.

I hate sadness. It's weakness.

So I get angry instead.

"Kai," I bark at the soldier in charge of getting the women settled in their new lodging. "Take my men, the prisoners, and these four females to Hailene. Make sure the women are fed along the way. Answer any questions they have."

"Yes, your majesty." He hesitates as he notices Maelyn still ensnared in my grip. "What about this one?"

"She wants to go home," I bite out. "I'm going to make sure she gets there."

CHAPTER 6

Maelyn

"Y͟O͟U͟ P͟R͟O͟M͟I͟S͟E͟ T͟O͟ T͟A͟K͟E͟ M͟E͟ H͟O͟M͟E͟?" I͟ S͟H͟O͟U͟L͟D͟ B͟E͟ relieved, but Zander's tone wasn't reassuring when he stated his intention. It was the way he spat *home*, as if there's an inside joke I'm not part of. As if he knows something I don't.

I'm confused, and this guy's mood swings are putting me on edge. One second he's tender, caring, and protective, then the next his expression is hard and unreadable.

I think he's mad at me, but I have no idea why.

"Well?" I prompt again, looking at the hand he has wrapped around my wrist. He's not squeezing hard enough to hurt, but it still reminds me of the rope. Of ownership. "You promise?"

"Yes." His tone is calm.

Too calm.

It's a total contradiction to the way his jaw keeps clenching. The way his nose is flaring. The way he nudges me along with him as we walk toward the woods.

Thayne, Marek, and another soldier are trailing behind us. Glancing back at them, I send them a helpless look. One starts to give me a comforting smile, but I stub my toe on a small rock and trip. Arms flailing, I close my eyes and brace for impact.

Halfway down, my free hand slaps onto hard muscle, stopping me from falling.

When I open my eyes, Zander's in front of me. He's down on his knees, sitting back on his haunches, literally putting himself between me and the ground.

And his wings are out. They're huge and covered in shiny black feathers. He's stretched them out and curled them around both of us, creating a dark cocoon of protection.

He must have reflexes like a cat. Or a bird, in this case.

He got onto the ground so fast.

I stare down at him, his lips parted as he looks up at me with concern.

A ripple of something pleasant courses through my body, and it takes me a couple seconds to realize it's attraction. My hand is still flattened on his shoulder, and my thumb involuntarily skates over his collarbone.

Closing his eyes, he groans quietly.

I swallow hard. "Are you hurt?"

A sliver of his irises appears through heavy-lidded eyes. "I believe that's what I should be asking you."

Even his accent adds to his sexiness.

"I'm good. Thanks." I straighten up, realizing he hasn't let go of my arm yet. Maybe that's a good thing. Maybe he's holding onto me so I don't injure myself.

As his wings retract, the feathers brush against my body as they shrink away. The silkiness skims over my butt before running along my arms.

I quiver.

Definitely experiencing some attraction.

I think I'm in shock. That's the only explanation I have for why the sensation causes goose bumps to skitter over my skin. Why it makes my nipples hard. Why I can feel my pulse in my clit.

"Are you sure you're all right?" Zander's tone is soft as he stands. "Do you need Marek to heal you again?"

His concern makes me smile a little. This side of him is way better than the one where he's stomping around and fuming.

"It's really okay. If the only pain I leave here with is a sore toe, I'll consider myself extremely lucky."

"Glad to hear it. This is as good a place as any. I'll need the portal now." Zander turns to Thayne as his wings completely disappear, and I lean to the side, trying to peek under the cloak to see where they went. They just literally absorb back into his body.

"A one-way?" The soldier lifts the little wooden box.

"No."

Clearly confused at the request, Thayne purses his lips. "How long should it stay open?"

"An hour. No more."

My eyes volley back and forth between them, having no clue why it matters if the portal stays open or not. It's not like I'm going to change my mind once I get through. There's no need to give me more time to decide.

Instead of passing the portal to me like he did with Jackie, Thayne drops it into Zander's waiting palm. The little thing looks like a flattened marble. It's shiny like glass, and the inside is an ever-moving swirl of milky white with some glitter.

I hold my hand out to accept it from him, but he doesn't give it over.

Zander stands completely still, staring straight ahead as if he can't see me.

Then he tips his hand, and the portal slips to the grass.

Shocked at the sudden bright flash ripping the air open, I react out of instinct and move closer to him. My hand ends up splayed out on his stomach, and he wraps an arm around my shoulders.

I'm a bit fascinated by how smooth and warm he is. I've never felt a guy up before, though I have an inkling most guys my age don't have abs like this.

Again, my fingers seem to have a mind of their own. They curl against Zander, and my nails dig into his skin. His muscles tense under my touch, and I quickly remove my hand. Tiny crescent shapes are left behind, evidence that I was there. I'm a bit mesmerized by my mark on him, and I shake my head at the ridiculous thought.

"Thanks again for saving me." I glance up at Zander's handsome face. "I really appreciate it."

You'd think the guy would be proud of himself for being a hero, but he looks so sad. The expression he wears now is different from broodiness or anger. His eyes are filled with pain.

There's a mysterious twinge of unpleasantness inside me when I think about never seeing him again, almost like I know I'm going to miss something I never had, which is crazy.

"Goodbye, Zander," I say, injecting confidence into the farewell. "I'll always be grateful to you."

Turning, I step toward the portal, but I stop so fast I almost trip again.

Because as I gaze through the watery film, I realize the other side is a location I don't recognize. In all fairness, I did tell Zander he didn't have to get me close to the city, but I don't see any buildings, houses, or roads. It's just another field and more flowering trees.

The lighting is different, though. Warmer. More dim, like it's a different time of day.

That makes sense. It was nearing sunrise when I was taken from the parking lot. I suppose if this is going to spit me out somewhere east of Dallas, the sun could be up already.

"Come along, Mae." Releasing the grip he has on my wrist, Zander slides his fingers until they're laced with mine.

He holds my hand intimately, the way lovers do, his thumb brushing back and forth along the inside of my wrist. I try to ignore the way my stomach tumbles and the unwanted butterflies erupting in my chest.

When he moves toward the portal, I ask, "You're coming with me?"

He doesn't answer, and it isn't long before fear replaces the butterflies.

Alarm bells go off inside my head as Zander steps through the opening like he's done it hundreds of times.

Staying planted where I am, I look at the way our hands are still connected with him on the other side. He almost looks like a mirage, distorted and wet.

He gives me an encouraging yank to get me to follow.

As I plunge through the portal, the air becomes cool and humid. A fine layer of mist coats my skin, and it smells like rain.

It's super weird entering a different world, but it's not painful. More overgrown grass flattens under my shoes, and approximately two seconds later, I realize we're not in Texas.

Not even close.

Dread falls heavy in my gut as I study my new surroundings.

These trees are full of pink blooms, and when the breeze blows, petals drift playfully to the ground. The air is unbelievably fresh and sweet-smelling. There's no hint of car exhaust, or other scents I'm used to in the city.

But it's not the beautiful scenery or the unpolluted atmosphere that tells me I'm far from home—it's the sky.

I tilt my head all the way back and gawk.

One half is night. The sky grows darker toward the horizon, and it's littered with stars.

In the other direction, there's a yellow glow, casting light on the peachy clouds with purple shadows.

Down the middle of the sky, there's an abrupt change between the two. It's like night and day collide in a strip full of prisms.

"Where are we?"

"Another realm." Zander keeps his hand twined with mine as he walks forward to make room for Thayne and the other guys coming through the portal behind us.

I gaze back at the field we were in before. The light is much brighter there, but it's dimmed down by the film of the portal.

"We're not in the Earth realm." It's a silly thing to say. Of course we're not on Earth, and Zander confirms it with an unamused twitch of his lips.

"It's called Dawn and Dusk. We're between the Day Realm and the Night Realm."

My hope withers. When Zander dropped that portal, I got so excited. I thought my world was just a few feet away. Now I feel farther than ever.

"Home?" I remind him, wondering if pestering the guy will annoy him into doing what I want.

Staying silent, he frowns and tightens his hold on my hand.

"Your majesty." The third soldier—I don't know his name—approaches Zander carefully, like he's afraid what he's going to say next will piss the king off.

This guy looks different than the rest. He has long dark hair, worn loose around his shoulders. Instead of black paint on his face, he has tattoos underneath his silver eyes. Black stripes go from his cheeks up into his hairline. More marks are on his forehead. At first glance, someone could find him extremely intimidating, but there's a softness about him that the others don't have.

Zander's shoulders are tense when he pivots to the man. "Yes, Torius?"

"What are we doing?" Torius' concerned eyes shift to me for a second before they land back on Zander. "We've broken protocol more than once today."

Since Zander is facing away from me, I can't see his expression, but whatever Torius finds there is answer enough. With wide eyes, the soldier backs off.

Confused, I glare at the men. I have no idea what's going on. Nothing about today has made sense. I just want to get back to my bed, take a long nap, then go on with my life as if none of this ever happened.

The last couple hours are going to take months of therapy to erase. Although, I suspect I won't forget Zander, no matter how hard I try.

Before I can ask any more questions, I'm being led to a tall bush.

Wait.

It's not a bush.

As we get closer, I realize it's a trellis. Ivy and other vine-like plants have grown over it after years of neglect, but I can see some white-painted metal peeking through in some places. It's strange that it's just sitting out here by itself in the middle of a clearing.

Once we get in front of it, Zander drops my hand and starts rummaging around in his bag.

"I need some strings," he grumbles to his men. "Leather or ripped fabric will do until I can find something more suitable."

Thayne takes a tan pack off his back. He reaches in and pulls out a whip-like tool. I thought the various blades were scary, but this thing takes the cake. It's obviously a torture device. The black handle is about a foot long, and attached to that, there are dozens of strips of leather.

Using his teeth, Thayne bites off two strings.

I suppress a gag when I think about where they've been. All the blood and skin they've had on them. Seeming to sense my discomfort, Zander frowns at the pieces when Thayne extends them his way.

That frown. I've noticed it's his default expression.

I wish I could see him smile, just once before I leave, but his lips turn down even more when he rolls the leather between his fingers.

"This won't do. Not for my queen. I'll use my shoelaces instead." Kneeling, Zander makes quick work of his boots, removing his brown laces and replacing them with the black whip material.

His queen?

Baffled, I just watch him with my mouth hanging open.

When he stands, he goes back to his bag and brings out a white chess piece. A queen.

Ohh. That queen.

Zander ties the shoestring around it and hands it to me. Then he does the same with the black king. Holding onto the ends of the string, he moves toward me with his arms outstretched.

I step back.

More frowning. "I need to put this around your neck."

"What for?"

"So you'll always have me with you."

That's… odd. Did the king form an instant crush on me or something? There were way more beautiful women in the group I came with. Sasha could've been a model, and she's the same as him—fae.

I have no idea why I've become special to him in such a short amount of time, but if it makes him happy to give me a gift before I go, I suppose it won't hurt anything.

I stand still while he secures the king around my neck and murmur, "Thank you," when he's done.

"Now you put the queen on me," he instructs, his voice dropping a little. The low rumble is sexy, and it does something to me between my legs.

Man, I really need to get away from him. This place is doing funny things to my body. My reactions are disconcerting, to say the least. I'm not a sexually driven person. I don't lose control of my impulses and I don't get urges to hook up with complete strangers.

Strangers with tan skin and brown nipples. An eight pack of abs. Those V lines by his hips.

Averting my eyes from his perfect torso, I wave the necklace at him. "You can't do it yourself?"

"It has to be a gift from you."

Fine. I'll play along.

Since Zander doesn't bend down so I can put it on him, I end up on my tiptoes as I try to reach behind his head. My front is pressed against his, and I'm suddenly very aware of our nearness while my fingers fumble to make a decent knot.

Zander's body is rigid, his chest completely still. I don't even think he's breathing, while I can't get enough air. With every inhale and exhale, my breasts push against his rock-hard stomach.

It makes me aware of my softness.

My vulnerability.

His face is dipped and mine is tilted up. Some of his inky black bangs fall to mid-nose over his crown, and I have to resist the urge to brush them back.

My cheeks get hot when I think about how close we are. Just a few more inches, and I could kiss him. I try not to look at his lips, but it's impossible not to.

He's not frowning now.

His mouth is relaxed, his lips parted slightly. It makes them appear even fuller than before. It still looks like he's pouting, but it's not the sad kind of pout.

It's the sexy kind.

And his scent… You'd think after a day of breaking up a sex trafficking ring and some fighting, Zander would smell bad.

He doesn't.

When I'm this close to him, I feel like I'm inhaling him. Fresh and alluring. Sandalwood and sunlight.

Speaking of smells, I bet I reek.

That thought convinces me not to linger. As soon as the string is tied, I back away from him, putting a few feet between us.

"Torius." Zander motions to a place in front of the trellis. "I'm putting you in charge."

With a hesitant expression, the warrior does as he's told.

Zander positions himself adjacent to Torius and extends his arms, palms up. "Take my hands, Mae."

I don't correct him on my name because it's not important. Staring at his waiting hands, I dig the toe of my shoe into the soft grass. "Is this part of the portal thing that'll send me home?"

Impatiently clenching his fingers, Zander gestures for me to come closer.

Okay, okay.

Slipping my hands into his, I startle a little when Zander speaks to Torius in a language I don't know. I'm fluent in Spanish, and I've dabbled a little in French and German. It's not any of those.

They go back and forth with each other. Torius' tone is confused and apprehensive, while Zander's clearly leaves no room for argument.

With a deep sigh, Torius relents to Zander's wishes—whatever they may be—and starts a longer spiel with the foreign words. It sounds… ceremonial. Maybe he's doing some kind of spell to send me home.

I keep waiting for the magic to happen, but it doesn't.

Impatient, I move a little closer to Zander to whisper, "When am I going to be home?"

"Very soon," he tells me.

Satisfied, I nod and let Torius finish.

Since I don't know what he's saying, I zone out a little, taking in the area as my gaze wanders. Thayne and Marek both stand on the other side of us, their shoulders squared with their hands behind their backs as they wear serious expressions.

Maybe frowning is a cultural thing here. Not all societies smile as much as Americans in the south. Growing up, I was taught it's polite to smile, even if I don't feel like it.

And I don't feel like it now, but old habits die hard. Wanting to seem pleasant and disarming to the two stoic soldiers, I send them a tight smile. Behind them, the forest in the distance becomes darker. Fog rolls in the shadows. Some stones are embedded in the grass, and when I focus on the area, I realize there are stairs. We must be on elevated land or something.

"All right, Mae." Zander gives my hands a squeeze. "Repeat after me, and you will be home."

The smile on my face turns genuine as I listen to the words he says. They're difficult to pronounce, but I try.

As I parrot the odd sounds back to him, I feel a little lightheaded and out of breath. Magic? My heart hammers as I stutter a few times, and he has to correct me on the last part, but eventually, I get it right. I know it by the grin on his face.

The man can actually smile.

And it's beautiful.

His teeth are white and straight, and I find out he has a tiny dimple near the right corner of his mouth.

Still grinning, he sways closer and flips the position of our hands so our fingers are pointing upward and our palms are pressed together. His fingers slide against mine until they're laced.

Locked together.

He lowers his face toward mine, and for a second, I think he's going to kiss me.

But he doesn't.

Touching his forehead briefly to mine, he says, "It was successful. I can feel it."

Huh? My head swivels from left to right, baffled over the fact that nothing happened and I'm still here.

All three soldiers get down on one knee at the same time and say, "Congratulations, King Zander and Queen Maelyn."

I let out a nervous giggle—a forced sound like my fake smiles. "Hang on a second. What?"

Keeping a firm grasp on one of my hands, Zander starts leading me back to the portal. "We should return."

Confused, I point at the bright opening as I drag my feet a little. "To there?"

As soon as we make it through the portal, I squint against the almost blinding sunlight and groan when it sends a sharp pain through my head. I cover my eyes, wishing I had some sunglasses.

Zander rubs the inside of my wrist. "I'm sorry, wife. It's dawn. The two suns in our kingdom collide on the east side twice a day, and the light can be difficult for someone who's not used to it."

My mind completely ignores his explanation about the suns, because I'm stuck on the word wife.

He called me *wife*.

The guys bowed down to me and said *Queen Maelyn*, which would imply that I married into the monarchy.

"Can I get a pause button?" I ask, still shielding the upper half of my face with my forearm as I narrow my eyes at Zander. "What are you talking about?"

"The suns—" he starts again, but I cut him off with a rude noise.

I'm done being polite.

As the convoluted pieces fall together, my heart pounds with a mixture of fear and anger.

Zander's been attached to me since he found me in the woods. He's been possessive, protective, and sweet. He showed signs of irritability when I didn't reciprocate his attention, but I figured that's probably because he's used to women throwing themselves at him.

When I think back on it, he was interested from the first second he saw me. He challenged that one dude who wanted to buy me. He played a game of chess and he won my freedom.

A terrifying thought comes to me. Maybe it wasn't my freedom he was playing for. Maybe it was… me.

In the other realm, the way he stood with me there, reciting words that sounded like rehearsed lines—it reminded me of a ceremony I've seen at least a half a dozen times in churches with family members and friends.

"What happened back there?" My voice shakes with emotion as I point at the trellis through the portal. "What did you make me say?"

Zander's face gives away nothing. "Vows."

"What kind of vows?"

"Wedding vows."

An unfamiliar sound—one of indignation and disbelief—erupts from my throat. "Wedding vows?" I gasp, feeling like I might pass out. "Why? Wh-why?"

"We're married now."

"But you promised you'd take me home." I probably sound like a broken record at this point. I've lost count of how many times I've asked them to send me back to where I belong. In my defense, they made it clear that getting me home is the goal.

"And so you are. You're my wife. Therefore, this is your home." He sweeps an arm toward the green grass, the forest, and the blue sky beyond.

"You tricked me!" I shriek, making more unattractive sounds I've never heard from myself before. "When I agreed to that ceremony, that's not what I meant, and you know it."

I tug my hand from his.

Zander's smile is gone now. I want it back. I want the kind words and the reassurance he gave me when I thought he was being a hero. I want him to tell me the things I want to hear.

Instead, his fingers shackle my wrist again. His hand is so big, his thumb overlaps his fingers around my delicate bone.

I can't get away.

Even if I fought with everything I have, I wouldn't be able to slip out of his tight grasp. "This is insane. You can't do this."

"I can, and I did."

No.

I'm going to have to figure out a way to convince Zander to undo the vows and pick someone else. He could literally have anyone he wants. I'm sure if he asked the girls in the group, one of them would volunteer to be his wife. He's incredibly hot. And a king.

Obviously, there's been a mistake, and I need to make Zander realize that.

I'm not like the other women. Evidence of the hard life Zander spoke of was clear on their faces. Their clothes. Their shoes. One girl looked like she hadn't had a good shower in weeks. I completely understand why they want to stay, but I have parents, a best friend, and a career to return to.

CHAPTER 7

Zander

"This is a big misunderstanding," Maelyn insists, dragging her feet as we go across the field.

"It's not," I disagree.

"Yes, it is. There's been a mistake. A really huge mistake. Earlier, you guys said the girls who get abducted have bad lives? They're chosen because they won't be missed? Well, they got the wrong person when they took me."

"I can assure you; you're meant to be here."

"And I'm telling you, they meant to get someone else."

"Who else would there be?"

Maelyn pauses. "You have to promise you won't go back for anyone when you return me. I don't want anyone else getting involved in this."

"I would never dream of taking someone in your place."

"I was in a less-than-reputable location when I was taken, and it's possible they were going after my friend Paige. We kind of look alike, though she's a lot taller than me. She's had a rough life. Her mom was an addict, and her dad was abusive."

"Her father hit her?"

"Sometimes. When she was ten, he left to go live with a girlfriend in another state. He never came back. I know it hurt her, but I was glad he was gone. Paige was better off without him. Besides, she spent more time at my house than her own growing up. Our sophomore year of high school, she ended up moving in with my family permanently when her mom got arrested. She's more like a sister than a best friend. We've had each other's backs through thick and thin. She helped me when I was younger, and I've been by her side in our older years. Even through all her bad decisions, which she's made a lot of in recent years, I've never abandoned her. She needs me. She's one of the reasons I have to go back."

This is intriguing. She speaks of this friend with such respect, love, and admiration. I want her to talk about me that way.

"How did she help you when you were younger?" I ask, wondering what it takes to be so revered in Maelyn's eyes.

"She protected me. Paige and I met halfway through second grade. I'd been getting picked on that year because I was so small—smaller than most of the kindergarteners."

"You were bullied? Who are these offenders? I want names and addresses."

She sputters out a noise close to a laugh. "I don't want you to go after anyone. Gosh, that was a really long time ago, and we were all just kids."

"They hurt you."

"Not physically. It was a lot of teasing. Some hair pulling, but mostly words."

"Words can hurt."

"True. Anyway, Paige showed up out of nowhere on the playground one day when I was getting hassled, and she announced that anyone wanting to mess with me had to fight her. She was so fierce and strong. She'd been held back a grade, so she was already a year older than most of the kids in our class. Plus, she was big for her age, so she was taller than some of the fifth graders."

"She sounds like a warrior."

"She was. She is. I wish I could be like her sometimes, but

that would mean going through everything she has… and I honestly think I would've broken under the circumstances a long time ago."

"You said your friend made bad decisions. What kind?" I'm honestly curious, and I prefer this conversation over Maelyn's constant protests.

The parallels of Paige's turbulent life to mine are peculiar. I've always thought of myself as damaged beyond repair but having the kind of love and loyalty Maelyn has given her friend would be healing, I imagine.

"A lot of partying, to start," Maelyn answers, a bit out of breath from the brisk pace I'm setting as we get closer to the forest. "I was mostly able to keep her out of trouble in high school because I refused to go anywhere with alcohol or drugs, but once we graduated, she branched out. While I was busy studying, she found other people to hang out with. I'm sure she's never dabbled in hard substances because of what she saw with her mom, but she drank quite a bit. Sometimes she'd call me to come pick her up from sketchy places. She's dated some pretty bad dudes, too. And then there's her job. I didn't agree with her stripping, but she didn't have the money to go to college and her grades weren't good enough to get a scholarship. I understand why she does it." She shrugs. "The Slippery Pole pays way more than any diner would."

"I still don't understand why you think she was the target."

"That's where the men got me—The Slippery Pole. I went to visit her, and they attacked me outside the building, so I can only assume they were supposed to take someone else. Maybe her."

She thinks she was brought to Valora by accident, but she's wrong.

I grunt. "Fate doesn't make mistakes."

"Fate?" Maelyn's tone is incredulous, as if I mentioned something that doesn't exist. "Fate didn't steal me. Those men did. Please, Zander. Jackie and Lupe—they got to leave."

"Some chose to stay."

"Well, that's not what *I* chose."

To say this isn't going as planned is an understatement. All the times I've imagined meeting my mate, it wasn't anything like this.

In my idealistic fantasies, she's overjoyed. My presence brings her happiness she's never known. The instant she sees me, she knows I'm her one and only, and she never wants to part.

But as I remember my clues, I realize I shouldn't be shocked.

You'll know her by her voice. She won't be with you by choice.

I'd hoped saying the vows would breathe some life into the bond. Although we haven't consummated it, the marriage should've strengthened our connection.

Yes, it was wrong of me to make Maelyn say the promise in the Old Fae language, but it's likely she wouldn't have repeated after me if she'd known the words.

From dawn 'til dusk, from dusk 'til dawn, I'll never love another.

Even though Maelyn doesn't understand the depth of the promise, the sacred oath isn't diminished. I can feel it in my soul. And, despite her objections, it gives me a feeling of peace, which is probably the only reason I'm not shifting right now.

Earlier today in the forest, my emotions almost got the better of me. My anger over the way my mate had been treated pushed me to the brink.

It's been at least a couple years since I lost control of the griffin inside me, and I don't want to tarnish that record. Especially not in front of Maelyn.

She can't know what I am.

Not yet.

As it is, she already fears me. Finding out I'm a monster won't help matters.

Shifting is unnatural, and people think of me as an abomination because of it. I'm right up there with Lycans, the murderous creatures that lurk in the Shadowlands. Even my best men, the ones who respect me the most, are put off by the griffin. As much as they try to school their features, they can't hide their fear and disgust once I'm changed.

"Torius, fly ahead to our spot and get the horses ready," I order. "We'll catch up to Kai and the others. I'd like to make it to Hailene by dusk."

The warrior does as I ask. Thayne and Marek are just a few steps behind me as we get to a break in the trees. A path that leads to a road.

Surely, news has traveled to the nearby towns and villages that there was another bust. These operations are happening less often than they used to, but some have been flying under my radar. Byris had at least two previous auctions before I got wind of his activities.

Unacceptable. "Thayne, I want a personal meeting with Gideon when we return to the palace. From the sounds of it, he's done business with Byris before and has more than one female in his possession. They must be stashed somewhere, and I intend to find out the location, with whatever means necessary."

"Ah, that won't be possible," Thayne says regretfully.

"Why not?" Hiking along the path, I tug Maelyn by her arm. I'd like to hold her hand instead, but her petite hand is clammy. I don't mind the sweat—it's going to take her a while to adjust to the heat in this realm—but it'd make it easy for her to slip out of my grasp.

Thayne awkwardly coughs, "Gideon got away."

I stop abruptly and turn around. "Excuse me?"

"He had a one-way portal. It seems he was prepared for things to go wrong and made a quick exit."

Son of a striker. He's the one I wanted most. Aside from Byris and Tarik, he's the one who deserves my wrath more than any other.

My anger rises up to dangerous levels again, and I start counting down to distract myself.

Ten, nine, eight, seven…

The telltale signs of an impending shift lessen as I get to zero. The bones in my chest stop rattling and the ache in my spine fades away. "Tell me we have Byris and Tarik."

"We do have Byris," Thayne confirms. "But Tarik perished by Torius' sword."

"No matter." I don't mind that the snatcher is dead, and I'm already thinking of all the ways I'm going to torture the answers out of Byris. "The auctioneer will tell us something useful if he values his head."

"Yes, your majesty."

Troubled, I continue our journey as I think about Gideon's escape.

I don't like the idea of hunting down a fugitive. Usually, the mission would give me a thrill, but everything is different now that I have a mate. Wherever I go, Maelyn will go, too.

I'd hoped to ease her into this world. Some leisurely time at the palace would do her good.

But if she's to be queen, she'll understand why we can't sit by and do nothing.

Maelyn tries to pull away from me again and fails. "Zander, please tell me you're kidding about the whole wedding thing."

"I'm not. I don't joke."

"You don't say," she grumbles out, and I recognize her facetious tone as human sarcasm.

There's a reason why I don't have a great sense of humor, and it's not just because I've always been serious.

Laughing isn't something I do.

Any extreme emotion, whether it's good or bad, can cause me to shift.

Because of this, I must keep my mood at a baseline that borders indifference. Apathy is my sweet spot. Anger and frustration are usually the main culprits for my accidental shifts, because I have difficulty controlling them, but happiness is a rarity I haven't had to worry about.

The air gets noticeably cooler as we get deeper into the forest where the shade is thicker. Frantically looking behind her, as if the field is Maelyn's last hope, she starts to struggle again.

Enough.

Pulling her to me, I let go of her wrist and scoop my arms under her back.

She gasps as she's hauled up into my arms. "What are you doing?"

"Carrying you."

"You're being such a caveman right now." She huffs as if she's frustrated, and she definitely is that.

But there's also something else flowing through the bond.

Arousal.

Being this close to me turns her on.

"What was the point of these necklaces?" Maelyn asks, flicking mine. She's probably trying to distract herself from the confusing attraction she has for me, but I'm glad she asked. "You gave it to me so I'd have you with me always, right? Well, that sounded like a goodbye."

"It wasn't a farewell," I inform her. "It was a commitment."

"A commitment," she repeats flatly.

"Yes. Objects of commitment, to be more precise. These pieces are the equivalent of wedding rings in your world."

Maelyn's voice quivers a little when she says, "I can't believe I trusted you."

Crying will do her no good, but her sadness stings and her feelings of betrayal burn. "You *should* trust me."

"And why is that? Because you're the king?"

"Because I am your mate, and you're mine."

"Whoa. Whoa, whoa. Mate? Like animals?"

"Soul mates," I clarify.

She gulps loudly. "I don't know what kind of drugs you're on, but you can't just go around telling people they're your soul mate."

"I'm not telling you. You just are. It's a fact," I state with confidence. "And that means I'll protect you. I'll kill anyone who tries to harm you or take you away from me."

"What if you're the one who's harming me?"

"I'm hurting you?" Horrified at myself, I stop walking and mentally inquire the bond for Maelyn's feelings. I take stock of where I'm holding her, but I don't think she's in pain. I'd feel it if she were.

Thayne and Marek are still with us, though they've fallen back, giving us more space to have a private conversation. Thank the suns. I'm already humiliated enough by Maelyn's rejection. If I were to injure my own mate on our wedding day, I'd consider myself the worst failure of a husband.

"No," she says, softer. "I didn't mean it like that. By not letting me go, you're breaking my heart."

She doesn't understand. As mates, we belong with each other, or else there will be dire consequences. Deadly side effects.

"You don't know the meaning of heartbreak," I tell her, and if her life is as good as she claims it has been, then it's true.

And that's good news for me. My dark soul needs someone pure and light. Someone whole and untainted.

Maelyn is that person. Fate got it right.

She's sunshine and I'm the shadows. She'll balance me out. We'll complement each other.

I decide we've done enough talking. Clearly, Maelyn isn't going to let the subject go.

We're almost to the small clearing where the horses are. Soon, we'll be on our way to Hailene. Once Maelyn sees the grandeur of the palace, she'll warm up to the idea of staying.

"Do you know how to ride a horse?" I ask. "Or would you rather ride in the wagon?"

She shudders so hard it shakes her entire body. "No more wagons. I'm actually pretty good on a horse. My parents sent Paige and me to horse-riding camp four summers in a row when we were teenagers."

I hate the thought of not being as close to her as possible, but we have a long journey ahead. A journey I'd rather spend in silence than hearing her pleas for freedom.

Maybe being separated from me for a time will give her space to realize I'm not so bad.

Reluctantly, I set her down next to a horse that's been fed and saddled. I already ache from her absence. My skin itches where we'd been touching, but I try not to let the displeasure show on my face.

"This is Gander." I pat the white steed. "He's yours now."

"Mine?"

"Yours."

"But—"

"No buts. He's fit for a queen and you deserve good things. He's one of many possessions you're automatically privy to as my wife." Before Maelyn can argue about our marriage or her length of time here, I put my hands on her waist and lift her. "Up you go."

She sputters as I place her atop the saddle. "I can do it myself."

I shrug before mounting my black stallion. Thayne gets on his horse and Marek hops up onto the driver's seat of the wagon.

I can practically hear the wheels turning in Maelyn's head as she runs her hand over Gander's neck.

What's she going to do next? Yell at me? Make a run for it? Neither will get her back to where she came from. The sooner she realizes that the better.

She says nothing. No more arguing. Just pleasant silence.

Feeling satisfied with myself for being stern, I give Onyx the cue to move forward and listen for Gander to follow.

He does. He's trained to. Even when he doesn't have a rider, he stays the course. Which means if Maelyn gets the idea to take off with him, he won't go.

Aside from the heat, it's a nice day for a ride. The first part of our journey will be shaded by trees, so I hope my mate isn't too uncomfortable.

A few minutes in, the bond flares inside me, causing my heart to thump erratically. There's an impatient buzzing traveling through my entire body, and my soul is unsettled. It isn't exactly painful, but it's unpleasant.

There's a yearning deep inside me. A gnawing in my gut.

Maybe I should've made Maelyn ride with me. If she's feeling how I am, she must be uncomfortable.

"Are you all right back there?" I call to her.

"I might pass out from dehydration, but yeah, sure. Just fine." More sarcasm.

Suddenly worried for her well-being, I yank on Onyx's reins and quickly turn around.

Of course Maelyn needs water.

What I'm feeling is her extreme thirst, not our separation.

I want to kick myself for not thinking of it sooner. She's human. Humans are fragile.

"There's a waterskin attached to the saddle," I say, reaching for my own. "It should be hanging to your left."

"Oh. Okay." Her voice cracks from the dryness in her throat and I feel even worse.

I've been so consumed by my wounded pride that I haven't thought of her enough. Guilt and insecurity replace the anger in me.

I've always wondered what kind of mate I would be. I'm not friendly and outgoing like the other kings of Valora. My cousin Kirian has always been charismatic in an effortless way. The Night Realm people literally worship the ground he walks on. Then there's Damon, The Dream Realm ruler. With his wit and humor, he can win anyone over.

It's no wonder that both of the other kings found their mates, broke the curse, and lived happily ever after. No, it wasn't an easy road for them, but their women were utterly devoted to them from the moment they met.

Sometimes love can make all the difference.

Or so I'm told.

I'd like to find out for myself.

But me? I'm just a surly asshole.

I almost feel bad for Maelyn for getting stuck with me.

"Oh!" Maelyn's exclamation comes out as a wet gurgle.

"Are you okay?" I trot over to her.

"It's cold," she says with wonder, and a bolt of satisfaction comes at me through our connection.

As she guzzles more water, her momentary happiness infects me, and a smile tugs at my lips. "Yes. It's waterfall mist. It stays cold always, and it's very refreshing."

"I-I drank the whole thing." There's a note of embarrassment and apology in her breathless statement.

"Then you can have mine as well." I untie the waterskin from my own saddle and extend it her way.

"You don't need it?"

"Not now. Plus, we have plenty more stowed away." Tilting my head toward the wagon, I indicate the traveling goods we have strapped on top. "We have more than usual because we had a trade meeting with the Night Realm delegates yesterday. Plus, I never leave home without a couple weeks' worth of essentials."

"You stay on the road that long?"

"Sometimes." As much as I like talking to Maelyn—especially when she's not trying to convince me we don't belong together—we've got places to be. "Let's get going."

I start to circle around again when she stops me. "Actually... the trail is wide enough for two horses to ride side by side, right?"

Turning my ear toward the leaves and trees rustling in the breeze, I calculate a twelve-foot distance between one side and the other. "Yes, I suppose so."

"Can I ride next to you?"

She wants to be near me. She likes my company. It's such a quick change from how she was acting before, but I'm not going to question it.

"Yes, of course." Motioning for her to join me—the hand command more for Gander than for Maelyn—I resume a steady pace and wait for her to say something. Hopefully something happy.

Fortunately, she doesn't disappoint. "Gander and Zander. Did you rhyme the names on purpose?"

"No. Gander was confiscated from a snatcher we caught. That was already his name, so I kept it."

"A snatcher. That's what you called the men who kidnap women."

"Correct."

"Do they do that a lot?"

"Not as often as they used to. It was more frequent back when my father was king."

"Why isn't he king anymore? Because he let it happen? Did the people revolt or whatever?"

Such a naïve little thing. Maelyn actually thinks the majority of citizens would overthrow a corrupt king.

She sees the best in people.

Even if we weren't a fated match, I'd find that quality incredibly endearing. And lucky, too.

Because I'm going to need her to see the best in me, even when it's hard to find.

The last thing I want to do is tarnish her blissful ignorance with the truth about our kingdom. Unfortunately, it's inevitable. The history of the Day Realm is, as humans would say, fucked up.

I decide to keep my answer short.

"He—" I pause, not wanting to tell Maelyn I murdered my own father. That I shifted into griffin form, hunted him down, and ripped his head from his body with my own beak. "—died five years ago."

"Oh, I'm sorry, Zander. That's terrible."

My reply is just a grunt. We meander along at a good pace for a minute, then she speaks again.

"You know, where I come from, people are supposed to get to know each other before they get engaged."

What is there to know? She's my mate. I'm hers. End of discussion.

I don't think she'd like that response, so I say, "If you could ask anything about me, what would it be?"

"Well, we just met, so it doesn't have to be deep or complicated. Simple stuff, like what's your favorite color?"

I'm not sure how to answer because I don't have a favorite color. When I'm in griffin form, I can see. I can see very well. I've just never thought of colors in a range of most preferred to least preferred.

To be honest, I don't have a favorite anything.

"Green," she guesses, bouncing a little, and I can hear the smile in her voice when she sings, "I bet it's green."

Well, I didn't have a predilection before, but I do now.

Now, my favorite color is green. I'll always associate it with the first time Maelyn was truly happy around me.

"You're smiling," Maelyn breathes out, seeming surprised by the grin I didn't know I was wearing. "I got it right."

"You did."

She squeals like she just won a contest, and my smile stretches wider.

The muscles in my face feel strange. Kind of tired and shaky, like they don't know how to keep this expression in place for this long. But it feels good.

The only thing that would make this moment any better is if I could see Maelyn's beautiful face beaming back at me.

I don't know what she looks like yet, but it doesn't matter. She's gorgeous. I can tell. I already felt her small soft body against mine, her silky hair tickling my arm when I held her to my side.

I can't wait to be that close to her again. My cock twitches at the thought, and as I catch a whiff of Maelyn's sweet, slightly floral scent in the breeze, my erection grows. My pants tighten. Wincing from the confinement, I adjust my position on the saddle to relieve the pressure on my aching balls.

Sweat breaks out on my forehead, and it's not because of the heat.

It's pure need, driven by the bond.

"Are you okay?" Maelyn asks, concerned. "You're shaking. Did you get hurt earlier?"

I try to speak, but a feral growl comes out instead. Maelyn gasps a little as her fear spikes.

Damn it. I hadn't even realized my chest was rattling from a threatening shift. I close my eyes, hoping to hide the way my irises change shape right before it happens.

Maelyn's presence is testing my control.

"I'm fine," I answer gruffly. "A busted lip and a couple bruises are bound to happen in a fight. Kai healed me, though, so I'm good as new."

"Glad to hear it." Her sincerity makes something twist in my chest.

"Did you—" I trail off, suddenly uncharacteristically shy.

"Did I what?"

"Did you feel it when I got hit?" I've been able to sense her pain all day, so I can only assume she felt mine as well.

There's a confused pause. "I'm sorry, I'm not sure what you're asking. Why would I feel something that happened to you?"

Hmm. Obviously, we're on different wave lengths. I wonder why I'm absolutely desperate for her, while she's fairly indifferent to me. I'm in tune with her every sensation and each shift in her emotions, but she seems completely oblivious to my feelings.

Maybe it's mind over matter. Too much rational thinking. Where she comes from, love is often a choice. Soul mates aren't connected in the same intense way as they are here.

The bond between fated pairs is magical. Irresistible.

How long will Maelyn be able to fight the pull? Will it be

the same with us as it has been with other mates in history? Will she be overcome by the drive and throw herself at me tonight?

Discreetly adjusting my hard-on, I listen closely for any hint that she's turned on. Quickened breathes. A fast pulse.

The fleeting attraction I'd noticed from her earlier is gone.

All I detect now is an undercurrent of nervousness, sadness, and determination. The fear has diminished, but the jubilation she should be experiencing is tragically absent.

I deflate.

Seems we won't be consummating our union anytime soon.

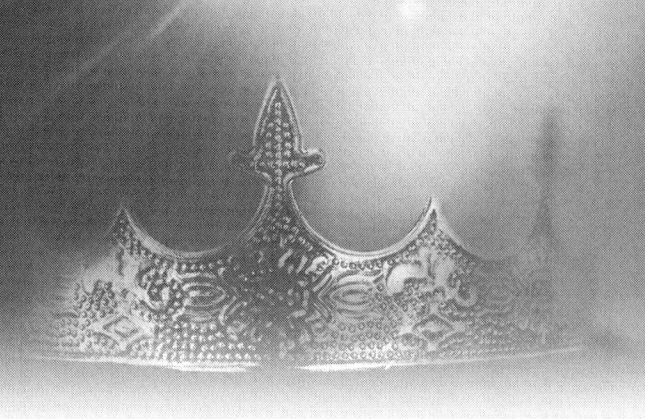

CHAPTER 8

Maelyn

I FEEL LIKE I'M BACK ON THE TRAILS AT CAMP. I DON'T HAVE to steer. The reins are useless in my hands. Gander seems to know this path, as if he could walk it in his sleep. I'm riding, but there's literally no skill involved.

I want to gallop. Feel the wind in my hair. Be in control.

My stomach gives a loud grumble, prompting Zander to point at another pouch attached to the saddle. "There's dried fruit and nuts in there."

He doesn't have to tell me twice.

I grab the leather bag and tug on the brown drawstring. My plan to charm the pants off Zander—figuratively speaking, of course—will have to wait while I stuff my face.

"I'm... sorry," Zander apologizes, the words stilted as if it's not something he says often. "I'm not used to thinking of others' needs. If there's something you want, speak up. I'll make sure you get it."

Except for leaving. He won't give me that.

I bite my tongue because begging isn't part of the plan.

I need Zander to believe I've accepted this situation so he'll let his guard down. He has to think I'm on board with this "marriage." And the only way to do that is to, well, just be myself. Really, it's not going to be that hard. I'll just be docile, sweet, and talkative.

And as soon as he turns his back, I'll escape.

It's all about waiting for the right moment. Maybe I could steal one of those portals from Thayne.

"And soon," Zander continues, oblivious to my internal scheming, "We should catch up to the others. By now, my men have stopped to hunt for fresh meat to feed everyone."

Hunt? "I take it you guys don't have a Walmart or something?"

"A what?"

"A store? That sells food?"

"Every town has a market," he replies, his brows furrowed. "But the vendors usually sell their goods outside."

"Outside?"

"From tents."

Absently, I nod as the strangeness of this world hits me all over again. "Do you have cars here? Television? Radio? Phones?"

Zander slowly shakes his head. "No. None of that. If we did, the sprites would die out from the fumes and frequencies."

"Sprites?"

Holding up his hands, Zander indicates a space of about eight or nine inches tall. "Little things that fly. They look kind of like people, but they're tiny. They're also very fast, secretive, and greedy. I suppose they're our phones, in a way. We hire them to relay messages to faraway places."

"Interesting."

I'll have to take his word for it because I don't plan to be here long enough to see one for myself.

It'll be a little harder to sneak off once we've met up with the others in the traveling party. More eyes will be on me, but maybe I could enlist the help of my fellow humans. Just because they want to stay, doesn't mean they won't assist my escape.

Sniffing, Zander tips his head and points to the road. "We're close and we're in luck. Lunch is still cooking."

I smell the air, trying to catch a whiff of what he smelled. After about twenty more feet, there's a hint of smoke. Like a campfire, and something savory.

My mouth waters.

When we get around a curve, two soldiers are standing on either side of the road in the distance. They're expressionless, their bodies stiff while holding spears as we approach.

"King Zander," they welcome in unison.

Zander sweeps an arm toward me with a hint of a smile on his lips. "And Queen Maelyn."

Their eyes bulge comically as their focus swings to me. Dropping to their knees, they greet me formally.

Flustered, I slash my hands through the air. "Oh, you don't have to do that. Really. Just Maelyn is what I prefer."

"She is the queen, and you'll address her as such," Zander contradicts firmly.

Embarrassed, I wave them up and shoot Zander a look. I wish he'd stop telling people that. The more people think I'm "special" the more they'll be watching me.

But the stink-eye warning I give him does nothing to stop him from telling the entire group. Within a minute, everyone in the large gathering has heard the news. Even the humans are kneeling and murmuring promises of undying loyalty as if they've been here their whole lives.

"Queen Maelyn!" someone shouts from inside a wagon parked up the road. It's about the length of a train car, and it's all metal. The small windows have bars on them, and from what I can see, it's packed to the brim with people.

It's the prisoners. One of them reaches through the bars, and his arm sizzles when it touches the metal, as if it's hot. "Have mercy on us. Please. My fantastical queen."

Chants for mercy start up from inside, quickly getting cut off when Zander motions with a finger across his throat.

For once, he and I are on the same page. They've really got

some nerve asking me for help. As if I could do anything to improve their situation.

As if I would.

Bless their hearts.

In a rare show of crudeness, I flip them the bird. Several of the humans snicker, but all the fae study my middle finger like they have no idea why I'm holding it up.

Apparently, the F-you gesture isn't universal.

Everyone's still kneeling, and I wriggle awkwardly. How long does this usually go on?

"I'm hungry," I say to no one in particular, and Zander nods.

"We'll eat now."

Thankfully, his wish for food gets his soldiers up and going.

Before I can slide off the horse, a warrior is stepping toward Zander. It's the scarred guy, Kai. "Your majesties, you might not want to loiter here too long. We got some information from Byris."

Zander sits up straighter in the saddle. "About Gideon?"

"Yes and no." Pausing, Kai glances at me.

"You can speak freely in front of the queen," Zander tells him, emphasizing the word as if he really enjoys saying it.

I refrain from letting out an exasperated sigh.

"All right." Kai shifts his focus between us, as if he's informing us both. "There's an unauthorized distillery south of Olphene."

A muscle ticks in Zander's jaw. "We can spare a few warriors. Send three or four men to take care of it."

"It's an *experimental* facility," Kai grits out, looking just as unhappy as the king. "And Gideon is the owner."

"Damn. We haven't had one of those in a while, but it doesn't surprise me that the scumbag is the mastermind behind it."

Kai nods. "It seems Byris is in the loop when it comes to underground networks."

"We'll use him to our advantage, then. Extract everything he knows about Gideon, including his whereabouts."

"Byris claims he doesn't know where Gideon lives or does business, but Pippin collected something from the auction site." Kai motions another guy forward.

Under the black liner smoked out around his eyes, I can tell Pippin is younger than the rest of the guys. He's lankier, his face is thinner, and instead of having the sides of his head shaved, there are intricate braids lining his scalp, while the blond hair on top is teased up like a frizzy mohawk, ending in a ponytail in the back. It's the most elaborate style I've seen yet. Overcompensation. Like he's trying to make up for his youth by having a great hair-do.

Smiling, he raises a stained white cloth, his turquoise eyes sparkling with pride. "This will help me find Gideon."

Zander wrinkles his nose, and I try not to notice how cute the action is. "Is that a bloody handkerchief?"

Pippin's excited expression falters. "It's Gideon's tooth."

Now I'm the one wrinkling my nose. I remember seeing the tooth fly up on to the stage. What I don't understand is why Pippin has it, or how that's supposed to help.

Clearly pleased, Zander's chest puffs up with a deep breath. "Good work."

The young soldier grins. "Would you like me to come along to the distillery?"

A few seconds tick by as Zander tilts his head from left to right, seeming to have an internal argument with himself. Like he's weighing the pros and cons of Pippin's offer.

He bites his bottom lip, sucking on it for a second. Heat infuses my cheeks when the plump flesh comes away wet.

I can't help imagining those lips on mine. Kissing me.

That annoying tightness in my nipples returns, and a throb starts between my legs.

As if Zander can sense my gaze, he glances my way. I quickly move my eyes to the trees because I shouldn't encourage this crush he has on me.

Finally, he says. "No, Pippin. Don't waste your power. If Gideon owns the distillery, we might get lucky and find him there."

"But if he isn't, I could help you locate him," the young soldier offers enthusiastically.

Zander looks to me and slowly shakes his head. "Let's tackle one problem at a time. The queen is going to be tired after this trip. Pack us some food and we'll be on our way."

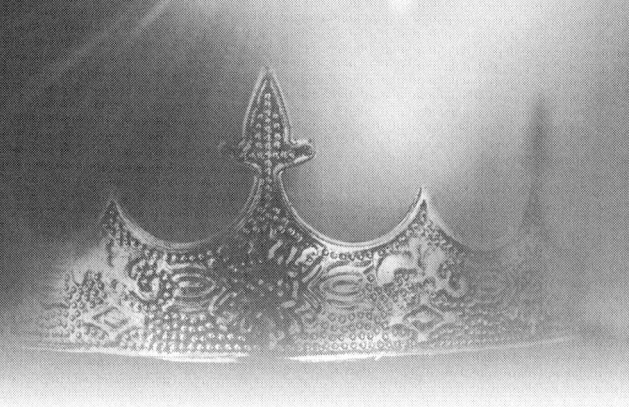

CHAPTER 9

Zander

THIS CHANGE OF PLANS IS UNWELCOME. I'M ABOUT TO introduce Maelyn to one of the ugliest realities of Valora.

"That guy said something about a distillery?" Maelyn pipes up next to me, seeming reenergized now that she's finished her lunch of roasted meat and fresh berries.

"He did."

"I went to a whiskey distillery last year on my birthday. It was the first time I got drunk. And the last. Holy hangover, Batman. Is it that kind of distillery?" She's keeping her tone light. Teasing, even. I can't even appreciate her playfulness because I'm in such a sour mood.

"No."

"He mentioned experiments. Is it a science lab?"

"You ask a lot of questions." Are all women this chatty?

"Hey, I didn't ask to be here. You can send me away if you'd like."

"Never."

"Well, you might as well tell me where we're headed and why you looked like you'd rather drink a bottle of castor oil than go there."

I sigh. I suppose I can't put the topic off any longer.

"There's history you need to know first. A long time ago, back when my grandfather Zed still ruled the Day Realm—"

"How long ago?"

"Over two thousand years."

Maelyn whistles. "I keep forgetting how long you people live."

"You'll be as old as me someday, and then you'll see a couple millennia isn't that long."

She scoffs, disbelieving. "Okay, sure."

"Anyway, a plague swept through the kingdom during Zed's rule. It only killed women of adult age, and—"

"Why only adult women?"

"Because it wasn't random. They were targeted on purpose. Remember, we don't have viruses here. It was a sickness curse from a powerful coven of witches."

"There are witches?"

"Yes, but this specific coven doesn't exist anymore. All except one of the members died a few years ago."

"How'd they die?"

"Do you always interrupt people when they're trying to tell you a story?" I ask, caught halfway between amused and irritated.

"Yeah, actually," Maelyn admits sheepishly. "My brain works faster than my mouth sometimes. I get excited and feel the need to get clarification or give input too soon, and then the topic goes off on a bunch of tangents. Sorry. I'll be quiet."

By the suns, she's adorable.

"I don't mind your questions, Mae," I say softly. "Sometimes it's hard to remember how confusing Valora can be for someone new. We're on our way to a Day water distillery. Glow is what people call the finished product. It's a volatile substance, and I have no one to blame but myself for its creation in the first place." I sigh. "The first time the plague came around, it lasted for several years before mysteriously vanishing. Then it reappeared about six years ago. When people were still sick and dying, I took matters into my own hands and invented the concentrated medicine. Day water can be healing, so I thought if I amplified those properties through distillation, it might cure the illness."

"Did it?"

"No. All I ended up doing is creating a new crisis. You've seen the powers some of us possess—like when Marek healed you. Well, fae abilities can be destructive, too. Some can wield fire, control the weather, or communicate with wildlife. Glow has a side effect—heightened powers."

"I imagine that could be dangerous."

"Very much so. On top of that, recently people have been taking the concentrated substance and distilling it further to make Blaze. That's why we try to destroy the facilities as quickly as possible—Blaze takes longer to produce, and it comes out in much smaller quantities. The sooner we can interrupt their process, the better. As it is, Glow is highly explosive if it mixes with stardust. Fortunately, stardust only comes from the Dream Realm, and we're as far from that kingdom as possible."

"How many kingdoms are in Valora?"

"Three. Day, Night, and Dream. The realm in between Day and Night is where we got married. It's a neutral territory, ruled by no one."

Maelyn becomes quiet as she processes all the information I've just dished out.

She's staring at me again. I can feel it. Because every time she studies me, I get these tantalizing sensations through our bond. Warmth in my heart and heat in my cock. My heart starts to pound and the hairs on my arms stand up.

If her eyes affect me this much, what would her hands do? Or her mouth?

"So, you were saying," Maelyn prompts. "The plague killed women?"

"Yes." I shake my head, willing my body to calm down. "It decimated the female population. Ninety-five percent, to be exact. That's when the kidnapping started. Our men wanted females, and they went to other places to get them. It became common practice. After my father Zarid took over, he pretended not to notice. He just… let it happen."

"They've been taking women from Earth for thousands of years?"

"No. Keep in mind the time difference between Earth and here—a year in Valora is one day where you came from."

"So that's…" Maelyn's voice is quiet, like she's talking to herself. "Two thousand something divided by three hundred and sixty-five… Like seven or eight years?"

"Sounds about right." I'm quiet for a beat, giving her the chance to speak if she wishes. When she doesn't, I continue, "Even with the abductions, the Day Realm never recovered. The ratio of male to female was seven to one when the plague resurfaced. We were able to contain it a little better the second time around with strict quarantines, but we still lost a lot of our citizens. Now the ratio is ten to one."

"Wow. That's a big difference."

I nod. "Fae fertility isn't good to begin with, so conceiving children can be difficult. After the second wave of the plague, the sex trade became worse than ever. That's when I took over, and I've been doing everything in my power to stop it since."

"The breeders," Maelyn says thoughtfully. "Sasha said something about the couples at the auction."

"Yes. They were there to purchase a fertile female with the intention of making her pregnant and taking the child."

She makes a sound of disgust. "Now, I'm not suggesting this as an option—*at all*—but if they want kids so bad, why don't they take babies?" A gasp escapes her as she clutches her stomach. "Or do they?"

"No, they don't take children. Their reasons might have more to do with their concern over sullying the bloodline than being moral. They'd rather impregnate a human woman with a baby who's half fae than bring a weakling into their family."

"A weakling." Maelyn chuckles. "I'm not sure if I should be insulted or not. That's my kind you're talking about."

"My kind, too."

"What?"

"I was born a halfling. My mother was one of the first human women to be brought here against her will when my father added her to his harem of women."

"Oh." Maelyn pauses, sounding sad. "But she chose to stay?"

"She had no choice." It's the simplest answer I can give at the moment.

I've said more than enough already. As much as I want Maelyn to get to know me, there are stories I'd rather save for later.

Later, when I'm not feeling so raw and exposed. When I've had time to adjust to the sudden change in my life. When I'm a little more confident Maelyn won't find me repulsive and inadequate because of the suffering I've endured.

"What do you mean she had no choice?" Maelyn swallows. "Like—like *I* have no choice?"

Her question slams me in the gut like a physical blow.

The comparison isn't the same. It's not. She's my fated mate. She's precious beyond words.

Yet.

Guilt eats at me.

I don't like it.

"The road might become narrower up ahead," I fib, careful with my wording so I don't hurt myself with a lie. "I'll ride up front until we reach our destination."

Squeezing Onyx's sides with my boots, I propel him forward, leaving my mate behind me. Her disappointment over the abrupt end to our conversation is another swift kick, but I don't want to talk about her captivity. Because it sheds light on one of my worst fears—that I'm more like my father than I thought.

CHAPTER 10

Maelyn

MY PLAN TO BE SWEET AND CHARMING IS unravelling fast.

Zander's refusal to acknowledge how he took me against my will is enraging.

Want to steal a woman? The least you can do is own up to it.

After he shut the conversation down and rode ahead, we traveled for a couple of hours in silence before arriving at a clearing where he said we'd set up camp for the night. In that time, I've reached steaming levels of pissed off.

I can't remember the last time I was this mad. Maybe when Paige drove off to see a guy she'd never met in a city two hours away. It wasn't just the fact that she wanted to hook up with a dude she only knew from the internet—I was angry because she was drunk when she left. Since she knew I wouldn't be cool with her meeting a stranger to begin with, she went without telling me. She never made it to see the guy. She ended up getting pulled over twenty minutes away, got arrested, and lost her license because of the DUI.

I'm not sure if it makes me a good friend or a bad friend, but I'd felt relief after that. Because of the cops, she didn't get into an accident and she didn't meet up with a potential serial killer. And she couldn't drive for six months, so it was easier for her to stay out of trouble.

Silver linings.

But there are no police here. No one's going to pull us over and stop this madness. The man who is the law has me under his thumb.

Or in his tent, if we're being literal about it.

This is more like "glamping." It's a real camp, with beans cooking over a fire and everything, but Zander's tent has all the comforts. The white structure is at least twice as big as the others for Thayne, Marek, and Torius. I'm sitting on a soft roll-out mattress that's as wide as a queen-size bed, and it's covered in white sheets and white furry pillows. Crates are set up on both sides like nightstands. Since the thick canvas keeps the bright daylight out, there are candles placed on each one.

Two chests line one of the walls. The trunks look old-fashioned, made out of intricately carved wood with curved lids.

Tiptoeing over to one of them, I fiddle with the latch.

I wonder if there're any portals in here.

There's a keyhole, indicating it's locked, but when I press in on the metal sides, the top pops open.

I stumble back.

Weapons. Lots of sharp objects lie within. Seriously, who needs that many swords and knives?

"If you're looking for clothes, it's the other one." Zander's voice makes me jerk, and I glance back to see him standing just inside the door flap.

My heart thunders from being caught snooping around.

Clothes. Right. Let's go with that.

Keeping up the pretense of searching for a new outfit, I go to the second trunk. When I peer inside, I only find big white shirts and khaki pants. "Do you have anything that would fit me?"

Zander frowns. "You can wear anything of mine."

I scan his wide shoulders and thick thighs. "That would be a no, then."

Thinking, he rubs his lip. "The shirts could be more like a nightgown on you. They'll be more comfortable to sleep in than what you have on."

"Okay." Lifting the clean, light-weight cotton, I ask, "Where's my tent?"

Zander raises his hands in a shrugging gesture. "You're standing in it."

"This is your tent."

"Ours."

Frustrated, I huff. "Can we just stop with this?"

"With what?"

"Pretending we're married."

"We are."

"Pretending everything is fine."

"It is."

I growl. "Pretending like you aren't keeping me here when all I want to do is leave."

Zander sighs tiredly. It's the same sound someone makes when they have to explain the rules of a game to a child four times in a row.

I know when I'm being gaslighted. Acting like I'm being irrational for throwing a fit when this is literally the worst day of my life is, quite frankly, shitty. My dad would say *ships and anchors* instead of shit. But I'm quickly learning life is too short for cuss word substitutes when you're seething.

"You seem like you're a good guy, okay?" I try to soften my tone, but I'm not doing a very good job of staying calm. "I don't believe you want to harm me. So just let me go."

Crossing his arms, Zander's gaze stays glued to the ground when he says, "No."

Moving forward, I invade his personal space. "The least you could do is look me in the eye when I'm asking you for my freedom."

He snickers, though there's no real humor in the sound. "No, I can't."

My face scrunches up. "What—"

"I'm blind, Maelyn."

I'm not sure what's more shocking—him telling me he's blind or him using my full name. Not Mae. Not queen or wife.

That's how I know he's serious.

Tilting my head, I look into his eyes—really look. The yellow glow doesn't creep me out anymore, so I study the variations in his iris. Most of the color is bright, like candlelight, but there are darker golden parts, especially around the center.

Focusing on his dark pupils, I shift my head to the right and notice how they move with me. But now that I'm paying attention, I notice a blankness there. It's as if he's looking right through me.

"You mean to tell me you can't see at all?" My voice is quieter now, his admission taking the wind out of my sails.

"Not even a little."

"But—but—" I stammer. "But you saw me on that stage."

"I heard you."

"You played that chess game with Gideon."

He holds up the white queen hanging from his neck and rubs the bottom. "Enchanted pieces. Each one makes a distinct sound when they get moved. Sounds only I can hear. Sounds I've memorized."

"You never run into things," I argue, as if pointing out his good mobility will somehow make what he said false. "You always know where I am." Raising my hand, I hold up two fingers. "What am I doing right now?"

"Giving me something humans call a peace sign."

I wasn't trying to convey peace, but he's not wrong. "How do you do that?"

"I've been without my sight since I was five years old. Fae already have heightened senses compared to humans. When we lose one, the others come forward. My hearing is especially good, and I've learned to use it to my advantage. Distance isn't difficult to estimate. The movement of air is very telling."

"If you don't mind me asking, how did you go blind?"

"The same coven that caused the plague—they cursed me."

"Why would they do that?"

"Revenge." Blowing out a breath, he shakes his head. "It's a complicated mess, but I'll try to explain. The witches didn't cause the plague for fun. The Night Realm paid them to. It was retaliation against us for crimes the Day Realm committed against them. Our kingdom and theirs were both in the wrong, and the witches got caught up in our war. Soldiers hunted the coven to punish them for the plague, and when the witches were found, their eyes were cut out. They were angry and wanted to hit the royals where it hurt—their children. So they cursed the princes."

"Is that why your eyes glow?"

"No. About ten percent of the Day Realm people have eyes that appear brighter. It's a genetic mutation. My father had it. It's one of the only traits I inherited from him, thank the suns for that."

"Why tell me about your disability now? Are you trying to get me to feel sorry for you?"

"I would never want your pity," Zander states, hard. "I'd rather have you hate me."

"You might just get that wish," I grumble.

"It's time for sleep."

"Is it nighttime already?" It's impossible to tell here.

"No, but you need a nap."

The audacity. I might be cranky, but I'm not a kid. "Maybe I'm not tired."

I am. I'm exhausted, but I'm also on an adrenaline high. I have been all day. At some point, I'm going to crash. I'm just not ready to be vulnerable yet.

"Sleep," he orders, his tone final as he pulls the sheets back on the bed.

"Are you always this bossy?"

He thinks for a second. "Yes. I'll wake you when it's time for dinner."

He points at one side of the mattress. It's not a suggestion. He's telling me to lie down. Like a dog.

Still clutching the nightshirt, I say, "Turn around."

"Why?"

"Because, privacy."

"I can't see you, Mae."

"Even if you are blind, I'm not getting naked in front of you."

"You're being ridiculous. Change." His tone is so haughty. So king-like.

My fists curl around the fabric so tightly I'm afraid my fingernails might pierce right through it. "I can't believe I actually thought you were handsome."

He lifts an eyebrow. "You think I'm handsome?"

"Thought. Past tense."

"I don't understand. How can you find me good-looking one minute, and not the next?"

"Because that was before you tricked me into marrying you."

"If you're attracted to me, you should be happy we're married."

I bark out a laugh. "Marriage is a lot more than attraction."

"You're right." Stealthily, Zander moves toward me, and I back up until the mattress behind me makes me buckle.

My butt lands on the soft feathers with an, "Oof."

Zander sits next to me, so close our knees are bumping. "My marriage to you is the linking of our souls. The promise to be together until the end of time. The vow that I will love you, unconditionally, forever."

With him this close, his body heat seeps into me. His scent surrounds me. If I'd met him a traditional way—at the gym or the grocery store—and he'd asked me out like a gentleman, I might've said yes.

Okay, probably.

Probably definitely.

I would've said yes.

But this unwelcomed arrangement is as untraditional as it gets in modern-day America. In less than twelve hours, I've gotten kidnapped, sold into sex slavery, rescued, then kidnapped again.

To top it off, I'm supposedly married to a stranger. Hell, I spent the day with Zander and didn't even know he was blind until five minutes ago.

Worst of all, he acts like I should be grateful to him for trapping me.

Leaning in, he inhales through his nose and exhales on a sigh. "I want to kiss you."

My heart does gymnastics inside my chest.

Is he crazy?

That's probably one of the worst things he could've said. Not only because we've been arguing and the timing is terrible, but because, regardless of our circumstances, I've thought about kissing him. I've wanted it—his pouty mouth pressed against mine—and I'm scared of the fact that I might like it. A lot.

And what would that say about me?

"I have a thirty-day rule," I blurt, admitting something I've only told Paige. "I don't kiss a guy for the first thirty days we're dating. If he's still around after that, then I know he really likes me and has good intentions. I know that probably sounds ridiculous and snobby, but I've seen women get used so many times. I've seen people give every single part of themselves and get nothing in return. My heart broke for them, and I never want to end up in a situation where I feel discarded. I'm cautious. Occupational hazard, I guess."

I predict Zander's going to ask more about my job or maybe spout off something about how we're not "dating" and we're actually married, but he surprises me.

"And who has passed your test?" Zander's facial expression darkens, and I swear his pupils do that thing where they look elongated for a second.

"One guy. He'd been a friend for a long time, and I knew he liked me. Honestly, I shouldn't have humored his idea to take it further. I never thought of him in a romantic way, but he was nice, and we got along. It was easy to hang out with him for a month because we already spent a lot of time together anyway, and he was totally devoted to the idea of being with me."

"And he kissed you?"

From the warning tone in Zander's voice, I get the feeling there's a wrong answer here. He doesn't like the thought of me kissing someone else—that much is obvious. But crap. It was in the past. A looong time ago. And it honestly sucked and ruined a friendship in the process.

"Yeah. It was… underwhelming." I shrug. "I knew as soon as we kissed it was pointless to try to have a relationship with him. I avoided him for a couple days after, then I broke things off. Friendship over."

Suddenly, Zander gets up and walks out of the tent. No explanation, no goodbye. He just goes outside.

Staying absolutely still, I wait for him to return.

Minutes pass.

Did he go get dinner for us?

I creep over to the doorway and peek my head out of the canvas flap. There's no one in sight. The fire's crackling under the cast iron pot in the middle of the camp. Every now and then, the lid clatters when steam escapes, but other than that, I hear nothing.

Well.

Apparently the way to get Zander to leave me alone is to talk about kissing other dudes. Too bad I don't have more stories about that.

But seriously. Who is he to judge? I don't even want to think about all the women he's been with. Where I come from, guys can sleep with dozens of women in a year, thanks to hookup apps. They might not have modern technology here, but Zander's a king. Kings don't need Tinder.

I'm not jealous. I'm not. Okay, maybe I am a little, but I don't want to admit that to myself.

More than anything, I feel a twinge of regret, because as maddening as Zander can be, I don't want to hurt him. And despite how many women he's had sex with, there's an innocence about him. An endearing-slash-infuriating cluelessness when it comes to women and romance.

But that cluelessness might be his downfall and my gain.

He's left me unguarded.

This might be my only opportunity to get away, and I better take it before he comes back.

CHAPTER 11

Maelyn

I'M NOT THE MOST PREPARED HIKER. IN FACT, I'M PRETTY sure my dad would give me the scolding of my life if he could see me right now.

Twigs and sticks scrape at my jeans as I trample through the overgrown woods. They snag on the nightshirt I tied around my hips, probably ripping it to shreds one tiny tear at a time. So much for having an extra article of clothing. I have a sheathed knife shoved into the waist of my pants and a pocket full of trail mix. One of those floppy canteens is attached to my beltloop, and it keeps hitting my hip as I stagger through the bushes. At least the water sloshing inside makes me feel a little more secure about this poorly planned escape.

Needless to say, I didn't get a portal.

It was risky enough approaching the horses on the outskirts of camp to snag food and water. I'd briefly thought about taking Gander with me, but I figured I'd have better success sneaking away on my own. Plus, I plan to avoid any roads, since it's easier to stay hidden in the trees.

A small branch whips across my cheek, leaving a sting behind. I reach up to touch it and a bit of blood comes away on my fingers. I should stop to clean it. The last thing I need is an infection, but I don't have time. I estimate I've been walking for about ten minutes—not long enough to stop yet.

If I can get to a town, I'll try to find a trustworthy person and tell them my predicament. Portals seem to be easy enough to come by; Thayne has a whole box of them.

"Ow," I hiss out my complaint when another stringy branch scratches my upper arm.

How are they cutting me so easily?

As I pass another close one, I lean away from it while studying the length of it for thorns. That's when I notice it's coming toward me. Almost like it's reaching for me.

I narrowly avoid getting cut by that one, only to be sliced by a different branch on my left.

"Son of a billy goat," I exclaim out of habit, before amending my statement. "Bitch. Bitch, bitch, bitch." The profanity feels good passing through my teeth, and it's completely warranted.

These trees are moving on their own.

Recognizing the specific type of tree that's harmful is easy because it doesn't have any flowering blooms like the others. With limp, ropey vines instead of true branches, they remind me of weeping willows.

I zig-zag to elude them, but there's too many, too closely together. It's no use.

"Stop it!" I whisper-yell, only to realize I'm talking to plants.

Keeping up my pace, I pull the nightshirt from my waist and slip it on. I don't take the time to button it, but it'll give me some protection on my arms.

As I take down my ponytail and shake my hair out to protect my neck, Thayne's initial warning comes back to haunt me.

It's too dangerous out there.

That's what he'd said about the forest. I thought he was talking about wild animals or exposure to the elements. Not murderous trees.

I turn in a circle to look back, wondering if I should just return to camp.

No.

I promised myself I'd get away.

Trudging further into the woods, I hunch my shoulders and try to make myself as small as possible while picking up my pace.

Ducking away from a few more scratching branches, I notice the vegetation starts to thin out a little. A small noise of relief resonates in my throat when I see a thin dirt path up ahead. It looks natural—not manmade. It probably doesn't go on for long and it's surrounded by more killer trees, but it'll allow me to run for a little while.

The second my shoes touch solid ground instead of a bed of leaves, I take off in a sprint. I revel in the burst of energy my body is exerting. The burn in my legs and lungs reminds me I'm alive. I might be a bloody mess, but I'm free.

I've only gotten about thirty feet when the ground suddenly falls away. My body lurches, and I close my eyes. Arms flailing, I wait for the pain of hitting something solid.

But there's no impact, and just as quickly as the path seemed to crumble, I'm standing on something solid. I'm anchored, my legs held in place.

When I glance down, I blink at the sight of my legs submerged in the dirt.

Only, it's not dirt.

It's sand.

Quicksand.

The stuff looks like dry, solid ground until it's touched. As soon as I skim my fingers over the wet surface, my dire predicament hits me hard.

I try to lift one of my legs, but I'm submerged up to my knees, and it's impossible. Grunting, I try again, harder this time. I put my whole body into the effort, wrapping my hands around my leg to lift it, but I lose my balance and almost face-plant.

I can't get out.

I'm stuck, and it feels like I'm being sucked in. Inch by inch, the level rises up my thighs.

Fast breaths heave in and out of my chest as I panic. "Oh, shit. Shit, shit, shit."

Fear, worse than anything else I've felt today, claws its way up my throat.

If I don't get out of here within the next few minutes, I'm dead.

Dead.

Using my fingers, I start digging around my legs, scooping the sand and tossing it away. It does nothing to help. Whenever I move any of it, more comes rushing in to fill its place.

Maybe I shouldn't move because the more I wiggle, the lower I sink.

It's almost up to my crotch now.

Realizing I should get rid of any extra weight, I throw the canteen, the knife, and the shirt about five feet away. They meet solid ground. So close, yet so far away. If I could wade over to it, I might be able to crawl out, but I'm completely immobile. My legs won't budge at all, and I'm afraid if I stick my arms in, it'll just pull me under faster.

I should chuck my glasses, too. I reach up to grab them, only to realize they're not on my face. The thick frames are gone, yet everything in sight remains sharp. Proof that what's happening around me is real and not a dream or a hallucination.

To add insult to injury, the killer trees start coming for me. They swarm around me, slicing my skin before dancing away. My forearms, my shoulders, my face.

Thinking I could use one as a rope, I try to grab onto it to pull myself out, but it slices my palm deeply. Crying out, I let go and clutch my bleeding hand to my chest.

The quicksand is up to my belly button now, and I have to raise my elbows up to keep them out of the wet sticky stuff. Even though having my arms in the air leaves them exposed to getting more cuts, I keep them there. I want as much of myself outside of this pit as possible.

For as long as possible.

At the rate I'm going, though, I'll be under in less than two minutes.

I let out an anguished sob.

There's nothing left to do. This is it. This is how I die.

All because I'm a stupid girl who couldn't just be okay with marrying a hot king.

My eyes sting when I remember how happy Zander looked at the ceremony. How hurt he was when I told him I wanted to leave. How he asked if he could kiss me, and I'd said no when—if I'm being honest with myself—I wanted to say yes.

He might be crazy, but at least he goes after what he wants. He doesn't live so carefully that he might as well not live at all.

Unlike me.

As I lose more of my body to the quicksand, my life flashes before my eyes, but not in the way people say it does.

I think about all the stuff I *didn't* do. All the parties I skipped. The countless Friday nights I spent inside, alone, because I was too afraid to go out and make mistakes.

And the kiss I really wanted from Zander... I'll never get to have it because of a dumb rule I made up when I was eighteen.

I missed out.

I'm going to die here.

Incomplete.

Bleeding.

Suffocating.

Big tears fall down my cheeks in hot tracks when I think about Zander realizing I'm gone. At first, he'll be mad. Then he'll be worried. He'll search for me and never find me, and he'll be devastated.

Unless...

I can't be too far from the camp. Zander had said his hearing is heightened. Maybe it's not too late for me.

"Zander," I call out weakly, my voice cracking as I cry. "Zander!"

The sand is up to my chest now, and the pressure it's putting on my ribs makes it hard to get a good breath.

"Zander!" I yell louder, but it still feels like my shout is getting swallowed up in the air.

I'm submerged up to my armpits now. I can feel the cool wet sand rising with every inhale I take. My collarbone disappears. It's as if the pit is greedy. It knows it's close to having me forever, and it starts sucking me in faster.

Within seconds, I'll be swallowed up and any chance of rescue will be gone.

Still, I try.

"Zander." It's barely a rasp. "Zander. Help, help, help." The breathless chant is all I can manage as the sand covers my throat.

Then I remember what Zander said about the chess piece that's still around my neck. When the bottom is touched, it makes a sound only he can hear.

Groping for the shoestring, I grasp it with my fingers and tug it out. I pull a muscle in my shoulder straining to get it, but I succeed.

Everything goes silent when the quicksand reaches my ears. Tilting my face up, I hold the black king in the air and rub the bottom in a frantic back-and-forth motion.

"Help." My eyes dart around, wishing for a glimpse of tan skin, dark hair, and yellow irises.

He's not coming.

The sand plays at the corners of my mouth as it coats my cheeks. More tears fall as I blink up at the bright blue sky peeking through the leaves above.

It's over.

I take one last breath through my nose, close my lips tight, and get swallowed up by darkness.

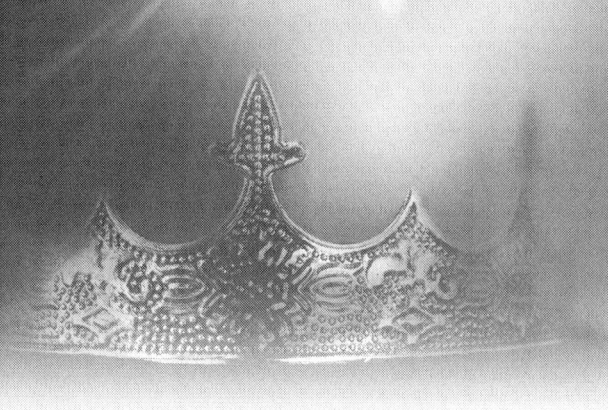

CHAPTER 12

Zander

FUCKING JEALOUSY.

I've experienced it before, but not to this degree, and the emotion snuck up on me. I've been jealous of my father; of the loyalty, power, and freedom he had. I've even been jealous of my soldiers, because their lack of rank means less responsibility. The weight of an entire kingdom isn't solely on their shoulders.

But I've never felt this way about a woman.

My rational side tells me Maelyn's interaction with the other male was in the past. And, from her retelling of it, she didn't enjoy it.

Of course she didn't enjoy it.

She's my fated mate. Not his. Being with anyone but me would never feel right for her, no matter how many boys she dated. She might not realize it, but that's the true reason she was never tempted by someone else.

Ashamed of my lack of self-control, I pace back and forth in the stream, hoping the cool water will calm me down. My paws splash heavily and make deep prints in the soft mud. Huffing out a breath, I scrape some rocks with my talons.

I'm disappointed in myself.

I shifted.

I didn't want to, but I knew it was going to happen when the bones in my chest shook until my ribs started to separate. At least I got to the cover of the forest before the griffin took over. I rushed there, kicking off my shoes, removing my precious necklace, and unbuckling my pants along the way. My soldiers saw it and made themselves scarce. They always do when I'm like this.

I should get back to Maelyn, but I need to be sure this tantrum is over before I return. If I'd shifted in our tent, I could've hurt her. There's not enough space, and the entire structure would've collapsed on us. Not to mention, she'd be so terrified, my chance with her would likely be gone. Any attraction she felt for me would've been obliterated.

Maybe she should be afraid. Maybe, deep down, she can tell I'm not right. A dangerous abomination.

"Zander." I halt all movement.

I could've sworn I heard Maelyn saying my name, but maybe it's wishful thinking. When I implore our bond, I realize it's difficult to feel her while I'm shifted. It's hard to tell if the pain lingering in my body is from her or the resettling of my bones, but I'm getting hints of overwhelming terror.

"Zander." There it is again.

It's faint, but the cry for help is unmistakable, and it's coming from the opposite direction of the camp. I look to the forest.

"Zander." Quieter now. Her voice is too far away.

What has happened?

Panicking, I take flight.

My wingspan is as wide as the stream, and the tips of my feathers clip against some trees as I rise above the forest and head east.

"Zander." Just a whisper. A desperate cry for help.

Maelyn's strength is fading, and her devastation pummels me.

She might even be dying, and I don't know where she is.

I yell out to her, but the only sound coming from my chest is a deep, menacing roar. Circling the area, I search the forest below. Somewhere among the bright green of the leaves, I look for a sliver of skin, clothing, or hair.

Another whisper floats on a breeze. I can't make out the words, but she's close. I dive through the trees and land ungracefully on a bunch of wild berry bushes.

I stomp around, sniffing for Maelyn's scent. She was here. Recently. Along with her sweetness, I detect the distinct metallic tang of blood.

Her blood.

This part of the Day Realm is filled with lashing trees. The cuts they inflict might not be deep, but they are many. Anyone who gets caught in a grove as big as this one can be left with hundreds of scratches.

The lashing trees don't mess with me. Last time one of them cut me while I was in griffin form, I snapped its trunk in half with my beak.

As I stalk past them, I search their shivering vines for a trace of red.

Then I see it. Moving forward, I count at least ten branches coated with Maelyn's blood.

If I weren't in a hurry, I'd tear down every single one that hurt her. They seem to know my thoughts, too, because they bend away from me as I walk by.

I no longer hear Maelyn's voice. Instead, there's a musical whirring I recognize from the chess piece I gave her. I follow the sound until I come to a path.

A waterskin, my dagger, and my nightshirt have been dumped on the ground. Confused, I scan the greenery for Maelyn.

Then I smell something musty and wet—a sand trap. As far as appearances go, the surface of the ground looks like regular dirt until it's touched.

My heart nearly stops when I see part of the black king

sticking out of the sand. I'd think Maelyn accidentally dropped it if it wasn't for the fingertip wiggling slightly beside it.

Suns and stars, Maelyn's in there.

I act fast.

Bracing my wings on either side of the pit, I hold myself up while reaching into the sand with my talon. After groping around, I find her body, wrap my claws around her middle, and pull.

I raise her mere inches.

Not enough.

I tug again.

These traps have consumed many fae over time. Even the most powerful faerie wings don't have the strength to fly away from it, but the stuff is no match for a griffin.

Very rarely am I thankful for my power. Today is one of those times, because Maelyn would be dead without me.

Beating my wings harder than I ever have before, I push off the ground with my back paws while holding on tight to my mate. Dust, dirt, and leaves go flying from the force of the air as I make it off the ground.

The top of Maelyn's head appears, and the sand bubbles and groans, protesting the loss of its latest victim. The pit seems to suck harder, but the sound of Maelyn coughing—and most importantly, breathing—encourages my motivation.

My back muscles strain as I get higher. Maelyn's legs are still caught, but they won't be for much longer. Just a few more feet…

As soon as she's released, we both shoot upward as though we were propelled from a catapult.

Maelyn screams, and the haunting sound is followed by a few sobbing wails.

I've never heard a better sound in my life.

She's alive.

She'll be okay. I wasn't too late.

It takes me a few seconds to regain my equilibrium, but once

I do, I head back to the stream. During the short flight, Maelyn doesn't fight me. She just hangs in my grip, trembling. Her legs swing limply, and I see she lost a shoe. Oh, well. Small price to pay for surviving a sand trap.

Once we get to the water, I lower us both into the three-foot depths. When I let Maelyn go, I expect her to run from me. I imagine her scrambling away and screaming, like so many others have done in the past.

She doesn't. She seems too focused on breathing and removing the brown gunk from her skin. I stand helplessly a few feet away, watching her cough and sputter while she splashes her face and scrubs her arms.

I want to help clean her off, but I'd probably end up scratching her. Which reminds me, I need to leave so I can shift back to fae form and come comfort her.

My anger from earlier has cooled. The near-death fright doused any petty jealousy I'd been harboring. Now I feel nothing but lingering concern for my mate's safety and gratefulness that I got to her in time.

Dipping backward, Maelyn rinses out her hair.

When she straightens, her eyes go directly to mine. She gasps and loses her footing, almost dunking herself in the water while getting a proper look at a griffin for the first time.

Trembling and wide-eyed, she stands.

I should move away, but I can't.

This is the first time I've seen her. Just as I suspected, she's perfection.

Her blond hair is darkened from being wet. The soaked strands cling to the skin on her neck and shoulders before ending a couple inches below her collarbone. The tank top she wears is pink. Her favorite color—I remember that tidbit from the auction. The fabric is light and thin enough that I can clearly see her bra through the material. Her jeans are like a second skin, tight and molded to her form.

I already knew she was petite, but seeing her small size is different than feeling it against me. She's so tiny. The shallow water almost comes up to her breasts and, even though it's distorting her figure, I can tell her body is shapely. She's thin, but the curves of her hips lead down to thighs I could squeeze.

My eyes travel up.

Her waist dips in at her middle. A hint of cleavage peeks out of her shirt. Every breath she takes makes her ample breasts strain against her shirt.

As beautiful as her body is, it's her face that does me in.

Her hazel eyes appear more vibrant from the tears in her eyes. Green—my favorite color—is the most prominent hue amongst the flecks of brown and blue.

I'm not sure if it's because she's crying, but her pale cheeks seem to have a permanent pinkness stained there, as if she's always wearing blush.

Her lips are like the rest of her—small but well-formed. The top lip has a pronounced cupid's bow, and the bottom is creased in the middle. The natural color is almost red.

I want nothing more than to know what it's like to kiss her, but I have no idea when that will happen.

A disappointed chuff leaves me, and the noise startles Maelyn. She stumbles back with a little splash, but she recovers quickly.

I start to back up and prepare for flight.

"Wait," Maelyn pleads, gazing at me with an expression I can't read.

It's not fear, and that shocks me to my core. Why isn't she running?

Tentatively stepping forward, she reaches out. When her hand is inches away from my face, her hand curls in on itself. Taking a deep breath through her nose, her lips press together, as if she's gathering courage.

Then she touches me.

Lightly petting my beak, she strokes me while I'm frozen in place. "Thank you. I don't know why you saved me but thank you."

She gives me a wobbly smile, and I notice her lips lift a little higher on one side. An asymmetrical quirk. Somehow, what could be seen as an imperfection adds to her beauty.

Being this close to her—watching her with my own eyes while she bravely stands before me—it's like a strong hit of Glow.

The one and only time I tested the drug on myself, I shifted into griffin form for two days straight. With a racing heart and energy through the roof, all I wanted to do was fly.

It's the same now.

I'm light-headed with euphoria.

I lean in and nuzzle Maelyn's shoulder. She stiffens momentarily, but then she relaxes and brings her hands up to the white feathers on my head.

"Wow, you're friendly." She laughs, albeit nervously.

And I'm jealous again. Of myself. Of the monster.

How can Maelyn accept him so easily? Is it only because he rescued her?

I saved her, too. Earlier today, I was her hero, but she ran from me.

She escaped from camp, preferring to take her chances with unknown dangers than be my wife. That thought sucks the happiness out of this moment, and I know I need to go.

CHAPTER 13

Maelyn

SHIVERING, I WATCH AS THE ANIMAL BACKS AWAY FROM me, its wings twitching.

"Don't go," I say, trudging forward on shaky legs against the current of the water. "I don't know where I am, and I need help."

I think I've lost my mind. Oxygen deprivation, maybe. I mean, I'm talking to an animal like it can understand me.

Before I can say anything else, it lets out a deep screech and jumps to the sky. The giant black wings block the suns for a second. In the shadow, I feel a sense of loss as a chill sweeps over my body.

Just as fast as the animal came to my rescue, it's disappearing over the treetops, its furry tail whipping in the wind.

Teeth chattering from shock, I stand in the water for a few seconds while I process what just happened.

I almost died, hopelessly sinking to my death. The quicksand had consumed me so fast. So ruthlessly. How could my plan go so horribly wrong?

I'd thought I was clever, getting away from Zander that easily.

Now I just feel like an idiot for underestimating nature.

I'm in over my head here.

Over my head.

Like the sand.

Hysterics take over, and I start to laugh and sob at the same time. My insane-sounding wails echo off the riverbank as I begin washing myself again.

I want to rinse the whole experience away. Sand is still in places sand should never go. In my nostrils and ears. Down my shirt. Inside my pants—I can feel the gritty little pieces in my underwear.

Just as I consider stripping, I hear Zander's panicked voice behind me.

"Maelyn!"

My heart leaps with relief when he emerges from the trees, looking frazzled with wild eyes and rumpled hair.

I'm not sure I've ever been happier to see someone. I don't even care that I've been caught. Maybe he'll punish me, but at least I'll be alive to experience it.

"I'm here," I announce weakly, wading over to the riverbank to crawl onto a flat rock.

"Where did you go?" He's breathing hard as he approaches me, and he doesn't have any shoes on.

My eyebrows furrow when I see his pants are partly undone. The top button hangs open, giving me an even better view of the dark happy trail under his belly button.

"I..." I think about lying. I could say I just went for a walk, but I'm too drained to be dishonest. "I ran away."

I expect him to be mad at me. To rage and yell. So I'm wary when he plops down in the mud next to me and simply asks, "Why?"

He knows why. He has to. And one glance at his eyes tells me I'm right. They're even sadder than usual.

Bringing his knees up, he props his elbows on them, linking his hands in front. It's a closed-off position. He's facing forward, keeping at least a foot of distance between us.

He's disappointed.

I'd probably be upset, too, if the person I thought was my soul mate ran for the hills.

"Are you going to hurt me?"

His face snaps my way, and his voice is sharp. "What?"

"For disobeying you," I clarify.

"I would *never* hurt you." The passion in his response sends funny sensations through my stomach.

Whether it's rational or not, Zander cares about me. His reckless devotion is ridiculous, but it's flattering, too.

He believes we're destined to be together. Even if I don't agree, it's real to him.

My gaze falls to his lips, and I remember one of my last thoughts before the sand pulled me under—I'd been mad at myself for not kissing him when I had the chance.

I'm probably not in the right state of mind to be making this decision, but I want that kiss. I've never wanted anything more. I need it.

Seriously, to hell with the thirty-day rule.

Rotating my shoulders to the right, I tug one of his arms down so I have an opening. Before I can second-guess myself, I clasp my hands around the back of his neck, rise up on my knees, and tug his head toward mine.

My lips touch his.

Softly.

Tentatively.

Unpracticed, since I've only done this once before.

His only reaction is a quick inhale through his nose, and he doesn't kiss me back.

The lack of reciprocation doesn't deter me. I continue with a second closed-mouth kiss, and I register the heat coming off him. His lips are so warm. His entire body is like a furnace.

Butterflies burst in my chest and my mouth tingles, but I start to feel silly because Zander's totally rigid, and it's like I'm making out with a statue.

Embarrassed, I start to draw back, but Zander quickly kicks into motion.

Looping an arm around my middle, he drags me onto his lap while his other hand goes to the back of my head. Within a second, I'm straddling him and he's pushing our faces together again.

The press of our lips is more confident this time.

Zander's mouth is soft and pliant, yet firm and controlling as he begins to change our kiss from chaste to passionate. His rhythm is choppy at first—just a bunch of closed-mouth kisses exploring my lips.

I'm trying to move with him, but I'm clumsy. Both of us are.

Then my bottom lip gets caught between both of his. We connect and pause, holding onto the moment as we fit together. He sucks on it and lets it go with an audible pop.

A whimpering sigh comes from my throat, and his grip on me tightens.

Holding me in place.

Although I'm the one on top, he has all the control as his mouth melds with mine. He's got me anchored to his body, one arm snaked around my waist and the other across my upper back with his hand placed at the nape of my neck.

And for the first time since I woke up today, I don't care if I'm trapped. For the moment, I feel safe.

Right now, I can let my worries go.

I don't want to think about the last ten minutes. I just want to have this. Him. Now.

My heart is racing a mile a minute, and I'm out of breath. When I open my mouth to draw in some air, Zander slips his tongue out. He licks the seam of my lips.

Heat explodes in my abdomen, and our kiss becomes a whole lot sexier. Instinct takes over, and I lose myself in him.

Scraping my fingernails over the short hair at the back of Zander's scalp, I meet his tongue with mine in a slow stroke. It's new and fascinating, and it feels so good.

We do it again and again.

Gripping my hair in his fist, Zander tilts my head to find a new angle—a way to go deeper. He captures my lower lip in between his teeth and tugs.

I moan. It's a quiet noise I didn't mean to make, but Zander takes it as an encouragement to do more. Reclining backward, he takes me with him as he lies on the ground, our lips still sealed together.

To brace myself, I put my right palm on the ground next to his head.

A sharp sting reminds me of the wound I sustained when I tried to use one of the vines to reel myself to safety.

"Ow," I softly cry out, the word muffled by the kiss.

Still holding onto my hair, Zander lifts my head away. "What's wrong?"

That's a trick question.

So many things are wrong.

Aside from my near-death experience, my body is reacting in a way it never has before.

The flames that were previously in my stomach have moved down, and I burn in all my most intimate places. The pulse between my thighs has grown to painful levels and straddling Zander isn't helping. He's hard. I don't have to be familiar with erections to be able to tell. The bulge pressing against me feels like a freaking baseball bat.

My body wants friction. Resisting the urge to rub myself on Zander like a cat in heat, I pant, "My hand. It got cut pretty bad."

You'd think a good make-out session would calm a guy down a little. For Zander, it's the opposite.

He's as frowny as ever.

Abruptly sitting up, he moves me off him. He's careful to set me down gently, but he doesn't let his hands linger. "Do you have any idea how dangerous this forest is?"

"I found out." Staring at the few inches between us, I suddenly hate the distance.

We'd just had our mouths, tongues, and hands all over each other, but maybe Zander's starting to realize I'm more trouble than I'm worth.

I should be happy about that.

I'm not.

My emotions are a raw jumble of confusion and cumulative devastation.

I've been through too much.

I need to sleep. To let my mind rest so it can filter through all the events. After a nightmare, everything is always clearer in the morning.

"I think I'd like to take you up on that nap."

"Get in the water first." Zander scoots forward, obviously expecting me to follow.

"I already washed off. I'd really like to get into something dry." And to get the sand out of my butt crack.

"You're bleeding all over, so I'm assuming you ran through a grove of lashing trees."

Holding my arms in front of me, I look at the dozens of scratches I obtained. There're too many to count. "Lashing trees. So the sadistic things have a name."

"Rightly earned, but don't take their intent to harm you personally. They go after anything that bleeds." With his back to me, he motions for me to come forward. "Day water is healing, remember? The scratches will seal up if you soak them for a few minutes, but we'll need Marek's help with your hand."

Being careful of my gash, I ball my hands into fists and crabwalk until I'm sitting next to him in the water.

"Can you—" I push down the urge to start crying again "Can you hold me?"

I don't feel like I have the right to ask Zander for physical comfort after rejecting him repeatedly and running away, but I'm so shaken.

Although I survived, my spirit is broken. I feel defeated and humiliated.

And the most depressing part is, I won't have the gall to attempt escape again. Not after what I just went through.

"Always," Zander grunts, surprising me and softening my heart.

Even when he should be furious, he's here for me.

Lifting his arm, he invites me in. I don't hesitate to lean into him. He draws me close, crushing my body against his.

The rush of contentment and safety I get in this moment is so strong it's jarring.

It's incredibly disarming.

I shouldn't be savoring the feel of my captor's arms, but I can't help it. I relax a little and rest my head on his shoulder. It just feels so nice to be supported by his strength and warmth.

"Want to tell me what else happened out there?" Zander asks, idly rubbing my arm while I let my hands glide under the water.

I shudder when I think about the quicksand. The darkness and the inability to breathe. The eerie silence.

"When I was little," I start, "my mom turned her back for a second when we were wading in the shallow end of a pool. I walked away from her, not realizing the incline made the water deeper just a few feet over. Suddenly, I was under water, and even though I couldn't swim, I tried. I kicked and moved my arms. It was probably less than fifteen seconds before she scooped me up, but it felt like a lot longer. Out there—" I hitch my chin toward the forest "—I fell into some quicksand, but it wasn't like drowning. It was like being buried alive. I couldn't thrash, couldn't do anything to help myself. It was crushing me."

Zander doesn't show fury or surprise, his default frown stubbornly present. "Very few people have ever escaped the sand traps. Since fae can't die from lack of oxygen, they get taken under, yet they survive, forced to live suspended in the depths."

Horrified, my jaw drops. "You mean, they exist in that until they die of dehydration or something?"

"Fae don't need water or food to live either. Eventually, they die of old age."

"But—but that could be thousands of years."

"Exactly. Your agony would've been ended much more quickly," Zander retorts gruffly. "Minutes, Maelyn. You were minutes away from ceasing to exist."

I start shivering again. "I know."

"How did you get out?"

"Something saved me."

"Something?"

"A big…" I wave my uninjured hand, "half-bird, half-lion thing."

"A griffin?"

"Yeah, I think so. That sounds crazy, doesn't it?" At first, when the strong talon wrapped around my torso, I thought it was Zander. I thought it was his arm reaching into the depths of hell to save me. Then I saw the claws once we broke the surface.

"Was it terrifying?"

"Yes." I blow out a breath and add, "But also kind of magnificent."

Shaking his head with disbelief, Zander chuckles a little. Maybe he thinks I hallucinated it.

"What? I'm serious. It was right there." I throw an arm out to where the creature had been just minutes before, and I'm a little shocked by the pink marks decorating my skin. Before, they were red and bleeding. Now they're closed, appearing as if they're days old.

Zander holds up a hand in surrender. "I trust you about the griffin. It's just…"

"Just what?"

"You called it magnificent. Why?"

"Because it was big and intimidating, but it was gentle, too."

"Would you say the same about me?"

I pause. Zander has a point. He's all those things.

Swaying my way, he lowers his head until his mouth is just an inch away from mine. "Would you say I'm magnificent, too, Mae?"

"Yes, but…"

"But what?"

"But the griffin didn't ask anything of me. It just saved me, made sure I was okay, then left."

Zander sighs sadly. "What am I going to do with you, wife?"

"Let me go." My voice betrays me. Because the demand has lost its fire, sounding more like a weak suggestion.

"What do you feel when I'm this close to you?" Zander asks, his breath wisping over my mouth.

It would be so easy to close the distance between us. To get lost in his kiss like I did before. In my wildest dreams, I'd never imagined kissing could be that good. That powerful.

For a glorious minute, I was blissfully unaware of everything around us as we made out. I know what Zander tastes like. How soft and warm his tongue is. How nice it would be to let good sensations eclipse all my thoughts.

And that terrifies me. "Scared."

"Nothing else?"

Oh, I feel lots of other things. Things I've never felt before. "I plead the fifth."

He frowns harder. "There's something wrong with our bond. My mate should never run from me."

"I'm sorry I did, if that makes any difference." Boy, am I sorry. What an epic failure.

"We're soul mates," he goes on vehemently. "You're supposed to be drawn to me. To ache for me as I ache for you."

There have been times when my body reacted to him so intensely that it hurt, but I don't voice that confession.

"I hate to admit it, but we need help," he mutters glumly.

"What kind of help?"

His lip curls with distaste. "The help of a witch."

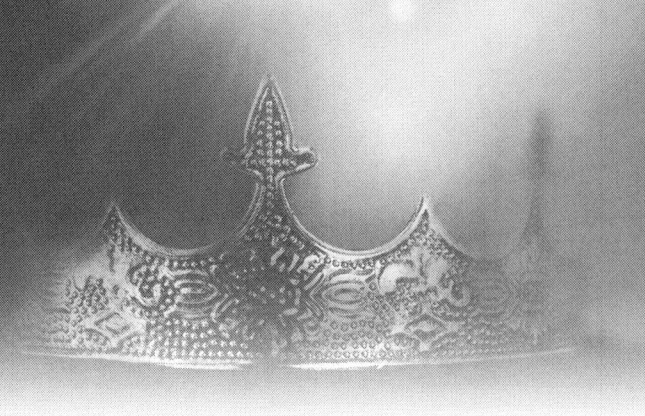

CHAPTER 14

Maelyn

EAVESDROPPING JUST INSIDE THE DOORWAY OF THE tent, I lean toward the canvas flap that ripples with the breeze.

"Find a messenger sprite and send her to the palace in Cassia," Zander tells one of his men. "Give her a portal. She's to give it to Astrid, and only Astrid. If she's quick enough, the witch should be able to use it to get here by tomorrow morning. I'll make it worth her while."

"Yes, your majesty," Thayne responds.

Apparently they're giving out portals to everyone but me.

Zander's quiet footsteps head this way, so I leap onto the mattress and sit cross-legged with my hands clasped in my lap. If Zander suspects my spying, he doesn't mention it when he comes inside.

"Did you get enough to eat?"

"Yeah." In fact, I might've overindulged on the bean soup that was served up for dinner. Camp food is supposed to be bland, but the soup was rich and salty, and even though I'm full, just thinking about it makes my mouth water.

Zander's lips quirk up. "You liked it?"

"It was pretty good," I admit.

"Are you in need of anything else?"

Thanks to Marek, I've been healed and I'm as good as new. I already took care of my personal needs behind a tree in the woods surrounding our camp, which was slightly embarrassing because Zander insisted on standing nearby and I'm sure he heard the tinkle.

My wet clothes are hanging from a rod holding up the ceiling of the tent, and I'm in another one of Zander's nightshirts. I have on a pair of his underwear, too. They're like boxer briefs, only shorter. Most of my panties are boy shorts, so it's not too dissimilar from what I'm used to, but I can't stop thinking about the fact that these have been on Zander's privates. And now they're on my privates. Yes, they're clean, but there's something super intimate about that.

It occurs to me again—technically, we got married today. I can only assume a traditional wedding night is the same for married couples here. Is Zander expecting sex? Will he push it, even if I say no?

Horrifying visions of him stripping me and roughly pushing my thighs apart while I'm powerless to stop it pop up in my mind. I know it's not a rational fear. Zander said he would never hurt me, and I'm inclined to believe him.

His amused expression immediately drops. "What happened just then? Where are your thoughts at?"

"You're not—" I cough as my throat gets tight with panic. "You're not expecting anything, are you?"

"Expecting what?" His face is blank.

"You know, it's your wedding night—"

"It's your wedding night, too." He cuts me off.

"Yeah. Well. What I'm saying is, you're a man. Are you going to—are you going to want—are you going to make me…?"

The meaning of my rambling finally sinks in and Zander's face gets hard. His eyes narrow and his teeth grind audibly. "I would never force myself on you. When we consummate our union, you'll be begging for my cock."

I cough again, this time from shock. No one has ever talked to me that way. I highly doubt I'll ever be begging for sex, but I don't say that.

"Okay. I'm all set, then."

"Good. Now you get to choose." Zander holds up some ropes. Two loops have been formed with knots, and the rough material is padded by thick white bandages. "You can sleep with these on, or I can hold you."

My eyes bulge at him like he's insane. "You're going to tie me up?"

"It's for your own good."

Clutching the covers to my body, I shake my head. "I promise I won't run again. Believe me, I learned my lesson."

He hikes a shoulder. "I can't be sure of that. Ropes or my arms?"

Helplessly glancing around the space, I try to come up with any other option. I'd thought maybe Zander would sleep on the floor, not in bed with me. I guess I could still ask him to do that, but then I'd be stuck with my wrists tied.

I don't want to go through that again, to be shackled like merchandise. Just thinking about the auction earlier today makes my stomach turn.

"Mae," Zander says, softer now, tossing the ropes down like he hates the idea of me tied up just as much as I do. "I just want to be near you. I will not hurt you. I won't… touch you inappropriately. That's a promise. Your well-being is important to me."

I allow myself to believe him, and as my anxiety drains away, I think of the way he held me in the stream earlier. How good it felt.

What he's proposing now sounds innocent, but my mind takes it somewhere else. Legs tangled together. Bodies pressed close.

My gaze roams his naked upper half, pausing on my favorite parts. The broad expanse of his muscular shoulders. His tight, brown nipples and the swells of his pecs. Every indent of his abs, plating his stomach like sculpted armor. That happy trail.

Inside his pants, the distinct outline of his dick is obvious. His hard dick. The erection is prominent against his thigh, trapped inside the khaki material.

Squirming, I try to quell the heat bursting in my core, but all I end up doing is making the cotton rub against my clit.

As if Zander can sense what's happening to me, the smirk playing at his lips broadens to a grin.

I blush and look away.

He can't know how I'm feeling.

Can he?

I've got to get a handle on my whiplash-like attraction. Mixed signals much? I can't insist that I want to leave him one second, accuse him of trying to rape me the next, then throw myself at him.

"I—I don't know if I can sleep with someone t-touching me," I stammer. "I never have before."

"Why don't we give it a try?" Zander drops a knee to the bed.

"You're going to keep your pants on, right?"

"It would be the proper thing to do."

That's not a yes or a no. Zander doesn't strike me as the type who adheres to anything proper, but he lies down with his slacks where they should be. Facing me, he places his head on one of the pillows and uncurls his arm. It lays across the mattress, his hand reaching out. Waiting for me.

"Look, I'm even on the outside of the covers." Zander motions to the sheet that would separate us. "Your virtue will remain intact."

I don't know any guy who could say that with a straight face, but Zander's not joking.

The Day Realm king doesn't joke.

Awkwardly, I roll toward him until he's behind me. Just like

I knew it would, Zander's arm fits under my neck perfectly. I let out a squeak when he hooks his other arm around my torso and pulls until my body is flush with his.

Keeping the covers around me like a chastity belt, I tuck them under me more snugly.

And then I melt.

All the tension leaves my body at the feel of Zander's warmth behind me. Even if it doesn't make sense, my system recognizes his nearness as a temporary reprieve from all the turmoil around me. The massive—multiple—adrenaline rushes from the day are finally catching up to me, and I'm ready to crash.

Despite my claim about not being able to sleep with someone so close, I feel like I could drift off right now.

Before slumber can claim me, I ask something that's been nagging at me all day.

"What did you make me say earlier today? At the ceremony? In English," I specify.

Zander's deep voice takes on a husky quality when he replies, "From dawn 'til dusk, from dusk 'til dawn, I'll never love another."

"That's a pretty intense promise. What makes it magical? They're just words."

"Here, every oath holds weight. Our souls reap consequences if we don't follow through. It keeps us honest."

"Or manipulative."

"Yes, or that." His fingers catch a wisp of my hair, and he starts curling it around his finger. "There's history behind it. A legend. But it was so long ago, no one knows if the story is accurate."

"Most legends come from truth, even if they change over time," I muse, getting more comfortable by the second. "Tell me."

"Yelissa and Conrad. It's the tale of the first fated mates in Valora. Back then, there were no kings and queens—just tribes that often warred with each other. Yelissa was a peasant girl, born to one of the lowest ranking women in her tribe. From the moment of her birth, everyone could see her beauty. She was gorgeous beyond words, and she was kind, too. When she was a teenager, she caught the eye of the tribe's leader and he swore he would have her for himself when she came of marrying age."

"But she didn't love him," I conclude, and Zander nods behind me.

"During her gathering trips to the mountain, Yelissa became friends with a lone wizard. Every day when she was sent to collect herbs and other plants, they would meet. He'd do magic tricks and make her laugh. Conrad made her happy. By the time she was almost twenty-one, they were in love. They knew their time was running out and the leader would make her his wife, so the day before her birthday, she packed a bag and ran."

"This is going to end badly, isn't it?"

Instead of confirming, Zander continues, "The leader's spies had been watching her, and they caught the lovers trying to flee. While the wizard had powerful magic, he couldn't overcome them when they ambushed him with iron nets and chains. The leader speared him through the heart with an iron sword, which is fatal for faeries. The iron poisons the blood, and they end up with a slow and agonizing death. They left Conrad there, bleeding and broken in the spot where the couple had first met, and they let Yelissa stay with him so she would witness his suffering. Conrad urged Yelissa to keep running before the men came for her. He wanted her to live somewhere else, free of the tyranny of her tribe, but she refused to leave his side. Five days went by before death finally came to claim him, but before it did, he offered to use what was left of his magic for one last spell. There was an enchantment he could create to bind their souls, but it meant when he died, she would perish, too. She begged him to do it, because she couldn't imagine living her life without him. And so he said those words—from dawn 'til dusk, from dusk 'til dawn, I'll never love another. When she said them back, she breathed her last breath, and they died together, wrapped in each other's arms."

"That's so sad."

"Fate recognized the tragic circumstances," Zander goes on, "and took pity on them. The promise became bigger than Yelissa and Conrad. Never again would a fated pair be kept apart if they were lucky enough to find each other. They'd be able to recognize their other half as soon as they looked into one another's eyes. Instantly, there was a wave of pairings all over the land. Even the leader, who inflicted the harsh punishment on Conrad, found his true match. Rival tribes had to come together because there were so many soul mates crossing over from one community to the next. Love won because of Yelissa and Conrad's sacrifice."

The story is beautiful and tragic. Part of me hopes it's not true, because why should some people have to suffer so badly for others to be happy?

"The fated couples," I begin. "You said all it took was one look for them to know if they belonged together?"

"Yes. Fate made it easy. No dispute, no questions. Just confidence."

"Is that why our connection doesn't seem real to me? Because you can't see?"

He grunts. "It wasn't an issue for the other cursed kings."

I'm quiet for several seconds, then I say, "It should've been my choice to say those vows, Zander. You took that from me."

"I know." Although he's finally acknowledging his wrongdoing, he doesn't sound sorry at all. Sleep is about to pull me under when he speaks again. "Maybe someday you'll say it and mean it."

CHAPTER 15

Zander

Dawn is here, which means we'll be interrupted at any moment. Astrid will arrive and, hopefully, I'll get answers. She might even be able to do a spell and fix the rift between my mate and me. Whatever's interrupting the bond needs to be repaired.

I don't like dealing with witches, but if I must, I'd rather it be Astrid. She assisted Kirian and Damon when they found their mates. Logic says she can do the same for me.

As long as she's willing, that is. I haven't exactly been nice to her in the past. My prejudice against her kind is rooted deep because of my experiences. First, the coven who took my sight away. Then the wizard who gave me my shifting power. Both were inflictions I never wanted.

Maelyn lets out a dreamy sigh, and I hold onto her a little tighter.

I don't regret the ultimatum I gave her last night. How could I when it worked out so well?

She had to be tied to something, and she chose me.

My presence must be calming because she hasn't woken once. At some point, she turned in my arms to face me and snuggled closer throughout the night. Her hands are curled under her chin. Even though the blanket still separates us, her leg is hooked over mine.

Every time a puff of air comes from her parted lips, it caresses the hollow of my throat, causing a ripple of pleasure to zing through my body.

I barely slept a wink all night, because I wanted to soak up every moment of this. Despite how many times Maelyn has voiced her rejection, I've never been happier than I am right now.

Unfortunately, even the best moments must end.

Right on time, I hear the whine of the portal as it opens somewhere on the outskirts of camp.

Ten seconds later, a raspy voice comes from outside the door flap. "Knock, knock. Better make yourselves decent before I come in."

"Do not enter," I say quietly, hoping Maelyn will sleep a little longer.

I want to consult with Astrid in private.

Carefully removing my arm from under Maelyn's head, I make sure the pillow is there to support her neck. When I slide my leg from between her ankles, the bond rebels at the loss of contact. My heart pounds against my sternum, causing a painful twinge in my chest.

"Damn," I whisper, rubbing the spot.

It's going to take me a while to get used to that.

After grabbing one of my tank tops from the storage trunk, I pull it over my head and exit the tent.

Outside, I sense several presences that weren't here yesterday. Behind Astrid's usual musty odor, I smell crisp night air, stardust, and autumn leaves.

"King Kirian?" I say. "King Damon? You're both here?"

"And us, too," Quinn speaks up.

Whitley giggles at something Damon whispers in her ear.

I'm surprised they all showed.

Kirian is my cousin by blood, and although we didn't start

forming a relationship until about five years ago, we've become close. Damon, on the other hand, has been a little harder for me to read. I don't see him as often, and I know he used to harbor bad opinions about my kingdom. I played a part in saving his life a few years ago, so that helped to clear the air between us.

Tilting my head toward the morning breeze, I try to detect others but find none. "The children?"

Kirian clears his throat as he steps forward. "Dani was still asleep when we left."

"Kallum, too," Damon adds. "The Dream Realm tri-annual festival is today, and they'll need their energy. Did you get your invitation?"

I nod. "I did. However, I've been a little preoccupied here."

"Preoccupied." The way the Dream Realm king says the word makes me think he has a different meaning in mind. "If that's what we're calling it these days." Snickering, he walks over and good-naturedly elbows me. "Congratulations, man."

"Thank you," I respond politely. "But the situation is a little complicated."

"How so?" Whitley comes forward to join Damon's side.

"Ah." Embarrassed, I scratch my temple. "She sort of can't wait to get away from me."

"That can't be true," Damon says confidently, and it's no wonder he thinks so.

He and Whitley hit it off right away. Even before they met, they had a deep connection in Whitley's subconscious when Damon went dream walking in her head.

Kirian and Quinn won't understand my predicament either. They've known each other since they were children, and even before they found out they were fated to be together, they were in love.

So, while I appreciate their moral support, I don't think they'll be able to answer my questions.

"Zander?" Maelyn's voice comes from inside the tent, and it causes a physical reaction in my body.

A tremor runs down my spine, and I have to clench my fists to keep from shivering. "Stay inside," I call to her. "I'll be back in a minute." I turn to the small witch. "Astrid, could I have a word?"

"That is why I'm here, correct?" Cheeky little thing.

I lead her over to Torius' tent. He'd said he was going to leave before dawn to go scout the distillery, so we can talk here while he's gone. It's smaller than my tent, and there's nowhere to sit except for a cot on the ground, so I just face the troll and get to my point.

"Maelyn was one of the kidnapped females in a bust yesterday. She's my mate—I'm sure of it—but she doesn't recognize the bond. In fact, she flat out denies it. I can't let her go, but she doesn't want to stay."

"My, my. That is a problem." Astrid's dress rustles when she fishes around in her pocket. "Can you tug the neckline of your shirt down. A little farther. Yes. Hmm." She leans in close, her face just inches away from my chest.

"What are you doing?" I stand completely still while she looks at… something. "What do you see?"

"My enchanted magnifying glass can tell me a lot about the soul."

"And there's something wrong with mine." It's not a question. Rather, a conclusion. Maybe I've told too many lies. Maybe I'm too dark. Too polluted.

Astrid makes a non-committal noise. "Your soul is fine. A little blackened, but it's intact. The bond, however… it's strong in you. It glows so brightly I can barely look at it."

"Is that good?" My impatience grows.

"What did you say you'll pay me again?" she backtracks.

I grit my teeth. "I didn't say. What do you want?"

"You once told me you don't do business with witches."

"I don't. I'm making an exception today."

She scoffs. "Don't lie on my account. How do you have an unlimited source of portals you can use on a whim? A witch, that's how."

"No. Thayne is a portal maker."

"A wizard?" She sounds impressed.

"Not exactly. That's his only ability. He can crank one out about every two weeks."

"Interesting."

"Yes. He's very valuable to my kingdom and the work I'm trying to do. With him, I don't need witches or wizards."

"Until now." I hear Astrid smile. "Now you need me."

"I didn't bring you here to listen to you gloat." Stepping back, I shove my hands in my pockets. "Can you tell me what's wrong with the bond or not?"

"Yes."

"Well? What is it?"

"I'm going to need a good grovel first."

"From me?"

"No, your horse," she spits sarcastically. "Yes you."

I knew our last interaction was going to come back to haunt me. It's been over three years since I spoke to Astrid, and our conversation didn't go well. She wanted a bottle of Glow. She wouldn't tell me what it was for, and at that time, very little was known about the volatile drug. I distinctly remember inadvertently insulting her when I refused.

But that was before I knew Glow could reverse iron poisoning if injected. Before we found out it's good for something. When used appropriately, it can save a life.

Frustrated, I spread my arms. "What do you want me to do? Get on my knees and beg for forgiveness?"

"That would be a start."

I bow to no one. An apology is out of the question.

"No." I step toward the door to leave.

Astrid catches my arm. "How about that bottle of Glow you owe me instead?"

My lips turn down. "You know how dangerous—"

"Of course I do," she harrumphs. "Do you think me an idiot? As long as it's not abused, you know how beneficial it can be."

She's right. It wouldn't be the first time I've given Glow to the other kingdoms for medicinal or magical use. As long as the person utilizing it practices caution, the substance can be helpful for healing or spells.

I've never given it directly to a witch, but I'm desperate.

"All right. You're talented and careful," I praise, hoping it will make up for the way I've snubbed her in the past. "You'll get your bottle of Glow if you can tell me something useful."

"Wonderful." She grins. "Your tether is defective."

Defective. Inadequate. Wrong. How many times have people referred to me as such in my life? Countless. And here it is again.

"Oh, don't pout," Astrid scolds lightly. "You're going to give yourself premature frown lines."

I scowl harder. "Our mate bond is defective?"

"Not on your end, King Zander. In fact, you're experiencing it doubly so. Do you feel Maelyn's emotions?"

"As if they're my own," I confirm. "Her physical sensations, too."

Astrid nods. "I can imagine it's quite intense for you. When I say your tether is defective, it has nothing to do with your soul. Do you remember when eight of the nine coven members perished?"

"How could I forget?" Damon and Whitley took them out, Dream Walker style. It was one of the most badass assassinations I've ever heard of.

"Well, when they died, some of the curses they created ended."

"Like the plague."

"Precisely. But we all know Merina's still out there somewhere."

"And we're assuming she's the anchor for my curse?"

"Yes. However, with the others gone," Astrid shrugs, "the bond became disconnected on Maelyn's end. Maybe someone else was her anchor. You're still very much fated, but she can't feel it."

I'd been afraid of this. When the coven was disbanded and their demise meant the end of the plague, I'd wondered about my own curse being altered. But the thought was too unpleasant, so I'd convinced myself I was wrong. Apparently not.

"Will Maelyn ever feel our connection?"

"Since it's the wonky curse that's blocking it, once the curse is broken, yes, I think so. All you have to do is the hanky panky, and everything will be right."

"The hanky panky," I deadpan.

"One of Damon's humanisms." Astrid waves a dismissive hand. "Have sex, King Zander."

I'm a little jarred by the blunt suggestion.

"Maelyn doesn't want me," I remind her, "which is the conundrum that brought you here. I can't bed her if she isn't willing."

"Well, I can't do love spells, if that's what you're after. They're not my forte."

"I wouldn't want that either." I shake my head.

It wouldn't feel right or real if Maelyn were coerced to fuck me.

"You're a good-looking man," Astrid says. "Can't you just seduce her?"

Thoughtful, I rub my lip when I remember Maelyn's desperate kiss and the way her body heats when we're close or when she studies me for too long.

"It's confusing. I can tell she's attracted to me. In fact, it's torturous for me. When her heart speeds up with excitement, when her nipples harden, when warmth floods her—" I end the sentence with a growl instead of going on about Maelyn's pussy. "Everything that happens to her, happens to me. I'm not only dealing with my own desire—hers is piled on top of it."

"She does desire you, dear king, but it isn't the bond making her feel that way. The physical attraction she feels is to you, not your soul."

I had assumed Maelyn's positive reactions to my body were a result of the bond. Now that I know that's not true, a notion I never considered is presented.

"You mean… she likes me for me?" The question sounds weird coming out because I'm not likeable, and it never occurred to me that my mate would fall for who I am as a person.

But I must admit, it has appeal.

Not relying on a mystical bond to yank me into Maelyn's heart would be ideal. If she could accept me there on her own, I would feel truly worthy. Chosen. Loved.

Obviously, she finds my appearance pleasing, so one half of the problem is already solved.

Sudden whispering comes from outside the tent.

"If he wanted us in there, he would've said so." That's Kirian.

"Why wouldn't he want our input? We're awesome." And Damon.

I should've known they'd be nosing around. I sigh. "Come in."

"See?" Damon says triumphantly to Kirian, not hesitating to step inside. "He totally wants us here."

I hold in another sigh. "How long have you been listening?"

Damon lays a hand on my shoulder. "Long enough to know you need a broment."

"A what?"

"Broment. We're your bros and we're having a moment. A heart to heart between dudes."

I shake my head at him, having no clue what he's prattling on about. "Okay."

Kirian shrugs. "So your mate is somewhat detached. It's not the end of the world. As long as you can get her to come around eventually, it'll be fine."

"Or else I'll die. Sure, no big deal." I inject sarcasm into my voice, knowing it's Damon's favorite language.

"There's an idea," Damon muses. "Play the sympathy card. Tell her your life depends on it."

"No," I dismiss firmly. "No pity."

I won't have Maelyn feeling sorry for me. It's why I didn't tell her that I'd regain my sight if we complete the bond, why I didn't fully explain the extent of the curse. If she's going to give her body to me, it can't be for any reason other than she wants to.

Kirian grunts. "Then you're just going to have to get her to fall in love with you the old-fashioned way."

If I could glare, I would. "Being fated mates *is* the old-fashioned way."

"In Valora," Kirian emphasizes. "But not on Earth. Maelyn doesn't understand our culture. You could use that to your advantage. Do things her way."

Date. That's what humans do. I've read enough books to know their romantic customs. Movies, dinner, long walks.

We don't have movies, but the other two are doable.

"Definitely," Damon tacks on. "Woo her with your charm and sparkling personality."

I aim a frown his way.

Now I know he's fucking with me. No one would ever describe me as charming in any way, shape, or form. "Not funny."

"He's right, Zander," my cousin says seriously. "There's a reason why fate chose the two of you to be together. Spend enough time with Maelyn, and she'll realize it, too."

"Well, she did marry me, so at least we're tied by vows."

There's a long, baffled silence.

"How did you ever manage that?" Astrid asks, fumbling with her magnifying glass again.

While she's busy trying to inspect my soul, I stab my fingers through my hair and grip the back of my neck. "Without telling her what it meant, I made Maelyn say the mate vow in the Old Fae language."

"You did what?" all three ask at the same time.

"It still counts." Defensive, I point at the other kings. "As if you wouldn't have done the same, had it been necessary."

They're quiet for a few seconds before Damon hoots with laughter. "Our wives are going to chew your ass so hard for this."

"No one gets to touch my ass except Maelyn."

"It's a figure of speech." He's still laughing. "Come on, Kirian. Let's go see how the women are getting along."

I can hear him snickering all the way across camp. Cheerful bastard.

Motioning for Astrid to go in front of me, I say, "We might as well join them."

"King Zander, there's one more thing. Something important you should know."

"Yes?"

"Since the bond is basically non-existent on Maelyn's side, if you were to send her back to where she came from, she wouldn't experience the effects of mate withdrawal."

Everything seems to halt. That's yet another instance that's never happened between a fated pair before.

"She could leave me, and it wouldn't hurt her?"

"Not physically," Astrid replies. "She might miss you, but it wouldn't kill her. She could go on with her life, none-the-wiser that she let her soul mate slip through her fingers."

"But for me? What would it feel like for me?"

"Absolute agony. You'd experience the withdrawal symptoms times two, and you'd probably die within a couple years."

Strike me.

Before, I reasoned that keeping Maelyn here was non-negotiable because I thought it would mean misery and death for us both if she left.

But if what Astrid says is true, I could give Maelyn what she truly craves—freedom—and she'd be fine.

I'm not selfless enough to make that sacrifice, though.

I've yearned for my mate for so long. I can't imagine letting her go now that I know what she smells like, what it's like to kiss her, the peace it gives me just to sleep next to her.

It might make me a heartless bastard, but I'm keeping her no matter what.

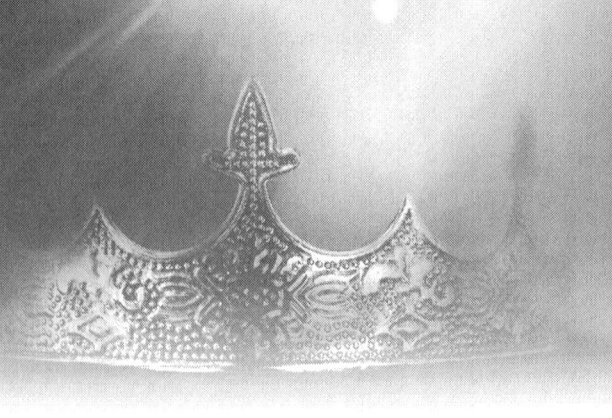

CHAPTER 16

Maelyn

"He forced you to marry him?" Quinn, the pretty brunette with the freckled face, gawks at me from where she made herself comfortable on the tent floor.

I rub my eyes, not sure I'm totally awake yet. "I repeated the words willingly. I just didn't know what I was saying. Is it legally binding?"

"Legal?" Whitley barks out a laugh as she runs her fingers over her very pregnant belly. "There's more to it than legality. It's an unbreakable oath from your soul to his."

"The concept is so absurd," I mutter. "Men can't just go around tricking women into marrying them."

Quinn and Whitley exchange an amused glance.

"What?" I ask.

Biting her lip, Quinn grins. "Kirian probably would've done the same thing if I'd refused him."

"Damon, too," Whitley agrees, shrugging like it's no big deal. "The fae are incorrigible, ornery, mischievous, sexy, secretive, and mysterious…" The sentence ends with a dreamy sigh.

"And you're okay with that?" They seem more than okay with it.

They're obviously very happy here and seem to think I will be, too.

As suspected, they both nod.

When they first came in and introduced themselves as the queens of the other realms, I'd thought they were here to whisk me away. They'd both jabbered on about being like me—human. At least, they were at one point.

"How long have you been here?" I ask, eyeing Quinn's casual attire.

While her ponytail shows off her pointy ears, her style is more like mine. Jeans and a nice tank top.

On the contrary, Whitley fits the role of fae queen well. She's tall and unbelievably beautiful, with vibrant red hair and striking facial features. The blue gown she's wearing enhances the sapphire color in her eyes, almost making them glitter the way Zander's do.

"I've been here for five years, so I'm fully fae now," Quinn replies proudly. "I have wings and everything."

"My answer is a little more complicated," Whitley states with a smile. "Long story short, I came here a little over three years ago and I became fae very quickly."

My eyes fall to her stomach. "And you're already having a baby?"

"This is my second," she corrects me, beaming. "Gonna pop any day now."

I look at Quinn. "Do you have kids, too?"

"I have a daughter, Dani. She's almost four, and I'm expecting again." Framing the slightly rounded bump on her lower belly with her hands, she smiles. "I'm only a couple months along but growing fast."

Flustered by their nonchalance, a string of questions fall from my lips. "You had no doubts about leaving your homes? No hesitation? No looking back? How is that possible?"

Whitley's happy face falls. "My parents died right before

I was brought here. We were in a car accident, and I don't have much family left. Damon saved my life, but that's not why I stayed. He's my soul mate. Where he goes, I go."

Before I can offer condolences for her loss, Quinn nods in agreement. "Kirian is my home. He took a portal to my woods when we were twelve, and it was love at first sight for me. He's been such a big part of my life, I can't imagine not being with him. Besides, with portals, I can visit Earth occasionally to make a phone call or two."

Sitting up straighter, I widen my eyes at her. "You get to go back?"

"Well, the timing can be complicated. Kirian gets to use one portal a year on his birthday. Otherwise, portals are very difficult to come by, and we don't have a portal maker like Thayne."

Portals are rare. Noted. Which means even if I had made it to a town yesterday during my escape, I wouldn't have found what I was looking for.

Quinn's face scrunches up as she thinks. "The last time I saw my parents was about six months after my wedding. Kirian went back with me but he had to wait in my treehouse, because to my parents, it had only been a half a day since they'd seen me. If I randomly brought home a man, they would've been suspicious. Also, I was about four months pregnant at the time, so I had to wear a baggie shirt to cover my stomach. In the years since then, we've visited Key West where my parents think I'm living. I call from there, but it'll probably be many years before I can see them face-to-face again. They think I work for a cruise ship, so I'm supposed to be out on the ocean right now."

"That's a pretty clever cover story." I pick at some fuzz balls on the sheets. "It's going to take me a while to get used to the time difference. I keep having moments of panic, assuming people are worried sick over the fact that I'm missing, but I haven't been gone long enough. I'd have to be here for months before anyone noticed."

"Yes!" Quinn pats her knees excitedly. "Don't you see, Maelyn? That's a good thing. You have nothing to lose by giving it a shot here."

"You think I should stay," I state, feeling a bit betrayed by my own people. They're definitely not taking my side. "Even when Zander is literally holding me captive?"

Quinn's face softens. "He loves you."

"He doesn't even know me."

"His soul loves yours," Whitley clarifies. "It's even deeper than conventional love. In Valora, when two people are fated to be together, it isn't a choice. Once you've met, that's it. You're connected forever. If you leave Zander now, he would—"

Suddenly, the door flap whips open and Zander's shadow looms in the sunlight. "That's enough chit-chat."

All of us girls squint and shield our eyes at the sudden brightness. I'm a little perturbed at the interruption. Whitley sounded like she was about to tell me something important.

"He would what?" I mouth at her, hoping she'll continue with what she was saying, but I don't get an answer because a tiny old lady pushes past Zander and comes straight to me.

Without asking permission to touch me, she grabs my wrist, raises my arm, and begins looking at my veins with a magnifying glass. I try to pull away, but she's surprisingly strong for her size.

She can't be much more than four feet tall, and she's rail thin. Her yellow dress hangs from her bony shoulders, like it's not quite fitted right. Long gray strands hang down to her waist, her skin is wrinkled, and her eyes are the color of whiskey.

This must be the witch.

"Um, hi?" I timidly break the stretching silence as I give my arm another tug.

She lets go this time. Slipping the tool back into her pocket, she spears me with her gaze. "You're human."

Confused by the obvious fact, I raise my eyebrows. "I know."

"One hundred percent."

"Right. Am I supposed to be something else?"

She looks to Zander. "This could be an issue for your position as king. She won't develop a power, and there's a chance she won't grow functional wings. Unless your father's genes come through, it's likely your children will have no fae ability."

"Does this mean I'm not Zander's soul mate after all?" I fold my arms protectively over my waist.

"Oh, no. You are."

I study her warily. "How do I know Zander isn't paying you to say that?"

"You don't believe me?"

"I don't know." Shrugging, I shake my head a little.

"Zander owes me all right, but not for telling you the truth. I'm not in the habit of proving myself to others, but let's see." With a smile, she rubs her hands together before pointing at yesterday's clothes hanging from the ceiling. "Are those still wet?"

Zander takes my jeans down, nodding as he feels the dampness. He tosses them to me so I can feel for myself. Yeah, it's going to suck wearing wet pants today.

Astrid makes grabby motions with her hands. "Give them to me."

After she's folded the jeans, she sits them on her hand while sprinkling dried flowers on them with the other. She closes her eyes for the beat of five seconds, her body swaying a little.

Then her eyes pop open and she dumps the heap, flowers and all, on the bed. When I pick the pants up, I'm surprised to find they're dry and warm, like they just came out of the dryer. They smell nice, too.

"Wow," I whisper, hugging the fresh fabric to my chest. "Thank you."

"You're welcome. That's the only freebie you get. So, rest assured, you're the king's fated mate." The confident little woman cups her ear, seeming to be listening to something outside of the tent. She turns to Whitley and says, "The portal is closing. We better get back. We don't want to miss the first ever fortune telling booth at the fair."

Smirking, Whitley plants a hand on her hip. "You just want to collect hair for your rugs."

"It's a reasonable payment for a reading from the queen."

"I feel used." Sniffing, Whitley tries to hide her amused smile behind her hand.

"You're going to love it. I've already seen the outcome—it's a hit. We'll be doing one next year as well."

Whitley rolls her eyes, but she laughs.

I have no idea what they're talking about, but the camaraderie between them is unmistakable.

Could I have something like that here? Could I make new friends, fall in love, and be as happy as everyone else?

Two men pop their heads in behind Zander. The brown-haired one immediately zeroes in on Quinn, while the blond guy's attention goes directly to Whitley.

Guess I know who's married to who.

For blind men, they sure are good at hiding the disability. Their eyes are clearer than Zander's, seeming to be focused on their wives.

When Quinn stands, Kirian comes up behind her and encircles her waist. "Hello, Maelyn." He doesn't even turn his head my way because he can't peel his lips away from Quinn's neck. "I'm Kirian, king of the Night Realm. We're so glad you're here."

"I second that," the blond man chimes in as he rubs Whitley's round belly. "I'm Damon, king of the Dream Realm. I'm also the funniest and most charismatic of the royals."

Kirian scoffs at the conceited statement. There's a backpack dangling from his hand, and Quinn accepts it from him with a kiss.

She looks at me and raises the bag up like it's a prize. "Maelyn, would you rather wear dresses or are you into casual clothes?"

"Casual, definitely."

She grins and tosses a triumphant look at Whitley. "Told ya. You owe me a fortune telling."

"Damn," Whitley bites out, pushing away the pack Damon brought for her.

Dumping the bag on the floor at the end of the bed, Quinn motions for me to peek inside. Keeping a firm grasp on the sheet, I make sure it stays wrapped around my waist like a skirt as I stand. Sensing my discomfort, Zander growls at the men and jerks his head to the door. Kirian and Damon take the message and clear out.

Shuffling over to the backpack, I undo the zipper. Inside, it's the stuff dreams are made of. Three pairs of jeans, two tank tops, and two t-shirts. There's even a sports bra, some panties, and a pair of sneakers. I look at the rubber sole and see the size '8' there. I'm a seven on my left. A six on my right. Close enough. Considering I lost one of my shoes to the quicksand yesterday, I'm going to need these.

I'm so touched by the unexpected kindness, tears spring to my eyes. "You brought me clothes?"

"You'll probably have to roll up the cuffs on the pants since you're shorter than me, but everything is stretchy for wiggle room. What I wouldn't have given for regular clothes the first week I was here," Quinn sighs with a smile. "I look forward to seeing you again soon, Maelyn."

"Yeah." Whitley starts inching toward the door. "If you need anything else, just send a sprite."

My face falls. "You're leaving already?"

"Like Astrid said, the festival is starting soon." Whitley shrugs. "You and Zander are welcome to attend."

My questioning gaze goes to Zander, but he's already shaking his head. "We have a raid this morning."

Damon—who might have a death wish—sticks his head back into the tent, and judging by the mischievous smirk on his face, I think he gets a kick out of badgering Zander. "Why don't you send Maelyn back with us for the day? Come get her after you're done. We'll make sure she's safe and has a good time."

"No." Zander shuts down the offer quickly.

"A raid is no place for someone who's still adjusting—"

"She's my mate. I'll make that call."

Reluctantly, Damon accepts Zander's refusal with a nod. The girls start to trail out, muttering goodbyes and wishes for good luck.

Quinn's the last to go. She sends a sad smile at me over her shoulder. I think it's meant to be encouraging, but she just looks like she feels sorry for me.

Dropping the sheet, I chase after them, forgetting to care about being pantsless. The shirt comes to my knees anyway. I want to watch them go through the portal, but Zander stops me just inside the tent. Hooking an arm around my middle, he keeps me in place. Making sure I don't run.

I wasn't planning to.

Part of me wants to be mad at him still, but I'm having trouble holding onto the anger. Sleeping next to him all night, combined with everything I went through yesterday, has made me associate his touch with safety. Plus, I'm crazy horny and being near him only makes it worse.

Maybe he really is telling the truth about the mate bond. If that's the case, my attraction to him can't be helped.

As Zander's fingers caress my waist, I suppress a shiver and back out of his hold.

I need distance. And clothes.

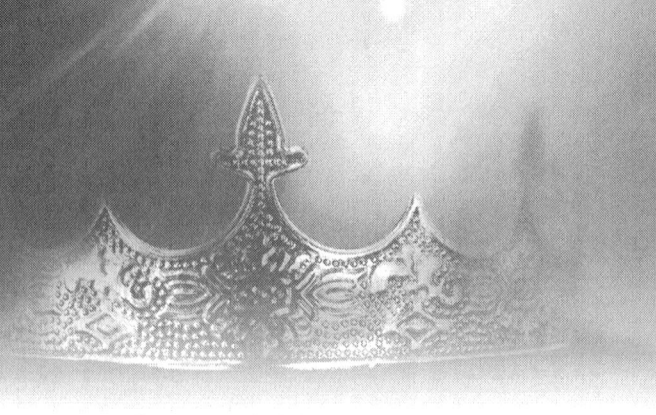

CHAPTER 17

Maelyn

I'VE JUST GOTTEN DRESSED IN A PINK T-SHIRT, A SPORTS bra, and jeans when Zander says, "I'm going to give you a chance to go back to your home."

"You are?" My eyes bore into the back of his head—I'd made him turn around while I changed—and he nods.

Swiveling toward his satchel, he picks it up and takes out the chess board. He drops the game onto the end of the bed. "You can play for your freedom."

I narrow my eyes. "Is this a trick?"

"Of course not." His signature frown appears. "But I gave the same courtesy to that lowlife gutter trash, Gideon. It's the least I can do for you."

Excitedly shifting from foot to foot, I watch as Zander kneels to unroll the board. The cream and black squares sit unoccupied, and all I see is an opportunity. Every blank space is a possibility. A future I haven't figured out yet.

I have an advantage, too—he has no idea how good I am at chess, so he's already underestimating my abilities.

I sit on the mattress. "So this is a bet?"

"A bargain." Zander begins lining up the pieces, putting the black team on his side. "If you win, you'll stay here for one month, without argument. If you still want to leave at the end of that time, I won't stop you."

A whole month?

"A week," I counter.

"Three weeks."

"Two." When Zander nods his compliance, I ask, "What happens if you win?"

"You stay forever."

Silence hangs between us as I contemplate the stakes. Five minutes ago, staying forever was the only option he'd given me. But if I beat him, I'll get a choice.

Like Quinn said, I could be here for a while before anyone back home realizes I'm missing. It'd be like a magical vacation where I'm not tied down by my own rules and expectations for life.

"Okay," I agree, and a flutter erupts in my chest.

Gasping, I rub my sternum.

"The bargain," Zander explains, touching his own chest. "Remember, promises are like solid entities here."

I felt something similar yesterday when he had me repeat our vows, but at the time, I was so jacked up on adrenaline, I'd thought I was having heart palpitations. Now I know something happened inside me.

I gulp when I realize I promised I'd never love another. No one but him.

If I win and I leave, would that oath follow me for the rest of my life?

Too afraid to ask, I steer the conversation elsewhere. "So, it's a problem that I'm human, huh?"

Zander tilts his head from side to side, appearing unburdened by the topic. "Astrid seems to think so."

"But Quinn and Whitley are, too."

"The other queens have fae ancestry to varying degrees."

"Oh. They do seem like they fit in here," I comment. "Do they have powers?"

"Quinn can tell when someone is being dishonest or evading the truth. It's a minor power, but it's useful during interrogations. She's the reason I knew about the auction you were in. She and Kirian come to the Day Realm every couple of months to help me question the criminals we catch. The underground has tight inner circles, and they often have information about upcoming events."

"And Whitley?"

"Whitley is a Seer just like Astrid. Both of them can tell the future and do spells."

Wow. Guess I can see why Astrid was so morose about my painfully average humanness.

"What about the other kings?" I ask.

Zander's hand pauses as he lines up my pawns. "Kirian can manipulate elements, like weather and nature. Damon is a Dream Walker. He can enter anyone's dreams as long as he has an object that belongs to them. Along with Whitley's help, they can control those dreams. They can even make people sleepwalk."

Blinking, I shake my head. "That's so cool. What's your power?"

Zander's frown deepens.

"I suppose if I want you to love me," he starts softly, "I'm going to have to tell you about myself, about my past. And not just my favorite color—deeper things. Things that make me… me. Things that make me weak."

"You? Weak?" I raise my eyebrows as my gaze drops to his chiseled arms and broad shoulders. "There are a lot of ways to describe you, but that's not one of them."

"In your world, physical strength, speed, or wealth is how power is measured, but here, being fae is everything. Magic is a person's defining feature."

He lets out a weary-sounding sigh as he gets up and comes to sit next to me. He takes my hand, gently toying with my fingers as if touching me gives him strength. And dang it, that makes me feel special.

"If a king is challenged for his role," Zander explains, "he can lose the position just as easily as he inherited it. Usually it's siblings or other close family members who try to take the crown for themselves, but any citizen could do it, and it's likely they will if they think they can win."

"Has anyone ever challenged you?"

"Not yet," he says, like it's an inevitability. "But I haven't ruled for very long. Having powers can make or break a king." Pausing, he lets several seconds tick by like a countdown to a bomb. "I wasn't born with one."

Roaming his muscles again, my eyes land on his sparkling orbs. "None at all?"

"None."

"Because your mother's human."

Zander nods. "I take after her, in looks and lack of magic. It was a great source of shame and embarrassment for my father."

"With me as your queen, you'll be even more of a target," I conclude, and Zander gives me a reluctant nod. "You could choose someone else."

His body goes rigid at the suggestion, and I have to admit, I'm not a huge fan of it either. Yesterday, I wanted him to pick one of the other girls. I should still want that, but when I picture him in the arms of another woman—someone who's tall, elegant, and fae—the thought causes an awful churning in my gut.

Swallowing my jealousy, I straighten my shoulders and speak the truth. "I don't want to be the one to drag you down, Zander. It's not too late to back out with me. I won't hold you to your vows. I'm not saying this because I want to leave you; it's not about me. This is about your future—"

"*Our* future." His fingers tighten around mine. "I can't give you up, Maelyn. I won't. I will *never* trade you for someone else."

Reaching up, he yanks the crown from his head.

"Maybe I should let go of being king." He turns the crown in his hands. Rotating it, his fingers touch the pearls and jewels.

"I never wanted this. I've tried so hard to fix this kingdom, but it remains broken."

I touch his wrist, stilling him. "This kingdom needs you. I've only been here for a little over twenty-four hours, but even I can see that. You've saved so many people from the auctions."

A humorless half-smile lifts on his face. "Try telling the people that. I'm hated in the Day Realm. The rest of Valora isn't a fan of me either, of the legacy my father left behind. The good citizens blame me for creating Glow, and the criminals want me dead for trying to put a stop to the female trade and the illegal distilleries."

"You're darned if you do, and you're darned if you don't. That's what my dad would say."

"Quite aptly put." His grip tightens around the crown. "It's so heavy, Mae."

Compassion bleeds from me, and I find myself scooting closer. "What about passing it onto a family member or something?"

He shakes his head. "My mother was burdened by being queen long enough. And Aunt Zephina—she despises the palace so much she refuses to live there."

I wait for him to list more candidates, but he doesn't. "That's it? There's no one else?"

Chewing the inside of his cheek, he mulls it over. "My grandfather, Zed, had an older brother. Ziah was the rightful heir to the kingdom, but he vanished when they were just barely adults."

"Vanished?"

"He didn't leave a note or take any of his possessions. Foul play was suspected, of course, but nothing could be proven. They eventually assumed he was either dead or he ran off to the human realm."

"The human realm? Your people trade all this—" I twirl my finger around in the air "—to live on Earth?"

"Not often, but it does happen. It means giving up the ability to fly while they're there, since their wings won't work outside of Valora. Some of their magic might remain for a time, but eventually they'll turn human. They'll lose the points on their ears and start aging as a human would. I've never understood why someone would trade the possibility to live thirty thousand years here for seventy or so there." He shrugs. "But maybe the long lifespan is too daunting for some."

"If your great uncle came back, he could take over." I'm trying to give the guy some hope here, but he doesn't seem lifted by it.

"He's dead, Mae. That's what I believe. Many who were alive back then say he was a good, righteous man. He was looking forward to leading our realm. He wouldn't have left of his own free will."

"Oh." My heart is heavy for Zander. For this responsibility he never wanted. For his inability to choose a different life.

He didn't ask to be here anymore than I did.

I told myself I wouldn't kiss him again. Told myself yesterday was a moment of weakness. I needed Zander. I took his kiss for comfort and distraction.

Now he needs me.

Tugging the crown from his grasp, I set it on the crate nightstand.

Then I lift a hand to his face and cup his sharp jaw. His dark scruff is rough and bristly, and I rub the coarse hair with my thumb. Closing his eyes, he leans into my touch, nuzzling my palm.

Curling my fingers around the back of his neck, I rise up to press my mouth to his in the slowest of kisses. It's so soft, our lips barely brush, but it still affects us both.

Wetness floods my center and Zander groans. His guttural sound only spurs me on, and I lick his bottom lip, hoping to get more of his addictive taste. I suck on the flesh, tugging it with my teeth before letting it go.

"Mae," Zander rasps, and suddenly, I'm on my back.

His weight presses me into the feathers underneath us, and one of his legs ends up between mine as he plunges his tongue into my mouth. His thick thigh rubs against my clit, and I buck my hips involuntarily.

My inner walls clench as more wetness seeps out. The new panties I just put on are damp now, but I'm too turned on to care.

As Zander continues to own my lips, his hand slides up my rib cage. The tips of his fingers graze the underside of my breast. Even through two layers of fabric, I can feel his touch as if it's on bare skin.

His palm closes over my breast and his thumb rubs my stiff nipple. Arching my back, I seek more contact, whining with relief when he repeats the action.

Panting and dizzy, I start to rock my hips faster.

I'm out of control.

I need more friction.

I need to come.

Heat builds in my lower belly until there's an intense pressure between my legs. Little spasms contract in my core.

I've never allowed myself to feel this way. Never let anything go this far. Never been tempted like this.

Until now, I'd been okay with that. My own fingers work just fine if I need a release. But I suspect with Zander, an orgasm wouldn't be like scratching an itch. It'd be like surviving an explosion. I'm afraid I'll come out on the other side, changed. Altered forever.

Running my hands up and down his back, I slip my fingers under his shirt. Glide over his muscles. Lightly scrape my fingernails over the ridges and bumps of sinew and bone.

I want his shirt out of the way.

With needy motions, I tug at it, and he helps me slip it off over his head. Our lips separate for the briefest second before his mouth descends on mine again.

Now that I have so much of his flesh available for my perusal, my fingers drift down to the dimples above his butt. Zander's tongue massages mine while I rub the indents in his lower back.

A feral sounding growl rumbles from him as he presses closer, his hard length digging into my stomach as he swivels his hips.

His mouth leaves mine to trail kisses along my jaw. Turning my head, I give him better access to my neck while absolutely losing my mind.

It feels so good—the suction of his lips, the scrape of his stubble. Zander latches onto a place below my ear, sending a jolt all the way to my clit.

Gasping, I roll my body against his, squeezing his thigh between mine as my orgasm approaches. I close my eyes, surrendering to it.

Suddenly, Zander's lips, his warmth, and his weight are gone.

I'm left alone, breathing heavily on my back, wondering how the situation escalated so quickly. Wondering why he stopped.

When I push up onto my elbows, Zander's facing away from me, his hands gripping the back of his neck so hard his fingernails might draw blood.

Unintentionally, my focus dips.

He's got what Paige would call a bubble butt. While I'm sure it's just as toned as the rest of him, the flesh is rounded.

Sexy.

"Zander, I—" I don't know what to say. Part of me wants to beg him to come back and finish what we started. The other half wants to thank him for not allowing it to continue.

If he'd insisted on more, I might've done it.

Releasing a ragged sigh, I sit up and run a hand over my face. My cheeks are hot. My lips are swollen.

"Are you ready?" All business, Zander pivots and motions to the game while removing the white queen from around his neck.

Okay. So we're going to go back to playing chess as if we weren't just dry humping.

Cool.

Great.

Not confusing at all.

I take off my necklace and we exchange the pieces.

After setting my queen in place, I fold my legs under myself, perch over the board, and muster up my most innocent tone. "Will you teach me the rules?"

I listen intently as Zander explains the different pieces—what they can do and how I can use them to my advantage. To his credit, he doesn't try to cheat by feeding me false information. He's thorough, even giving me a practice start and showing me an example of how to capture his king.

Now that we've officially started, I tap my lip, keeping up the appearance that I'm unsure of the move I should make. I open with a pawn to D4.

Zander mirrors it with a pawn to D5.

Choosing a more aggressive approach, I move my bishop to G5.

Zander blinks twice. It's the only indication of surprise, but it's enough to assume he's suspicious that I downplayed my skills. Maybe I shouldn't have given myself away so early, but I want to throw him off. He recovers with a pawn to C6, clearing a path for his queen to move. His bishop could come out, too.

After I move my pawn to E3, he chooses the bishop, sidling it up next to mine.

As our pieces shift around the board, I realize I'm having fun.

I need to stay serious because high stakes are on the line, but playing feels a little like flirting. It's like a dance. A push and pull. Without words, I assert my power. Zander takes it from me. I snatch it back.

I like watching the facial expressions he isn't aware he's making. A scrunch of his nose. A twitch at the corner of his lips.

"Your majesties." A voice comes from right outside the tent.

"It's time to get going. We need to pack up, and we'll have to eat breakfast on the way to the—"

"Just a few minutes," I call at the same time Zander barks, "Not now."

We share a small, secretive smile.

It's my turn and our pieces are spread out all over the board. He's captured several of mine, but I have more of his.

I nudge my queen one space diagonal, forcing Zander to move his king.

"I thought you didn't know how to play," he says darkly, though I catch a hint of amusement in his voice.

"Did I say I didn't know how?"

His lips curl up with an impressed smirk. "No. You certainly didn't."

Refusing to be distracted by how hot he is when he smiles, I look back at the game. "My dad taught me when I was five."

"I learned from my mother. You're a formidable opponent, wife."

Oh, my nickname got an upgrade. It's not the first time he's called me his wife, but the way he says it now sounds like a reminder. He doesn't want me to forget I'm his.

And that tells me his confidence is shaken. I might actually win.

I start thinking about how I'll spend my two weeks here. I'd like to see the palace. See some sights. Visit the other humans and make sure they're settling in okay.

Sadness flickers dimly in my mind when I picture myself back in my room—in my bed—alone. Zander might be a brute, but he's a brute who's made his affection and intentions very clear.

Guys in my world aren't like him. Girls are a dime a dozen, and no one can keep their focus on me long enough before getting distracted by someone shinier.

Someone *more*. More outspoken, more assertive, more

spontaneous, more willing to give them the physical fulfillment they don't want to wait for.

And I can't deny there's something between Zander and me. Whether it's the magical mate bond or natural attraction, I'm drawn to him.

I broke my rules for him. He's the one man I've ever caved for, and I don't regret it one bit. In fact, my body's still buzzing from earlier, as if it's complaining because we didn't go further.

I steal a glance at Zander's serious face as he stares blankly at some spot above the board.

Rubbing his lower lip, he moves his queen. "Checkmate."

My heart drops as disbelief ripples through me. "What?"

Frantically searching the game for the ending I didn't see coming, my eyes dart around the board.

I was so deep in thought, I missed the fact that Zander had a direct line to my king. Even if I move it, it won't change the outcome.

I got distracted and cocky. Total rookie mistake. How could I let this happen?

Oh, yeah, I know how. My vagina is basically in the driver's seat right now.

"It was a good game." Zander's consolation is soft and sincere as he collects the pieces and rolls up the board. "I enjoyed going up against you."

"Rematch?" I need to redeem myself and get a second chance at my choice.

"I'd like that sometime, but only for fun."

"Double or nothing," I insist, sounding desperate. "I'll agree to a month instead."

Zander shakes his head. "The deal is done."

Done.

Final.

My fate here is sealed.

"It was a crappy proposal from the start," I point out, realizing

I'm being a sore loser. "You thought I was an amateur. There's no honor in wiping the floor with a beginner."

"But you're not a beginner, are you?" he shoots back.

No, I'm not. I actually thought I had a chance at beating him, but I was too busy drooling over my opponent to concentrate.

My uncontainable attraction to Zander will be my undoing.

It already is.

Muscles rippling, Zander takes the white queen—still attached to his shoelace—and slips it over his head. He puts on his cloak and straps his weapon holster across his chest, securing the long sword to his back.

Flicking his unfocused eyes my way, he gives me a heated look filled with possessiveness and triumph before he goes outside.

He's happy because I'm truly his now. I gambled. I played his game and lost.

As I put my own necklace back on, Quinn's words come back to me.

What do I have to lose by being here?

The answer is loud in my head.

My family. Paige. Independence.

My virginity.

My heart.

Basically everything.

But as I remember Zander's lips on mine and his claim to protect me, there's a sudden, surprising, hopeful whisper in my mind—because if Zander, and Astrid, and every-freaking-body else is right, I have something to gain, too.

My soul mate.

I just wish I didn't feel like his prisoner.

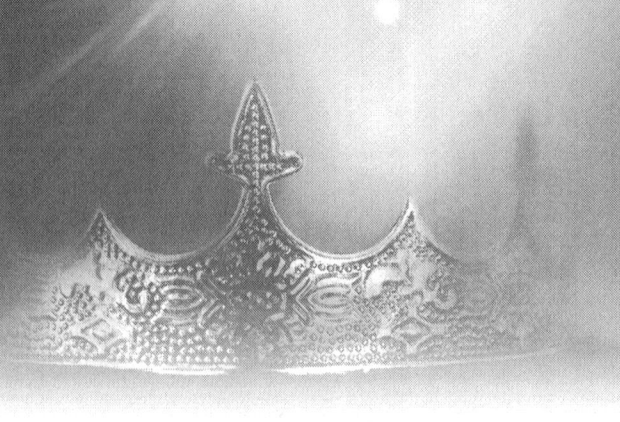

CHAPTER 18

Zander

MAELYN'S MELANCHOLY EATS AT ME AS WE RIDE TO OUR destination. I feel it in my stomach, in every breath I take. She's been quiet, nursing her wounds after the loss.

I won't apologize for winning. Our game was fair.

To be honest, she could've been victorious. Once I realized I'd severely underestimated her, she had me sweating a little. I'd like to blame the fact that I'd almost come in my pants mere minutes before, but it wasn't sexual frustration that had me mentally scrambling to keep up with the game.

My wife is good.

Smart. Strategic. Surprising.

And I'm falling for her. The bond has nothing to do with it. It's all her. When I told her I wasn't born with a power, I expected disappointment. Instead, I got her support.

She even offered to sacrifice her title of queen for me.

A more cunning woman would try to use her position to her advantage. She could demand jewels and other material luxuries. She could order my men around or try to make up rules that benefit her.

Not Maelyn. She oozes compassion and acceptance, even though I don't deserve it.

I couldn't even give her the orgasm she needed.

This morning on the bed, she was so pliant and willing beneath me. She writhed. She moaned.

For me.

I wanted to keep going, but we couldn't.

I couldn't.

I became so overwhelmed, I almost shifted.

Which was shocking. Self-pleasure has never caused a shift before. I can assume that's for two reasons. One, it's not amazing or exciting when I'm by myself. And two, with the bond feeding me Maelyn's sensations, it's almost too much to bear.

I don't know what to do about that.

Repeated exposure and desensitization, I suppose. I need to touch her. Often.

Unfortunately, I'm not going to accomplish that while we're on separate horses.

Turning my head to the right where Maelyn's riding alongside me, my voice is stern when I say, "Listen, I'm going to have you wait outside with Thayne when we get to the distillery. I'm trusting you to stay put."

"Okay." I hear her shrug.

"I'm serious, Mae. These missions can be dangerous, and I need to keep my head on straight."

"You don't have to worry about me. I'll be good."

"Good girl."

A flush hits her face, heating mine as well. Maelyn is flattered at hearing my praise—maybe even a little turned on by it. The thought of calling her *good girl* when she's naked makes my cock stiffen.

Gripping the reins harder than necessary, I force my mind back to the matters at hand.

Now that Maelyn has promised her cooperation, I can breathe easier. I won't allow her to come close to any of these hellholes. That's what these testing facilities have become, and Maelyn's too pure to witness the atrocities within. However, depending on how many captives are inside, I might need her help afterward.

"You said you're a counselor," I muse. "Does that mean you're good at calming people when they're in distress?"

"I just started at my job a couple months ago and I was only a volunteer before that, so I don't have a ton of experience, but I'd like to think so."

"The people we're rescuing—there's a good chance they've been through a lot of pain. They might be drugged or injured. Marek can heal their outside injuries, but we can't fix their mental wounds. The best we can do is offer them a meal and safe travels."

Maelyn takes a second to absorb what I've said. "I'll do what I can, but emotional damage doesn't go away with a glass of water, food, and a hug. It can have lasting effects. Post traumatic stress disorder can go on for years. For life."

She's not wrong. Two trolls died by suicide last year after they'd spent a month in a testing facility. I wasn't sure if the Glow experiments altered their state of mind or if they were just too broken to go on. Either way, I feel responsible.

"What would you suggest for treatment?"

Maelyn hums thoughtfully. "Well, ongoing therapy is a good idea. Sometimes medicine is necessary. Do you have a hospital where they can go to recover?"

"Hospitals? Not exactly. Since we don't have natural illness in Valora, it's never been necessary. Some survivors of the plague have lingering physical ailments, and because of that, there's a healer or a doctor in each town to give out tonics for pain."

"You need medical centers where everyone can access them," Maelyn states, sounding queen-like with her no-nonsense tone. "It's not uncommon for the mind to be forgotten about. Mental illness is neglected in my world, too. In my opinion, you should set up a large hospital in a central location, then branch off with smaller clinics elsewhere. And you should be involved."

"Involved?"

"You know, stop in every now and then to see your people

and check on them. I know you said you're generally disliked, but that would change if you formed friendships, if you showed them you have their backs."

See? Smart, strategic, surprising.

"I believe you're right, wife."

Excited by my encouragement, Maelyn continues to ramble, her thoughts seeming to tumble out of her. "The new human arrivals could use something like this, too, only like a rehabilitation center. Giving them housing and jobs is great, but there's an adjustment period. They can't be expected to jump from one life to another without time to process the change. A little extra care could go a long way."

"If I were to put you in charge of this project, would you like that?"

More enthusiastic waves come at me. "Really? You'd trust me with your people?"

"Our people," I correct. "They need you, too."

She doesn't respond to that, but there isn't time for more discussion anyway, because we're close to the distillery. I can smell the stink of it. Sulphur, burning coal, and wet dirt.

Olphene is just a couple miles north. Gideon likely chose this spot to set up shop because many people travel in and out from this side of the city. More traffic means more buyers.

Unfortunately, I'm not optimistic about catching him here today. The distillery owners usually hire workers to carry out their unpleasant tasks, knowing if there's a bust or an accident, someone else will take the fall.

I slow my horse as I veer toward the side of the road. There's a clear area with enough room for the horses and the wagon. Sometimes a peddler sets up shop here. Perhaps they're not present today because they know the distillery means trouble.

"This is where you'll stay with Thayne," I tell Maelyn. "No matter what happens, do not move from this spot."

After making sure the horses' reins are secured to a post, I approach Maelyn. As she stands in front of me, I sense her anxiety, but I don't know what it means.

I tilt my head. "Are you worried about me?"

"Well, if it's anything like yesterday, there'll be lots of fighting. Are people going to get hurt?"

"Yes," I answer honestly.

"Even you?"

"Maybe."

There's no telling what we'll find inside. If we're lucky, the place will be empty except for one or two workers, but it's rarely that simple anymore.

I reach out to caress Maelyn's cheek. "I'll be back soon, wife."

I lean down to kiss her.

She's initiated our kisses so far. It's my turn.

Spanning my big hand along the side of her delicate neck, I grip the back of her head with my fingers while tilting her chin up with my thumb.

Then I crush my mouth to hers.

It's not like the other times we've kissed. It's harsher. Needier. Quicker.

I don't even care that my men are here to witness it. If they know what's good for them, they'll avert their eyes.

Palming Maelyn's waist, I press my growing erection against her stomach while licking inside her mouth and tangling my tongue with hers.

Taking Maelyn's bottom lip between mine, I bite down.

The brusque way I'm handling her might be too aggressive, but I need to get used to physical contact with her. The sooner the better.

It's just too easy to forget where we are.

It's too hard to stop, especially when Maelyn's little fists grab at my cloak like she needs something to hold onto. Like she wants to pull me closer.

Strike me, repeated exposure and desensitization aren't

supposed to feel this good. At some point, I'm just going to have to go for it and let the repercussions happen.

My head is light and I'm buzzing all over, and the bond is flaring with the need to be fulfilled.

Finally breaking the kiss, I rest my forehead on hers and try to catch my breath.

"Don't move," I command her, backing off before I do something foolish.

Like rub my cock on her until I lose control and turn into the griffin.

After putting my hood up, I point at Thayne as I start to walk away with Marek and Torius. "Guard her with your life."

"Always, your majesty."

No one comments about my public display of affection. If my men and I were friends, they might have the courage to tease me. But we're not comrades. They serve me because they respect me and I pay them well. Friendship isn't part of the equation.

"I'll go first," Torius starts, all business, "and disband any booby traps I find. Marek, you come in behind me and incapacitate the workers."

This is the typical plan, minus Thayne. He's usually behind me to guard my back, but someone needs to be with Maelyn. I'm not so worried about her running off at this point; my main concern is that someone would snatch her up. Ransom for the new queen would be high.

Rounding a patch of thick trees, we arrive at a flat field. I don't sense any raised land, which means they dug out a place underground instead of hollowing out a hill.

Damn.

These are the more dangerous distilleries. The criminals who construct them aren't engineers or architects, and the rooms they build aren't safe.

Before these bastards started testing on people like lab rats, raids were easy. We could just arrive with a stardust launcher and blow the place to smithereens. If the distillers were killed in the explosion, even better.

But now they have hostages. When the experimentations began a few years ago, they would capture fae who tried to sneak in and steal from them. They figured thieves deserved to be caught and tortured.

Innocent trolls have been targeted recently, so I have to be careful. I don't want to lose any more citizens, whether they're fae or not.

Crouching, I flatten my hand on the grass. There are subtle vibrations below, and if I can detect the differences in the ground, I'll eventually find the hidden door.

Torius and Marek are quiet next to me as I feel around.

There.

Silently, I motion ahead and slightly to the right, flashing my hands twice to indicate twenty feet.

We discover a hatch under a bush.

Sweat trickles down my temple as Torius quickly disables a wire attached to a trap that would've shot arrows at us from a nearby tree. Then he lifts the door.

Immediately, odor hits me. It's comprised of charcoal, unwashed bodies, and blood.

Torius carefully lowers himself into the dark hole, stepping on a ladder that's been embedded in the mud. Once we get down about fifteen feet, we find a tunnel with a low ceiling. Each of us have to bend over just to make it through.

Without any wind, it's more difficult for me to estimate the distance, but from the way our breathing echoes, I'm guessing it's only about ten feet until we'll find another door.

Two more booby traps are disassembled along the way.

Since Torius and Marek aren't used to being in the dark, they communicate through taps on the hand. I hear Torius' finger make contact with Marek's palm with the signal that he's going in.

We bust through the door.

There are three shouts of dismay. I also register three gasps and groans—sounds of suffering—along with one body expelling shallow breaths.

Three arrests and four rescues. Not the worst raid we've ever had.

"Marek, now," I order.

Blood-curdling screams follow as Marek uses the destructive side of his power.

Yes, he's a healer, but he can do harm as well. Very few people possess opposite sides of the same power. His twin brother had the same ability, but Tibbult was killed years ago in the line of duty for King Damon. When Tibbs died, his power transferred to his brother. Marek told me he could feel it when it happened. While he was devastated to lose his only remaining family, he vowed to use the heightened power for good and pledged himself to me as a faithful warrior.

Honestly, I couldn't do this without him.

Bones snap as he breaks the criminals' bodies from the inside out, and they collapse to the dirt floor. They crawl, trying to get away from the pain, but there's no escape for them now.

Angling my ear, I listen to the quieter sounds of the facility. Sizzling coals, bubbling water, and a constant dripping indicates five barrels of Glow.

Some of it has probably been concentrated from the original formula to make Blaze. We'll have to be careful about disposing of it. Sometimes getting rid of the stuff is the most dangerous part. Since it can pollute lakes, streams, and crops, I have a crew of sailors who dump the liquid out on the Endless Seas.

Torius usually leads that mission because I know I can trust him, and since his power is influencing water and aquatic creatures, he's experienced with sailing.

Speaking of the man, he's already tending to one of the captives, so I go to the table nearest to me and start undoing the straps trapping a female troll. "What's your name?"

"Synda," she answers, and she sounds young.

Her wrists are bound so tightly, I wouldn't be surprised if the circulation has been cut off to her hands. I free her ankles. "You're safe now. Can you walk?"

"No. They broke my leg."

Striking assholes. Their pained screams sound like music to my ears.

"Marek will fix you as soon as we get out of here," I tell Synda. "For now, I'll carry you."

As I scoop her light weight up, I hear the unbuckling of leather while Torius releases another troll. He herds two of them over to me before going to the last one.

More screams echo around us as Torius shouts over the commotion, "The fourth troll is unresponsive!"

"I can carry another."

"I've got her. I'll meet you outside. Just get them out before this place caves."

All the shouts are disturbing the dirt above us. Every time the ground shakes from the slightest bit of vibrations, dust and clumps of mud rain down.

After giving Torius a nod, I begin shuffling toward the door with the little people. They cling to me, grabbing my pants and my cloak as if I'm a life raft on the Endless Sea.

One of Marek's victims roars out a battle cry as his nails scrape over the side of a wooden barrel. The container tips over, spilling the contents with a loud splash. The liquid coats the floor, making the mud soft and squishy beneath my boots.

A whiff of something familiar makes me halt in the doorway; I smell it before anyone else sees it—the scent of night. It's faint, but unmistakable. And it's the last thing anyone should have near distilled Day water.

The criminals must have some stardust on standby for an occasion such as this. Rather than being caught, they'd prefer to die and take us all down with them.

"Stardust!" I yell out the warning, shielding the trembling trolls against the wooden doorframe the best I can. "Get dow—"

BOOM.

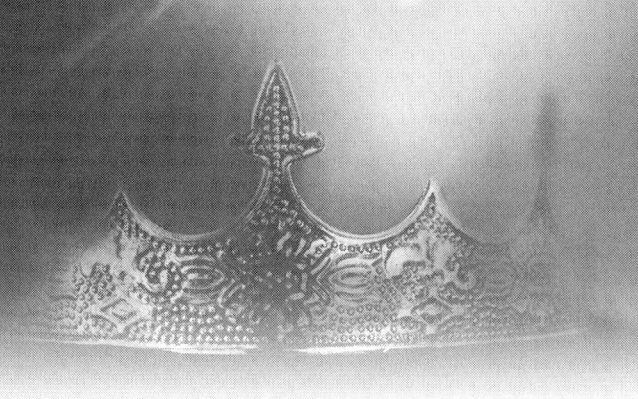

CHAPTER 19

Maelyn

Awkward silence. There isn't much for Thayne and me to talk about. I've tried to start conversations about the weather, which were met with grunts. When I've asked anything about where we're headed next, I'm given one-word answers, or my favorite response—the king will tell us.

I've taken to pacing my anxiety away. Every time I get a little too far, Thayne tenses and steps toward me as if I'm going to take off at any moment.

Please.

For one, as if I could outrun him. The guy has wings.

And two, I'm not taking my chances in the forest again.

Three, I'm too worried about Zander. Because if something bad happens to him, what would happen to me?

Without him, I have no place in this world.

And to be honest, I don't want to imagine this world without him in it.

Chewing the tip of my thumbnail, I crane my neck and try to see around the curve in the road where the men disappeared about ten minutes ago. Too many trees are in the way.

"Don't fret, my queen," Thayne says, softer now. "This is all routine."

Nodding, I try to let his reassurance calm me, but I won't be satisfied until Zander's back.

Suddenly, the ground shakes. The first tremor is quickly followed by a loud rumble, and I almost lose my balance when the road seems to shift under my feet.

Spreading my arms to steady myself, I glance over my shoulder at Thayne. "Wha—"

A deafening crack splits through the air, and I instinctively topple to my knees while covering my head. I hear a ringing, and it takes me a second to realize my eardrums are reacting to the loud sound.

Pressing my palms to the dry dirt to steady myself, I try to make sense of the rippling quakes beneath the surface. Pebbles dance across the road as everything seems to settle.

And then it's so quiet it's almost eerie.

Disoriented, I blink up at the sky. A dark plume of smoke is rising over the trees.

"Queen Maelyn." Thayne hauls me up by my elbows. "Are you all right?"

"I'm guessing that wasn't part of the plan?" I shout my concern at him over my ringing eardrums, and my need to worry is confirmed by the alarm in his eyes. "Zander. Is he in trouble?"

Flattening his lips into a thin line, Thayne just nods once as he quickly escorts me back to where the horses are freaking out.

Gander and Onyx both tug at their restraints and stomp their hooves. I'm able to calm them a little, but the ones hooked up to the wagon decide to bolt as soon as they get their reins to break free. Before we can even try to stop them, they're flying past us on the road, kicking up dust as they disappear in the distance.

I swallow hard. Thayne saved me just in time. If he hadn't gotten me out of the road, I might've been trampled.

"Your majesty." His voice sounds so far away. "I need to save the king and the others. Stay here. Please."

I just wave him on, feeling the urgency of the matter.

Thayne wanders ten feet away, then he throws down a portal. The other side is completely dark, and he pushes against it, as if he's having trouble getting through. As his arms reach in, he gropes around before bracing his feet on the ground and pulling backward.

Suddenly, a body falls to the road along with a ton of dirt. The small figure coughs and rolls around in her stained dress, but Thayne goes back to digging before checking on her.

I know he told me to stay, but surely he didn't mean exactly right here.

I can help.

Running forward, I hook my hands under the person's armpits. She's light, like a child. They have kids in the facilities? What kind of evil people are we dealing with here?

I catch the sight of blood on her face and decide to pick her up instead of yanking her away. She's heavier than she looks, but I'm able to cart her to safety. When I set her down next to a tree, I push brown shoulder-length hair away from her face to reveal honey-colored eyes.

"Are you okay?" I scan her dress for any large amounts of blood, gasping when I get to her calf. The bone is crooked, and the flesh around it is dark purple and swollen. "Your leg."

"The others," she rasps. "Help them."

I look behind me. Two more small bodies are crumpled in the growing pile of dirt.

After two more trips, I've got three children huddled together and almost zero knowledge of what just happened or how to help them.

Water.

I rush over to Gander and soothingly pet his neck as I loosen my canteen of waterfall mist. Quickly bringing it over to the kids, I extend it in offering, unsure of who to give it to first.

Unanimously, the two boys push it toward the girl. She gulps four times before passing it off to them.

Scanning them for more injuries, I frantically ask, "Why would they want to hurt kids?"

"We're not youngins," one of the males replies, his voice surprisingly deep. "We're trolls, miss."

"Trolls," I parrot, and now that I look at their faces, I notice the evidence of age. Crow's feet and laugh lines decorate their skin. It was hard to see at first under all the dirt, but as I peer closer, I realize one of the men has graying hair.

There are also some differences in their facial features, setting them apart from humans or fae. Their noses are a little longer, and their eyes are slightly closer together. They remind me of Astrid.

And that's when it clicks. Astrid is a troll, too. I thought she was just a really small person. It's not like I'm much taller than these people. I've got maybe half a foot on the men. Who am I to judge someone for being short?

"Speak for yourselves," the girl snarks, smiling, then wincing from pain as she tries to get more comfortable without disturbing her leg. "I could pass for a teenager."

I swallow hard. "How old are you?"

"Twenty-one."

"Hey, me too. I'm Maelyn." I manage an awkward wave.

"Synda of Troll District Four in Olphene," she introduces herself, then points at me. "Let me guess—human, right?"

"That obvious, huh?"

All three of them nod before Synda answers my original question.

"Trolls are a popular choice for the facilities because most of us don't have powers. If we don't have powers, they can use Glow on us without worrying that we'll be a threat to them once we're amped up."

"I'm so sorry." The apology stumbles out as I crouch down. It would've been nice to get a little more background information before heading into this, but I'm learning to take things in stride in this world. "What happened to you in there?" I'm not sure who will answer first, and I don't care. My gaze pings from one distrusting face to the other. "You're safe now. I promise."

"I was captured a week ago." Synda sighs. "The bad men cut me up a little and gave me Glow to heal my skin. Then they broke my leg and fed me Blaze last night."

"The concentrated Glow." I remember when Zander told me about it. At least I know that much.

Nodding, she gestures to her mangled bone. "Anyway, as you can see, it didn't work. Then some men came rushing in a few minutes ago, and we were about to be rescued, but there was an explosion and the whole place collapsed."

"I'm glad you made it out." I try to smile but it's more like a grimace. "Part of me hopes the guys who did this to you won't survive."

"Fae are very difficult to kill." Synda sounds so disappointed about that. "My guess is they'll be just fine."

"Zander won't let them get away with it."

She glares at the name. "Zander?"

"Yeah. I'm… accompanying the king."

Synda's eyes go wide. "The king?" She points at a spot over my shoulder. "Is that him?"

Rolling from my knees to my butt, I glance back at Thayne. There's a new body—a big one—lying on the ground. All I see is charred skin on an expansive back and light-colored pants that appear to have been burned away in large patches. The hair on his head has been completely singed away.

"Zander," I whisper, my heart in my throat.

I push up so fast I almost fall forward, but I right myself and run to him.

Forgetting any first-aid training I've ever learned in my life, I panic and jerk his seared shoulder, pushing him onto his back so I can see his face.

Only, his face isn't there. It's gone. Blown off.

Blood, bone, and bits of brain are all that's left.

I cry out, slapping a hand over my mouth so I don't vomit. My stomach twists and churns violently, and tears suddenly flood my eyes.

He can't be gone. He can't. He can't.

"No, no, no." Memories of the past twenty-four hours lash at my heart, ripping it open with a pain I've never felt before.

Zander's mesmerizing eyes under his dark hood. His infuriating, stubborn frowns. The passionate kisses we've shared. How he held me last night, so tight and secure, like I might disappear at any second.

During the little time I had with Zander, I spent most of it resenting him.

Yeah, I had good reasons. He went about obtaining me the wrong way, but he never wanted to hurt me.

He adores me.

He *did*.

Now he's dead.

If he really was my soul mate, that means I'll spend the rest of my life feeling incomplete. Any man I meet in the future will pale in comparison to the broody king.

A barking sob lurches from my throat as I touch his cold upper arm. The warmth I've gotten used to is painfully absent. Fae might not die easily, but it's clear there's no life left in him.

Thayne shakes my shoulder gently, snapping me out of my grief. "Your majesty."

Unable to look away from Zander, I only manage another sob.

"That's not the king," Thayne says, making my heart leap.

"It's not? Well, who is it then?"

"No one we know."

Sniffling, I scrutinize the body with a new outlook. His skin is paler than Zander's—though I'd just attributed that to him being dead—and the hair on his chest is blond. The white queen necklace isn't there. There's no dark happy trail leading into his pants.

"King Zander might be angry at me for asking you to get your hands dirty." Thayne's voice is strained. "But I could use your help if you're able."

As I blink away my tears, I look to him. "What do you need?"

He's trying to pull someone else out of the portal. Half of an arm hangs out. The back of the hand is badly burned, but underneath the coating of dirt is bronzed skin.

I gasp with happiness. "Zander?"

Nodding, Thayne instructs, "Give the king a pull while I reach in to find his other arm. He's really wedged in there."

More relief floods in as soon as I wrap my hand around Zander's and he squeezes back.

Yanking with all my strength, I dig my heels into the ground and use my body weight as I lean back. With Thayne's help, we're able to pull Zander out until his head and shoulders are free.

The dazzling crown is still intact on his head. That band is so tight, even an explosion can't knock it off.

"Don't be upset, Mae," Zander coughs out, and I never thought I'd be so glad to hear him call me by the shortened name, but I am. "I hate it when you're sad."

"Do you have any idea how ridiculous it is for you to be thinking of my feelings at a time like this?" I half-laugh, half-sob.

"I'm always thinking of you." Pushing himself out of the portal with a grunt, Zander starts passing information to Thayne. "The space was about twenty feet by thirty before it caved in. There are three distillers to capture. Torius should be about ten feet behind me. A troll is with him."

"Shouldn't I retrieve Marek first? Your injuries—"

"Are not that bad," Zander finishes for him, freeing his legs and plopping onto the ground.

Nodding once, Thayne takes another portal out of his box and walks several paces away before dropping it. A new dark hole opens, and he continues his search for the others, scooping out huge chunks of mud.

Leaning up on an elbow, Zander shakes his head, sending clumps of dirt flying. "Mae?"

"I'm here." Kneeling next to him, I scan his body for more injuries, but I find nothing significant. The only places he seems to be injured are his knuckles. His pants look charred, but not enough to have burnt him. The cloak is askew on his shoulders, and I quickly check under it.

Smooth, untarnished skin. He's going to walk away relatively unscathed.

"I thought you died." I can't keep the quiver out of my voice.

"I'm not the one you need to worry about." Sitting up, he grabs my hand with a sense of urgency. "There were captives in my care. Three trolls. I tried to shield them. My cloak is fireproof, but—"

"You saved them." I stop his panicked rant. "They're over there, on the side of the road."

He blows out a breath like the weight of the world just left his shoulders. Standing, he brushes himself off. "It wasn't supposed to happen that way. There was a stardust bomb."

"Well, one of the bad guys sort of lost his head." I cringe. "Or half of it anyway. He's definitely dead."

"I'm sorry you had to see that. Maybe Damon was right—I shouldn't have brought you here."

"I'm not sure I agree with you," Synda pipes up from her spot. "This woman helped us."

Zander gives me a questioning tilt of his head, and I manage a humble nod. "I just carried them to a safer area."

"And she gave us waterfall mist," Synda adds, smiling a little at me. Then her tone turns colder as she looks at Zander. "I would suggest having a nice woman in your army at all times. If not for her assistance, we might've been crushed by the more valuable species your man seeks to procure."

Zander's eyebrow goes up, but he doesn't chastise Synda for her snooty tone. "More valuable species?"

"Faeries, your majesty. We know you think you're above us."

"I can assure you, I do not."

I'm torn between blushing from Synda's praise and bristling because of her snide admonishment of Zander. Obviously, she's not a fan of faeries, but she was just saved by some.

"My queen will be with me always." Placing his hand at the small of my back, Zander ushers me over to the trolls.

Synda's eyes dart to me. "You're the queen? You married him?"

Not knowing how to answer, I open my mouth and draw in a breath, preparing to release a string of oversharing and overexplaining.

"Yes, she is," Zander interjects for me, preventing the ramble.

It's for the best. Telling Synda I'd been plucked from an auction wouldn't earn Zander any brownie points.

He crouches in front of the trolls, putting himself at their level. "I already met you." He nods at Synda before talking to the others. "What are your names?"

"Teegan," the oldest man replies.

The weak one whispers, "Tomas."

"You'll all be healed, escorted home, and compensated for your trouble," Zander informs them curtly, and an awkward silence ensues.

So his bedside manner could use some work. He's obviously not the type to coddle, but these people just went through something horrific.

Now might not be the time to assert my queen status, but oh well. Zander put me in this role. If he really wants a wife, he's going to have to take everything that comes along with it—my opinions included.

"Unless," I drawl, "you'd like to come back to the palace with us as our guests. If you need time to recover in comfort, we can provide that for you."

Clearly unimpressed, Teegan sniffs. "The offer is generous, your majesty, but I have a family to get back to. Children and grandchildren."

Synda nods, though she looks tempted by my offer. "My mother is worried sick, no doubt."

Tomas has dozed off, but his breathing is a little shallow.

"Is he okay?" Bending down to check his pulse, I find a rapid thumping under my fingers and glance at Zander. "Is his heart supposed to be beating this fast?"

"Tomas was in the facility before I was," Synda supplies. "He was in and out of consciousness for most of it."

Teegan gives his fellow captives a worried look. "I was the last to arrive, just yesterday. They only dosed me once, but Tomas had lost count of how many times they'd injected him."

"Dosed you with what?" Zander asks. "Blaze?"

Nodding, Teegan rubs the side of his neck. There's a faint puncture mark on the skin by his artery. "It was like being injected with the sun. It spread through my veins like lava. I screamed until I couldn't anymore. I woke up this morning to find them doing the same to Tomas, but he didn't even have the energy to make a noise."

"They used the last of the Blaze on him," Synda says. "I heard them arguing about needing to make more. That's probably why the blast didn't kill us all."

"I shielded you," Zander says flatly.

Teegan huffs. "Glow wouldn't even exist if it weren't for you."

"I tried my best to keep you safe."

I detect annoyance in Zander's voice. It's not fun to be unappreciated, and I feel a niggling of guilt, because I've treated him with the same contempt the trolls are showing now.

I see what Zander means when he says his people don't like him. And it's a shame. He invented Glow with the intention of saving people, not hurting them. It's not his fault people suck and try to abuse it.

Using these trolls as lab rats is awful, but it's not Zander's doing.

I'm confused about why it's being done, though. My sad eyes go to Tomas, who's looking grayer by the second. "What were these guys trying to accomplish by injecting him repeatedly?"

"To see if a tolerance can be built up," Zander fills in. "I've heard rumors of death by too much Blaze. The distillers are trying to figure out how much the body can handle. There's a fine line between amplifying their powers and being overloaded with toxins."

"Tomas." I gently jostle the man's bony shoulder, afraid he might die right in front of me, but he's unresponsive.

Then Thayne discovers someone else in one of the many portals he's got going. Torius.

The warrior is lugging a limp troll under his right arm as he drags himself out with the other. "Take her."

Thayne cradles the small unmoving body to his chest while Torius crawls out.

As soon as Torius is on his feet, he takes the troll back and glowers at the ten dark holes ripping through the air. "You shouldn't have wasted so many portals on me, Thayne. It might've taken me some time, but I could've dug my way out."

"I wasn't sure if you lived through the explosion." Thayne throws down another portal a few feet away.

Torius scoffs, seeming unaffected by the massive burns on his arms and back. "You should know me better than that by now. Unfortunately, I don't think this one made it." He lowers his ear to the female troll's mouth before coming to the side of the road to place her on a patch of soft grass. "She was barely hanging on when I got to her. The blast knocked us both down pretty hard."

"I know CPR," I offer, but Marek spills out of a portal a second later.

He can help her more than I can. The soldier just dusts himself off and strolls our way, not a scratch on him.

Guess that's the perk of being a healer. You can fix yourself.

Spitting dirt out of his mouth, he comes over, hands out as he reaches for Zander.

"Not me." The king dismisses Marek's attempt with a flick of his charred hand toward the troll with Torius. "Her first."

When Marek lets his hand hover over the chest of the little battered and bruised body, he bows his head. "She's gone."

Blowing out a breath, Zander asks the trolls, "What was her name?"

"We don't know," Synda replies. "She wasn't awake the entire time we were there, and none of us recognized her."

At that, Zander frowns and directs Marek to Tomas. "Him next. He needs to be cleansed. Then you'll fix Synda's leg and tend to Teegan. From the smell of burnt flesh coming from Torius, he'll need you as well. Treat me last."

My heart does a weird flip. Selfless acts—they get me in the feels. Zander won't let Marek come near him until everyone else has been healed.

He might not have wanted to rule a kingdom, but he's good at it.

I see how much he cares.

As soon as Marek starts to heal Tomas, the troll jerks. Without waking, his entire body trembles. The motions become more violent until he's convulsing. Horrified, I cover my mouth as foam and vomit spill from his mouth and nose.

"What's happening?" I whisper harshly.

Standing, Zander pulls me up with him, looping an arm around my waist to lead me away. "Marek has to force the substance out of Tomas' bloodstream. The process isn't pretty, but he should be fine after it's gone from his system." He rubs my arm reassuringly. "It's been a trying time for you, wife. If I had a choice, the first glimpses of my world would've been wonderful for you. Not this."

He motions behind us at the carnage.

Tomas is still being cleansed. Smoke is smoldering from the explosion site. Thayne is going from portal to portal, searching for the other criminals' bodies.

I wasn't prepared for any of this. When Zander talked about a raid, the picture in my mind was more like a meth lab being surrounded by a SWAT team. They'd shout from the outside that everyone is busted, and the druggies would come out with their hands up.

Nope. Not even close.

At least Zander and his crew are okay.

Winding my arms around his middle, I give him a hug. For a minute there, I wasn't sure I'd ever be able to touch him like this again.

I press my cheek to his chest. Dirt and a dusting of hair are rough on my skin, but he still smells good. Underneath the distinct scent of mud and sulfur, there's sandalwood and sunshine.

Sighing, Zander gently pets my hair while hugging me back. "I promise I'll show you the best Valora has to offer. We just need to get home."

Home.

The word conjures up images of my mom's white ranch-style house and the fields that surround her one-acre property. And Dad's log cabin, just four houses away from my mom's place. I remember all the times I walked back and forth between the two after the divorce, happy my parents were still so close.

I don't know if I'll see those places ever again, but it's not the walls and roofs I miss. It's the people. The memories.

My family.

And I'm not sure if the best castle in the world could make up for that.

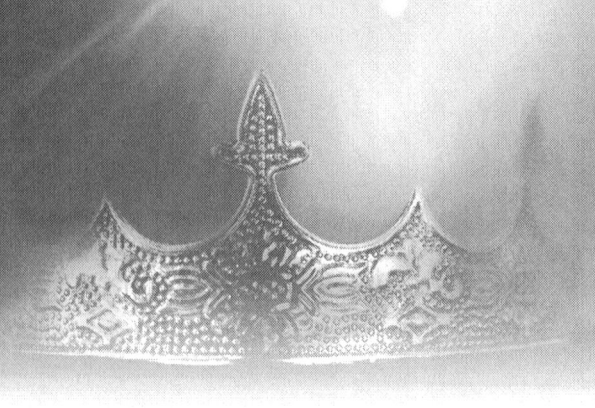

CHAPTER 20

Maelyn

Okay, I hate to admit it, but the castle is even grander than I'd imagined.

The homesickness I've been feeling all day ebbs away as I gawk at the shiny, cream-colored marble spires. The stained-glass windows. The rose bushes lining the perimeter and the ivy climbing up the sides.

It's magical.

There's a huge circular fountain out front, surrounded by cobblestone walkways that veer off in different directions through a garden with a hedge maze.

The Day Realm palace is straight out of a storybook.

However, exhaustion pushes against my excitement, and I yawn.

It's been a long day.

After confirming that two of the distillery workers were dead, we had to give up on the third. Thayne couldn't keep using portals, and we needed to deliver Synda, Tomas, and Teegan to their villages. None of the trolls accepted my offer to come to Hailene.

Zander wasn't kidding about the disdain the townspeople have for him, and I witnessed the hostility firsthand. Even though we were heroes, we got a lot of dirty looks from the trolls as we brought their missing people safely to their doors. Most didn't even come out of their little houses. They just glared at us through their windows.

To make up for the trouble the criminals had caused, Zander passed out goods—jugs of waterfall mist, bags of grain, and baskets of fruit.

Still, their silent sneers were evidence of the blame they place on his head. Synda was the only one who said thank you throughout the entire day, and even then, she directed it at me, not Zander and his men—the people who actually deserve it.

We spent the rest of the afternoon searching for the identity of the troll who didn't survive. Zander wanted to lay her to rest in her hometown, but after stopping by a dozen troll districts with no luck, he became concerned about how worn out I was and asked Thayne for a portal back to Hailene.

I insisted on seeing our mission through to the end, but Zander said Marek and Torius could handle it. The mystery troll could've been from anywhere, and it might take some investigating to find out where she's from.

I yawn again.

With the constant daylight, I have trouble remembering what time it is. I paid attention to the suns throughout the day, and the two orbs seem to circle around the world in opposite directions. I've concluded they cross paths four times a day. Twice in the west, twice in the east.

I'm pretty sure dusk came and went hours ago. The suns are circling back around, almost opposite of each other in the sky.

"How can you tell the difference between morning and evening?" I ask. "Don't you get them mixed up?"

"You listen for the morning birds."

"Morning birds?" I glance at Zander's profile. "Isn't that what the guy doing the auction called me?"

"Yes. In the Day Realm, the birds sing for about an hour

before and after dawn. Sometimes longer if they're in a good mood. If the suns are colliding in the east and it's quiet, then it's dusk." Slipping his arm around my shoulders, Zander guides me up the walkway leading to the door. "Let's go inside."

We pass several guards stationed along the way, and they each give us a robotic bow before returning to stoically staring ahead with long spears in hand.

I recognize the soldier at the door. It's the young guy who was with the group yesterday. The one with the turquoise eyes.

"Your majesties," he greets us. "Good to see you've returned so soon."

"Hello, Pippin." Zander doesn't brief the warrior on the complications we came up against today, but he does inquire about the human girls from the auction.

"They've been delivered to the dorms, as requested."

"Maelyn had a good idea," Zander announces proudly, surprising me. "She thinks a sort of rehabilitation center might be more appropriate for the new humans. Can you set up a meeting with Zephina?" He turns his face toward me. "Aunt Zephina handles immigrant affairs."

"Yes, your majesty." Pippin nods. "Is there anything else I can do for you this night?"

"Where's my mother?" Zander lowers his voice, as if he's worried his mom might hear him asking about her whereabouts.

"Asleep, as are most of the staff." This guy might be young, but he's clever, catching onto Zander's desire to avoid people without missing a beat. Sending us a wink, he says, "If you take the secret hall to your bed chambers, I bet you could make it there without being seen. I can have someone bring you some dinner."

I'm a bit relieved. It's not that I don't want to meet Zander's mom. I'm just overwhelmed by the day, and I need some downtime.

Instead of going through the door, Zander takes me around to the side of the castle.

Tall, trimmed hedges hide us as we walk along the perimeter, staying snug to the wall. We pass a few windows before coming to a stop next to one of them.

Zander pats a rectangular stone along the windowsill. "Have you ever opened a puzzle box before?"

I nod. "At a science museum once."

"Feel here." He takes my hand and guides me through a series of movements on the windowsill. Mechanical clicks follow as we put pressure on the ledge, shifting the stones in a certain order. "It's like a combination lock, and we're the only ones who know the code."

With a final clank, the wall separates, and a five-foot slat opens underneath the window. Fascinated, I peer into the dim hallway. It's made up of gray stones, and the window gives off enough light to see a stairway about thirty feet ahead.

"How cool is that?" My whisper echoes in the silent corridor, making the discovery seem even more forbidden.

Zander motions for me to go ahead of him. "After you."

Since I'm a shorty, I barely have to duck to go through. Zander folds himself into the opening behind me. He closes the secret door, and as it latches, the snap ricochets down the hallway.

The painted glass panes behind us throw colors on the floor—yellow from the sun, pink from the flowers, and green from the leaves and ivy in the design.

I give Zander a small smile. "I guess a castle wouldn't be legit without secret tunnels."

"The passages weren't always here." Taking my hand, he walks me toward the stairs. "Back before the first plague, my grandfather Zed was loved by many, as was his wife, Lynea. But she succumbed to the illness within a year of its appearance, and King Zed went mad from heartbreak. Paranoia ruled his mind. He thought everyone was out to get him, so he had a bunch of secret tunnels built in case there was an uprising and he needed to flee with his children. But his children were victims of his insanity, unfortunately. His daughter Zella ended up being fated to Keryth, the king of the Night Realm. Because of the tension between our kingdoms, Zed wanted to keep them apart. When Zella ran away to be with Keryth, he hunted her down and tried to kill her."

"Yikes. Talk about dysfunctional."

"He wasn't right in the head."

Not sure I buy the insanity defense. A lot of people lose their spouses and go on to lead healthy lives. "Did Zella and Keryth get to be together?"

"Yes. They ruled the Night Realm for a time, and they're the parents of Kirian."

"What happened to Zed?"

"He died. My father—his son—Zarid put him out of his misery."

My eyebrows jump as we climb the steps. "His own son killed him?"

A muscle in Zander's jaw twitches when he clenches his teeth, and he's quiet for the rest of the climb.

And it is a climb.

I'm actually glad he stopped talking so I can focus on breathing.

I thought the stairs would plateau, turn, and start another flight, but it just keeps going in a straight line. Up and up we go. There are no windows or lights, so it's gotten quite dark. That doesn't bother Zander, but I'm worried I might trip. Gripping Zander's hand, I lift my legs a little higher than necessary, making sure my feet clear each step.

"How long does this thing go on for?" Huffing and puffing, I gesture toward the seemingly endless stairwell.

"To the fourth floor." Of course, he's not winded at all. "Not much longer now."

Finally, there's a hint of light. When we get to the top, a glow comes from underneath a door straight ahead. It's just the thinnest line, but I can tell the room on the other side must be bright.

I stand behind Zander on the small area, estimating the platform is about four feet wide and five feet long. When he puts our hands on another stone puzzle on the wall, he ends up showing me how to find a secret box with a key.

"The other palaces in Valora have been upgraded with enchanted locks," he tells me. "The doors can be opened with a touch of the kings' hands. But I won't allow it here. I don't put my trust in wizards or witches."

"You trust Astrid."

Zander makes a noncommittal noise as he inserts the key. "When I don't have any other choice."

"Did she tell you anything useful?" I ask. "Aside from the fact that I'm a super weak human?"

Zander doesn't laugh at my self-deprecating joke, and he doesn't answer with anything more than, "Yes."

As he pushes the door open, a beautiful room comes into view.

The large king-size bed is covered in a fluffy black comforter and furry pillows. The walls and floors are made of marble. There are decorative columns embedded in the walls every ten feet or so, and they stretch all the way up to the incredibly high ceilings. A fan hangs down where a light should be, slowly rotating.

Candelabra sconces are attached to the walls in various places, but the candles have never been used. The wicks are white and new. I suppose they wouldn't need to be lit in a place where it's daylight all the time.

Dark-blue curtains frame tall windows that overlook some gardens. Glass double doors lead to a semi-circular balcony. A wooden armoire sits to my right, and to my left, there's a work desk with several blank sheets of paper and an inkwell.

I walk over to it and lightly touch the black feather of the quill pen.

I'm used to the drab beige walls of my apartment, my twin-size bed, and the baby monkey poster I have above my desk that says, 'Hang in there.'

While Zander's place beats mine in luxury, it's incredibly impersonal. Like a hotel. There are no mirrors or decorations.

As if he can read my mind, he offers, "You can decorate it however you like."

I glance back at him as he shuts the secret door with a soft thump. With the way the marble is cut, you'd never know there's a passage hidden in the wall.

First, Zander drops the backpack Quinn gave me into a basket next to the armoire. Then he lifts his weapons off and unties his cloak before setting them with my stuff.

"We'll take showers." He starts unbuttoning his pants. "Then I'll tell you anything you want to know."

Squeaking, I move my gaze to the window. "Separate showers, right?"

Air whooshes out of Zander as he walks by me with his fly hanging open, and I spy a ghost of a smile on his lips.

Did he just sort of... laugh?

"We might not have electricity, but we do have hot water," he informs me as I follow him into the en suite bathroom. "Air conditioning, too. Some of the criminals we've caught are given the option of hard labor while they await their sentencing. Good behavior can help them avoid execution. They work in shifts, stoking the fire under the water heater, while others ride stationary bikes to keep the water pressure up."

He demonstrates this fact by turning a knob inside the glass shower. The spray starts, and steam billows up a few seconds later, fogging the gold-framed mirror over the sink.

"Sounds like a job from hell," I comment, and Zander thoughtfully rubs his jaw.

"It kind of is. While cold doesn't bother faeries, excessive heat is uncomfortable. Better than being beheaded, though."

I'd been wondering about the punishments for all the people they wrangled up at the auction. I'm curious about how they handle the justice system here, but I'll ask about it later. I need to be clean and well rested before I start thinking about death sentences and prison terms.

Plus, I'm suddenly very aware of the grime accumulated on my body. That soak in the stream cleaned me off last night, but I need soap.

After rummaging around in a drawer, Zander places a new wooden toothbrush and a jar of paste on the counter next to the sink. Then he gestures toward a stack of fluffy white towels on a wicker shelf. "Take as long as you need."

I wait until he's gone, then I strip out of my dirty clothes like I've got fire ants in my pants.

The shower is huge. Probably big enough for five people. When the hot water sprays my scalp, it feels so good I actually moan.

I stand here for a few minutes, just letting the heat relax my muscles and wash away the day.

As the water rushes over me, my mind clears. My thoughts always make more sense in the shower, and I'm able to look at my situation a little more objectively.

All the events from the last two days still seem totally bizarre, but a startling realization comes to me.

I'm not the same person I was before I came here.

If I left now, knowing everything I know, experiencing everything I've experienced… I couldn't return to my old life as if nothing happened. I've had too many emotionally charged, life-shattering moments.

The kind that change someone.

When I thought Zander died today, I've never felt grief like that. Even if it was only for about a minute, it was sixty-some agonizing seconds of devastation I've never known.

It was a turning point for me.

I'm not going to ask to be sent home again. I want to know more about Valora, and after today, I feel like I could have a purpose here.

And I want to get to know Zander better, too. In all ways. I want to trace every line and indent on his body. I want to find out how it feels to have his muscles quiver under my touch. I want to learn what makes him smile and why he doesn't laugh.

I was right before the auction yesterday—I'm weak.

So weak, I'm not even a candidate for Stockholm Syndrome. I just sailed right past it, barely stopping along the way to having the hots for my captor. Someone might as well give me a notebook so I can draw hearts and stars around Zander's name on every page.

Shame should swallow me up.

It should.

It doesn't.

Instead, I feel a strange sort of acceptance.

There's a small part of me that still rebels against my attraction to him. A small part that tells me to fight against my growing affection. To run, if not for my freedom, then for the principle of it.

But that voice isn't loud enough.

Even now, when I should be enjoying my time alone, I can't stop thinking about Zander.

Water trickles down my chest, and for a second, I let myself imagine it's his fingers trailing over my nipples. Arousal sparks inside me, warming the place between my legs.

I'd been so close to getting off with him this morning, and my body never seemed to get the memo that it's not going to have the orgasm I so desperately needed. I've been on edge all day from it.

I could touch myself and fix the problem.

Sliding my hand down my stomach, I bury my fingers in the trimmed hair over my mound. I slip my middle finger between my lips and press down on my clit. It jumps at the contact, and my inner muscles flutter.

Closing my eyes, I picture Zander's hand wedged in my thighs, his wrist twisting as he plunges his thick, tan fingers into me.

I'm so sensitive down there, I'm barely able to suppress a whimper. With another soft nudge to my clit, my knees almost buckle, and I slap my palm on the marble tiles to steady myself.

Three loud thuds on the door have my eyes snapping open.

"Are you all right in there?" Zander's voice comes from the other side of the wood, and my guilty hand sheepishly retreats.

Did I make a sound I wasn't aware of?

"I'm fine." I try to keep my breathing normal. "Just give me a few more minutes."

What am I doing? This is what I mean when I say I've changed. The previous me would never masturbate to thoughts of a guy while he's in the next room.

I wash quickly, rubbing my body with sandalwood soap. There's an unlabeled leather tube on a ledge—like a mini version of the waterskins. After squeezing some clear goop into my palm, I realize it's shampoo.

Unfortunately, I don't see any conditioner. It won't be the first time I've gone without it, but I know my hair will be a frizzy mess in the morning.

Next, I grab the toothbrush.

While scrubbing my teeth, involuntary quiet humming gurgles from my throat through all the minty bubbles in my mouth. I've always had a habit of singing in the shower. My mom told me I used to do it even before I'd graduated from the baby tub. Happy, sad, sick. Doesn't matter. I'll sing.

And the acoustics in here are great. Who knew marble, gold, and glass are so good for sound reverb?

Just as I rinse my mouth out, my stomach grumbles, reminding me we haven't had dinner yet.

I shut off the water. After drying off, my eyes land on a white robe hanging from a hook on the back of the door.

Oops.

In my haste to get clean, I forgot to bring clothes in.

That's Zander's robe. It's been on his naked, wet body.

You've already worn his underwear.

Reaching for the white terrycloth, I snag it and slip my arms into the fluffy sleeves. After tying the belt at the waist, I walk out to find Zander in nothing but his boxer briefs.

His back is to me, and his muscular butt flexes when he pulls out a bottom drawer of the armoire. He stands with a white nightshirt in his hand and turns my way.

"For you to sleep in." Stalking over to me, Zander holds the garment out. "I like you in my clothes."

I go to take it, but he pulls it back. Furrowing my eyebrows, I step closer and swipe for the shirt. Again, he moves it away. Now it's behind him, and we're almost chest to chest. Or his stomach to my chest, in the case of our height difference.

I gasp a little when his erection prods at my belly button. I didn't see it before because the shirt was in the way, but there's no mistake. He's hard and huge.

Resisting the urge to look down, I tip my head up and focus on his serious face. "Are you going to let me have it or not?"

Bending down, he runs his nose over my hair and the side of my face before finally passing the shirt to me. "I like it when you smell like me, too."

Did he seriously just play a game of keep-away so he could sniff me? And is he literally trying to mark me with his scent and clothes?

I'm strangely flattered instead of freaked out, and I'm hyper-aware of how naked I am under this robe as Zander swaggers past me to the bathroom. My nipples are stiff, and the rough fabric rubs against them. There's a dampness between my legs that has nothing to do with the shower.

Before he disappears behind the door—which he doesn't bother to close all the way—his thick thighs bunch with every step, his butt tightens, and his muscular back ripples. This is the first time I've seen him without shoes or socks on, and even his feet are sexy.

As the shower starts up, it occurs to me that Zander's left me unattended again. Is he so confident I won't run? Or is he just positive I'd get lost in the palace?

I lean against the bed and stare at the main door of the bedroom. It's probably locked. Curious, I toss the shirt down on the bed before tiptoeing over to the only way out.

I'm not planning to take off. I just want to find out if I'm trapped in here.

I'm about to grasp the knob when a knock comes from the other side.

I freeze, unsure if I should answer it.

There's more rapping, followed by a female voice. "King Zander, welcome home. I have your dinner."

My stomach practically shouts at the mention of food.

I turn the knob. The latch smoothly retracts as a deadbolt slides open.

So it was locked, but only to someone from the outside.

When I crack the door a few inches, there's a blond woman on the other side with a large golden tray in her hands. Her hair is perfectly curled and bunched together on one side with a white ribbon, and she's wearing a fancy yellow gown. It's a lot like the dresses the fae women were wearing at the auction, only I can tell hers is probably more expensive with all the silk.

She's taller than me by a good eight inches, so I have to tilt my head up to see her face. My eyes connect with hers. They're brown, but there's a glittering quality to them. The way they sparkle is obvious in the dim hallway.

Her eyebrows dip as she openly scowls at me. "Where's Zander?"

"In the shower."

Her focus falls to the robe I'm clutching over my chest. "So it's true. Zander finally brought a woman home."

Finally? She says it as if female guests aren't a regular occurrence for the king. But that can't be true. Maybe Zander's just discreet about all his hookups.

Ignoring the I-want-to-claw-your-eyes-out vibes I'm getting from this woman, I step back and make room for her to come in. After all, she has my food.

Gracefully gliding by as if she's floating on air, she studies me from head to toe in a slow once-over. Her scrutinizing gaze stops on my wet limp hair and travels my face. Whatever she sees, she's not impressed.

"I'm Maelyn," I supply.

"I'm Carielle." She breezes over to the desk and sets the tray down before whispering, "I've known Zander his whole life. He can be impulsive, though I must say this takes the cake."

She's looking at me in that way again. Like I'm less. A bad decision.

The shower shuts off. Her eyes light with interest, and she tries to look past me to the bathroom. Unwelcome jealousy tightens my gut.

Has she been with him? Do they have a romantic history?

I shift a couple paces, hoping to preserve Zander's privacy. My small frame won't do much to block her view, but I can distract her. "Zander says I'm his fated mate."

"Says?" She cocks her head. "You don't know for sure?"

I pick at some imaginary lint on my sleeve. "Until yesterday, I didn't believe in other worlds, magic, or soul mates. I'm… adjusting to everything."

"No one wants to contradict a king." Sighing heavily, she shakes her head like Zander's an ornery child who doesn't know what he wants. "Wishful thinking can be a bitch."

I have a feeling she can be, too. "Are you implying he's wrong?"

"Desperation makes people do desperate things." She gives a nonchalant shrug.

I don't like her. I'm not one to pass judgement so quickly—ever—but there's something about her that rubs me the wrong way.

Carielle motions to the two covered plates and the glasses of water, resuming her haughty tone. "Zander usually eats at his desk. There's only one chair. I suppose you could sit on the floor."

"My wife will not eat on the floor."

We both jump at Zander's hard declaration.

"King Zander," Carielle breathes out. "There you are. And wait—what? Your *wife*?" She pins me with a look.

"Yes." Zander strides forward in nothing but a towel. "We were married on the wedding ridge yesterday."

Losing her composure, Carielle gapes like a fish. "Does your mother know about this?"

"I would assume not, since I haven't told her." There's a warning in his words. He wants to be the one to announce the news and Carielle better not spill the beans.

"Well." Her knuckles turn white as she balls her hands into fists at her sides. "The rumors are already out."

"I trust you can be discreet." It's an order. I'm not familiar with this world, but even I can recognize that.

"Of course, your majesty," Carielle agrees with a curtsy.

While openly checking out my husband.

My husband.

I seriously just referred to him as that in my head. But it's true. He is. Carielle doesn't know the reluctant circumstances of our union, and it's super rude for her to ogle the guy when he's practically naked.

That towel's barely long enough to make it all the way around his waist. It's rolled inward, staying in place by sheer chance. His dick print is obvious, and his skin is still wet. The white queen is around his neck, and I'm guessing he showered with it on because the shoestring is soaked. A rivulet of water drips from it, trailing down his tan skin. A drop gets caught on his nipple and Carielle licks her lips.

Okay. That's it.

I move in front of him, pressing my back to his front. He hooks an arm around my waist like it's the most natural thing in the world.

"We can eat on the bed," I suggest, hoping Carielle will go away. "Thank you."

"That'll be all." Zander dismisses her with a flick of his hand.

Her face is red as she relocates our dinner, then she leaves the room.

"Who was that?" I ask, attempting to keep the question casual so I don't give my sudden internal tantrum away.

Zander releases me and easily perches on the end of the bed, while I have to climb up because it's so high off the floor.

"One of the women trapped in my father's harem," he replies. "When he died, some of them decided to go back to the human realm. Others had nowhere to go, so my mother gave them jobs in the palace or in the dorms. Carielle's the royal event coordinator. Since we don't have many events to plan, she also does some light servant work, too."

"Oh." Now I feel like a jerk. "She's suffered, huh?"

"Did she treat you badly?"

"Define badly."

His face darkens. "Did she insult you? You were jealous."

Wanting to deny the—very true—accusation, I sputter, "Jealous—I wasn't—I just…" Sometimes it's kind of cool how he's so in tune with me. Other times, it's just embarrassing.

"I'll fire her right now."

"No! I'm not gunning for her to lose her job. Geez, Zander. You can't go all off-with-their-heads every time I don't get along with someone."

"Why not?"

"Because." I take the dome off my plate to find a sandwich, some circular fries that look a lot like chips, and a small bowl of green grapes. "Because I don't want you to."

"She must've said something to make you feel..." Zander's eyes blankly dart around while he decides on the right word. "Threatened. If Carielle overstepped, I'll—"

"I just got a weird vibe from her, that's all," I downplay it. "She seemed to have doubts about us being fated mates."

"It's not her place to have an opinion on the subject. And you? Do you still refuse to acknowledge our connection?"

Exhausted and stressed, I rub my temple. "I know I care for you. I can't deny that."

"Why do you say that as if it's a problem?"

"Because I shouldn't." I laugh, but there's nothing funny about this. "You forced me here, yet I like you. And this whole ordeal has made me realize how malleable I am." Sadness floods in when I think about my ruined career. "Even if I did go home, at this point, I can never go back to my job. How could I when I'm a fraud? How could I look those damaged women in the eye every day and tell them how strong they are for leaving their abusive partners? I'm a hypocrite."

Zander scowls. It's more intense than his frown. "Why do you compare yourself to these females? I would never hit you, Mae. I'd rather die than cause you pain."

"Abuse isn't always physical. Sometimes it's psychological, too."

"And you feel—" A muscle ticks in his cheek "—abused by me in this way?"

"No, not exactly, but you robbed me of my free will when you took my choice away."

Eyebrows pushing together, Zander looks confused. "I did give you a choice."

I scoff. "What? When?"

"I presented options to the humans. You left my side. You

walked away from me. You chose wrong, so I had to correct your mistake."

I make a sound of indignation. "The fact is, I didn't have a say in the matter."

Looking pained, Zander briefly closes his eyes. "I don't want to be like my father."

"You're not," I say gently. "I didn't know the man, but I've gotten to know you. You fight so hard for a better kingdom."

"But when it comes to you, I'm a selfish bastard. Even if you'd rather be somewhere else, I'm glad you're with me. I won't apologize for that, but I'm asking you, in earnest, to give me a chance." He softens, his face ditching the frown as a hopeful expression takes its place. "I need you to choose me. To be here willingly. It'll kill me if you think of yourself as my prisoner. I just can't handle that. Choose me. Please, Mae. Please."

I've never heard him sound so desperate. So open. Zander's baring himself to me in a way that makes him vulnerable to my rejection.

"If I say no, will you still keep me?" I just want to test the theory.

"Yes." And he's just being brutally honest.

He has zero remorse. He's so self-assured and unrelenting when it comes to my captivity.

But didn't I already decide to stay?

It's pointless for me to fight against it, but there is a request I won't budge on. "Could I ever go back to Earth for a visit? Not to stay, but just to see my parents on a holiday or something. Quinn said she does it."

Zander tips his head from side to side as he considers it. "I've never been to the human realm. Never had an interest in it. But as long as you'll allow me to accompany you, yes, we can visit."

Surprised by his agreement, I jerk back. "Really?"

"I swear it."

"Okay," I exhale roughly.

Zander looks stunned. "What?"

"Okay, I'm giving you a chance. Not because you're forcing me to, but because I'm curious about this fated stuff, and like I said, I like you."

The man really does have a gorgeous smile, and he gives it to me then.

CHAPTER 21

Zander

I feel like Maelyn has just gifted me with the suns. Sure, she reduced me to begging for her cooperation like a peddler trying to sell sunshine in the Day Realm, but my pride is the last thing on my mind.

She's willing to stay.

In return, I'll give her everything I can, including my secrets. No, not all of them. But I'll tell her enough to pull her further into my life.

"It needed to be done," I say, thinking back on our conversation in the stairwell.

"What did?" Maelyn happily munches on her sandwich, unaware of the tragic story I'm about to dole out.

"Zarid killed his father to save his sister's life. If Zella had died that day, the repercussions to this world would've been massive. The rift between Day and Night would've been bigger than ever. War would've broken out. Trade would've stopped which means, at the very least, we'd have no cold beverages." Raising my glass of water, I let the ice from the Dream Realm clink around. "Everything would be different. Zarid made the right choice when he ran his father through with an iron spike."

Drawing a deep breath through the nose, Maelyn chews her fried potatoes. "Well, it does sound justified."

"Truly?" I'm surprised and skeptical.

It's obvious my wife is soft, which isn't a bad trait. She's sweet. Untainted by how evil people can be. I like her innocence.

But she's accepting the brutal crime way more easily than I expected.

"I'm not a fan of the death penalty," she states, "but in domestic abuse situations, there are times when getting away isn't an option. In the worst-case scenario, someone gets killed, and I'd rather it be the abuser than the victim. If your father killed his father to stop him from hurting Zella, then it was a form of defense."

Defense. The excuse rolls around in my mind.

Is that what it was when I hunted my father down? When I flew above him on Battle Field in griffin form, reveling in the fear on his face when he spotted me in the sky? When I bit down on his neck with my beak, tasting his blood and feeling the crunch of bone as I severed his spine?

"I murdered him," I blurt the confession. "Zarid, I mean. Five years ago, he struck an under-the-table deal with the princess of the Night Realm. Traded a bunch of Glow for a good number of their females. Kirian was furious and banished his sister for the crime, and I knew it was up to me to rescue the women because my father was willing to fight to keep them. The resulting battle with the Night Realm served as the perfect opportunity for me to carry out my father's execution. He never saw me coming until it was too late… and I ripped his head off."

Maelyn gasps. "W-with your hands?"

I let out a sound that's neither a confirmation nor a denial, but she takes it as a yes.

Her soft fingers cover my fist. "That must've been awful for you."

A humorless laugh leaves me, but it's more like a grunt. She's unbelievable, in the best way. Even after I've kept her against her will and forced her to marry me, she's in my corner. No questions asked, she's on my side.

What a perfect queen she is.

"I'm certain it was worse for him," I say sardonically.

"You were abused, weren't you, Zander?" Maelyn's soft question hits me right in the heart.

Abused? The word isn't ugly enough for what my father did to my mother and me.

I close my eyes as I recall his thundering shouts. His fists pummeling my ribs, my back, my head. His belt, cracking across my skin. The times he would use his fire power to burn me. Even worse, I remember him directing his wrath at my mother, her blood dripping onto the pristine floors while the scent of her seared flesh hung in the air.

"Yes," I rasp. "Throughout my childhood, my father used my mother and me against each other. If I defied him, he would make me watch while he tortured her. If she was disobedient, he would go after me. We had to play by his rules. Or else."

"What rules?"

"For one, my mother wasn't allowed to speak her original language. She barely spoke any English at all when she came here, and she had to learn quickly."

I've lost my appetite, but I force myself to take a few bites anyway. Once I've finished half my sandwich, I continue telling Maelyn the terrible truths of my life.

"You already know how my mother came to be here. She was from Brazil. She loved her home and had a great family—she was the oldest of four sisters. She just happened to be in the wrong place at the wrong time. The snatchers plucked her off the side of the road when she was going for a walk. They picked her because she was beautiful. Only the best for King Zarid. He wasn't willing to wait for his fated mate, but he wanted an heir, so he formed a harem of about fifteen human women, hoping to impregnate one or more. My mother was the first and only one to conceive, and he married her to make it legitimate. How unlucky for her to be tied to such a heartless man."

"But something good came out of it," Maelyn declares optimistically. "She got you."

I scoff. "If there's one thing I could change about the past, it would be her kidnapping. It would erase my existence, but at least she wouldn't have had to suffer."

A bolt of sorrow travels through the bond, and although I don't want Maelyn to be sad, I like the fact that she cares.

"Is that what your mom would choose, too?" Maelyn asks. "Would she turn back time and give you up?"

I know the answer immediately. "No. She loves me more than anything."

"Then you need to stop thinking about a different outcome. Accept her love and know that you're a good man. She raised a great king, and I can't imagine this world without you in it."

There's so much conviction in her compliments that I believe her. I'm in awe of her ability to lift my soul with words. "Is this what you do when you're working? Build people up?"

"When someone has been beaten down, they need to hear positive affirmations. Everyone craves kindness. Some people just need it a little more than others."

"You're very good at it."

Blushing from my praise, she flits around her plate before biting into a grape. "What other rules were there?"

"I wasn't allowed to leave palace grounds. First, it was because my father was ashamed of my lack of power. Then it was because I was blind. Then it was because—"

I stop, realizing I'm about to give away one of the secrets I don't want Maelyn to know yet. I want her affection for me to be deeper before she finds out I'm a monster.

"Because what?" she prompts.

"That's why so many citizens of Valora don't recognize me," I veer our conversation off course, hoping she won't point out my deliberate avoidance. "Until my father died, hardly anyone had seen me past the age of five. Fae powers can emerge in infancy, but sometimes they take until someone is four years old to become present. When my fifth birthday came and I still had no power, my father went into a rage. There was no celebration. No presents or cake. He shut me in my room for an entire day while he trashed the castle and beat my mother. After he was done with her, he came for me. Up until then, I'd wished for his approval and love. I had spent many months looking at my useless hands, wishing they could conjure fire like his, but my hope died that day."

"Oh, Zander. I'm so sorry."

I sigh heavily. "Less than a year later, the witches cast the curse and I lost my sight. So, on top of being weak, I was disabled. Father didn't want the kingdom to know he had a defective son, so I was prohibited from leaving. I didn't mind sticking around home at first. I had my mother, good food, teachers, and a library. Aside from the abuse, I was privileged and sheltered. This isn't a bad place to be."

Continuing to listen attentively, Maelyn eats her dinner while I talk.

"I missed out on battles, trades, and bonding with my citizens, but I had a reason to stay. Once I was big enough to take my father on physically, I fought back. I protected myself and my mother. If I was here, he couldn't touch her. That's one reason why he kept his harem. He couldn't take my mother's body, so he got his needs met elsewhere. I think he was hoping to impregnate another woman. If he'd been successful in doing so, he might've found a way to get rid of us. But, unfortunately for him, I was his only child." Feeling lighter now that I've gotten all that off my chest, I take a deep breath. "I had to end him, just like he had to with his father."

"What made you wait so long to go after him?" Maelyn asks between sips of water. "I'm not judging. I'm just wondering how the timing played out. Was the shady deal with the Night Realm the last straw?"

"I wish I could say I killed my father for noble reasons—justice for my mother and me, or to save the Night Realm females. But that's not true. I did it for you."

Inhaling her drink, she coughs a little. "Me? You didn't even know me then."

"But you were a possibility." I smile a little when I remember the burst of hope I got when Kirian found his fated mate. "Up until several years ago, I believed my life to be meaningless, and I didn't think the curse would ever be broken. Many times, I contemplated suicide." Before she can scold me for such thoughts, I push on. "The only reason I didn't kill myself is because I couldn't leave my mother, but everything changed when Quinn broke Kirian's curse and restored his sight. He gets to rule with his other half at his side while surveying his kingdom and looking upon his people. Then the same happened for Damon—"

"Hold up." Maelyn's hand cuts through the air. "They're blind from the same curse as you, right?"

"They were."

"But the curse was broken? How? I didn't even know that was possible."

Squirming uncomfortably—and chastising myself for the action because kings don't *squirm*—I clear my throat, realizing my deliberate attempt to leave out such a large detail is going to come back to 'bite me in the ass', as Damon would probably say.

"Every curse has a way out." I poke at my grapes. "The stipulations of said curse are to be blind forever unless we find our fated mates and consummate the union."

"Sex. You mean sex."

"Precisely."

"Don't you think that's something you should've told me yesterday?" The mattress jostles as Maelyn sits up straighter.

I aim my unseeing eyes her way. "I'm not looking for a pity fuck."

"Good. Because I wouldn't pity fuck you." The dirty word sounds so pretty coming from her sweet mouth.

My cock stiffens as all my blood rushes to my lower half, making it difficult for me to think straight. Although I hadn't planned on divulging so many details, now that we're talking about it, I can't seem to stop.

"In addition to having sex with the right person—the only person in the universe meant for me—it has to be her. *You*. If I so much as kiss someone who isn't my soul mate, the curse will be permanent, and I'll be blind forever."

"Oh." Maelyn deflates. "So, you didn't tell me because the curse is permanent for you."

"No. Why would the curse be permanent?"

"Because you've kissed someone else before me."

My face scrunches up. "Who?"

"I don't know. Someone." Maelyn's voice pitches up before lowering to a whisper. "There's no way yesterday was your first kiss."

"And why is that?"

"Because you're you."

"What does that mean?"

"You're—you're hot. Zander, you might not be able to see the looks girls give you, but you get noticed. A lot. And you're a king and you're all broody. You're like catnip for women."

My male pride swells. "You flatter me, wife, but I assure you, you're the first and you'll be my only."

Positive feelings flow through the bond. Warm affection mixed with happiness. There's a new lightness to Maelyn's tether, and I realize some of her armor has fallen away since she consented to being here.

"Anyway." I get back on track to our previous conversation. "Kirian's success gave me hope that the same could happen for me, but if there was even a slight chance that I could find you, my father had to go. And I did find you. You're here, and by my side is where you'll stay."

"I want to add a condition to my choice," Maelyn states, sobering me.

"Yes, wife?"

"If you want me to be your partner, I need you to be open with me. I have a lot to learn about this world, and I don't want to be blindsided by any surprises. The fact that you could get your sight back? That's a big deal and you should've told me. No more secrets."

"No more secrets," I agree, and it hurts.

Because that was a lie.

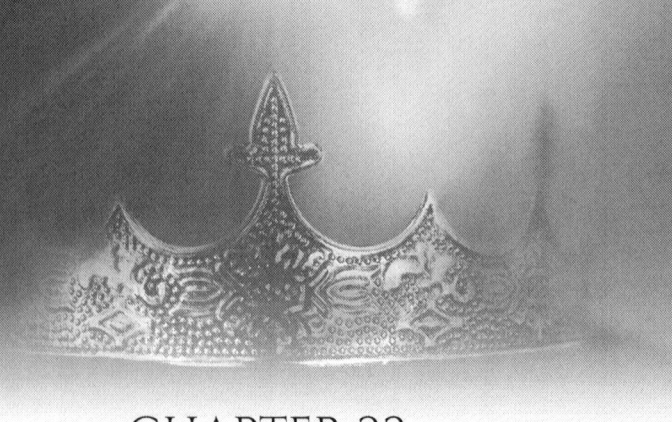

CHAPTER 22

Maelyn

I squeeze my thighs together as I slip under the covers. My stomach is full, and my body is clean, but I'm far from satisfied.

The ache between my legs won't subside.

Out of the corner of my eye, Zander nudges the dinner tray into the hallway before shutting the door and locking it.

Although it's dark in here because he closed the curtains, there's enough light glowing from behind them to see.

He's still wearing that towel, and somehow, it's hanging on by a thread. As he saunters over to the armoire, the material suddenly drops, and his sculpted butt is there in all its glory.

I hold in a squeak and raise the blanket to eye level. I can't seem to bring myself to hide behind it completely, because then I'd lose my view.

Zander's shoulders shake and a series of puffs silently exhale from his body.

Is he laughing at me?

Even if I'm the butt of the joke—pun intended—I'd welcome his teasing. Anything to hear some booming joy from this man.

After learning what he went through as a kid, my heart hurts. I could tell it was difficult for him to open up the way he did. His story had come out clunky and stilted, as if he'd never told the tale before. And that's a tragedy in itself—to hold all that in for so long.

It took all my self-control to keep from leaping over our plates and giving him a hug. Maybe a few kisses, too.

Now he's walking toward the bed wearing only those white boxer briefs. With me in just a nightshirt and panties, that could result in some skin-on-skin action under the covers.

"You're not wearing pants," I say quietly.

His normally broody face lifts with a lopsided grin. "I usually don't in my own bed."

"I could sleep on the floor."

"My wife will not sleep on the floor."

Every time he calls me *wife*, my chest constricts with an unidentifiable emotion. I sort of love his possessiveness.

Lying on my side, I keep my back turned as he gets in. The mattress dips behind me. Warmth emanates from his body. Anticipation thrums in my veins as I wait for him to get closer.

When he slides his palm over my hips and around to my stomach, heat explodes inside me. It's like a million tiny flaming butterflies take flight, spreading outward, through my arms to my fingers. From my abdomen to my wet core.

I've soaked my panties.

"It's okay if I hold you, right?" Although Zander poses it as a question, there's no inflection at the end, making it seem more like a statement.

He doesn't wait for me to nod, but I don't say no either.

Melding his front to my backside, Zander slides his other arm under my head like he did last night.

Unlike last night, we're not separated by layers of blankets and clothes. His erection is like a steel rod against my lower back.

My toes curl as I try not to wiggle against him.

His thumb brushes my belly over the fabric of the shirt. Back and forth. An idle caress.

A whimper gets trapped in my throat as I clench my teeth and grab a corner of the pillow.

I strongly suspect he's working me up on purpose. My mind is fuzzy with desire, and my lungs are working faster to keep up with my thundering heart.

How am I supposed to sleep when my body is so revved up?

As if Zander knows exactly where my mind is at, he asks, "Is there anything you need?"

"No," I whisper.

"Ah, ah. I thought you said no more secrets." His warm breath tickles my ear. "It should work both ways."

I'm way too shy to tell him I need to come. "I can't say it."

"Why not?" Sliding his hand up, he bumps over my ribs.

"I just can't."

When his fingers graze the underside of my breast, I almost tell him he's going to have to take the lead, be the one to make a move. Kissing him was out of character for me. He's the exception to the rule, and I hope I didn't give him the impression that I'm the type to throw myself at someone.

Zander's fingers walk their way up my sternum, stopping at my collarbone. His wrist is trapped between my breasts, buried in my cleavage. More heat floods my center, making me feel swollen and puffy down there.

Zander softly rubs the hollow of my throat. "What if we were to play a game?"

"Like chess?"

He hums low, a sexy rumbling in his chest. "A game where I tell you to do something. If you truly want to do it, you obey. If you don't want to do it, you tell me to stop."

The terms sound harmless enough, but it doesn't take a genius to realize he's talking about something physical, and my entire body lights up at the thought of doing more than kissing.

"It wouldn't be appropriate for us to go very far," I say weakly, unsure if I really mean it.

"We're married. We can do whatever we want."

He's not wrong, and my resolve is cracking.

"How about this?" Zander proposes, pushing up on an elbow. "I won't touch you unless you ask me to."

I wrinkle my nose. "I thought the whole point of the game was so I wouldn't have to say anything. What are we going to…?" My question trails off as Zander gets up from the bed.

He heads over to his desk and grabs the pen from the inkwell. Watching him, my eyebrows pinch with confusion as he wipes the ink off. Idly twirling the feather, he starts back toward me.

"This is from my own wing," he says with a hint of pride.

"If there was a contest for best feather, I bet you'd win." He really would.

It's over a foot long, and the black fibers are so shiny they glint from the glow behind the curtains. When he waves it at me slowly, like a conductor leading an orchestra, I realize what he intends to do.

He might not touch me, but the feather will.

And I want that.

I want the silkiness gliding over my skin.

Zander stops by my side of the bed. "Lower the blanket."

I do as he says, pushing it to my knees.

Clucking his tongue, he shakes his head. "All the way. I need your feet, too."

"I'm very ticklish," I warn, kicking the covers to the end of the mattress. "If you're hoping to make me laugh, you might accomplish it."

His lips quirk up. "I love your laugh, but I'm hoping to hear some new sounds from you tonight. Tell me how this feels."

Taking the feather, he touches the tip of it to my left knee and drags it upward along my inner thigh.

I shudder, closing my eyes at the soft sensation. "Good. It feels good."

My heart speeds up as he repeats the action a few times. Down. Then up. Down. Up again. Slowly. Softly.

On every upward stroke, he goes a little higher, nudging the nightshirt out of the way.

With the next pass, my legs automatically spread.

A silent invitation.

My eyelids are heavy as I peer up at Zander, and I know something is going to change between us tonight.

I've already surrendered my freedom. Now my body is putty in his hands. Er, putty under his feather, I guess.

Either way, I want more.

I *need* more.

My heart is going a mile a minute, and this type of exhilaration is something I've never experienced before. It's drugging, making me light-headed and giddy. I've never been an adrenaline junkie, but who needs bungee jumping when you have a sexy fae king looming over you?

"Unbutton your shirt," Zander orders.

He's testing the waters. Wanting to find out if I'll stop the game.

Swallowing hard, I pop the first button out by my neck. Then the second. And the next.

Soon, the shirt is open along my front. I don't peel back the fabric to bare my breasts. I let it cover me, the exposed strip of skin ultra-sensitive to the cool air.

Zander points the feather to the hollow of my throat. It doesn't linger long. Satisfaction and desire punch through me as it takes the path between my breasts and down my stomach. Briefly dipping it into my belly button, he swirls it, then continues his descent.

The light touch skims over my panties before stopping right above my clit.

I moan.

Pressing my fingertips to my mouth, I stare up at Zander, wide-eyed. I hadn't meant to make that sound.

"There it is," he says huskily. Approvingly. "I could listen to that for hours."

Continuing the wonderful torture, he repeats the slow, dragging motion along my torso a few more times.

It's not enough. This game isn't helping—it's only making my self-control crack. Words I've never even thought about saying are on the tip of my tongue.

Take off my clothes. Touch me. Make me come.

I'm trembling. My fingers keep clenching, balling into fists at my sides. The dampness in my panties has gone from a puddle to a pond. I can feel the wetness seeping down to the bed, and my inner thighs are sticky.

At least I'm not the only one affected by this erotic game. Zander's erection is prominent inside his boxers, tenting the fabric. His cock is so long and thick, it's partly trapped in one of the leg holes, and there's a dark rounded shadow sticking out. The tip.

On the next pass down my sternum, he pauses, wisping the feather against my skin a few times before flicking the shirt. The cotton covering my right breast falls away.

I hiss.

Unguarded by the fabric, my nipple hardens painfully, and I don't get a chance to recover before Zander's circling it.

My breath comes out in a series of broken pants. "Zander."

"Yes, wife?"

I just whimper, not knowing how to explain what I'm feeling. My face and fingers are starting to tingle. Goose bumps decorate my entire body and sweat dots my forehead.

I ache. I hurt. Everywhere.

But the worst pain is between my legs. My core throbs fiercely, demanding attention as it spasms around nothing, and I can't think clearly. All my needs are centered on the empty space.

Zander pushes the other side of the shirt away, but instead of playing with my nipples, he moves the feather down, running it along the elastic of my panties.

"Do you want me to stop?"

"No," I whisper shakily.

"Then take these off."

I hook my thumbs into the waistband and push them down while wiggling my hips. The white panties end up dangling from one of my toes as I hang my leg over the bed, and Zander snatches them before they can drop to the floor.

Balling them in his fist, he brings the material to his nose. He inhales, then shudders.

With rapt fascination, I gawk while his tongue darts out to lick the material. The material that's damp with my arousal.

Sucking it into his mouth, he growls. Deep. Like an animal. It's so loud, vibrations travel through the wooden bedframe and shake the mattress.

I'm sure that sound has made grown men run for their lives, but for some reason, it just turns me on more.

I can see why women fall for the bad boy. There's a forbidden rush of knowingly putting your own life in peril, while thinking you have a safety net underneath you.

In my line of work, I've often wondered what it would be like to get lured in by a dangerous man, to miss all the red flags and throw caution to the wind because of a pull I can't deny. It happens to women all the time.

But Zander isn't bad. Not really. He's dangerous, there's no disputing that, but he's not a danger to me. If there's one thing I know for sure in this confusing world, it's that Zander cherishes everything I am.

He loves the same way he hates—with utter abandon. With passion. With his whole heart.

His gentleness and his violence are two sides of the same coin.

Love isn't something he's had a lot of, yet he still finds an endless well of it inside himself, as if he's spent his whole life saving it up for me.

That's why I chose to stay. Why I said yes to the game. Why I'm so infatuated with him.

Rules and responsibilities are a far-off whisper in my mind as Zander grazes my slit with the feather. It tickles the overly sensitive skin of my lips and it just barely skims my engorged clit. The touch is too light. Too soft. I need more pressure.

"Legs wider," Zander commands, and I immediately comply. "Bend your knees and spread those sweet thighs. Bring your heels up to your ass. Yes, just like that. Now wrap your hands around your ankles. Hold yourself open for me."

All the air leaves me in a whoosh as I do what he says.

Clenching his jaw, he sniffs the air and another growl rumbles from his throat. The panties fall from his grasp, and the hand holding the feather shakes.

I'm glad I'm not the only one being driven crazy here.

Zander's head drops back, and he rasps, "You want more."

"Yes," I agree on a whimper.

"I could use my fingers instead." He lets several seconds pass, waiting for me to refuse him. "But remember, you have to ask for it."

I'm past the point of embarrassment. "Touch me?"

"If you insist." Carelessly discarding the quill pen to the floor, Zander puts a knee on the mattress. My heart hammers and my body jostles as he smoothly climbs on the end of the bed. Turning to face me, he sits on his haunches, his knees between my feet.

I'm completely bared to him. Not that he can see it, but I'm still a little scandalized at my own view—my knees spread wide, my hands holding my legs in place.

The first caress on my ankle makes me jolt. It's just a fingertip, for Pete's sake. But it's Zander's finger, and I'm so wound up.

"Are you ready for this now?" Zander's tone is almost teasing. "Or is it still inappropriate for me to touch my wife?"

"Just do something," I pant out. "Please."

"Say please again." His finger goes up a few inches, torturing the inside of my calf.

"Please."

Although his face is cloaked in shadows, his golden eyes glow with excitement. "Again."

"Please," I whine, contemplating grabbing his hand and shoving it where I want it.

He lets out a satisfied hum and goes higher, leaving goose bumps in his wake as he makes it to my inner thigh. "That's what I want to hear—my eager wife begging me to finger fuck her."

Gasping a little at his dirty talk, my jaw drops open and heat infuses my face.

"Don't be embarrassed, Mae," he coos. "It's normal for you to want me this much. I'd move mountains to get to you." His middle finger traces the crease where my thigh meets my pelvis. "I'd burn the entire world to the ground for this pussy."

Before I can say anything else, he presses his thumb to my clit with unbelievable precision.

My back bows, and I moan again.

"You're so wet," he praises, his tone full of wonder as he rubs up and down. His mouth parts with a groan as he explores my slick entrance and the soft flesh of my lips.

He stops above my clit. With his forefinger and thumb, he pinches the cord of nerves and rolls it in between his fingers.

I choke out a gasp.

I've never touched myself like this before. Usually, I focus only on the main part of the clit, not the areas around it.

But this…

Going a little higher, Zander continues pinching and rolling. Hitting all the right notes while blowing my mind. Maybe I could get off from this, but I don't think that's his goal.

He wants to drive me to the brink of madness, and he's achieving it. Toying with that string attached to my clit, he plays me like he's practiced me for years.

Every woman is different. We all have personal preferences, which is what makes it so difficult for men to please us. At least, that's what Paige says. Many times, she's complained about having to teach her boyfriends what she likes, which is why I suspect she stays with the losers she dates long after the expiration date is up.

But Zander knows my body better than I do.

With just the right amount of pressure and speed, his touch is perfect.

My breathless voice is full of accusation when I say, "For someone who's never done this before, you're very skilled."

He stops rubbing. "You think I was lying when I said I've never been with someone before?"

"How do you know where I need to be touched?"

"During my exile here, I spent countless hours in the library researching anatomy. I probably know the female body better than you do. Erogenous zones. Nerve endings. Though I've never practiced, I'm quite capable of kissing, among other things." He starts playing with me again. "Also, there's the matter of the bond. I feel an echo of everything you feel."

To make his point, he taps my clit three times.

"See?" He raises his eyebrows. "I felt that."

"What do you mean?" I slur, almost drunk from desire. "Felt it how?"

"Put your hand on me." Dipping his chin lower, he indicates his cock. When I don't comply right away, he drawls, "Or we could stop playing."

"No," I say too quickly, then I sit up and raise my trembling hand to his crotch.

Shy and completely unskilled, I touch it lightly. Zander lays his hand over mine, forcing my fingers around his girth through his boxers. God, he's so thick. I can't even get my fingers all the way around his cock.

"Stay there." Zander taps my clit again, and my eyes go wide when his cock jumps in tandem under my hand.

"You literally feel everything I do? Sexually?"

"Not just that. Pain. Emotions. All of it."

"Can you tell when I'm happy?"

"Yes."

"Do you know when I'm turned on?"

"Every single time."

I gasp. "So you knew when I touched myself in the shower?"

His smirk is wicked. "Oh, yes."

"You interrupted me on purpose."

"I couldn't let you have all the fun without me."

That's a little embarrassing. Here I've thought I was doing a good job of concealing my growing attraction. He knew all along.

It's so intimate to be connected in this way.

I've never been flayed open like this before. A rough swallow works down my throat, and my arm drops to my stomach as I hold myself in a protective gesture. A shield, as if I can hide myself from the imposing man in front of me.

A man who looks at me like I'm the center of his world. A king who's bowed down to me. A warrior who would give me his last breath.

And now I have tangible proof of his claim. "We really are soul mates, huh?"

He doesn't answer with words. Instead, he continues the sweet torture, tracing my wet slit. I lie back again, and my breath hitches when he stops at my entrance and plays with the hole. He nudges it, igniting nerve endings but never pushing inside.

Lightly trailing through my folds, he purposefully avoids the places where I need him most.

Flustered, I grab a fistful of my hair. "You're teasing me."

"Do you want me to stop?"

"No!"

He chuckles, mischief bleeding through the sound. Getting closer to a laugh.

"I'm going to kiss you now," Zander murmurs.

I look down just in time to see him slide off the bed, grab my hips, and yank me to the end of the mattress. I yelp in surprise.

Kiss. He doesn't mean on the mouth.

Zander's so big that even on his knees, his chest is taller than the ginormous bed. His handsome face is situated in the V of my legs. When his warm breath puffs against me, I dig my heels into the mattress and curl my toes.

One at a time, he drapes my legs over his broad shoulders.

Excited and nervous, I press my fingers to my lips as I wait for him to put his mouth on me. I've often wondered if oral sex is overrated. Girls talk about it as if it's the eighth wonder of the world. According to Paige, it depends on the guy. Not all of them are great at it.

Zander will be, though.

Tense silence stretches between us. His breathing is fast like mine, and every exhale is another teasing caress to my center.

I can tell it isn't easy for him to hold back. His big hands are wrapped around the tops of my thighs, his fingers digging into my skin as he holds my legs in place. Turning his head, he kisses my inner thigh, then licks the area that's damp with my arousal.

He groans, slowly dragging his tongue over the same place again. Tasting me.

I wriggle impatiently. "Well? Are you going to do it or not?"

"What should you say?" He quirks an eyebrow.

"Please?"

"Please what?"

"Just—please!" I burst out, exasperated and desperate. "Tell me what to say and I'll say it."

He grins. It's one of his rare smiles, but he totally looks like the cat who caught the canary. "Please, husband, lick my pretty pussy."

I make a strangled noise. "What?"

"You heard me."

My throat clogs as sweat trickles down my temple into my hair. I don't know if I can get the words out.

As if to entice me further, Zander's thumbs start rubbing the place where my legs meet my butt. He's so close, yet so far away.

Forming his lips into an O shape, he lightly blows. My inner muscles clench hard when the air hits me, angry from being so neglected.

"Okay!" I shout at the ceiling, unable to look at Zander's face when I grumble, "Please lick my pussy."

"Pretty pussy," he corrects.

"Pretty pussy."

"Husband."

"Huh?"

"You forgot that part."

"Husband," I whimper, my heart doing a weird flip as the word passes from my lips.

"All together now."

This man. This infuriating, sexy, stubborn man.

I let out a growl that's not even a fraction as menacing as his. "Please, husband, lick my pretty pussy."

As soon as the sentence is finished, Zander attacks. I cry out when his mouth fuses over my clit, sucking in a pulsing rhythm.

Growling against me, Zander moves down a little to drag his tongue over my entrance. Stiffening it, he licks inside.

The pressure is amazing, and it only gets better when he replaces his tongue with a finger, inserting it up to the second knuckle. He massages the inside, curling it upward, stimulating a place I've never touched before.

While he keeps that up, his lips go back to my clit.

The dual sensations are enough to make my eyes roll back in my head, and I've completely lost control of myself.

I'm no longer worrying about the sounds I'm making. Moaning, I writhe and arch and rock my hips, chasing the orgasm I know will come.

All my limbs are jerking, and my leg starts to slip off Zander's shoulder. Catching it with ease, he reaches behind his head and locks my ankles together, tapping them in a 'stay' command. Then he lightly bats at my knees, making my legs fall open even more.

I like that he's in control. It takes out any guesswork for me. I almost want to test the theory that he'd stop if I asked him to, but I don't want to risk ruining the moment.

This is a big deal—the first time a man is going to get me off.

Needing something to do with my hand, I reach down and spear my fingers through his messy dark hair. He groans out a sound of approval, and the vibrations from his mouth cause little spasms in my core.

"Zander," I pant.

He removes his mouth long enough to say, "You'll call me husband when I'm inside you."

"H-husband," I obey.

I'm rewarded with a second finger. There's a bit of a sting in the stretch, but the pain heightens all the other sensations.

Zander's tongue is lashing my clit. One of his thumbs is pulling on my lips, spreading me open wider. I feel the rough scratch of his facial hair on my thighs.

"Who am I?" he grumbles low.

"Husband."

Suck, suck, suck. "Whose husband?"

"Mine."

"Good girl." *Lick, lick, lick.*

As my climax builds, my breath comes out in high-pitched pants and I start thrashing. Zander's arm hooks over my hips, banding me in place while he works me like a pro.

When a third finger pushes in and all those digits put pressure on what I can only assume is my g-spot, my pussy clamps down with an orgasm so strong it actually hurts.

Tilting my head back, my entire body locks up as I scream. One wave of contractions crashes into the next, and Zander shouts loudly against me when I gush on his face.

I sob toward the end of it, my lungs fighting for air as every muscle burns from tensing so hard.

As the last flutters taper off, I go slack. I jolt from a couple aftershocks, and I'm trembling.

Wait. The trembling isn't coming from me. It's Zander. He's shaking so hard his arm is practically vibrating where it rests on my stomach and thighs.

He slides his fingers out of me and stands.

Still trying to catch my breath, I gaze up at his serious face. It's shiny and slick with my arousal. He licks his lips, totally unconcerned with the mess.

"Zander, I—" Thank you won't cut it. "That's the best thing I've ever felt. Ever. I mean, I've heard of mind-blowing orgasms before, but I wasn't sure it was real. And you…"

My rambling trails off because he turns his back and stalks to the other side of the room. At first, I think maybe he's going to grab a towel to clean himself up, but he makes a bee line for the balcony doors. Bright light floods in when he throws them open.

"I'll be back later," he says gruffly before walking out.

Huh?

I hear the flap of wings. Scrambling off the bed, I quickly rebutton the shirt.

My legs are still wobbly from what Zander did to me, but I manage to stagger over to the open doors. When I get there, the balcony is empty.

Day Realm heat wafts at me as I creep forward.

Making it to the railing, I set my hand on the smooth marble, looking down as I search the ground four stories below.

From up here, so much more of Hailene is visible. The city beyond the palace walls stretches for miles. Cobblestone streets and Tudor-style houses make up the grid, spanning off in all directions.

There aren't many people out and about, but when a yawn threatens to emerge, I remember it's the middle of the night. The suns are close to colliding in the west, and it makes the clouds a bright yellow-orange.

Lifting my eyes, I scan the sky.

Zander's nowhere to be found.

And I'm confused.

Did I do something wrong?

Disappointment filters through the high I'm still riding. I might not have experience with men in the bedroom department, but I'm fairly positive leaving immediately after a sexual act is considered rude.

I glance back at the disheveled, empty bed.

I'm too amped up to sleep.

More sweat runs down the side of my face, and when I reach up to wipe it away, my hand gets caught in the damp tangles matted to my scalp. My hair's a complete mess. Guess I could occupy myself by searching for a decent brush. Of course, that'll mean rifling through Zander's drawers, but if he didn't want me snooping around his room, then he shouldn't have left me alone.

Sighing, I turn to go back inside while feeling a little sorry for myself.

CHAPTER 23

Zander

When I was twelve, my stuffy math tutor had a coughing fit while drinking his tea, and it shot out of his nose. I couldn't see it, but the sounds were highly amusing, and I couldn't stop myself from laughing. In fact, I laughed so hard, the boisterous pressure in my chest quickly turned into an impending shift. Right there in the library, I went full-on griffin in front of Ontarius, which only made him sputter harder as he looked at me with terrified eyes. He quit that day, demoting himself back to the kitchens so he didn't have to be around me.

I hated my power then, and I loathe it now.

The memory darkens as I stalk across the rooftop of the palace, my talons digging into the stone. Father was so angry at me for scaring off one of my teachers, I had to guard Mother around the clock for a full month to make sure he wouldn't take it out on her.

I'm always being punished for what I am, and tonight is no exception. What should've been a glorious moment was interrupted.

At least I resisted the shift long enough to get Maelyn off, but I lost control when her thighs shook. When her hips bucked. When she came undone on my face.

I felt her bolt of pleasure shooting through me. It was so strong that it triggered my own orgasm.

And two things happened: I came harder than I ever have before, my seed coating my underwear and running down my thigh. And the first tremors of the shift began.

I had to get out of there before Maelyn saw it. Luckily, I made it up to the rooftop before the griffin took over.

Peeking over the five-foot stone wall, I gaze down at my woman, watching her as she looks for me. She's wondering why I took off without an explanation.

As she should.

What an asshole move.

I wish it didn't have to be like this. I want nothing more than to have her in my arms as we relish in the moment we shared together. And I will after I calm down.

Fortunately, I won't stay shifted long. My heart is already slowing as the rush fades. Soon, I'll be lying with my wife, sleeping peacefully, just like we did last night.

When Maelyn's head tilts up to study the sky, I move back, out of sight.

"I'm surprised to find you up here."

I growl at the voice behind me, turning to see Carielle standing inside the doorway of one of the four spires. Her hip is popped, her flirtatious smirk is in place, and she's twirling her hair around her finger.

If I could roll my eyes in griffin form, I would.

She's putting on her act for me, just like she used to with my father.

"I thought you'd be with your new little wife," she tacks on, taunting.

As I prowl her way, her eyes widen with genuine fear.

Not many people can stand in front of me when I look like this without wanting to soil themselves. My mother is the only person who's ever been able to accept me as I am, no matter what form I'm in.

Maelyn did, too, in the stream. But that's because she'd almost died. She wasn't in her right mind.

Going over to a storage bin attached to the wall, I knock the lid back with my beak and lift a pair of pants out.

Chuffing at Carielle, I whip my head to the side.

Avert your eyes.

Everyone knows I don't like to be watched while I shift. I'm too vulnerable, unable to hide the pain as my bones snap into place.

Not to mention, I'm naked.

Once Carielle has her back turned, I start the process of changing.

My beak cracks as flames ignite across my face. Agony shoots through my head, the plates in my skull breaking apart. Shards of bone tear through tendons and muscle while my legs and arms fold in on themselves.

When it's finally done, blackness descends in my vision once more. I'm on my hands and knees, my limbs unsteady as I hang my head. I take a few deep breaths, allowing my rib cage to expand with my lungs. My fae wings are out. I'll need them to fly back to my room, so I keep them where they are.

Grunting, I push off the stone and get dressed.

"So, Prince Zander ran off and got married." Carielle's overly sweet tone puts me on edge as I button my pants.

"*King* Zander," I correct harshly, turning toward her. "And yes, I did."

"Why her?"

"She's my mate."

"Doubtful."

Fury flares through my chest, but I keep my temper at bay. "The correct sentiment is 'congratulations.'"

"There's no way she's your destined match," she goes on, having no clue how close she is to being thrown off this rooftop. She has wings. She'd be fine. But it would be a clear message on how much I enjoy her company. "I saw the way she looked at you. It's not the way a woman looks at a man she loves. If she's your mate, she'd look at you with the suns in her eyes. Not… indifference."

I smirk. Maelyn wasn't so indifferent a few minutes ago. "You don't know what you speak of."

"Maybe she bewitched you."

"She's a human, Carielle. She can't bewitch anyone."

"Even more reason for you to reject the idea of being with her. She'll make you weak."

She's provoking me, and I shoot her a warning glower to convey the sentiment. "Lay off her. You were human once."

"But not completely though, right? I must have some fae heritage or I wouldn't have changed as much as I did."

It's true. I can only assume Carielle has some fae blood running through her veins. Several years after her arrival, she grew white feathered wings. Her eyes became more vibrant, and she developed a minor power. She can move objects with her mind—only a little, though. Nothing heavy or cumbersome. Her power is equivalent to a strong gust of wind. And, true to fae nature, she can be manipulative and charming.

All reasons why she was one of my father's favorites. That, and because she always seemed very enthusiastic about pleasing him.

I sigh, sick of her pursuit of a romantic relationship with me. Ever since she was released from my father's ownership, she's been proposing a union between the two of us. Time and time again, I've made it clear it's never going to happen.

Carielle's been conditioned to use her body as a means to an end. She's floundered since being set free, but my mother has given her a purpose here. One that doesn't include fucking the king to earn her keep.

I feel sorry for her, but my sympathy only goes so far. Maelyn obviously sensed something untoward in Carielle. Perhaps the woman has overstayed her welcome here. There are other places for her to go. Hopefully far away from me.

"The rooftop is all yours." I gesture around us. "I'll leave you in peace. Goodnight."

"The masquerade is in five days," she drawls, following me to the ledge. "Would you like to go over the menu in the morning?"

"My mother can approve the food choices."

"Are you attending?"

"I don't know. After Maeyln has time to settle in, we're going back out to hunt down a fugitive."

"You're taking her with you on a dangerous mission?"

"Of course. She's the queen."

Despite what happened earlier at the distillery, I haven't changed my mind about keeping Maelyn at my side. Yes, this world is brutal and gruesome, but Maelyn surprised me today. She was compassionate and brave. The trolls might've been less receptive to my assistance had she not been with me.

Carielle trails her fingers down my forearm. "If you'd let me, I could make you so happy you'd forget about her."

"Don't." My grip is harsh when I catch her wrist and remove her hand from my arm. "You will not touch what's not yours."

"How did Maelyn react when you told her about your ability?" she persists, and I stay silent, mostly because it's none of Carielle's fucking business. She tsks. "Oh. You haven't told her yet. I can't imagine that's going to go over well. And what about after you've completed the bond? If she truly is your mate, will she experience your pain every time you shift?"

It feels like the wind has been knocked out of me. Carielle just brought up a point I hadn't considered. Astrid said Maelyn and I would be connected like regular mates after we consummate the bond. But would she suffer during my transformations? No others are like me. I have no one to ask about gifted powers and how it will affect Maelyn. By mating with her, I could be exposing her to the excruciating reality I face every day.

Another pressing question—will I shift every time we're intimate? That'd be inconvenient, to say the least.

I shove all my insecurities out of the way.

None of that matters.

Fate chose Maelyn for me. Chose me for her. We're meant to be.

After she's fallen in love with me, I'll be able to show her all sides of myself. I'll come clean about my power and we'll figure it out as fate intended—together.

"I can make you feel good," Carielle tries again, stepping into my personal space.

Bile rises in my throat.

She's like another mother to me. All the women in my father's harem were. While I was growing up, they'd dote on me, basking in the untainted innocence only a child can bring during a dark time.

Tapping into the griffin, I let my eyes flash at her, my irises stretching to oblong slits. She stumbles back, reacting the way I knew she would, and I enjoy in her terrified gasp.

"If you touch me again, you'll find yourself on the streets as a beggar."

She harrumphs. "Fine, but when she leaves you, I'll still be here, and my offer stands."

As her angry footsteps fade away, I effortlessly pounce up onto the ledge.

Warm wind ruffles my hair, and rays from the suns heat my skin.

I lick my lips.

Maelyn's essence is still on my face, her honeyed taste like pure bliss on my tongue. Regardless of the intense orgasm we both had minutes ago, I'm not sated. I want nothing more than to go back to my room and pleasure her over and over, but I don't want to shift again. I already ache from changing back so quickly.

Plus, Carielle has put me in a foul mood. She fanned the flames of self-doubt I've been wrestling with, and the wrongness of her proposition churns in my gut.

After the masquerade, I'll do another loyalty sweep through my staff and guards. I'll need Quinn for that. I sent Kirian an invitation to the upcoming ball, but I don't know if he and the Queen of Honesty will be attending.

Either way, Carielle will be among the first to be sent packing. Her time at the palace has expired. My mother might object to it, but I'm the king now.

Every decision is up to me whether I like it or not.

As much as I don't want to be away from Maelyn, I need to blow off some steam. A vigorous flight might do me some good.

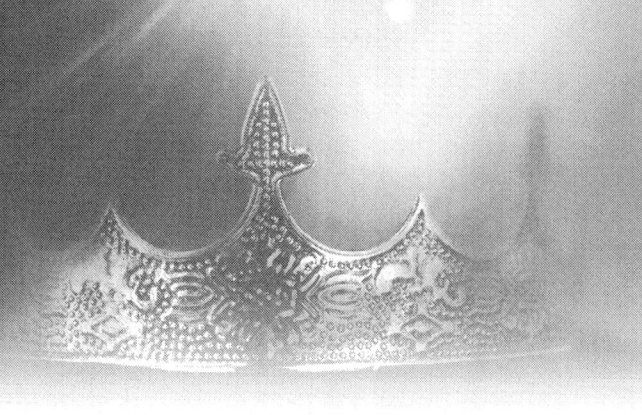

CHAPTER 24

Maelyn

I'M BALANCING ON THE EDGE OF SLEEP. I CAN'T REMEMBER exactly what I dreamed, but Zander was there. He was with me in Texas. We were in the field behind my mom's house, and he was laughing. Just like I imagined, the sound was deep and joyful, and it made my heart lift with happiness.

But I'm not in Texas. If the satiny sheet under my cheek isn't any indication, the merry singing of the morning bird is. Somewhere outside, I hear several of them whistling away.

Rolling over, I blink against the bright light coming through the windows. The curtains have been drawn back.

And I'm alone.

I pat the empty side of the mattress next to me.

Still warm.

Zander was here recently.

Last night, I tried to wait up for him. I stayed awake for as long as I could, detangling my hair with a comb I found and unpacking some of my clothes.

Eventually, exhaustion won out and I rested on the bed with drooping eyes until sleep took over.

Somehow, I know Zander held me throughout the night. It's as though I can still sense his arms around me.

Sitting up, I push my messy hair out of my face as I scan the quiet room.

There's a tray of food sitting at the desk, along with a tall glass of water. When I putter over to it, there's a note for me. A piece of paper has been folded and it's leaning up against my drink.

Wife is scrawled across it in calligraphy-like lettering. Obviously, the quill pen was used for this, and my cheeks heat when I look at the black feather sitting oh-so-innocently in the inkwell where it belongs.

I open the note. For someone who's blind, Zander's penmanship is good. Meticulous and precise. Controlled.

Just like him.

I didn't want to wake you. I have a meeting with my men this morning, but you'll have lunch with me at noon.

It's signed *Husband*.

Even his notes are bossy.

Palace food is way better than what we got on the road. Breakfast is more like a small feast. There's a basket of rolls, three different types of jam, scrambled eggs with cheese and sausage mixed in, some bacon, and a bowl of fruit salad.

After picking at my dinner last night and eating so much trail mix on the road, I'm starving. My body wants all the carbs.

Going for the rolls first, I break the bread open and steam rises out. They're fresh, and my mouth waters. When I slather on some of the red jam, I expect it to taste like strawberries. I'm surprised when I get a fruity flavor that's tangier, sweeter, and richer at the same time.

I switch to the eggs, taking three bites before I reach for more bread.

I'm sort of glad Zander isn't here right now. The very unlady-like stuffing of my face is real. I haven't even sat down yet. I'm just hunched over the desk like an animal.

Sticking my finger in the blue jam, I scoop up a good dollop and make a surprised noise when I taste citrus instead of berries.

I've cleared half my plate and four rolls when my stomach hits its limit.

Licking some of the sticky jam from my fingers, I wander over to the armoire and open the doors. Underneath a row of hanging khaki pants and some stiff-looking vests, a few piles of my clothes are folded, separated by pants, shirts, and undies.

I choose some light wash skinny jeans and a lavender t-shirt with a wide boat neck.

Once I get them on, I tuck the front of the shirt into my waistband. One of the shoulders keeps falling off to the side, but with the sports bra underneath, it looks intentional.

Now for my hair.

I poke around at my somewhat crispy locks. I really shouldn't have fallen asleep with it damp. My hair isn't super long, but it's thick. Somewhere between straight and curly, it's a nonsensical heap of waves.

I sigh, because I've got my work cut out for me.

As I'm heading for the bathroom, a knock comes through the door.

I stop in my tracks, wondering if I should answer it when, "Room service," comes through from the other side in a sing-song voice.

Oh. Glancing at the rumpled sheets on the bed and the hamper of dirty clothes, I realize I should've assumed Zander would have a maid come tidy up. First breakfast, now this? Talk about the royal treatment.

When I open the door, I find a woman about my height. Long black hair falls around the tan skin on her arms, and her smile reaches her soulful brown eyes.

And I immediately know who she is, because she might be female and petite, but the resemblance is uncanny.

"You're Zander's mom."

Grinning, she nods. "Just kidding about the room service. I wanted to meet you."

I step back and motion for her to come in. "Zander told you about me?"

Her happy expression falls a little, and her fingers tighten around a porcelain case in her hands. "No. I haven't seen my son since he returned, but the rumor mill at the palace is working overtime. When I heard he snuck in with a woman last night, I had to see you for myself."

"Oh." Well, this is awkward. I haven't left the room yet and I'm already doing the walk of shame. "It's not what it looks like."

"What does it look like?" Her eyebrows lift, and before I can answer, she points at the chess piece around my neck. "It seems the two of you got married. Object of commitment, right? Zander carved that king, and all the pieces of his board, with his own hands. He wouldn't give it to just anyone."

There's no judgement in her voice. No disapproval.

I blow out a breath. "Yeah, you got it. In my defense, I had no clue what was happening at the time."

Confused, she tilts her head, then gestures to the bed. "Why don't you sit and let me help you with your hair, and you can tell me all about it."

Nodding, I scurry over to throw the covers up to the pillows in a poor attempt to make the bed before we sit where Zander did dirty things to me last night.

Our eyes meet when we haul ourselves up onto the high bed, and we both giggle a little because we're so tiny compared to the ginormous furniture.

It feels good to laugh with her. Like she's a friend. I have to remind myself that she's thousands of years older than me and technically my mother-in-law, but she doesn't look a day over twenty-five. She really is beautiful, with high cheekbones, thick lashes, and full pink lips.

"I'm Rowan, by the way. I mean, Rosita." With a laugh, she shakes her head the way someone does when they're correcting themselves. "I was Rosita before I came here. Then my name was changed. I recently decided to change it back, but sometimes I forget. You can just call me Ro. Rosita works fine, too. Just not Rowan, please."

I like the way she rambles. It reminds me of myself.

"You've probably already heard, but I'm Maelyn. Zander likes to shorten it to Mae, but he's the only person who can get away with it."

Hope fills her eyes. "Can he see now? Is the curse broken?"

"No." I glance down. "I—he—we haven't—"

"I see." With an understanding smile, she stops me from awkwardly explaining that I haven't banged her son yet. "Sit in front of me here."

She pats a spot on the comforter. Opening the lid on her case, she picks up a small spray bottle and a brush. I move into position and she starts squirting the most tangled places in my hair first. The mist coming out smells good. Like roses.

She uses her fingers to work the liquid into the strands, and as she drags the brush through the bird's nest on my head, I wait for the snag, but it doesn't come. The bristles glide easily through each knot, without any resistance at all.

In fact, it feels nice. Comforting. Whatever's in that bottle must be magic, because I can already tell it's smoothing my hair.

Even after Ro has worked through the mess, she keeps brushing.

It brings me back to the times when my mom used to do my hair when I was a kid. Her mother had been emotionally distant when she was a child, and she'd never learned how to French braid until she had a daughter of her own. I remember how clumsy she was at first, sometimes accidentally pulling my hair too hard, but eventually she became really good at it. The first time she got it perfect, she'd beamed with tears in her eyes, jumping up and down because she was so proud of herself. Then she hugged me and thanked me for being hers.

I hadn't done anything special. All I'd had to do was sit there and be patient with her, but she was so grateful to have me.

I miss her.

Suddenly, emotion wells in my chest and my throat tightens. Blinking rapidly, I try to swallow around the lump in my esophagus, but it's no use.

A tear trickles down my right cheek.

Sniffling quietly, I wipe it away, but Ro misses nothing.

"Oh, dear." She gently grasps my shoulders. "What's wrong?"

Before I know it, I'm spilling everything. Babbling through a few sobs, I tell her about waking up in the wagon. The auction, the other girls, the rescue. If I were anywhere else, I'd sound like a crazy person talking about portals, enchanted marriage ceremonies, and trolls, but Ro just listens, nodding as she lets me get it all out.

"And then we came here," I finish, wiping under my eyes. "Sorry. I'm just really overwhelmed. I don't know how to be a wife or a queen, and if what Astrid said about me is true, I'm probably going to bring Zander down just because I'm human."

Ro's face is serious as she gives me a motherly rub on the back. "You were ripped from your life, and you're worried about my son?"

I shrug and nod at the same time.

Her eyes change, going hard as a snarl lifts her top lip. "I'm going to throttle that boy."

That's all the warning I get before she's rushing for the exit. Her long white dress swishes violently around her legs with her strides, and she's still holding onto the brush, her knuckles white from the tight grip.

Oh, ships and anchors. I just ratted Zander out. I didn't mean to do that.

"Wait!" I call out, running through the door.

Ro's going so fast, I barely catch a glimpse of her disappearing around a corner at the end of the hall.

I follow. "Ro, wait."

We descend two flights of stairs—actual flights, with turns

between each level—and by the time she's marching down a hall I think is on the second floor, I'm puffing from exertion.

Without pausing her tirade, she kicks a wooden door, busting it open with surprising force.

Like Chuck freaking Norris.

The frame cracks and splinters, and I step back to avoid getting hit by any flying debris.

"You!" She points into the room, brandishing the brush like a weapon, before letting a few Portuguese expletives fly.

And I thought Zander had a temper.

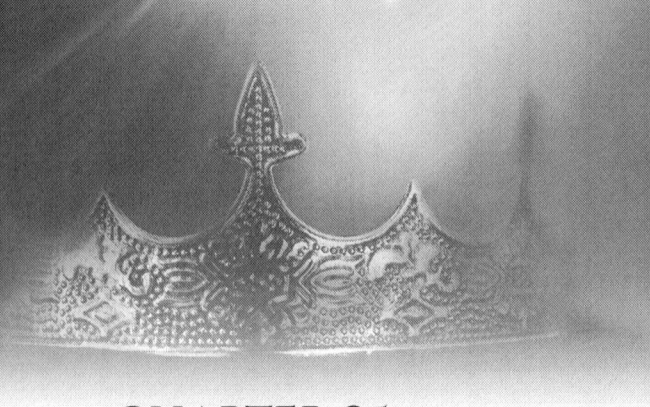

CHAPTER 25

Zander

"Gideon doesn't have a registered address," Thayne informs me from two seats down.

I'm not surprised. All the records we have of the bastard are sketchy at best.

It's unusual for someone to be off the grid. Every member of the Day Realm has some sort of traceable footprint—a job, a marriage, or family members. But Gideon's like a ghost.

The only information we have on him is that he was born in Azerdeen and he's a Pyro. His parents aren't listed because the orphanage he was raised in burned to the ground when he reached adulthood, and along with it, all their lineage books. How convenient. And suspicious.

Did he set fire to his records on purpose?

Ultimately, it doesn't matter where Gideon lives. With Pippin's Seeker power, we'll be able to find him.

"Marek, what's the news with the deceased unnamed troll we recovered?"

"Found her family in Azerdeen," he replies. "She'd been missing for six weeks."

I rub my lip. "She was pretty far from home, then."

Marek nods. "My theory? She was transferred from the abandoned distillery we found there last month."

"Which means Gideon has been around more than we realize."

"He's barely trying to cover his tracks," Torius chimes in. "It's almost like he wants to get caught."

I grunt out an agreement. "Or at least cause as much trouble for me as possible. Something isn't sitting right with all this. For him to be so cocky—"

Suddenly, the floor tremors beneath my boots. This room is soundproof, so I can't hear any commotion coming from outside in the hallway, but the thuds are rhythmic. Like stomping footsteps.

There's an ear-splitting pop as the wooden door caves inward.

Alarmed, I almost reach for the sword I keep strapped to the underside of the table, but my mother starts yelling at me.

I relax.

Apparently, she's met Maelyn. I knew she'd be upset if she found out about my wife from anyone but me. I'd meant to go to her this morning before the meeting, but I couldn't seem to pry myself away from Maelyn until the very last second.

"Hello, Mother. Good morning to you, too."

"You kidnapped a girl?" Her practiced accent slips, reverting to the one she knew so long ago. "And you married her against her will?"

Strike. I'm in trouble.

It hadn't occurred to me that she'd discover so much detail about my indiscretion.

"Excuse us." I gesture to my men, and they immediately get up and evacuate the tactics room.

No one wants to be around when my mother loses her composure. Although she doesn't have a fae power, she possesses the ability to make grown men feel about two inches tall with her no-nonsense attitude.

"Please, Ro." Although Maelyn stays planted outside the

room, her close proximity makes my veins sizzle. "I wasn't trying to tattle on him. It's just been a rough few days for me."

"Don't defend him," Mother shoots back, her tone gentler for Maelyn's benefit. "There's no excuse for what he did."

Facing Maelyn, I motion across the hall. "There's a library through that door. Go explore a little and I'll join you soon."

There are things my mother and I are going to say to each other that I don't want Maelyn to hear. Usually, I'd just close the door to this room for some privacy. That door is currently in about a hundred pieces.

"Okay," Maelyn agrees softly, and I hear her bare feet pad across the hall.

Once the door to the library closes with a click, I turn to my mother. "She's my fated mate."

"So?" she retorts, shocking me.

"What do you mean, so? So, that explains why I have to keep her."

"But you tricked her into a promise she should've been able to make when she chooses to." For emphasis, she marches over and pokes my shoulder. "No excuse. None!"

"Mama, aren't you happy for me?" I deliberately use the name I was only allowed to call her in private, when it was just the two of us.

Softening, she huffs. "There are better ways to go about this. If she's your fated mate, then you shouldn't have to resort to trickery."

"I had to because there's something wrong with the bond," I grit out, pacing away as I stab a hand through my hair, knocking my crown off in the process. Even after years, I still forget it's on my head. It clatters to the floor, and I hope it breaks. I know it won't, though. The damn thing is indestructible.

"Sit." Mother's command leaves no room for argument. "Explain."

Sinking to my chair, I roll up the map of Valora before

tossing it to the middle of the table with the registry book. "When the coven members died, there was a fracture in the curse."

"A fracture?"

"Yes." With a hushed voice, I relay what Astrid told me—how Maelyn can't feel the bond, while I'm getting it multiplied. "At the time, I thought I was saving Maelyn's life by making her marry me. We'd already met, and I couldn't send her home to die from mate withdrawals."

"Yes, there is that," Mother agrees reluctantly.

"Only, there isn't that. The curse is so damaged that it messed up our tether. Turns out, if she were to leave now, before the bond is complete, she'd be fine."

Several seconds tick by. "Are you going to let her go, then? And what about you? How would you fare without her? I don't approve of what you did, but I can't let you die either."

I almost smile at her rapid-fire questions without letting me answer. My mother and Maelyn have that endearing verbal spewing habit in common.

"Last night, Maelyn agreed to stay," I tell her. "Which is good, because if I let her go, the mate withdrawals would be more intense than usual and quite excruciating for me. According to Astrid, I wouldn't have much time left."

Mother sighs. "What are we going to do about it?"

"*We* aren't doing anything. This is between Maelyn and me."

"I understand that, but I'm still your mother. I'm conflicted about all of this."

"So am I."

"I'll do everything I can to make her feel at home here," Mother says, drained of her anger. "Girl time, lunches, spa days. I'll let her know she's wanted, but if she decides to go back to the human realm…"

"That isn't an option."

"You can't hold her hostage here forever."

"She isn't a hostage. She's my wife. Maybe I went about it the wrong way, but I can woo her. I'll get her to fall in love with me."

Before our intimate encounter last night, I might not have been so confident. But now I know what I can do to Maelyn's body. The pleasure I can bring her.

Although, I'm not sure if we'll be having a repeat anytime soon. Running out on her once is confusing enough. If it becomes a pattern, she's going to have questions.

Nodding enthusiastically, Mother places her hand on mine. "Just be yourself, let her get to know you, and her heart will follow. I'm sure of it."

Of course she'd think that about her only child. In her eyes, I hung the suns. Our love is forged deep. I was her one light in this life, her protector and savior. Her safety and well-being were dependent on me for so long.

"Let's have dinner in the garden tonight," Mother suggests. "Just the three of us."

I nod, knowing she'll guilt me into it if I say no. Admittedly, I like the idea of Maelyn and my mother becoming close. The more friends my wife has, the better.

Now that this discussion is over, I should call my men back and resume our planning. But there's a tug on my heart, pulling me to the library where my mate is. I left our bed a little over an hour ago, and I already miss her.

I walk across the room, stopping when my boot bumps into something in the way. Picking up a section of the broken door, I set it on the long table. "Have someone fix this."

"I will," Mother responds, then adds, "You need to tell her."

"Tell her what?" I play clueless.

"About your gift."

Gift. I want to scoff at her word choice. What the wizard did to me is a curse I'll never break.

Keeping my back to my mother, I tap the doorframe while trying to keep an air of innocence. "How do you know I haven't already?"

"Because you're my son. You've never embraced your power."

"I did once," I say without turning around. "Just once, I enjoyed the pain as I shifted. I smiled while my bones snapped and my skull broke apart. And do you know why?"

"Why?" Mother whispers, and I suspect she can predict what I'm going to say next.

"Because I was going to kill Zarid. Being a beast was the only way to defeat him, so for one day, I loved it."

"And how did it feel to love who you are?" It's a rhetorical question, and she continues, "How wonderful would it be to feel like that all the time?"

Impossible.

Continuing out the door, I don't answer her. I let the silence speak for itself.

My self-loathing causes my mother pain. I know this, yet I can't change it. I've hated who I am for so long, the hate is a part of me.

Walking to the double doors of the library, I slip inside and shut myself in. If I had my sight, I'd see rich browns on wood-paneled walls. Golden domed ceilings. Navy-blue rugs on the marble floors. The darker colors are a respite for the eyes. With how bright the Day Realm is all the time, people need a break from the light, and this library is the perfect place for that.

It's quiet in here. The scent of books is comforting, and Maelyn's shuffling footsteps are like a soft whisper as she moseys around the history section. Valora's history, to be exact.

I hear a page flip as I approach her.

"This room has some major *Beauty and the Beast* vibes," she says, looking up from the book.

Beast?

Did she hear my mother and me talking? Does she know?

"What?" I ask a little too gruffly.

"Oh." She laughs lightly. "It's a popular fairy tale. A prince is cursed to look like a beast, and he kidnaps the woman he loves and shows her his amazing library." She comes closer to me and teasingly bumps me with her hip. "Sounds familiar, huh?"

I realize she's pointing out the similarities to our own story, but she doesn't know she hit too close to home.

"A company called Disney made a movie about it," I supply, keeping the focus on the film she speaks of and not on my beastly qualities. "Among other stories that always end with a happily ever after."

"You know Disney?"

"It's all there," I point ahead and to the left, "on the entertainment shelf. Earth is the third row from the bottom."

"You study Earth?"

"I study everything. I probably know more about your world than you do."

"Books are great, but they're not the same as experiences," she refutes, her tone light. "Smells, for instance. You don't know what it smells like in my backyard during a hot summer day, right after a heavy rain when the sun comes back out to dry up the grass. Or a late fall evening, how crisp the air can be."

"You're right," I concede. "Maybe someday you can show me."

Her happiness spikes. "You really meant it when you said we could visit my parents?"

"Yes. I wouldn't lie about that."

However, I did lie about not keeping secrets, and I'm still experiencing the consequences today. Usually, dishonesty doesn't affect me for long, but maybe deceiving your own mate has harsher consequences. The pain in my stomach is lingering. My appetite hasn't been as good, and I'm feeling a bit feverish.

"What are you reading?" I change the subject.

"The history of fated mates. I found the legend of Yelissa and Conrad." Maelyn's fingertips bump over the raised dots on the pages. "Do all the books have Braille for you?"

"Yes. It took decades, but eventually we had every single one adapted for me. Would you believe this used to be just a small office?" Spreading my arms out, I indicate either side of the big window overlooking the garden. "Walls used to be here and here. I knocked them down one day when my father was gone on a trade. The other rooms along this side of the hallway were guest quarters that never got used. I figured since I was stuck here, I might as well have a place to keep busy, so I expanded the library with four additional rooms."

Setting the book on a side table next to a leather chair, Maelyn turns to me, and her voice becomes a little more serious. "Am I going to be an afterthought in your business dealings?"

"What?" I'm confused by the abrupt question.

"You say I'm your partner, and you talk about this relationship as if we're a team. Equals. Yet you leave without telling me where you're going, and you don't include me in meetings." She waves a hand dismissively, as if she's trying to make it seem like it's not that big of a deal. "I'm just wondering. I want to know what to expect. Whatever your answer is, it's fine."

Apparently, it's not fine. She's upset about last night. About me leaving her alone. And it seems she's not too keen on waking up by herself either.

I haul her to me, and my body comes alive when her front smashes against mine.

"You were tired," I say, referring to this morning while purposely avoiding my reason for leaving last night. "If you want to be included in military briefings, that's more than okay. But I warn you, the talks can get gruesome." I bump my forehead to hers. "We're not planning tea parties."

She rolls her eyes so hard I hear the muscles straining inside her head. "I didn't assume it's pleasant."

"I suppose we could add tea," I muse playfully, "to boost morale. But not all my men like tea, and if someone doesn't like tea, they must at least contribute polite conversation."

"Did you just quote *Alice in Wonderland*?" Maelyn gasps a little. "Are you—are you making a joke?"

"Do you find tea parties to be funny? Tea parties are no laughing matter around here," I deadpan, my lips twitching. "Everyone must take it seriously. Or else."

"Or else what?"

I finally crack a smile. "Off with their heads."

Laughing, Maelyn shakes her head. "You're funny today. And you really do know your Disney."

"I'm familiar with the novels associated with the film adaptions." I bring my fingers up to her mouth and feel her smile. "I like it when you laugh."

She cups my face. "Do *you* ever laugh?"

Before I can answer her, there's a soft knock at the double doors. One swings open, and a wheel on the food cart squeaks as it's pushed into the library.

"Your mother said you might like to have lunch in here," a scratchy voice says.

It's Tabitha. She's a troll and one of our most valued dawn-to-dusk staff members. She's been at the palace since the days of King Zed and Queen Lynea. At her old age, she should've retired about a hundred years ago, but she stays on for me and my mother.

"It's not lunchtime yet. And why are you serving us food, Tabby?" I can't muster up a scolding tone in my words, because I'll always have a soft spot for the elderly woman who nursed my injuries after my father's tirades. Rolling the cart away from her, I lift the plates and set them on the round table. "You're supposed to be in the textiles." I pivot toward Maelyn to explain, "Tabitha is the head of the royal couturier department, and her talent is unrivaled. She designs all my mother's dresses."

"Oh." Tabitha titters. "You flatter me, King Zander."

"Thank you for serving us. I appreciate it." I expect her to leave since her task is done, but she lingers.

"And who is this lovely lady?"

Ah. So this errand is personal. Seems everyone can't wait to meet my bride.

I keep Maelyn plastered to my side, my arm firmly wrapped around her waist. "This is Maelyn, my wife."

Tabitha lets out an ecstatic squeal. "Oh, I'd hoped it was true. I didn't believe it, and I had to see it for myself. Congratulations, your majesties." She clasps Maelyn's hand. "What a beauty you are."

I almost laugh then.

Beauty and the beast, indeed.

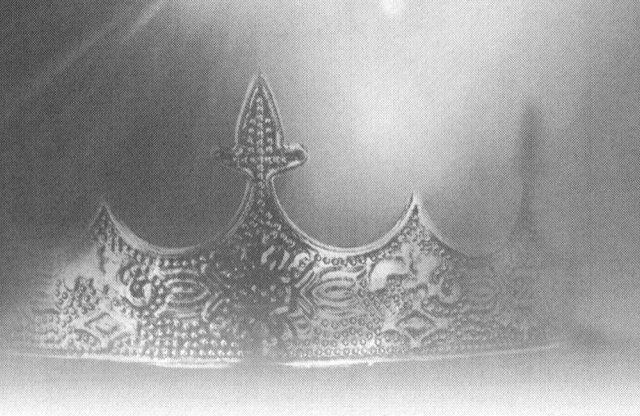

CHAPTER 26

Maelyn

"What's that building?" The gray rectangular structure is out in a field all by itself. To get a better view, I almost press my nose against the glass of the window at the end of the hallway on the second floor.

"The only certified Glow distillery in Valora," Zander answers behind me. "That's where it's produced safely and stored in a secure vault. The alchemists dilute it down to one percent, and citizens can use it for medicinal purposes or recreational activities."

"Do they get high from it?"

"It's basically the equivalent of being a little drunk."

"Interesting. What's that big shadowy area?" I point to the crater I can see in the other direction.

"The execution courtyard." Zander gathers me in his arms to sweep me away from the window.

"Are you going to take me there?"

His eyebrows furrow as we walk toward the staircase flowing into the two-story foyer entrance. "I'd rather not."

"Why?"

"Nothing good happens there."

"Is this like *The Lion King*, when Mufasa warns Simba not to go to the Elephant Graveyard?"

He shakes his head. "Not even close. The sunken amphitheater has been soaked with more blood than you can possibly imagine. It's an inevitability that you'll see it someday, just not today."

Okay, that does sound pretty morbid.

"I definitely want to see the prison, though," I insist. "Is that where we're going next?"

After all, Zander promised to show me the castle after lunch, and I've already seen most of the inside. A tour should include everything, right? I'll let the execution courtyard slide… because it's far away, and we're having dinner with Ro soon.

"You mean the dungeon?" Zander looks apprehensive.

"It sounds so ominous when you call it that." I tip my head back to stare up the crystal chandelier in the grand entrance. Just like all the other decorative light pieces, the candles have never been lit.

Apparently, in a realm where thirty percent of the people have Pyro power, house fires are all too common, so they utilize the daylight instead of flames whenever they can.

"That's because it is ominous, Mae. The lower levels of this place house a literal hell. You don't want to see it."

"Yes, I do." Tugging Zander's hand, I pull him to a stop at the bottom of the wide, red-carpeted stairs. "I'm not saying I'll want to go back down there ever again, but I need to look at it. Just once."

Blowing out a breath, he spears his hair with his fingers. He's not sporting the crown this afternoon, and I'm glad. Wearing it seems to make him cranky—well, *crankier*—plus it gets in the way of his bangs. I love how the inky black strands fall in front of his eyes.

I reach up to toy with them. "Please?"

He kisses my palm. "All right. But I'll show you the ballroom first."

My stomach flips with anticipation as he leads me to our left. Up ahead, the golden double doors are closed, and I'm not prepared for the elegance and beauty when one of the guards sees us going that way and opens them for us.

An actual ballroom.

It's where the masquerade will be held, and I can't stop my building excitement. Tall windows framed with dark-blue curtains line the large oval space, and the sun shines brightly, sparkling on the gold-infused marble floors. The elegant room has a second story made up of individual theater-style balconies overlooking the lower level. And the ceiling… a night sky is painted there, and the stars seem to shine and twinkle. I can imagine when the curtains are closed, it feels like night.

Two thrones sit on an elevated platform at the far end.

"Once a year," Zander begins, "a theater troupe comes to perform for the winter solstice. The stage is cleared off." He gestures to the thrones and then points to the closest balcony. "We'll have the best seats in the house. The queen gets the privilege of choosing the show."

I give Zander a smile.

I know he's trying to make the palace sound as appealing as possible. Even though I told him I'd stay, he's still in convincing mode, which is probably why he doesn't want me to see the unsavory places.

The tour started on the fourth floor. Zander and his mom occupy that level, but there are several empty rooms up there.

Nurseries.

For children.

Zander's children. And mine, too, if we're getting technical.

The third floor is filled with rooms belonging to the staff. I was pleasantly surprised at that. The maids and cooks aren't treated as second-class citizens. Their rooms are just as fancy as the rest of the palace, though a bit smaller in size.

Since I already got an unplanned tour of the second floor

when Ro literally busted up Zander's meeting, we popped into a few unoccupied guest rooms across from the library. All the while, Zander talked about parties and fun events, even though I get the impression he hates the social functions.

What he doesn't realize is, he doesn't have to entice me with masquerades and theater shows. Sure, that stuff is fun, but after last night? Honestly, he could just haul me up to his bed and convince me with his tongue.

We go back through the foyer and into a formal dining room that has rich brown walls, dark blue curtains, and a table that seats twenty.

Cutting through the kitchen, we head to a back door. Several staff members bow as we pass, and I just smile while my hand flops with an uncoordinated wave. There's a reason why I was never a pageant queen. Aside from my rambling, I couldn't get that wave down.

As we make it outside, I self-consciously tug at my t-shirt. My hair's behaving much better since Ro sprayed that stuff on it, but I tied it back into a high ponytail, and with my jeans and sneakers, I look more like I'm ready to go hiking than sit on a throne.

Even the staff wear nice clothing. I know Quinn meant well offering her casual wardrobe, but I'm sort of wishing I'd asked Whitley to give me those dresses.

As if Zander can read my mind, he says, "You can meet with Tabby before the masquerade. She'll make you the finest dress this realm has ever seen."

"How did you know what I was thinking? Does the bond tell you that, too?"

"I can sense your embarrassment and you keep fidgeting with your clothes."

Perceptive.

"I'm not as pretty as the women here." I shrug. "It's not just about what I'm wearing. They're tall and willowy. Some of them have eyes that sparkle. I can't compete with that."

"Mae, they don't hold a candle to you. You're beautiful, and your eyes are amazing. The variety of hues…" Zander shakes his head. "I could get lost for hours trying to name all the different colors in your irises."

Confused, I stop. "How do you know what my eyes look like?"

Zander stiffens.

It's a small reaction, but I notice. "Zander, you've never seen my eyes. Right?"

"I had someone describe them to me." A breath puffs from his flared nostrils as a grimace flits over his face. His lips thin and his eyes narrow.

Pain.

I've seen women try to hide it in the shelter where I worked.

I put a hand on his forearm. "Are you okay?"

He just gives me a tight smile and links our hands as he walks me to a cellar-type door. Two guards on either side of it greet us formally before taking out some keys and unlocking a heavy-duty bolt. The metal slab is embedded in the ground at an angle, and the hinges creak loudly when one of the men pulls it upward.

An unidentifiable stench wafts out as I gaze down at moss-covered stone steps.

Even with the suns behind us, it's pitch black down there, as if the darkness swallows up the light.

A shiver zips through my spine.

"Are you sure you want to do this?" Zander asks, placing his hand at the small of my back.

Reluctantly, I nod. "Just a quick peek."

One of the guards picks up an unlit torch and puts his hand over it. Much to my surprise, smoke wisps up, right before the wooden sticks catch fire.

Nifty.

Zander accepts the torch with a nod and guides me forward.

As we descend the stairs, the air becomes hotter. Heavier. Thicker.

THE FAE KING'S PRIZE

I'm breathing, but I can't seem to get enough oxygen. Thumps and clanks echo from below. The distinct smell of something burning reaches my nostrils.

"The water heater is down here," Zander reminds me.

Right. When we make it off the last step at the bottom, I see the source of the heat. Far down the hall, a huge pile of embers glow underneath a giant vat. The bucket-like container is at least eight feet tall and ten feet wide. A pipe runs from the top of it up into the concrete ceiling.

A guard stands off to the left with a spear in hand and various weapons strapped to his belt. Keeping his stoic expression in place, he mops at his sweaty face with a rag. Man, it must suck to have his job. I hope Zander pays him extra to be down here.

Around the water tank, four people are chopping wood. Two more are taking the logs and inserting them into the fire. A group of people are taking turns cranking a long lever up and down in a constant, steady motion. Three others are peddling on what looks like stationary unicycles.

All of them shine with perspiration. Gray, tattered clothes hang on their gaunt frames. A ball and chain is attached to their ankles, limiting their movement, and there are similar iron shackles at their wrists and necks.

Barred cells line both sides of the dungeon. I count sixteen in total, and several are occupied by sleeping lumps on the hard floor. There are no windows. The only contraptions I see that closely resemble toilets are six-inch holes in the floor in the corner of the cells, leading to who knows where.

"Don't feel sorry for them," Zander says seriously. "These are the people who would have raped you day in and day out until they ripped your child from your arms."

Now that I look closer, I recognize one of the women from the auction. Her blond hair is a mess, plastered to her sweaty face and neck. Brief eye contact is shared between us before she looks away and goes back to stoking the fire. Dark streaks run from the metal bands she wears. Blood. Now she knows what it felt like for Sasha.

"Is it necessary to keep them in pain at all times?" I wince at the thought of being burned 24/7.

"It's not about their suffering, though they do deserve it. The iron weakens them, keeping them from using their powers against us."

I need to stop forgetting how dangerous these people can be. "Gotcha. They look awfully thin. Are they fed?"

"Once a day, to keep their strength up. Fae don't need food the same way humans do. Starvation won't kill us, but hunger is unpleasant."

"There's so much misery down here."

"I warned you. This is about as far from a tea party as you can get."

I lightly elbow him in the ribs. "Although I like your jokes, the timing is highly inappropriate."

Unaffected by my ire, he shrugs. "I'm serious. They're being punished. If they're lucky, they'll complete their sentence and become reformed from their wicked ways."

"And if they don't change?"

Zander's face is completely impassive. "They die."

"Just like that?"

"Just like that."

Harsh.

Zander can't hug me, because he's carrying that torch, but I think he wants to. He moves closer, presses a kiss to the top of my head, and murmurs, "There's a time and place for compassion, but it's not here and now. These people are dangerous. Their sentence can either make them realize the error of their ways, or it can fuel a grudge. With all the other crimes happening in this realm, revenge isn't something I have time for."

I get it. I do. Safety of the innocent citizens comes first. Doesn't mean I like thinking about people dying, though.

One of the men chopping wood turns around and his eyes lock with mine. Byris. He sneers, and suddenly, I don't feel so bad for them anymore.

The smell is starting to get to me, and I swallow down a cough. "I'm done here."

With a nod, Zander squeezes my hand, and we start toward the stairs. The light at the top beckons me, and I eagerly put my foot on the first step, wanting to get away from the dungeon.

"How do you determine if someone has learned their lesson?"

"Quinn," Zander replies. "She's able to read their true intentions. Faeries try not to lie because it has physical consequences, but it is possible to be deceiving if they're able to mask the pain."

Lies cause pain. Noted. I think of the way Zander's expression pinched earlier when he said he'd never seen me before. Since he's blind, I know it's not possible for him to know what I look like, but why would he lie about someone describing me?

He could ask me for a description, but he hasn't. And I find that odd.

I think there's something he isn't telling me, but I have no idea what it could be.

Then again, maybe I'm just being paranoid.

"Are you satisfied with your tour, my queen?" Zander asks as we ascend the last few stairs.

We're almost out of this hellish place, so I decide to lighten up our conversation.

Taking on the most somber tone I can muster, I say, "Well, there's somewhere else I'm needed right now. A perilous, treacherous situation I can't escape."

Drawing his eyebrows together, Zander looks genuinely worried. "What are you talking about?"

My lips curl up with a teasing smile, and I lean in to whisper conspiratorially, "Dinner with my mother-in-law, who I know for a fact can throw down like Chuck Norris."

A loud sound barks from Zander—causing me to jump back and press my spine to the mossy stones—while the biggest grin stretches over his face. All his teeth are on display as his stomach spasms and more hearty chuckles follow.

"You—you laughed," I say with awe, stepping forward to lift my fingers to his smiling mouth. "I made you laugh."

"That you did."

And I fall for him a little more. In the most unlikely place, too. Here, in this disgusting, dirty dungeon full of despair, surrounded by pain and darkness, I found one of my favorite moments ever.

CHAPTER 27

Maelyn

THE GARDENS ARE FULL OF FLOWERS. OF COURSE gardens usually are, but the complicated maze takes it to new heights. As Zander leads me through the twists and turns constructed from trimmed hedges, thousands of roses and lilies peek out from the leaves and branches. All colors, too, like an artist speckled the walls with rainbows.

Loose gravel crunches under our steps as we turn a corner and come to the center of the maze. The round area features four fountains, and a marble gazebo surrounded by roses of varying purple hues.

"The bride and groom." Face lighting up, Ro stands and greets us from a small round table under the shade of the gazebo.

Her sincere smile puts me at ease instantly. Whatever little chat she and Zander had this morning, it seems she's not pissed off anymore.

When we get closer, my eyes land on plates of steaming sliced meat, roasted vegetables, and more of those yummy bread rolls.

"Please, sit." Gesturing toward the two other chairs, Ro takes her own seat and raises a crystal glass filled with red wine. "Celebration is in order. To my new daughter and the queen who will rule this kingdom with kindness and wisdom."

Since I don't normally drink alcohol, I just politely clink my glass against hers before setting it back down.

After we've had a few minutes to eat—I started with the rolls first—Ro sets her fork next to her plate and looks at me. "I've been told you have interest in working with the new human women."

Trying not to talk with my mouth full, I nod as I swallow. "That's right."

"Zephina could certainly use the help. My sister-in-law has dedicated the last several years of her life to getting the women settled. Looking out for their well-being, making sure they have success," she lists. "But it's been difficult. She doesn't understand humans the way you do. Most of the conflict she has with them are because she doesn't know the life they came from."

"What kind of conflict are we talking about?"

"Mostly minor offenses. Some stealing and food hoarding. They don't realize they don't need to worry about their next meal. Then there's breaking curfew. Individual freedoms are a big deal to humans, and these newcomers don't realize how dangerous this world is if they go off wandering alone."

I hear that.

Man, did I learn my lesson in The Lashing Forest.

But it's strange that Ro talks to me as if I'm the only one at this dinner table who knows what it's like in the Earth realm. She came from there, too, but maybe it's been so long she's forgotten.

She's a survivor. It's possible she blocked out her old memories to protect herself, but it doesn't have to be like that anymore. She isn't a prisoner now. She's free.

I wonder if helping others would help her, too. Being around people who are healing could be therapeutic. Or it could go the other way and be triggering for her.

"Would you like to join me on this project?" I invite hesitantly. "I mean, it's something we could do together."

Ro's happy face falters a little and her eyes get distant. "I haven't been outside of the palace walls."

My jaw drops. "Ever?"

Slowly, she shakes her head. "At first, it was because I wasn't allowed to. Then I was afraid." Her eyelashes flutter as she looks down at her plate. "I should be there for the women, I know that."

I lean forward. "You do what feels right. Do what makes you happy. You deserve that much and more."

Her gaze flits up. "Yes, I do deserve that." She gives a nod as the stormy look leaves her face. "I'm so glad you've come. You'll be what they need."

"If you ever want to join me, just say the word." I go back to my rolls.

"Has—" Ro fidgets with her napkin as she seems to work up some courage. "Has the world changed much since I've been gone?"

Zander, who's been quiet throughout our exchange, looks concerned as he continues to listen to our conversation.

Poor Ro. Like me, she left a loving family behind. How could I possibly think she'd forget them? Many of the humans who come here don't have a great life to hold onto, but Ro and I do. We have that in common.

"Some things never change." I grin wryly. "Politics, religion, fighting. All those go hand in hand. Technology has advanced, though. Cell phones, for instance. They're not just for calling or texting anymore. Phones are everything now. People use them as cameras, they watch movies on them, conduct all their business from just one little device. It's crazy."

"Wow," Ro sighs wistfully. "I would've loved to see that."

Sipping my water, I glance at Zander, and I notice he's barely eaten anything. Picking at his dinner with his fork, he just moves the food around the plate. He's paler than usual and there's sweat on his forehead.

"Zander?" His mother speaks up before I can, leaning over

the table to touch the back of her fingers to his face. "Are you all right? You're warm."

"I'm always warm."

"Warmer, then." Keeping the scrutinizing stare only a mother can manage without looking totally bitchy, Ro tilts her head to some hedges a good distance away. "A private word, dear son?"

Reluctantly, he nods and pushes his chair back. He drops a quick kiss to the top of my head before following his mom away.

Straining to hear their conversation, I watch their body language. Zander's got a hand stuffed in his pocket, while the other one absently rubs at his stomach. Ro throws her hands up and starts dabbing his forehead with a handkerchief.

Among her louder exclamations, I catch the words *lie* and *sick*.

Guess my paranoia wasn't unwarranted.

Zander did lie to me, and now he's hurting because of it. Why?

"More wine?"

I jump at the voice that comes out of nowhere, and swivel toward the woman.

Carielle.

I shake my head and eye my full glass. "No, thanks. I'm good, but it looks like Ro could use another."

"Ro," Carielle drawls, filling her cup to the brim. "My, my, you've gotten comfortable quickly."

The statement itself is fine. Her delivery, however, isn't. I once learned that tone of voice is ninety percent of what someone says. And the bitter note in her voice is revealing.

"That's the name she prefers," I defend. "Plus, I'm her family now."

"Family," she repeats flatly. "Speaking of that, how's the honeymoon going?"

"Wonderful," I exaggerate a little.

"Really?" Carielle's tone is disbelieving. "Is that why your husband was on the roof with me last night?"

I feel like someone just punched me in the stomach. Jealousy, so intense and swift, burns me from the inside out. "You're lying."

"I'm not. I've never been a good liar."

I study her for signs of pain or discomfort and find none on her smug face.

Maybe she's telling the truth, but I don't think it's what she's making it out to be. Wherever Zander went last night, it wasn't so he could cheat on me. I know that much.

If Carielle's so big on honesty, let's see how she reacts to my straightforward questions. "Did you have sex with Zander?"

Her smile drops, and she hesitates.

"Well?" I push. "Did you?"

She grinds her teeth, and her hand tightens on the handle of the gold wine pitcher. "No."

"Did he kiss you? Touch you?"

"No."

Lowering her gaze, she looks hurt. Lonely.

Everything Zander told me about Carielle surfaces, and it's hard not to have sympathy for her. This woman needs someone to talk to. Three minutes with her is more than enough for me, but it might help her to sit down and purge herself of the bitter memories she's holding onto. She's a victim, in the worst sense of the word.

Back on Earth, captives don't live long. Even if their basic needs are met, eventually the spirit breaks. In general, human lifespan is short anyway. But abuse can shave off decades.

In Valora, someone can be forced to endure thousands of years of torment with no end in sight.

"Carielle," I start gently. "I'm a counselor for domestic violence victims. I know what you went through was awful—"

"You don't know anything about it," she snaps under her breath, glancing at Zander to make sure she wasn't overheard.

Chastised by her hostility, my face heats with something close to embarrassment. "You're right. I don't. Just—I'm here if you need me."

It's not unusual for survivors to dislike the title of victim.

The word can make the situation feel too real, make someone feel weak.

She looks me up and down again, and I'm not sure if she's trying to figure out if I'm being sincere or if she's glaring at me like I'm a bug under her shoe.

So much for trying to reach out.

Setting the pitcher on the table, Carielle sways closer to whisper, "You think I'm a wounded damsel in distress who needs saving? You're wrong. I was the king's favorite. He loved me. He wanted to marry me, but he couldn't because of that cow." She nods toward Ro.

I'm insulted on Ro's behalf. "She's your friend. She gave you a home here."

Carielle snorts. "Oh, how wonderful of the great queen. I was once revered and respected. I was waited on hand and foot, given gifts beyond my wildest dreams, and had a man who treasured me. Now I'm a servant."

The pure venom in her voice is startling.

Maybe I was mistaken about her. I'd assumed her bitterness stemmed from the trauma she suffered, but it sounds more like grief and anger.

I don't know what to think.

To give Carielle the benefit of the doubt, I could assume she was conditioned early on, leading her to believe she loved Zarid, but it's possible she and the former king found a kindred spirit in each other.

Whether she was abused or not, though, she's dangerous now. I think about what Zander said about revenge in the dungeon.

Clearly, Carielle wants to stir up trouble. First with her uncalled-for comment about seeing Zander on the roof. And now she's admitted she believes Ro took something from her.

That sounds like someone with a grudge.

Zander and his mom seem to be wrapping up their conversation, and as they start this way, Carielle takes the pitcher and disappears behind a hedge without another word. Her quick appearance, coupled with how she slinked away, gives me a bad feeling.

A prickle of suspicion raises the hairs on the back of my neck as I stare at the deep red wine she poured just a couple minutes earlier. It might be my imagination, but I swear I see a swirly film floating on top.

Carielle didn't refill Zander's drink, even though it's half empty.

Call it instinct or whatever—I don't know why I do it, but I quickly switch my glass with Ro's. Then I panic and toss the liquid outside of the gazebo.

I don't want to go accusing anyone of anything, but at the same time, I can't take a chance on Carielle poisoning the former queen.

Plastering on a fake smile, I set the empty glass next to my plate as Zander and Ro rejoin me.

"Was that Carielle?" Ro sounds confused as she takes her seat.

"Yes," I answer slowly.

"Strange. She's off duty tonight."

My gut flips and clenches as I stare at my—formerly Ro's—wine glass a few inches away. She happily drinks mine, totally unaware of what I suspect.

Maybe I really am being paranoid this time.

Still, I need to talk to Zander.

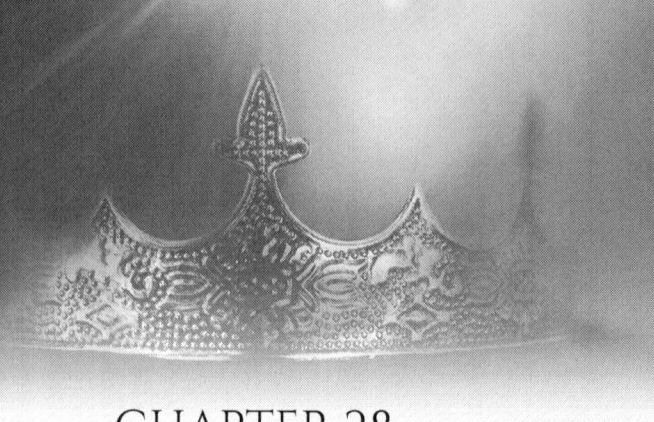

CHAPTER 28

Zander

"Are you sure you're feeling okay?" Maelyn asks for the tenth time from where she sits atop Gander.

My lips twitch with a smile. She's cute when she frets over me. Maybe I should lie more often and make myself ill.

On second thought, no. Yesterday was awful. I hadn't felt that bad in a long time. I actually thought I might vomit during dinner. Dishonesty has never affected me so severely.

While I was speaking with my mother, we determined that lies do matter more when it's your mate and I was probably feeling it twice as much because of the fucked-up bond.

To make my guilt worse, Maelyn tended to me so sweetly after we got back to our room, and I feel bad about greedily soaking up her attention. I didn't deserve the cool rag she pressed to my forehead or the soothing tune she hummed as I drifted off.

I took it, though. Everything she had to offer.

From now on, I'll try my best to be honest with Maelyn. Not just because I don't want to be sick, but because I owe her the truth. Or at least a version of it.

"I'm fine," I tell her. "But even if I wasn't, we can't put off this mission. It's too important."

Every hour that passes, Gideon could be hurting the females

in his possession. Or he could be moving them to a new location. It's best to find him sooner rather than later.

If we don't arrest him today, we'll be going home empty-handed. I'm not dragging Maelyn all over the Day Realm when she should be enjoying the comforts of the palace.

Not to mention, the masquerade is in three days, and I won't let her miss it. Whenever she talks about it, excitement comes off her in intoxicating waves. Apparently, she basically missed her senior prom, which is a big deal to teenaged humans. Her friend had snuck a flask of liquor into the dance, and Maelyn ended up taking a belligerently drunk Paige home before the crowning could happen.

So strange... Schools dubbing certain students as fake royalty. What's the point?

"Speaking of important." Maelyn interrupts my thoughts. "We need to talk about Carielle."

"Again?" My eyebrows furrow.

Last night, on the walk back from dinner, Maelyn had peppered me with questions about the woman. At first, when I sensed her jealousy, I suspected Carielle might've acted out of turn. And I was right about that. For Carielle to imply that she and I were together in any capacity is infuriating. I almost turned around right then to hunt her down and toss her into the dungeon, but Maelyn convinced me not to.

Once we got to our room, she dropped the subject and switched her focus to my self-inflicted pains. Like the wonderful wife she is.

"You said she's at the market today gathering supplies for the masquerade?" Maelyn asks.

"Yes."

"And she'll be there all day?"

I nod, more confused by the second. "Planning the ball is a huge undertaking. Very time consuming. Why do you ask?"

"I think she might try to hurt your mother." Her panicked statement comes out in a rush, as if she's been holding it in.

My veins turn cold at the notion. "What leads you to believe such a thing?"

"Some stuff she said to me last night when she came to the dinner table. She's unhappy—rageful, even—and she blames your mom." Maelyn sheepishly tells me about the wine glass switch, and profusely apologizes for even thinking such a thing about Carielle. "I know she's been through a lot. I'm just trying to play it safe. I'm sorry."

"You don't need to be sorry, Mae. I value your opinion and I'm glad you brought this to my attention."

"But?"

"No but. I'll have someone watch her closely over the next couple days. If she's up to something, she'll be caught and stopped."

"Okay," Maelyn says softly. "That makes me feel better."

"After the masquerade, I'll have someone escort her from the palace and present her with other living options."

Maelyn sputters. "Just like that? All I have to do is tell you I'm suspicious of someone and they're gone?"

"Were you lying?"

"No. Of course not."

"Then why wouldn't I take what you say seriously?"

"I just—I thought I was going to have to convince you. Her home has been at the palace for thousands of years."

"That doesn't make her loyal. You have to understand—in this world, constant loyalty is hard to come by. Traitors are common. That's why I'm so glad we have each other. I'll protect you, always. And now I know you'll do the same for me."

Several beats pass as we travel on, and I absorb what Maelyn has said. If she's correct, Carielle will be punished with more than a scenery change. When I said *other living options*, I meant the dungeon. Possibly death.

No one can taunt my wife or harm my mother and get away with it. After what I did to Zarid, everyone knows that.

A question still nags at me. It's petty for me to press the issue, but I need to know.

"So, you're not mad because Carielle came onto me?"

"She came onto you?" Maelyn practically screeches.

"Wife, my faithfulness to you will never be in question. I'm yours. You're mine. Carielle's advances started long before you came along, and they've been an annoyance I've had to suffer."

"She's pursued you since you came back with me? Knowing you're married?"

A smile grows on my face because she's acknowledging our marriage. I think that's the first time I've heard her say it out loud without complaining. Minus the minutes my tongue was on her pussy, of course. She didn't mind calling me her husband then.

She huffs. "Glad you find this funny, because I don't."

I reach over to take her hand. "My heart and soul belong to you forever. No one can ever change that. Besides, it's not me Carielle wants. She's after a position only a king can give her. She's just desperate for a lifestyle she'll never have."

Tugging Maelyn closer, I kiss her knuckles. Our legs bump as our horses crowd each other. I want to pull her onto my saddle and kiss her. I want her straddling me, rubbing her hot center on my stiff cock. But I need to keep my thoughts focused on the mission, so I let her go.

"Where are we now?" Maelyn takes out the map we had in the tactical room this morning for the briefing.

Paper crinkles, and I hear her fingers bump over the raised shape of the castle, the rough texture of the forests, and the smooth expanse of land. All the nooks and crannies of the terrain get explored by her acute attention. My fingertips have memorized it as if it's the back of my own hand.

"About an hour from Azerdeen, a coastal city where we import most of our fish," I inform her. "It's a great place to trade goods."

"Including women, I assume."

"I can only hope we don't make it to the water. If Gideon has a brothel set up on a ship somewhere, we're in trouble." The Endless Sea is dangerous, and I refuse to take Maelyn out where monsters lurk beneath the waves and even the best navigators find themselves lost.

"Yelissa's Peak," my mate utters with wonder as she touches the northwest mountains of the realm. "Can we go there someday?"

"The area is forbidden," I say regretfully, "even for a king and queen. It's said that strange incidents happen when people trespass in the area. Disappearances. Mysterious injuries."

"Oh, bummer." Maelyn's stomach rumbles, reminding me it's almost time to stop for lunch.

The sounds of the forest are around us as we near our destination.

The morning birds stopped singing a few hours ago, and we've been traveling south toward Azerdeen. Behind us, Kai and Marek are driving the wagon. Thayne is flying overhead to keep watch from a distance.

"Pippin," I call ahead to the soldier riding in front of me. "How much farther?"

"We're getting close."

"Did you get much sleep last night?"

He coughs awkwardly. "Uh, a few hours, your majesty."

"I told you to get to bed early."

"I did."

"Your *own* bed." If he thinks I wouldn't hear about his visit to the female dorms, he's mistaken.

"Sorry. I was just trying to make sure the women were settling in okay."

Torius barks out a laugh next to him. "Is that what we're calling it now?"

Pippin just grumbles, knowing he doesn't have the rank to talk back.

"You better not be taking advantage of anyone," I warn.

"I'm not, I swear. They came on to me."

"They?" I quirk another brow, wondering how much fun he's been having in his free time.

It's not uncommon for young fae to experiment with their sexuality, because not everyone finds their fated mate. In fact, it's the exception these days, especially in the Day Realm. When the coven inflicted us with sickness and so many females were lost, lives and futures were altered forever.

So, I don't blame the kid for being carefree with his body.

At twenty-two, Pippin hasn't reached the full maturity of a man yet. Life is new. Adulthood is exciting.

Normally, I wouldn't take someone his age into my military, but he's the only Seeker I know.

His ability to find someone—as long as he has an object of theirs in his possession—is a rarity. However, because of his youth, his power isn't fully developed. If someone uses a portal more than once to change locations, he'll lose their trail. The only way to pick it back up again is to find another possession the fugitive has touched recently.

Eventually, he'll be able to find anyone, anywhere, with no limitations. But until then, I need him well-rested and at full bodily strength.

Suddenly, Pippin whistles.

Apparently, he was right about being close. He always lets out the first signal when we're about a hundred yards away from our target.

Forests, fields, and the occasional country estate make up this part of the kingdom. Good. A remote location means it's less likely any innocent citizens will get caught in the crossfire if our confrontation goes badly.

Pulling back on Onyx's reins, I slow, veer off to the side of the road, and tell Maelyn, "I'm going to have you wait here with Torius."

Anything could go wrong. After what happened at the distillery, she saw how plans can go awry. Ideally, Gideon will be caught off-guard and the women will be easily found. We'll arrest him, load the females into the wagon, and be home by dusk.

I highly doubt it's going to play out like that, though.

Just as Maelyn dismounts her horse, Thayne lands on the road several feet away. "Your majesty, there's a house up ahead, just around the bend in the road." He flips through the registry book. "It's unlisted."

"An abandoned property, perhaps?" I muse.

"Definitely not. The wooden shingles haven't even been rained on enough to darken."

Considering it rains four or five times a year, that would make the house less than a year old. "Did you see anyone outside?"

"No. The little cottage is well-hidden in a grove of trees. A few candles are lit inside the windows. There are flowers planted around the front, and a creek runs through the backyard."

As far as appearances go, it doesn't sound suspicious. With the candles lit, it indicates someone is home and it seems the property is cared for.

Maybe Pippin is off his game, and we're at the wrong place.

After securing all the horses and assuring Maelyn will stay where she's supposed to, I head off on foot with my men.

I motion for Marek and Pippin to go ahead.

We come to the entrance of a lane. Overgrowth from the trees on either side of it make it somewhat hidden, but we lift the branches out of the way and carry on.

Once we get to the yard, Pippin walks slowly as he wanders off to the left. He idles at a grassy place by the tree line. Untrimmed weeds wisp against his boots.

"Gideon came out through a portal here. I don't feel his presence in this place, though." Unwrapping the tooth from the handkerchief, he holds it up and walks a few more paces. He heaves out a defeated sigh. "He's not here, and I'm not sensing his new location."

Damn. We can only hope Gideon left something of his at the house for Pippin to track him with again. Fortunately, we can use his absence to our advantage. If the females are staying here, we can rescue them. We'll worry about Gideon's arrest later.

"I'll head inside first, your majesty," Marek announces, always willing to lead the way.

His footsteps pad over the cobblestone walkway up to the door. Cautiously, he turns the doorknob, finding it unlocked.

Too easy.

Too quiet inside.

Something's wrong.

Before I can shout a warning that I think it's a trap, Marek steps over the threshold.

Immediately, his body seizes up and crumples to the floor. Agonized screams and staticky crackles follow.

He activated an electrical forcefield around the house, and now he's stuck in it.

"Get me a rope!" I shout at Thayne.

Fucking sorcery. An electricity enchantment is difficult to accomplish, especially on a dwelling of this size. Gideon must be friends with a powerful wizard, which would explain all the portals he has at his disposal.

Marek continues to scream, and he won't stop until we get him out of there. Once someone has breached an electricity barrier, they're rendered immobile. I've heard it's excruciating. It won't kill him, though. No, it will just cause endless pain for as long as the spell lasts. Depending on the strength of the wizard, it could be years.

Desperate to help his friend, Kai reaches in to grab Marek's boot. Mistake. He should know better. His screams join Marek's.

Even though his arm is the only part of his body that's submerged, it will make him useless. Pippin tries to help. He gets zapped as soon as he touches Kai, falling back with a pained shout.

Thayne rushes past me, the rope he grabbed from the wagon dragging in the grass behind him. He might be able to lasso Kai to tug him away, but Marek is probably too far inside for it to work.

Pippin comes to me, and his tone is urgent when he says, "Shift, your majesty. You're the only one who can breach the barrier. It's the only way."

He's obviously desperate. This is the first time any of my men have ever asked me to be the griffin, but he's not wrong.

This is one of those rare instances when my power actually makes sense.

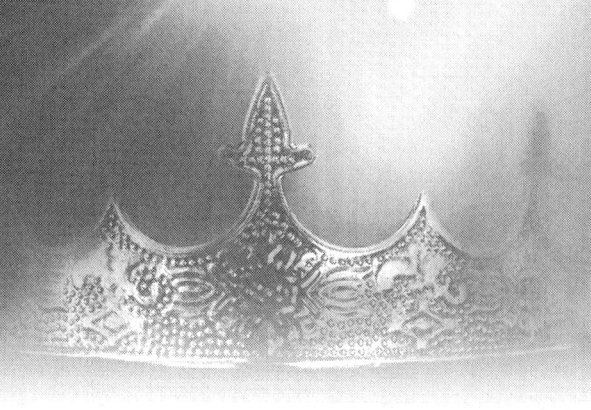

CHAPTER 29

Maelyn

Torius looks torn as Thayne sprints away with the rope. The panicked man had shouted something about an electricity spell, and I can hear blood-curdling screams echoing from somewhere ahead. They don't stop or let up. Birds and other wildlife keep evacuating the area, just as freaked out as I am by the awful sounds.

"You have to go help," I tell Torius, my eyes wide with terror.

He shakes his head. "I can't leave you alone."

"Then we'll go together." I start marching down the road, but Torius puts his big body in my way. "Move. We're wasting time."

"I'm following orders." Torius crosses his arms over his chest.

"Okay." I do my awkward pageant wave, trying to seem queen-like. "You have new orders from me, the queen. Go forth and help. Or whatever."

He deflates, and I know I have him. He has to do what I say. I hate throwing my weight around like that, but he forced my hand.

I take off in a run, following the pained cries that grow louder with every foot of distance I close between me and the house.

When I round a cluster of trees and stagger my way through some low branches, I see chaos in front of me.

Pippin is standing back, his hands stressfully gripping his hair while Thayne tries to get the rope around Kai's leg without touching him, but every time, the loop doesn't stay tight enough and slips off.

Poor Kai is on the doorstep, his entire body jerking as he shouts guttural noises. His arm is caught in a web of sorts. I squint and step closer, only to realize it's not a web like spiders make. The glowing blue network reminds me of those electricity globes in a science museum. When a certain part is touched, all the electricity is drawn to it.

Inside the door, I spy boots belonging to another person. He's caught in the web, too.

Frantically whipping my head around, I search for Zander. I don't see him.

"The king is safe," Pippin tells me, reading my worry.

"Where?"

He doesn't look away from his friends. "He should be back any second now."

Relieved, I nod. I wouldn't wish pain on anyone, but I'm glad it's not Zander in the house.

Torius sidles up to Pippin. "What can I do?"

"Nothing." Pippin shakes his head. "It's being taken care of."

All of a sudden, a deafening roar comes from the sky, and we all glance up.

Black wings. Paws and talons. A large beak and a lion's tail whipping in the wind.

Shocked, I cover my mouth. "How many of these things do you have in Valora?"

"Excuse me, your majesty?" Torius sounds confused.

I barely spare him a glance because the animal is descending on the house. It begins tearing at the roof with its beak, sending chunks of it flying.

"A griffin saved me the other day." I point at it. "It looked just like this one."

"There's only one in the Day Realm," Torius informs me curtly. Gently grabbing my elbow, he pulls me to a safer distance as shingles and wooden beams are tossed to the grass.

As soon as the opening is big enough for the griffin to crawl inside, he drops into the house.

Concerned, I press a hand to my pounding heart. "Won't it get hurt, too?"

Thayne gives me an odd look, like he's surprised I have to ask. "Spells can't touch him."

Well, how am I supposed to know something like that?

Griffins transcend magic. Got it. I file that helpful tip away as loud bangs and thuds come from inside the house.

A few seconds later, Kai and Marek get nudged out of the doorway. The griffin uses his beak and talons to push them away. He's too big to fit through the door, but he sticks his head out as far as he can, making sure both men are at least a couple feet from the stoop.

The web disappears once the bodies aren't touching it anymore, and Kai and Marek's screams have stopped. They lie still, except for their chests rising with gasping breaths.

I expect the creature to climb back out through the roof, but a minute goes by.

"Are you sure he's okay?" I ask to no one in particular. "He isn't coming out."

"I'm guessing he's checking for anyone else who might be inside," Kai rasps, rolling onto his stomach to push up from the ground.

A noisy clatter comes from inside, followed by a crash. Through the window, I catch a glimpse of the griffin stalking around. His massive size is like a bull in a china shop. Furniture gets tossed out of the way as if it weighs nothing. There's a crack and a creak when he breaks a door from its hinges.

Fascinated, I move to the side to keep him in my sights through a window. When he turns around, his tail hits a lantern. Glass breaks. Flames erupt.

With a warning roar, the griffin scampers away, heading to a kitchen at the back of the house.

"Fuck," Pippin curses.

"That's bad, right?" I give the men a worried glance. "Or is he fireproof, too?"

Grinding his teeth, Torius grips the back of his neck. "His feathers. They're too flammable for him to be walking around in that." Stepping closer to the house, he cups his hands around his mouth and shouts, "Get out! Get out now!"

Dark smoke rises from the hole in the roof, and the silence that follows is unnerving.

All the men are tense, their muscles bunched. Their fists are clenched as they watch the burning home. They can't go in, or they'd be right back where they started in the first place.

I start to panic along with everyone else. Because if these guys are losing their cool, it must be bad. Obviously, this griffin works with them. Maybe he's even a royal pet of sorts.

"There's a creek around back, right?" Torius speaks up. "I can—"

Finally, the griffin busts through the top of the house on the backside, his wings smoking in certain areas. His flight is choppy as he goes over us, and it's obvious he's been injured. He crash-lands in an open area of the yard, tearing up grass and dirt as he skids to a stop with his claws.

We all rush toward him. A few objects drop to the ground, falling from his talons and beak. A comb, a toothbrush, and some clothes. Pippin runs to the pile like it's a precious treasure and scoops everything up. Then he backs away so quickly he almost trips over his own feet.

He's not the only one keeping distance from the griffin.

Kai and Marek aren't at full strength yet. Still breathing hard, they're a bit hunched as they recover about ten feet away. Torius is standoffish, too.

So maybe the griffin isn't a pet.

While the guys do look concerned, they don't seem to have any warm feelings for the animal.

Before anyone can stop me, I walk over to the griffin. Keeping my motions slow, I circle his body, making sure I don't spook him while I get a better look at his injuries. Some of his black feathers have been charred, exposing the intricate bones of his wings. There are burns on his hind legs, and the furry puff on his tail is singed badly.

Going around to his front, I lightly touch his beak. "You poor thing."

Chuffing out a groan, he leans into my touch.

I glance behind me. "Does he have a name?"

Thayne gives me a tight smile. "I think he would prefer to remain unidentified."

"Kai? Marek? Can you guys heal him?"

"Griffins are immune to magic," Kai replies, shaking his head. "That includes ours."

"What are we going to do? We can't just leave him here like this." My head whips back and forth between the creature and the men. "Could he come back to the castle with us?"

I'm met with blank stares and awkward silence. Something's up with them. Why are they being so weird?

Then I realize they're scared, shifting from foot to foot, fidgeting with their hands. These big, bad warriors are afraid of the griffin.

"He's really nice," I insist, demonstrating the fact by scratching the side of his feathered neck. "See?"

A hand lands on my shoulder and starts guiding me away. It's Torius. "Please, come with me, Queen Maelyn."

"But—but—" I extend my arm, reaching for the wounded griffin as I dig my heels into the grass. "I want to help."

"Good, because I could use your assistance with something. It's very important."

The sincere urgency in Torius' voice gets me to stop resisting, and I watch Kai inch toward the griffin. Standing an arm's length away, he awkwardly pats the griffin's head and assures me, "I'll take care of him the best I can."

"You're not going to kill him, are you? Like putting down a lame horse?"

Kai looks horrified. "What? No." He throws his hands up. "Why does everyone always think I mean to murder?"

"It's your face," Torius quips light-heartedly, chuckling a little.

"I can't fix my scars," Kai growls.

"Not that. You look angry all the time. Resting bitch face is what Quinn calls it."

Quinn's not wrong there. Kai's constant pissed-off expression is worse than Zander's frowns.

Speaking of the frowny king, where is he?

As if Torius reads my mind, he says, "Zander should be back soon, and he'll know what to do with the griffin."

"Okay." Reluctantly, I let him lead me away.

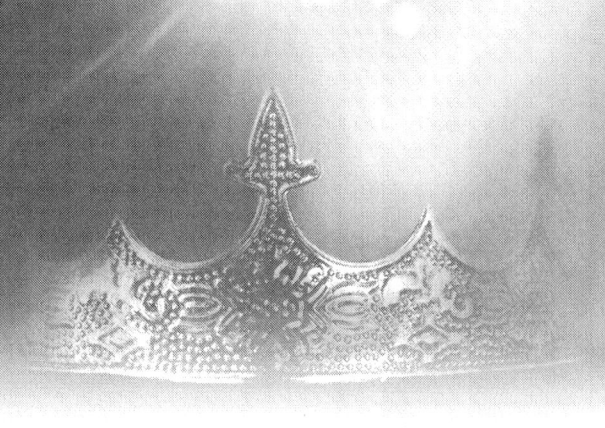

CHAPTER 30

Zander

I SHOULD'VE BEEN MORE CAREFUL IN THERE, BECAUSE HOUSES aren't built for monsters like me.

Other monsters, though… Gideon is most definitely a wolf in sheep's clothing. He might look like every other fae on the outside, but there's something sinister inside of him.

The innocent-looking cottage is really a house of horrors. Gideon's not running a regular brothel—it's a sex dungeon, a masochists' playground.

Before I knocked the lantern over, I found two bedrooms besides his in the cottage, and they smelled of sex and despair. Leather whips were strewn about, some hanging on the walls and others discarded on the floor as if the wielder had left in a hurry. Ropes were tied to the headboards, and the knots were draped over red silk sheets.

Red. I bet Gideon chose that color so the bloodstains wouldn't show.

When I tore the cellar door from the floor in the kitchen to make sure there were no females being held down there, I smelled blood and urine down in the dark depths. Chains and shackles hung from the stone walls, but it was vacant. He moved the females recently. From the strong scents, I'd say they were there yesterday.

We missed our opportunity, but we'll get another.

We won't stop hunting him. If not for the women he's hurting, then for my mate.

If he'd had his way, Maelyn would've been one of his slaves.

I feel sick just thinking about it.

At least the rage muddies the effects of my injuries.

Once I was back in regular form, Kai was able to heal my burns. However, my wings are damaged, and the feathers I lost will have to fill in on their own.

I roll my stiff shoulders, getting used to the slight difference in the way they fit when they're folded inside. Good thing the griffin has more feathers than I do. When my wings shrink down to regular size, it's hard to tell there are any missing just by looking.

Thayne tosses me a new shirt from a storage trunk on the wagon. It's identical to the one I was wearing before, so Maelyn won't notice I've changed.

Until a few minutes ago, my men didn't know I'd been keeping my power a secret from Maelyn, but her cluelessness clued them in pretty fast.

Luckily, they took it all in stride. I heard Torius taking Maelyn around the back of the house to the creek. He can manipulate water, and he made it seem as if he needed her assistance to put out the fire.

I'm grateful for his quick thinking. He simultaneously made her feel needed while giving me the time I required to shift back.

"So, she doesn't know," Thayne concludes quietly.

I should've told him. He's the head of my guard, so he should be aware.

"No." I don't provide a detailed explanation, and Thayne turns away like he's going to let it go. But then...

"Your majesty, if I may..."

I adjust the white queen around my neck. "Spit it out."

"She seemed very accepting of your condition."

She did.

For the second time, she came to me while I was in griffin

form. For the second time, I got to see her up close. Those kind hazel eyes. Light wispy hair framing her face. That cute quirk of her asymmetrical lips.

She made me forget about my pain.

She pet my beak.

My cock stirs at the recent memory, and optimism fills my chest.

The time she approached me in the stream could be written off as a fluke. But twice now? It's not a coincidence. She's not scared of what I am.

I feel like a weight has been lifted.

I can tell Maelyn soon. I just have to find the right time. I might give it a few weeks to let her feelings for me grow, because now I have to explain my lie.

Her voice floats down the road, beautiful, like wind chimes blowing in the breeze. When she sees me, her happiness sparks through the tether.

"Zander, where were you? I was worried. And did you take care of the griffin? I told you I saw one the other day."

My smile ticks up. "And I told you I believed you."

"Is he okay?" She closes the distance between us quickly, her shoes squishing audibly with each step she takes. The scent of creek water coats her hair and clothes.

"He is. Why are you wet?" I ask, changing the subject.

"Oh, Torius needed help putting out the fire. He made this super cool cyclone thing out of mist." Her hands are moving animatedly, and she proudly adds, "I had to tell him where to direct the spray."

I restrain a grin. I won't tell her Torius is a master at manipulating water, and he could've done it without her.

"Well done." Engulfing her in my arms, I bring her in for a hug. I mouth a silent thank you to Torius before rotating toward Pippin. "Did you pick up a new trail?"

"Yes. The comb the griffin gave me is fresh. Gideon left by

portal on the outskirts of the property, but he's far away. I sense a great distance between us."

"What is it with this guy and portals?" Thayne murmurs, probably wondering where Gideon is getting them. "Elusive prick."

"Either Gideon's a lazy asshole who doesn't like to travel the old-fashioned way," Pippin supplies, "or he knows about me and my weakness. He's using portals to throw us off."

I frown. "We've been secretive about the limitations to your power."

Pippin shrugs. "Could be a leak."

That would imply one of my men aren't loyal to me. I'd thought I weeded out the bad ones in the most recent sweep.

"And you've told no one else?" I ask Pippin.

"Ah, well…"

I raise my eyebrows at him.

He clears his throat. "The women in the dorms are very chatty. When I show up, they expect riveting conversation."

"So you compromised our mission."

"Not on purpose. I was in a… precarious position."

I run a hand over my face. I don't even want to know what he means by that, but it sounds kinky.

I thought he was smarter than this, but maybe his loose lips aren't to blame. "The newest humans have only been here for three days. I don't think they would've had the opportunity to leak important information."

"It's not the recent arrivals I'm referring to." He's sounding guiltier and guiltier. "I was at the other dorm last week. And the week before that."

Other dorm, meaning the bigger building that houses the well-adjusted humans who've been here long enough to turn fae. It's also where several of my father's captives chose to live after release. Women who would sell Pippin's secrets with zero remorse because they have no attachment to his soul.

"I'm incredibly sorry, your majesty," he grovels, dropping to his knees dramatically. "If I'm the cause of our troubles, I'll never forgive myself. I deserve punishment. I'll take dungeon duty for as long as you say."

I've got a better idea. "A vow of celibacy."

"What?" His head snaps up, and he's so aghast, you'd think I just sentenced him to death.

"Keep your cock in your pants and your mouth closed."

"For how long?"

"Until I decide otherwise." Lacing my fingers with Maelyn's, I start to lead her over to the horses and clap Pippin's back on the way. "It's not so bad. I did it for thousands of years."

Adequately chastised, the kid gets to his feet and scrapes some rocks with his shoe. "Yes, your majesty."

I turn to my best warrior. "Thayne, how many portals do you have in stock?"

"Six."

We've used more than usual in recent days. I want nothing more than to be back at the palace with Maelyn now. With her in our bed. But it's time to slow down with the portals or else we might run out. "Save them. We'll travel back to Hailene the way we came."

Wrung out from the electrocution experience, Marek and Kai trudge over to the wagon. Torius and Pippin mount their horses, and Thayne leaps to the sky to be our lookout on the way back.

I keep a firm grasp on Maelyn's hand as we go to our horses. Physical contact, even non-sexual, is blissful with her. I hate it when we're not touching.

As we pause next to Gander, neither of us move away from each other.

I gently skim my fingertips from Maelyn's shoulders to her elbows, needing to touch her. Needing to reassure myself that she's mine, now and forever.

Sometimes I'm scared I'm dreaming. That I'll wake up and find out none of this is real.

I'm about to order her to ride with me when she says, "Can I…" Shyness overcomes her, and she trails off. "Never mind."

"What is it, wife?"

"Can Onyx handle two people at once? No. I'm being silly. I'm soaked, and I don't want to get you all wet, too."

Smiling a little, I brush my thumb over her lips. "What are you rambling about?"

She huffs. "Gander's great, but I…"

I want to be with you. I miss your touch. I love you.

My mind fills in the blanks with all the possibilities, but I don't force her to finish the sentence. If Maelyn wants to be close to me, she doesn't have to explain herself.

Placing my hands at her waist, I lift her up to Onyx's saddle. When I join her a second later, she melts into me, her entire body relaxing as she rests against my chest. I enjoy the coolness of her damp clothes and the sweet scent of her hair.

We might not have won today, but I feel like the most victorious man in all of Valora as I ride away with my wife.

CHAPTER 31

Maelyn

"Rook to F4, please."

The maid, Miria, nods, her wheat colored bun bobbing up and down. She moves my piece on the chess board, then she glances at me over her shoulder. "Good move, your majesty. And you don't have to say please every time."

"I do, and I will." I smile warmly down at her from my pedestal, but the seamstress at my feet clears her throat, irritated with me for not standing up straight. "Sorry," I tell the woman who's crouching near the hem of my dress.

Tabitha is next to her, stitching as they go. "You don't have to apologize either," the little troll says, her voice tinged with amusement. "Queens don't have to know those words."

"Well, I'm going to set a new standard for queens, then," I say, trying to be as still as possible while they finish my gown for the masquerade.

Talk about cutting it close.

We have minutes to spare before the ball begins.

When Zander said the couturier department could design a new dress for me, I thought for sure there wouldn't be enough time. Who can make a ball gown in mere days? Apparently, Tabitha and her team can. As soon as we returned from the mission three nights ago, they took my measurements and got to it.

Squaring my shoulders, I try to keep my chin up as Tabitha works around the silky fabric. I haven't looked in the mirror yet, but I can already tell it's the most beautiful gown ever. At first glance, it looks ivory, but there's a slight pink tint to it. It's almost pearlescent, the way it shimmers in the light. A pattern of jewels decorates the skirt, and I wonder if they're real.

I wouldn't put it past Zander to adorn me in thousands of diamonds.

The balcony doors of Zander's room are wide open, letting natural light in so the seamstresses can see what they're doing. Along with the sunshine, music from outside carries in. There's a string quartet set up near the main entrance of the palace, playing cheerful tunes as guests arrive.

I'm a bundle of excitement and nerves as I wiggle my toes inside my shoes. My correctly fitted shoes, designed for my uneven feet. Although I'm not a fan of heels, I'd requested them. The little chunky wedges beneath my feet only raise me up one inch, but it's an extra inch I'm grateful for.

This is the first time many people in the realm will meet me. Important people. I'm so anxious, I might not be able to eat, and that'll be a shame. According to Zander, no expense is spared on the food. Hors d'oeuvres will be brought around the room by the staff, but the main spread will be on a long table—savory snacks and sweet desserts of all kinds.

I focus back on the chess game as Ro reaches across the board. She takes my rook, like I'd hoped she would. Her mischievous brown eyes flit to mine.

She's probably going to beat me. Just like her son does every single time we play. And we've played a lot. I'm taking a serious hit to my record here.

For the past few days, Zander's been at my side almost constantly and he's kicked my butt at chess at least a dozen times.

Chess isn't the only game he likes. I've discovered that behind the muscly exterior and the frown, the king actually has a playful side. We've spent hours playing hide-and-seek in the maze, which usually ends with him kissing me breathless once we find each other.

We've enjoyed breakfast in bed every morning, lunch under the gazebo with Ro, and dinner in the formal dining room, just the two of us.

At night, we lie in bed and talk. I tell him funny stories about Paige and me from when we were kids and not-so-funny tales from when we were older and she got into trouble. He answers all my questions about Valora in detail, although his firsthand knowledge about the other realms isn't as great as it should be. While he's visited them a handful of times since his father died, there's simply too much ground to cover. Almost everything he knows came from books.

Yesterday, we spent several hours in the library. It started with a yummy chocolate custard dessert after lunch, which was followed by a heated chess match. After I accepted my defeat, I read aloud to him while we snuggled in an oversized chair.

Spending time with him has been amazing, but one thing we haven't done? More than kiss. Much to my disappointment, every time our make-out sessions start to get a little hot and heavy, Zander pulls back.

And I know he knows I'm frustrated. I'm sure the mate bond communicates that quite clearly.

So why won't he make a move?

Speaking of the Day king, the door opens, and he saunters into the room. "How's it going?"

God, he's so handsome it's ridiculous.

He's wearing a more formal outfit. It's not a suit—that would be way too hot here—but the crisp fabric of the white collared shirt fits his body well. His sleeves are rolled up on his muscular forearms. A tan vest is secured over his middle with pearly buttons. The crown is on his head, appearing uncomfortable as always.

I want to take it off. Mess up his hair. Undo the buttons over his chest so I can slip my fingers inside and feel the coarse hair on his smooth body.

"Almost ready," Tabitha announces, her response muffled because of the pins she's collecting in her mouth. "Queen Maelyn looks gorgeous."

"I have no doubt about that." Zander's mouth ticks up with a smirk as he aims his unfocused eyes at me.

I wish he could see me now. The way my hair is curled and swept to the side with a pearled clasp. The dark mascara on my lashes. The mauve lipstick.

I've never felt more beautiful, and when Zander does get his sight back, this is how I want to look the first time he sees me.

Soon, the curse will be broken.

It could happen tonight. What's stopping me?

For all intents and purposes, I'm already his wife. Waiting is pointless.

Sometimes I forget I started out as Zander's captive. No one has ever made me feel as special and treasured as he does, and during our short time together, he's gone from being an unwanted husband to my friend. My best friend.

"All done," Tabitha spouts proudly as she ties off the last stitch. She beams up at me. "This is my greatest work."

Zander reaches out to help me down from the pedestal. As I pass the chess board, I move my knight.

Then I stop in front of the oval standing mirror Tabitha brought in.

I really do look amazing. I hardly recognize myself.

Turning slightly this way and that, I admire the way the light plays on the iridescent fabric and how the jewels catch the sunlight. I have cap sleeves covering my shoulders. The corseted waist is cinched, so my curves are enhanced. My breasts are pushed up in an almost lewd way, my cleavage on full display.

Yeah, Zander and I need to get it on tonight.

This is an opportunity that's too good to waste.

Stepping up behind me, Zander loops something around my neck.

My black king.

The shoestring is gone. It's been swapped out for a silver chain. Diamonds glitter from the custom prongs that hold the precious piece in place.

Once the necklace is secured, Zander takes advantage of my hairstyle, kissing the side of my exposed neck. Just a gentle caress of his lips does obscene things to my body. Closing my eyes, I tilt my head, giving him more access. Begging him to take it.

Instead, I feel something velvety and cool on my cheeks, nose, and forehead.

When I open my eyes, I see a pearlescent mask covering the top half of my face. It's the same color as my dress, with matching diamonds outlining it. Zander secures the ribbons behind my head, cleverly weaving the silk through my hair so the bow is hidden.

"Maelyn, you're absolutely stunning," Ro says from her seat.

"Thank you." My cheeks heat under the mask.

"We might have to finish this game another time. I'm sure everyone is anxious to meet our new queen."

There's a strange note in her voice. Not sadness. Almost... nostalgic. I wonder if she's thinking of her own introduction to the kingdom. I'm sure it wasn't a happy one.

She's been acting kind of weird all day. Maybe social events make her uneasy. She hasn't changed for tonight yet, so it's safe to say she might be dreading it.

"Three more moves," I insist as Tabitha and her assistant leave with their baskets of sewing supplies. "Then we'll call it a draw."

Thanking Miria for sitting in for me, I take her seat and study the board for a few seconds, then move my queen. To be honest, I haven't been paying much attention to the game, but Ro's seemed distracted, too. Even now, her eyes are trained on some spot outside the window, her gaze blank. Like she's deep in thought.

"Ro? You planning some epic checkmate on me right now?"

She glances at me, some of the distance clearing from her face as she shakes her head. "Sorry. A lot on my mind."

She moves the pawn I was planning to take.

Then I see it.

An opening. A trap. A clear path to her king.

Several beats pass as I stare at all the positions and possibilities, wanting to make sure I'm not seeing something that's not there. But, clear as day, I'm going to win.

"Checkmate. Oh my God, checkmate!" Squealing, I bounce a little.

That seems to snap Ro back to focus, and she narrows her eyes at the game. "Really?"

"Yes, look." Just to demonstrate my win, I slide the queen across the tiles and lay her king on its side.

Seeming shocked, Zander comes over and touches the wooden trim along the board. This isn't his enchanted set, so he can't tell where anything is. Still, he seems shocked as his fingers touch the remaining pieces.

Clapping, I stand up and do a victory dance.

I'm usually a gracious winner. I don't gloat. But I just beat the grand master.

I stop my jig and give Ro a suspicious look. "Did you let me win?"

She's blinking at the game like it betrayed her. "No." She sends me a smile filled with motherly satisfaction. "You did this on your own. Congratulations, Maelyn."

While I'm glad she's genuinely proud of me, she and I both know this shouldn't have happened.

"Are you feeling okay?" I ask, still concerned about Carielle's ongoing presence here. Although Zander's guards have been spying on her, it wouldn't be impossible for her to try something.

"I'm fine." Ro's smile brightens. "I better go get ready."

"Mother has never liked parties," Zander tells me, extending a hand to help his mother up while suggesting, "Perhaps you could slip away after all the introductions."

Patting his fingers, Ro nods. "Perhaps."

"Would you like for us to wait for you?" he offers. "We can all go in together."

"No, that's not necessary." Pausing to smooth his vest, she says, "My handsome son. I do love you so."

"And I love you." He reaches out to lovingly palm the side of her head. "Mama."

The sweet exchange between them almost brings tears to my eyes. They've been through so much together. They've survived, and when I think about being in their family, it feels right.

It feels like I'm a missing piece they've been waiting for.

"Well." It seems I'm not the only one who's gotten emotional, because Ro wipes at the corner of her eye before saying, "I have a present for you, Maelyn." Bending down, she pulls a flat wooden box from beneath her chair. "This was mine. Now it's yours."

When she opens the lid, a dainty tiara glints at me. It's rose-gold and not as gawdy as Zander's crown. With a few diamonds and pearls, it's perfect.

I suck in a breath as Zander picks it up and sets it on my head. Prongs on the back of it make it feel more secure in my hair, and I turn to get the full picture in the mirror.

"Lovely," Ro gushes. "You two have the best time tonight. Enjoy each other."

She smiles at us both through glistening eyes. I could write it off as a mom getting emotional about a monumental event, but as she quietly leaves the room, I can't help feeling like something's off with her.

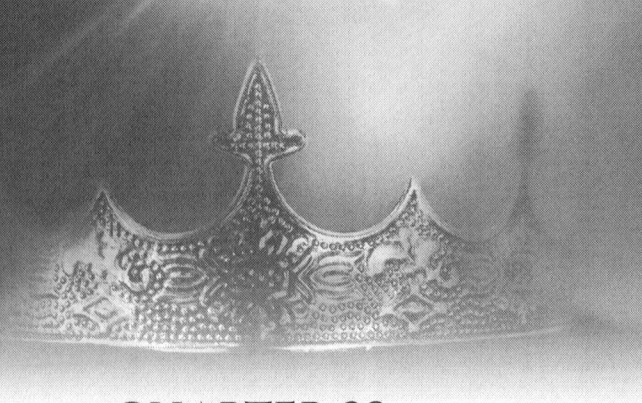

CHAPTER 32

Maelyn

Okay, so I can see why Ro was apprehensive about this event.

I gawk as we stand just a few feet from the ballroom entrance. I've never seen so many glamorous people packed into a room at once.

Gowns of every color. Jewels and elaborate hair-dos. And everyone is so tall.

Ornate masks cover the top half of the guests' faces, just like mine and Zander's. Glittering. Shining. Some have feathers added for extra flair.

All the curtains are covering the windows, keeping the light out. It's as dark as night in here, and it adds to the magical atmosphere.

The candles have finally been lit. Flickering wicks are everywhere; on the three giant chandeliers, on wall sconces, and the best part of all—tree boughs are attached to the walls in various places, making it appear as though the branches are growing inward. Twinkling votives wrap around the hanging limbs.

My hand tightens on Zander's arm as the announcer shouts our arrival.

Every single set of eyes snap our way, and a hush falls over the room.

Luckily, we don't loiter in the doorway for everyone to just gape at us. Zander strides forward confidently, with an air of entitlement about him. Sweeping through the ballroom, he doesn't stop long enough to have a conversation with anyone.

Instead of my pageant wave, I give subtle nods and quiet hellos as I pass people.

Soon, we stop in front of the thrones, and Zander gestures to one, indicating I should sit.

Gulping, I stare at the golden masterpiece. It's so huge, it's going to swallow me up. My legs will be dangling like a child's.

"I feel like this is something we should've practiced," I hiss quietly, hesitating.

"It's just a chair, Mae." Humor drips from Zander's tone. "Watch me."

He effortlessly folds himself into the contraption. No rituals or special movements. Simple enough.

I mimic his action, though I'm sure I don't achieve it as gracefully as he did. And just as I thought, my feet don't touch the floor. Scooting forward a little, I try to fluff my dress so my small size isn't so obvious.

Extending his arm between the chairs, Zander uncurls his fingers in an invitation to hold his hand.

I take it.

At this point, any physical contact with him is welcomed. And torturous. As he rubs my palm with his thumb in soft circles, my body awakens. Memories of the night he used the feather on me bubble to the surface.

My nipples harden to painful points when I remember how he trailed it over my breasts. Wetness floods my core at the thought of his face buried between my thighs.

I squeeze my legs together.

A low growl comes from the throne next to me.

He's feeling what I'm feeling.

Good.

Maybe I should keep thinking about that night. Maybe if I get turned on enough, he won't be able to resist a repeat.

Unfortunately, people start lining up in front of us. Bows, curtsies, and introductions follow. Since everyone's faces are obscured, it's unlikely I'm going to remember who anyone is later, but I do what I think a queen would—I thank them for coming and utter words of agreement when they praise the food, even though I haven't tasted any of it myself.

The greetings portion seems to last forever. By the time the line finally thins out, I'm squirming with the need to pee.

A woman with white-blond hair and lavender eyes shining from behind her silver mask stops before us. "Your majesties."

Zander perks up at her voice. "Maelyn, this is my aunt. Zephina, meet my wife, Queen Maelyn of the Day Realm."

A member of Zander's family. Guess that makes her mine, too. "It's so great to meet you, Zephina."

"Please, call me Phinney, and the pleasure is all mine. You've been sitting for so long. Would you like to take a walk about with me?"

I'm nodding before she's even finished the offer. My butt's numb, my bladder is full, and I want some food.

I glance at Zander and he dips his chin with permission. "Don't keep my mate away for too long."

As soon as I stand, Zephina hooks her arm with mine and begins sashaying through the crowd. People part for us, stepping out of our way with murmured words of respect. I don't think it's all for me. Zephina's loved in this kingdom.

"I can't tell you how happy I am to have you here," she exclaims as we duck under a branch. "Rowan mentioned your interest in acclimating the humans to our world."

I don't correct her on Ro's preferred name, but I do emphasize it when I say, "Ro is great. Yeah, I'd be happy to help. I've been thinking about it, and maybe a couple days a week, they could come here to talk to me about how they're doing. Just to get some traumas off their chest or chat about their future."

"You could make it a luncheon," Zephina says happily, then her smile falters. "Although maybe that would just make it all stuffy and formal."

"A quiet, relaxed, private meeting might be good at first," I provide thoughtfully, "but we could work up to luncheons."

She sighs. "I'm going to be forward here—I'm struggling with the new girls. I always do. We promised these girls a better life, and it kills me when I feel like they're just as miserable here as they were in the Earth realm."

"Speaking from experience, being uprooted from the life you know and brought here is overwhelming and scary and confusing. What's the biggest challenge you face in the first week with them?"

"Where do I start?" She forces a laugh. "Sometimes they don't get along with each other, and we have to switch roommates around until we find suitable pairs. We just don't have the room for everyone to have their own space."

"Then we need to make more space," I state firmly. "I'll talk to Zander about expanding."

"Fantastic. Also, the girls are resistant to the dormitory rules. They might accept their restrictions better coming from you. As much as I try to discourage male overnight guests or sneaking out, they manage to do it, and I'm pretty sure they think I'm the biggest prude they've ever met."

I smile wryly. "I've been accused of being a prude many times, so I'm not sure I'll be much better than you in that department. But I could just tell them about the time I got my butt kicked by a bunch of lashing trees and almost died in a sand trap."

Zephina blinks at me, and I get the feeling she's going to ask about the full story another time. "That might be effective for the sneaking out. The men however..." She sighs. "There's no such thing as birth control here. While it would be rare for one of them to get pregnant by a man who isn't their fated mate, it is possible."

"Do you have kids?"

A flash of pain enters her eyes, but it disappears quickly. "I do not. That time has passed for me."

"I'm sorry."

"Don't be. In many ways, the girls who come here are like my children."

"Are you married?"

"I was once, but a century after my husband and I wed, he met his fated mate. Staying with me wasn't an option, so we went our separate ways."

"Ouch."

Surprising me, she just laughs and shrugs. "She was his mate, and he and I were never a love match. It was a marriage arranged by my father and I accepted it because I'd hoped for children while I was still of conceiving age."

I notice we've made it all the way around the room, putting us near the thrones. Leaning to peek around a group of people, I look at my handsome husband. Several stragglers are still lingering in front of him, seeming pleased as punch to be getting his time.

Zephina turns to me and takes my hands in hers. "It was lovely to meet you. I won't keep you any longer. Let's meet up next week to discuss plans going forward."

"Sounds good."

"Would you like me to walk you back to King Zander?"

"Actually, is there a bathroom around here?"

Nodding, Zephina points to a darkened alcove behind me. "Just through there. The door is on the right."

"Thank you."

After giving my arm a friendly squeeze, she lets go and glides away. I turn, my sole focus on getting to the bathroom so I can return to Zander.

I pluck an appetizer off a gold tray on my way there. As soon as I stuff it into my mouth, I wish I'd grabbed more. It's like a mini twice-baked potato.

Just as I dart around a group of laughing people, I bump hard into someone's chest. Firm hands steady me by the shoulders, and I glance up at familiar turquoise eyes behind a black mask.

"Pippin, hi. Sorry I just rammed into you like that. I'm a woman on a mission." Huffing out an awkward laugh, I motion toward the restroom. "When nature calls, amiright?"

Peering around him, I realize the alcove is more like a hallway. I catch sight of a few couples. Shadows in the dark, leaning against the wall. Bodies pushing together as lips connect and limbs tangle.

They're making out—and probably more—right there for anyone to see.

My eyes go back to Pippin, and I think I spy a smudge of lipstick on his white collar. "Are you under cover tonight?"

Zander had told me warriors aren't invited to the masquerade, but maybe he wants some of his men on the inside. Security has been bumped up. No reason in particular, except for the fact that introducing new leadership can cause some citizens to become disgruntled. He'd assured me we have no reason to believe anyone would be upset about my new role as queen. If anything, people view me as a symbol of hope and stability, because I can break Zander's curse.

A happy king equals a prosperous kingdom.

"Queen Maelyn." The silky way Pippin says my name sends a shiver of unease up my spine, and the feeling only increases when he rubs my arms. "How good to see you."

I'm about to ask him if he's been drinking too much wine when he gives me a departing bow and smoothly walks away.

Weird.

Moving on, I push through an ornate white door with gold trim to see a series of stalls along the back wall. They're large and completely enclosed. Private, closet-like rooms. How extravagant.

To my left and to my right, there are sinks with pearl-framed mirrors. I'm walking past a woman fixing her hair when I recognize the reflection.

"Carielle."

Son of a billy goat. I didn't mean to say her name out loud. I would've preferred to pretend I didn't see her and ignore her all together.

Her eyes meet mine in the mirror. Lipstick is smeared across her cheek—the same hot-pink shade I saw on Pippin's shirt—and her mask is askew, dangling from a pin in her hair.

Did she and Pippin…?

So much for his vow of celibacy. Zander's going to be pissed.

"What?" Carielle barks. "Did you come in here just to stare at my beauty?"

"This is the bathroom," I deadpan, breezing by. "What do you think I'm doing?"

She doesn't answer, and I shut myself in my stall. A couple seconds later, I hear the main door open and close. I release a breath. It's not like I expect anyone to bow down to me—still getting used to that—but Carielle's hostility is totally unwarranted.

Oh, well. Tomorrow, she'll be gone and I won't have to worry about her anymore.

CHAPTER 33

Zander

K IRIAN AND QUINN ARE HERE. THE ANNOUNCER JUST shouted the arrival of the Night Realm king and queen, and I get a whiff of autumn and honeysuckle as they approach.

Royalty waits for no one, and there's a hush amongst the crowd as they cut to the front of the line.

Day Realm citizens are still acclimating to the friendly relationship I have with the other kings. They're skeptical, wondering how long the alliances will last.

Can't blame them. Until a few years ago, they'd never known true peace in Valora, but true peace they will have. I can give them that, if only they'll give me a chance in return.

Like my mother, I've never enjoyed these events. Balls and parties rarely happened under my father's rule, but when they did, I was expected to be the perfect, compliant son. To make a quick appearance. Satisfy everyone's curiosity, prove that I was alive and well, and then leave before anyone could notice there was something wrong with me.

I stand to shake Kirian's hand. "I'm glad you're here."

"So are we," he responds.

"Damon and Whitley wanted to be here, too," Quinn says, "but she went into labor this morning."

"That's great. I'll be sure to send a sprite with a gift for the new baby." Impatient to skip niceties and cut to the chase, I tell Quinn, "You're needed."

"I am?"

I nod. "I suspect one of my staff of treason, and there are new prisoners to be interrogated as well. How long are you staying?"

"We planned to leave in the morning, but we can put it off until tomorrow night," Kirian offers.

"Stay until the day after tomorrow, and I'll get you home by portal."

It's a good deal. Even if they're traveling by flight, my way will allow them to return around the same time, and their wings won't be exhausted.

"All right."

"Where's Maelyn?" Quinn asks, sounding eager to steal my wife away for a social call.

Good question.

"I'll go find her." Thankful for an excuse to vacate my spot, I tune out the complaints of the nobles in line behind Kirian. They probably want to talk about land expansion or a dispute with a neighbor.

They can wait.

Ten minutes away from Maelyn, and I'm antsy and itchy.

I thought having her at my side would make the masquerade more tolerable, but with so many people swarming her and dividing her attention, my need to claim her has only heightened.

I need to get her alone.

Now.

Straightening my vest, I follow the buzzing in my veins. Vibrations pulse beneath my skin as I eat up the space between me and my wife. Her desire is so intoxicating it makes me jittery.

For the past few days, I've deprived her while denying myself. She wants my body, and the suns know I want hers, but I've avoided sexual satisfaction. All because I'm afraid I'll shift after we've reached release.

In the restroom corridor, moans, smacking lips, and rustled clothing tickles my ears as lovers have trysts in the shadows. The gyrating couples are so caught up in each other, they don't notice me as I reach the bathroom door.

I hear the sink running, and the woosh of the faucet gets louder when I slip inside. Immediately, I pounce, capturing Maelyn from behind.

A sliver of fear shoots through her until she sees my reflection in the mirror.

"Zander." Her body softens against mine. "What's up?"

"You were taking too long."

"Is it time for dancing?"

Technically, yes.

The string quartet has set up inside near the buffet table, joining the harpist who's been playing serene music for the introductions. I hear the first few notes of a merry tune, setting the mood for a waltz. No one will dance until Maelyn and I have, but they'll have to wait.

Right now, I want my mate all to myself. "It's time for us to go somewhere private."

Heat and sunshine immediately warm us as we dash out the kitchen exit and run across the cobblestones. Maelyn's giggle floats up behind me. With her hand caught in mine, she's struggling to keep up with my fast pace.

I spin, haul her up into my arms, and keep speeding toward the garden as I carry her.

Passing some guards, I order, "I need someone stationed at the entrance and exit of the maze. No one goes in."

"Are you crazy?" Maelyn laughs. "We just left our own party."

"So?"

"What are we doing?"

Not getting to our destination fast enough, that's what.

If only I weren't wearing this confining outfit, I'd let my wings out right now and fly us to the middle of the labyrinth.

That's something Maelyn and I haven't done yet—fly together. She hasn't asked; maybe she's not ready for it. And I haven't offered, because my wings are healing from the fire. I haven't tested my flying ability, but this morning I had Marek take a look at my wings. Downy, gray feathers are growing in on the burnt patches.

"We're playing a game," I reply, rushing through the hedges.

The air becomes cooler as Maelyn and I pass under the shade of the tall flowery walls. We haven't gotten ten steps into the maze when I set her down. Since the movement is so sudden, she sways, disoriented. I splay my hands across her back to steady her.

Although she doesn't have wings, the design of the dress accommodates for them, sweeping low, exposing her spine.

I trail my fingers over her delicate bones while pressing a kiss under her ear. "Hide-and-seek. You've got sixty seconds."

"What happens when you find me?" Breathless, she drags her fingertips up my chest, fiddling with the buttons of my shirt. Driving me to the brink of madness.

"I win."

My cock is hard and throbbing. My heart thunders. Desire and lust make the tether feel heavy. Heady. Like a saturated rope pulled taut.

And there's something deeper between us.

Love.

I don't know if Maelyn feels the same, but I love her. Not the idea of her.

Her.

Her silly swear words and her ability to turn a simple sentence into a minute-long ramble. The graceful way she accepts defeat every time I beat her at chess, and her determination to try again and again. Her willingness to take me as I am: grumpy, blind, mysterious.

Rotating her body so she's facing forward, I let my lips skim the back of her neck. "Run, wife. When I catch you, you better be ready for me."

Her breath hitches, and she hesitates.

"One," I count. "Two…"

She takes off. Gravel kicks up as she sprints aimlessly into the maze.

The seconds go by as I listen for the skittering pebbles under each footfall. Pulse pounding, I track her whereabouts with my ears. She takes the first right turn. After arriving at a dead end, she backtracks and goes left, then right again.

From the sounds of it, she's going to end up near the gazebo. Perfect.

Fifty-eight, fifty-nine, sixty.

The hunt is on.

Taking my time, I leisurely stroll through the zig-zags, inhaling Maelyn's scent as I go. All is quiet now. She must be hunkering down somewhere, and I can't wait to discover her.

As I get closer, her heartbeat is audible. A quick and strong pitter-patter.

I love this.

Every time we play in the maze, my body is frenzied by anticipation. I enjoy chasing her down. There's something primal about it, and it speaks to my inner beast.

Silently creeping along the hedge wall, I stop a few feet away from one of the openings into the courtyard. Maelyn's on the opposite side of me. Leaves and branches separate us, and her breaths puff out loudly.

It's time to collect my prize.

Darting around the wall, I encircle Maelyn with my arms.

She shrieks, then laughs. "That was fast."

"I was motivated," I tell her. "What's my reward?"

Suddenly becoming serious, she turns and laces her fingers around my neck. "Me. You get me."

I dip down to capture her lips, but she playfully pushes me away before I can make contact.

Giggling, she runs toward one of the fountains. "Catch me."

"I already did." Lunging forward, I try to grab her dress, but the silk slips through my fingers.

She dances around the circular marble structure, quick on her feet as she leaps away from me again and again. I'm about to say to hell with my clothes and jump through the water and just cut straight through to her, when she skids to a stop.

Her heart does a strange flip as she stands completely still. I can feel her eyes on me as a sense of wonder and happiness infiltrates my bones.

"What?" I ask, stalking around to her. "What's going on in your head?"

"You were laughing." Her response is sobered, but joy bursts through her emotions.

"Was I?"

"Yeah. The big kind." She's a little choked up. "The real kind."

"And this makes you cry?"

After removing my mask, I reach up to lift hers away before dropping both to the ground. I feel her face. Her cheeks are dry, but there's a small bit of wetness under her eyelashes.

"It makes me happy, Zander."

"Mae," I whisper, dropping my forehead to hers.

My chest is full, and I get that surge of love again. I'm not sure if it's coming from me or her or both of us, but it feels good.

With my woman, I finally know what it is to feel powerful. Invincible. Wanted.

I was a worthless king without her. Now, I'm unstoppable.

Maelyn gasps as she looks over my shoulder at the gazebo and notices my surprise. My lips tick up with a knowing smile.

"You planned this?" she asks, seeing the twinkling lights hanging from the ceiling and the fluffy blanket I'd had one of the staff members lay out underneath them. There's a picnic basket filled with snacks from the masquerade.

Maelyn grabs my hand and tugs me along. "Oh, you are *so* getting some tonight."

I laugh again, and I like the foreign sound. "I didn't do this just to get under your skirt. I wanted some time alone with you. Are you hungry?"

"Food can wait."

Agreed.

Suddenly, the days of holding back have caught up with us. Our patience has run out.

When we get up the steps, Maelyn practically climbs my body to kiss me. Her arms wind around my neck and one of her legs hooks over my backside.

Growling against her mouth, I palm her supple ass through the layers of her dress.

While my lips crash into hers, our tongues melding, her fingers go to my belt and I get to work on her corset.

Only, I hadn't realized the laces could be so complicated. Along with the strings criss-crossing over her back, there are buttons and ties. I could rip it, but I refuse to ruin the dress. Tabitha worked hard on it, and we still have a party to get back to.

Frustrated, I chuckle. "Apparently, I should've spent some of my time in the library studying women's apparel, because I can't get this off you."

Maelyn snorts.

I've managed to loosen the bodice enough to pull the fabric away from her breasts, and I dip my fingers inside. She moans when I find her pebbled nipples.

"Looks like we'll have to improvise around the dress," I rasp, replacing my fingers with my thumbs as I draw circles on her peaked breasts.

The sensations coming back at me are nothing short of divine.

I moan.

"You know, I haven't gotten to touch you yet," Maelyn complains, her lip jutting out in a pout.

I take the opportunity to suck the flesh and bite it. "So touch me."

Bold, Maelyn reaches into my pants and fists my erection. My entire body jerks from how good it feels to have her smooth fingers around me.

Releasing my cock from my boxers, her movements are tentative and awkward as she explores my length. She finds out she can't get her fingers all the way around my girth. She discovers the ultra-sensitive skin around the head.

When her thumb brushes over my slit, smearing away some precum, I hiss.

Even with her unpracticed ministrations, I could come right now.

I already know the griffin will take over when that happens, but I have a plan for that—one of the reasons I brought Maelyn out here is so I can safely shift afterward without her realizing it. While the hide-and-seek game is fun, it's a decoy. A chance for me to get away and calm down as she searches for me.

"Zander." Maelyn kisses my jaw while pumping my cock. "I—I want to make you feel good."

I almost laugh, because her tone implies she's failing, which she most certainly is not. "What do you think you're doing right now?"

Her hand stops and her confession is a whisper. "I want to do something that's for both of us."

Sex.

By the suns, I want it so badly my chest aches. But our first time won't be a hurried coupling. A quick fuck, half-clothed, in the middle of an event where we have to go mingle among others afterward. I won't share our post-coital bliss with a bunch of strangers.

Besides, once we complete the mate bond, my power will surge as my soul rides the high, and I might not be able to shift back from the griffin for a while.

"If we had more time, I'd make love to you out here." Bunching her dress in my hands, I lift the material up so I can get to her pussy.

Only, there's more gauzy stuff in the way. How many striking layers does this gown have?

"I want that. I want you." Maelyn starts panting when I finally breach her panties, discovering she's soaked.

"Mae, when I make your body mine, we'll be in our room. All night. Just you and me."

My finger finds her clit, and as I circle it, she rubs my cock. The double pleasure is almost too much, but I keep at it.

Suddenly, Maelyn drops to her knees in front of me, taking her pussy away from me. Leaving my fingers, wet with her juices, bereft.

I don't have time to be disappointed, though, because her mouth is level with my cock.

It bobs heavily in the air, and I can feel her warm breath caressing my tip.

When she licks the head, I groan. The groan turns into a shout when she sucks me into her mouth. Swirling her tongue, she nearly brings me to my knees.

"Mae." My fingers tangle in her hair.

"Yes?" she asks coyly, before wrapping her hand around my shaft and sucking on me again.

She starts a rhythm with her head, fitting me into her mouth again and again, until I hit her closed throat.

"Fuck. Fuck, Mae."

She pops off. "Is it good? I don't know—I'm not sure what men like, and—"

"Don't talk about other men," I say harshly. "I'm the only one for you. Do you understand?"

"Yes."

"Yes, what?"

"Yes, husband."

"Good girl. You're so good, Mae." Pulling her face back to my erection, needing to feel the silky warmth of her tongue, I whisper, "Just keep doing what you were doing." Holding onto her head with both hands, I set the pace, guiding her as she takes my cock. "That's it. Suck me. Suck your husband."

She whimpers, and I shove farther in, wanting to see how deep she can take me. When her throat opens, her gag reflex kicks in, but the way she contracts around my shaft only makes it better for me.

I'm not going to last much longer. Already, my balls are tight and tingling with the need for release.

I step away, my breathing ragged. "I can't let you finish me like this. I don't want to leave you unsatisfied."

"You can do me next."

If I were a regular man, her suggestion would be completely fine. Taking turns makes sense. But she doesn't realize I won't be in any shape to return the favor after I come.

Reaching out to remove her tiara, I take off my crown as well and let them both drop to the blanket.

Then I get down and lie back. "I've got a better idea. Come sit on my face."

CHAPTER 34

Maelyn

Sixty-nine. That's what Zander wants to do. Hesitating, I try to work out the mechanics in my mind.

I'm all for it, but this stupid dress has proven to be quite the cock block so far.

"You won't be able to breathe under all this." I shake the material around my legs.

Unconcerned, Zander hooks an arm around my waist and manhandles me into the position he wants. My legs are on either side of his head, and I'm facing the massive erection lying against his stomach.

"I'm fae. I can't die from lack of oxygen." As he talks, the air from his mouth teases my pussy.

Without anymore discussion about it, Zander gets to work. He pulls my panties to the side and licks my clit.

Okay. So we're doing this.

Lowering my upper half, I press my lips to Zander's tip. A bead of precum has collected on his slit, and my tongue darts out to taste it. I expected it to be gross, but it's not. In fact, I want more. I lick the area, making sure I don't miss any.

Zander groans under me, his hand gripping my thigh hard enough to leave bruises while he sucks my clit. Hard.

My entire body jolts as my inner muscles spasm, and it's harder and harder to keep my hips from rocking.

Zander gives my butt a light slap, encouraging me to move. When I start to rock my hips, he rewards me with a finger. He massages my opening before pushing inside.

Surprisingly close to orgasm, I focus on his monstrous dick. Can't forget I'm supposed to be reciprocating. Poor guy's giving it all he's got, and here I am, just panting on him.

Nuzzling his sac, I note his scent is stronger down here. Muskier. Sexier.

I cup his balls with one hand while fisting the base of his cock with the other. Closing my lips around the head, I sink down a couple inches. My jaw stretches uncomfortably, but I want to make this good for him.

Time for me to stop testing the waters and just go for it.

I take him in as far as I can, sucking as I go. I'm not even halfway down his length, but I make up for it by using my hand, too. Matching the speed of his finger pumping in and out of me, I bob up and down on his cock.

I must be doing something right. Zander's reactions are hot. Every time he tenses his thighs, all the grunts and growls, the involuntary thrusting of his hips—for the first time, I have the upper hand in our relationship. I'm the powerful one.

Though, I'm at his mercy, too.

There's something obscenely erotic about having his fingers filling my pussy while my mouth is stuffed with his cock.

I like it.

I like feeling as if he's everywhere at once.

Stiffening his tongue, Zander flicks it over my clit in quick strokes.

Oh.

Right there.

Faster…

He knows exactly what I need, and he gives it to me. Adding another finger, he speeds up.

Fucking and sucking. Owning me. Loving me.

Every part of my body tightens as my orgasm builds. It's almost as if time enters slow motion as I feel it approach.

I can't breathe. I'm aware of the burning in my lungs, but I'm frozen. My legs are locked around Zander's head. My eyes slam shut. My toes curl inside my shoes.

Zander's still pumping his dick into my mouth, using my head and hand for his own pleasure.

Then it happens.

White-hot light bursts behind my eyelids as my pussy clamps down, and my clit jerks inside his mouth.

Drawing in air through my nose, I'm finally able to get the oxygen I need. My exhale is a series of moans and muffled shouts, muted around his length.

I work him faster, wanting him to get there with me, but it isn't even a second later before he's coming, too.

His pelvis jerks, shoving his cock deeper. Hot salty jets coat my throat and tongue. I try to swallow all of it, but there's so much. He keeps coming and coming.

And he's not quiet about it.

His uninhibited raspy groans against my wet flesh are the sexiest sounds I've ever heard.

My world suddenly flips when Zander rolls us. In a flash, I'm on my back, blinking up at him as he crawls over my body. Looming above me, he gives me a strained smile before placing a quick kiss on my lips.

"It's your turn," he rumbles out. "Count to sixty."

And then he's running away.

Confused, I sit up, my hair in total disarray, my dress hanging loose around my breasts. Pressing the fabric to my chest, I try to calm my racing heart while the pleasure trance Zander put me in evaporates.

He wants to keep playing our game?

Now?

Glancing around, I take stock of the rumpled blanket and my wrinkled skirt. My shoes fell off at some point.

I'm an absolute mess. Even if Zander and I are the only ones in the maze, I can't go running around like this.

Standing on wobbly legs, I slip my feet back into the shoes. It's impossible for me to tighten my corset, but I try. Reaching behind me, I yank on the laces until the fit is decent enough that my breasts aren't on display.

It'll have to do for now. Maybe Zander can help fix me up, but I have to find him first.

I haven't been counting, but I'm guessing it's been at least a minute.

Smoothing my gown, I start down the stairs, having no idea which way to go. There are four separate breaks in the hedges. Four different paths to take, and I was too out of it to pay attention to which one Zander took.

Tapping my chin, I consider the one I came through to get here. Might as well go that way. It's the one I'm most familiar with.

I'm walking across the cobblestone walkway when I hear rustling on the other side of the gazebo.

I turn around. Some leaves shake in the hedges.

"Zander?" Hopping in that direction, I ask, "Are you trying to make this easy for me? I appreciate it, but I could've found you on my own. Maybe. Okay, probably not. We've been gone a long time, though. We really should get back to the party."

He doesn't say anything, and I smirk when I imagine rounding the corner and tackling him. He owes me a cuddle. Two, actually. After all, this is the second time he's bolted, leaving me alone while I'm a defenseless heap of satisfied goo.

Just as I'm about to exit the courtyard, an arm shoots out from one of the hedges and hooks around my neck from behind.

For a second, I think Zander's toying with me, but I'm assaulted by smells that don't belong to him. Sulfur and dirt.

I'm jerked backward.

Definitely not Zander. He'd never handle me so roughly.

Cool mist coats my skin as the scent of rain invades my nose, and a familiar wooziness comes over me as I'm taken from one place to another.

A portal.

Someone pulled me through a portal, but my confusion increases when I realize we hopped out on the other side of the gazebo. We're still in the garden, and that means Zander is close by.

Scratching at the arm over my throat, I kick and thrash while being dragged a few feet away. One of my shoes drops off my foot in the scuffle, and I desperately try to scream. My airway is completely cut off, though, and my open mouth produces nothing but silence.

Before I know it, my attacker and I are plunging through another portal, taking me to a place I've never seen before.

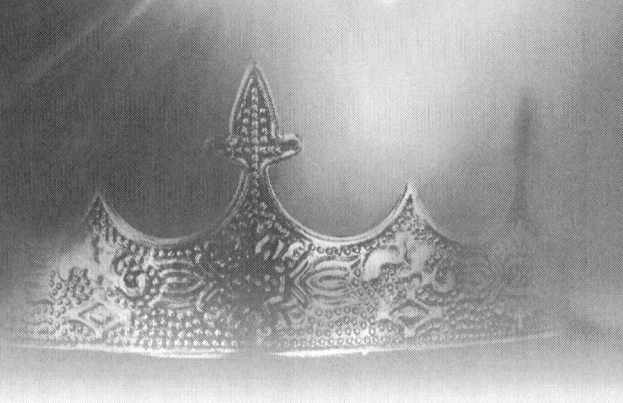

CHAPTER 35

Zander

I MANAGED TO SHED MY NECKLACE AND CLOTHES BEFORE the shift. Just barely.

Grumpily stalking through the maze, the flowers, leaves, and branches of the hedges scrape at my sides. I didn't take into account that I'm almost too wide to fit in the walkways.

Calm down.

The sooner I shift back, the sooner I can be with Maelyn.

My wonderful, beautiful, playful, caring, talented wife.

I owe her the truth. I hadn't planned on telling her tonight, but I can't handle this guilt. As soon as I get back to her, I'll sit her down and reveal my secret.

Her confusion floats through our tether as she wonders where I went, and I hear the teasing lilt of her voice. At any moment, she'll come looking for me.

Taking a deep breath, I stand still and mentally push the change. My body protests, not wanting to experience the pain again so soon. I've never shifted twice in the same minute before, but I can do it for Maelyn.

Just as my chest starts to rattle, panic and fear shoot through our tether, and the distinct sound of gravel spraying makes it to my ears.

Did she fall?

Immediately, I push off the ground with my lion legs, leaping to give my patchy wings a head start over the hedge walls. The fire damage is worse than I thought. Because of my missing feathers, I have to flap double time to get my heavy body up high enough to survey the maze.

I soar above it, quickly searching for my mate.

Maelyn is nowhere.

That can't be. There's no way she found her way out so quickly. Perhaps she's in the gazebo.

I dive toward it, preparing myself for her surprised reaction when I land so close to her in griffin form. Only, she isn't there. The blanket is rumpled where we lay before. Our crowns still sit side by side. But Maelyn is absent.

Something shiny catches the sunlight on a cobblestone by one of the fountains.

One of Maelyn's shoes. It's laying on its side, shockingly out of place without Maelyn nearby. I sniff around it, finding her lingering scent... and something else.

A portal.

Two, actually. It's a classic Gideon move.

Rage descends on me swiftly as realization hits.

He took her.

Roaring, loud and long, I emit the call my soldiers know means trouble. If I could breathe fire, flames would be shooting from my mouth. For the briefest moment, I wish that were part of my power. I want to destroy everything around me. The gazebo, the maze. The entire world.

Burn it all.

Nothing means anything without Maelyn.

I know that's partly the insanity talking. Just the thought of never being with Maelyn again drives me crazy, and I get a bitter taste of the mate madness as I pace back and forth.

Less than thirty seconds later, several warriors are flying

through the sky, weapons at the ready as they land in the courtyard next to me. Assessing the threat, their alert eyes dart around the space.

Now I need to shift back. Tell my men what I know. What I don't know. How I failed my mate.

I left her unguarded.

All my fault.

Crouching, I push through my tumultuous emotions and mentally will the shift.

But just before I begin changing back, I look straight ahead. Wilted flowers are in my direct line of vision. One of the rose bushes surrounding the gazebo is dying. Dried leaves hang limply, shriveled and dark.

It's the bush right behind where Maelyn had been sitting at dinner with my mother. Right where she'd tossed the wine with suspected poison.

Carielle. She has something to do with this.

This time, I revel in the pain when my bones crack and crunch. I enjoy the fire licking up my spine and through my head.

I deserve to be punished for my stupidity. For my dishonesty.

All. My. Fault.

As I come back to fae form, I lie sprawled out on the ground, the rough rocks beneath my face digging into my cheek.

"Your majesty." Sounding concerned, Thayne tries to help me up.

I bat his hand away.

Enough wallowing.

Self-pity isn't going to get Maelyn back.

"Someone apprehend Carielle. Bring her to me in iron shackles. The queen has been kidnapped." Pants get tossed to me once I get to my feet. Fisting the fabric, I stab my legs in while shouting more orders. "Shut the doors to the ballroom. No one leaves until we figure out what has happened. Tell the Night Realm king and queen to come, too—I need their counsel."

A flurry of action ensues while I stand at the scene of the crime, utterly helpless. Time passes quickly and slowly at the same time. Every second that goes by is another moment my mate could be harmed. I don't feel any pain through the bond, but I do sense something else: distance.

She's far away, and my soul aches from it.

"Please!" Carielle's panicked voice is music to my ears as she's dragged through the maze. "What is the meaning of this? What's happening?"

She's about to face wrath she's never known. I can already smell the blood and burnt flesh from the iron on her skin. If I didn't need information from her, I'd kill her on the spot.

A guard drops her to the ground at my feet.

"Roll call. Who's here?" I don't normally allow my lack of sight to be so obvious. Usually, I'd sniff everyone out, but I don't have the patience for it.

Thayne, Marek, Torius, and three palace guards make themselves known. Two of them take off to alert more of my men. A second later, Kirian and Quinn come flying from overhead.

Kneeling, Carielle sobs, "King Zander. What did I do?"

"Your lying and scheming ways have finally caught up with you," I bark at her. "Queen Quinn, step forward." Kirian growls a bit at my rude tone, always protective of his wife, and I add, "Please."

I don't have it in me to muster up gentle words right now. He must know that. The *please* was more than I'd usually do anyway.

"Carielle, are you in cahoots with Gideon?" I start the interrogation.

"Who's Gideon?"

"Did you try to poison my mother and Maelyn?"

Carielle cries harder, playing the victim quite well. "Why would I do that?"

It doesn't go unnoticed that she's answering questions with questions. I turn to Quinn and raise an inquisitive brow.

The Queen of Honesty says, "I sense deceit. There's something she isn't telling you."

"Try again, Carielle." I motion Marek over. "Or we could use more barbaric methods."

"No! All right. I steeped some lashing bark in the wine the other night. I wasn't trying to kill anyone. I just wanted to make them sick."

"That's the truth," Quinn intones. "Absolutely."

"A treasonous offense," I drawl, enjoying her whimpers of fear. "Tell me another."

"I don't have any others."

"Tell me where my wife is!" I thunder out.

"She's missing?" Carielle sounds genuinely shocked. "I don't know anything about that. I swear."

"Then how could she be snatched from me so quickly? Did you know we would be out here? Our rendezvous spot was a secret." I throw my hand toward the romantic setup under the gazebo. "Maelyn was here one minute and gone the next. If you were a part of a plan to kidnap her, by the suns, I'll—"

"I—I don't know." The chains rattle as Carielle rubs her temples. "I wasn't part of any plan."

"It's a half-truth," Quinn supplies. "There's honesty, but there's also an omission. She might have suspicions about what happened."

Carielle finally drops the victim act, breaking down in earnest as she spills, "It's true—I knew you'd be here tonight. I overheard one of the maids talking about your surprise. But I only told one person!"

"Who?"

"Pippin."

My jaw ticks. Her answer isn't good enough. My men know my whereabouts most of the time. While I didn't directly tell Pippin my plans for tonight, it wouldn't have mattered if he found out.

"You tell me nothing," I spit. "Take her to the dungeon."

"Wait." She scrambles as they lift her to her feet. "Listen to me. He was acting very strangely. We were in the alcove at the masquerade..." The way she draws out her voice tells me they were doing more than talking. "And he kept asking questions about you and Maelyn. I just wanted him to shut up and fuck me, so I told him about your plan to bring her out here."

I'm speechless for several seconds. One, because Pippin disobeyed my celibacy order. And two, because he wasn't even supposed to be at the masquerade tonight. He was stationed on the fourth floor along with another soldier to make sure no guests snuck off to explore the palace.

"She's telling the truth," Quinn says quietly.

Betrayal burns hot in my chest.

Ever since my men had graciously helped me keep my secret days ago, I'd started to think of them as friends. Pippin included.

Yesterday, I let him lead a mission without me. Putting my pride and personal vendetta aside, I tasked my men with finding Gideon because I wanted to stay home with Maelyn. Pippin used the objects we'd gathered at the cottage, but he returned with bad news. He'd lost the trail in Olphene because of Gideon's portal hopping.

Maybe he was lying.

Maybe he's been deceiving me all along.

I gave him a chance when I let him into my army. Took him under my wing, so to speak, and now he's betrayed me in the worst way.

"Your majesty." Speak of the devil. Pippin sounds out of breath as he flies over us and lands hard on the ground. "The queen—"

"Chain him, too." I point at the traitor.

"What?" he hisses when the shackles clasp over his wrists. "What's going on?"

"Sorry, man." Torius' voice holds remorse. "You fucked up."

"I didn't make her leave," Pippin protests. "She wanted to go."

"Like hell she did!" Getting in his face, I punctuate each word. "My. Wife. Would. Not. Leave. Me."

"What?" Seeming confused, Pippin shakes his head. "I'm not talking about Queen Maelyn. It's your mother. She's gone. Here." A paper crinkles in his hand. "She left a note in her room. When I heard the queen was missing, I wasn't sure which one they were talking about, so I went to Queen Rowan's bedchambers. She'd never made it out for the masquerade, so I wanted to check on her. She wasn't there."

"What the fuck is going on here?" Beyond distressed, I tug at my hair. "What does the note say?"

I pace back and forth as Thayne reads, "My dear son, the time has come for me to go home. To Brazil. To the place where I'm sure my family mourns my absence every day. You finally have a queen to rule at your side. I've been waiting for this day, not just for you, but for myself as well. That first dinner with Maelyn, when she said I deserve happiness, I know it to be true. But before I can be happy, I need to find the part of myself I lost when I came here. That part of me is somewhere in the Earth realm. Please don't be sad. I love you. Maelyn, take good care of my boy." He clears his throat. "It's signed by her at the bottom. It doesn't look like a forgery, and I have reason to think this was planned."

"Planned how?"

"Your mother asked me for a portal yesterday. I didn't question her intentions. It wasn't my place to ask her what it was for, but it makes sense now."

I spin back toward Carielle. "Did you have anything to do with this?"

"I didn't. I swear."

I don't need Quinn to tell me the verdict. While Carielle is guilty of trying to do minor harm to the women most important to me, she didn't make Maelyn disappear or force my mother to leave.

The real culprit is just to her left. "Pippin, you're going to tell me where Maelyn is. If I can get her back tonight, I might make your execution swift. Never mind the fact that you were at the masquerade breaking rules. I'm only concerned about the well-being of my wife."

"Masquerade? I wasn't there."

"Carielle attests differently."

"Your majesty," Thaddeus, who was stationed with Pippin, speaks up. "He's been on the fourth floor with me since dusk. Neither of us have left our post."

"Truth," Quinn pipes up.

I growl, because nothing is adding up. "How can someone be in two places at once?"

"Umm, something weird is happening." Carielle licks the corner of her mouth while her head tilts with thought. "Pippin was missing a tooth before. He's not now."

Missing a tooth…

"Fuck," several of us fling the cuss word.

Because there's one man we know who's missing a tooth. One man who has it out for me.

A man who has access to portals, electricity enchantments, and now, mimicking someone's appearance.

It can only lead me to one conclusion.

Gideon is a wizard, and he's just played the biggest checkmate of all.

See, the game of chess has it wrong. The rules say it's over if the king is defeated, but that's not how it should be. When the queen is captured, the king should surely fall. Because without her, he has no future.

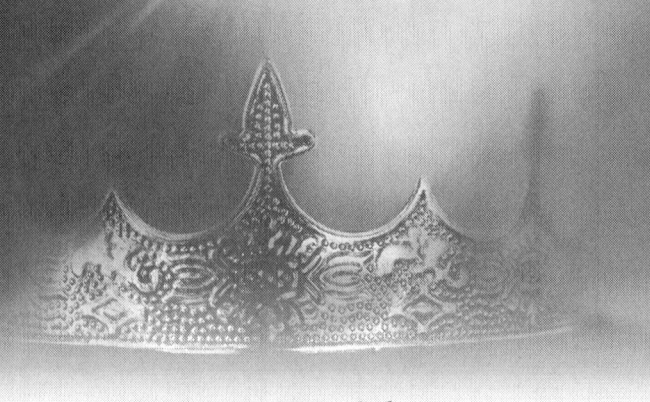

CHAPTER 36

Maelyn

"WHERE ARE WE?"

The grip on my elbow tightens as I'm yanked through a cave of some sort. Torches are the only source of light, throwing dancing shadows on the rust-colored rock walls. Uneven grooves decorate the sloping sides around us.

It's cold here. And dark. Very much unlike the Day Realm I've gotten used to.

"Pippin, please." Attempting to appeal to the guy I've gotten to know, I say, "Zander respects you. He values you. Don't betray his trust."

He laughs, though it's not cheerful or light-hearted.

Tossing his mask to the ground, he looks me in the eye. "You're so gullible, it's pathetic."

I hold in my frightened gasp. As my eyes bounce around his face, I realize he doesn't look all that much like the young soldier. His eyes are the same color, but the bridge of his nose is slightly wider. While Pippin is usually clean-shaven, this man has coarse stubble on his jaw.

"You're not Pippin." I gasp. When he grins, there's a wide dark gap where his incisor should be. "Gideon? That was you with Carielle at the masquerade. You used her."

He doesn't confirm it, but I know I'm right. As the seconds go by, he looks less and less like Pippin. Somehow, he'd changed his face before, but it's wearing off now.

Deeper and deeper he pulls me into the darkness. The ground has a slight incline, and I feel like he's leading me to the depths of hell.

But there's hope.

If the real Pippin is still with Zander, that means they can find me. Gideon doesn't know I lost my shoe between the first and second portals. If Zander and his men find it, they'll be able to track my location.

Trying to keep my steps even, I walk on the toes of my shoeless foot. I grimace when sharp rocks cut into my skin, and I hope I'm not leaving a trail of blood. If Gideon notices something of mine got left behind, all he'd have to do is toss me through another portal.

Zander might never find me if that happens.

He will come for me. I know it. Until then, I just have to be a good little captive.

Funny how I've come full circle from when I first got here. A week ago, I was ready to comply and behave. Whatever it took to survive. Then I rebelled, got myself into some trouble, and found my way—not just out of the sand trap, but into Zander's heart.

I didn't know it at the time, but my life was just beginning.

Now I need to survive so I can live it.

"You're making a huge mistake," I say, parroting the same argument I tried with Zander when he first took me. Only this time, I know it to be true. "Zander's going to be unbelievably angry at you for taking me. It's a death sentence. If you let me go now, you might be able to get away."

"I've already gotten away with it, dear queen," Gideon drawls. "It was so easy. I infiltrated the ball, figured out where you'd be, then I took you. Simple."

"Okay. I realize you wanted to buy me, and you might be

upset that Zander won at the auction, but he had no choice. I'm his fated mate."

Snarling, Gideon suddenly stops and jerks my arm so hard my shoulder socket throbs. "Fate did come to a head that day, but don't flatter yourself, sweetheart. This is not about you."

"Then why am I here?"

"You're just collateral damage in a much bigger picture."

"Collateral damage?" I want to keep Gideon talking. "Sounds personal. Is this about revenge or something?"

"Of course."

"But Zander doesn't even know you."

His evil chuckle sends a chill through me. "Oh, but I know him. I've been waiting for the opportunity to take from him, just like he took from me."

"I don't understand."

"I was four years old when King Zarid murdered my father."

I freeze. So this grudge goes back a lot farther than last week. "What does that have to do with Zander? Listen, from what I've heard, Zarid sucked, okay? Zander didn't like his dad either."

"Doesn't matter. Zander's the reason my family was stolen from me. My father was the best wizard to ever exist in this realm. When King Zarid hired him to gift his little pipsqueak of a son with a power, it didn't go as planned. The spell didn't turn out to his liking, and the great Zarid couldn't have a son who was more terrifying and more powerful than him, so he hunted my father down. Stabbed him in the heart with an iron spike right in front of my mother and me."

Power? Gift? Spell?

This guy's insane. Just babbling nonsense.

Confused, I shake my head. "Zander doesn't have a power."

"Oh." Gideon looks at me like he feels sorry for me. "Sounds like your husband has been lying to you, pretty bird. You really are daft. Pity. I'd thought about keeping you for myself. It would've been the ultimate revenge to fuck you as you slowly die, knowing Zander's dying, too."

I tremble. "You're going to kill me?"

Now his assessing eyes turn confused, like we're not on the same page. "Didn't you know? Fated mates can't live without each other. Being separated means certain death. Usually takes a few years. At least, it did for my mother. Don't worry. Madness will set in long before you perish. You'll be so consumed by insanity, you won't even know your body's being used up like a whore."

His words chip away at my soft heart. In more ways than one. Aside from the whore comment, he's told me some important facts Zander didn't.

I'd already known Zander was hiding something from me. I'd told myself it was his business and he'd talk about it when he's ready.

But his secrets directly affect me. Apparently, my survival depends on his and vice versa. There had been hints about the consequences of separating mates. I remember when Zander mentioned how his grandfather went crazy after losing his wife. At the time, I'd thought grief was a ridiculous excuse for the way Zed acted in the years following his mate's death, but maybe it really wasn't his fault.

And I'm disappointed that I had to find this out from Gideon, of all people.

That's not the biggest lie, though. Zander has a power because of something Gideon's father did.

I'm afraid to ask what that power is. Instead, I question, "Why now? Why wait so long to get your revenge?"

"Until Zander finally grew a pair and offed his father, he'd been under strict guard at the palace. But ever since he killed dear old daddy, I've been making as much trouble for him as possible—creating unrest, turning his citizens against him, fueling the crime." Gideon looks so proud. "All while staying under the radar, too. I'd never even met the king until last week, yet I'd been making his life a living hell for years. Then you came along, and you're the key to completing my plans. You'll be the end of Zander, and I won't even have to lift a finger to make it happen."

Before I have a chance to pry more information from Gideon, we get going again, even faster as we turn into a tunnel with a low ceiling. Gideon has to duck down just to make it through. When we come to an exit, the cave opens into a big room. A round dome.

A couple torches are the only source of light. The rock walls are bare and rough. There's another cave opening opposite of us, leading to who knows where. A canvas hangs over it as a makeshift door.

My stomach lurches when I see several cages on the floor. They're small, reminding me of the crate my family used to keep our golden retriever in when he was being potty trained. Person-size lumps are inside.

One of those lumps moves.

A head lifts, emerging as a threadbare sheet falls to her shoulders. Brown eyes peek at me through dark ringlets framing her face, and the girl watches me as I'm led to my own prison next to hers.

"In you go," Gideon orders, and I'm not going to fight him on this. Being inside a tight space might be uncomfortable, but it's a barrier between him and me. I'll take it.

When I crawl inside, I'm extra mindful of my dress, making sure my bare foot isn't discovered.

Hunched over, I scoot to the back of the cage and sit cross-legged as I take stock of the area. I count six cages in total, and while two of them are empty, it's obvious one was occupied recently. A thin blanket is balled up on the floor.

A shiver races up my spine, and not just because it's chilly. I don't want to think about where the missing girl is. What she's being forced to do right now.

Gideon secures a padlock on my door.

"Get some sleep, pretty bird. You have a performance in the morning." He grins, and any familiar characteristics of Pippin have faded away completely.

I can't believe I thought Gideon was good looking at one point. When I first saw him at the auction, he was my preferred choice. I'd seen his smiling face and mistaken his grin for friendliness.

Striding away, the psycho whistles as he whips the canvas to the side and disappears into the mystery tunnel.

Unlike the day I woke up in the wagon, I'm not going to be a fearful mute this time. I need to ask questions and figure out as much about this place as I can, so when Zander does come, I'll have info to help him take down the operation.

"Hey," I whisper to my new neighbor. "Where are we?"

"Hell," she responds, monotone.

"Yeah." I blow out a breath, having no idea what she's been through. Maybe a glimmer of hope would help her talk. "We're going to get out of here, okay?"

She turns her face toward me, and she's gorgeous. Her brown skin is smooth and flawless, she has high cheekbones, and even in the dim lighting, I can see how long and thick her eyelashes are.

She blinks at me. "There's no way out."

"You were brought here recently, right?" Grasping the bars between us, I think about the house we busted the other day, and how we'd gotten there too late.

"Yeah, but I was captured a long time ago. Probably months, but I can't be sure. We've been moved four times, but this place is the worst. No running water. Hardly any food."

"Well, what did you see when you came here? Landmarks or forests? Anything?"

"A mountain."

"Okay." I nod encouragingly. "That's a good start. What about the weather?"

"Kinda chilly, I guess."

"And the sky—was it day or night?"

"Hard to tell. We came out of a portal into a deep valley. I guess I remember seeing blue skies, though."

"Good," I say excitedly. Blue skies mean we're most likely still in the Day Realm. "If we got free, would you be able to find an exit?"

Shaking her head, she lies back down, resting her face on her folded hands. "There's no way in or out. We had to use a portal to get in. Besides, there are so many tunnels, you could get lost forever if you go wandering off. It's like a maze in here."

"My husband is the king, and he has experience with mazes," I tell her. "What's your name?"

"Sloan." She points across the way. "That's Milana and Ivy." Her finger flicks to the empty cage. "Annie's working tonight."

I swallow hard. "What does work entail, exactly? What are we expected to do?"

"Entertain."

My gut roils. "Sex stuff?"

"After we perform, yep. You got a talent?"

Remembering Gideon's persistent questions as I stood on the stage, I whisper, "I sing."

Sloan nods. "So does Milana. I dance—ballet." Silky pink straps cover her shoulders, and I scan her blanket-covered body. Pointe shoes peek out from the rough-looking material. "Ivy plays the piano. Annie's a chef. While we do our thing, Gideon auctions us off. It's like a three-ring circus around here." Her eyes get distant, but her armor finally cracks when she rasps, "There was a girl named Bette, too. But she's gone now."

"What happened?"

"Died," she croaks. "A customer got too rough with her. He was on Blaze, and something went wrong with his power. He burnt her up really bad. I've never seen someone in so much pain before. Took her a whole day to finally pass on. She begged me to kill her, but I couldn't." She breaks down, sobbing as she covers her face. "I couldn't do it, and she suffered."

"I'm sorry." I shudder, wishing I'd stayed ignorant. Maybe not knowing what lies ahead would've been better. Because I'll definitely have nightmares if I do manage to sleep.

As I draw my knees up to my chest, I try not to cry along with my new roommate.

Morning is hours away. Depending on where we are, it could take a while for Zander and his men to travel here. All I can do is hope they arrive before it's too late.

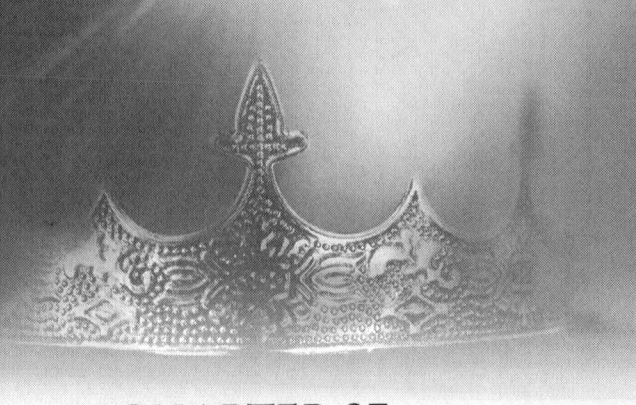

CHAPTER 37

Zander

Now that it's been confirmed Pippin isn't a traitor, I have his shackles removed.

"We don't have time to waste," I say, shoving Maelyn's shoe into his hands. "Can you sense her?"

Immediately, he nods. "Whether it was an accident or intentional, Maelyn left this between the two portals. I detect a long journey to the north. If we fly, we might be able to make it there in three or four hours."

I release my wings. "Thayne, Marek, Torius. I need you all with me."

Someone tosses me their belt, and when I catch it, I feel the heavy weight of a sword. It won't be like having my own strapped to my back, but I'm not about to eat up precious minutes by retrieving my weapon from my room.

"I want to come with you." Kirian steps up to me.

I shake my head. He's got a family. I can't let him risk himself.

Instead, I suggest, "Stay and sit in for me. Let my guests carry on with the masquerade as if nothing's amiss. With my mother gone, I have no second in command. My kingdom will be vulnerable in my absence."

My mother running off is another catastrophe I'll have to

deal with when I get back, but it's not the most pressing matter. If she went to the human realm, it could take days to find her there, which equals years here. I'll have to choose a special warrior for the task. Someone who doesn't mind leaving Valora for such a long time.

Kirian lays his hand on my shoulder. "I'll do this for you, cousin."

"And I'll owe you."

"Yes, you will." He gives me a hearty pat. "Now go get your wife. By this time tomorrow, she'll be here, and all will be well."

Without hesitation, my warriors and I take to the sky with Pippin in the lead. Thankfully, my wings are performing better in fae form, and I don't have to work as hard to go high and fast.

Below, I can hear Carielle screeching as she's dragged away. Some time spent in the dungeon will do her some good. I haven't decided her sentence yet, but I won't go easy on her.

As we fly north of Hailene, all my wrath shifts to Gideon. I let myself stew on the punishments I want to dole out. My thoughts swirl around death, torture, and destruction.

He'll pay with his life.

Maybe I'll hunt down a necromancer and have Gideon raised from the dead just so I can kill him again.

Hours pass. My men and I barely speak. The only words exchanged are necessary for our planning.

By the time Pippin starts shouting about being near, we're almost to the northern shore of the Day Realm. The only landmark separating us from the Endless Sea is Yelissa's Peak.

I grimace.

Of course. What a perfect place for Gideon to take my wife—the only place in the realm that's sacred and off-limits. The only place we wouldn't have looked.

Soaring, we descend to the ground just outside Mate Valley.

"Pippin?" I need him to be positive we're in the correct spot, though I already know the answer.

I can feel Maelyn. She's cold. She's scared.

My chest bones tremble, and I force myself to breathe through the rage. I'm barely keeping myself in check.

"She's here, but there's a barrier in our way." Pippin gazes up at the tall peak. "Possibly, she's inside the mountain. Or underground."

"Lead the way."

He gulps, no doubt worried about the myths and superstitions associated with Yelissa's Peak. Maybe it's all hogwash, and we're about to test that theory.

We traipse through the valley for minutes, getting higher with each step.

Dawn is here. The bright glow from the suns colliding on the other side of the rock wall make the shadows seem darker. Mist kisses my skin. The land is elevated, and clouds linger around us.

Pippin halts, and my heart flips. "I've been looking for a way in," he says, sounding discouraged. "A crack in the wall or disturbed grass on the ground. I'm not seeing it."

"If Gideon's a wizard," Thayne starts, "then he could get inside the mountain with a portal."

Which would be quite sneaky. His operation would never be found without a way in.

My hearing is better than all of my men combined. Placing my hands on the mountain, I press my ear to the cool rock wall.

Every three feet or so, I knock, listening for a difference in sound. On the fourth try, I hear an echo.

"It's hollow here." I point. "Thayne, quickly."

He throws down a portal, and we cross over the threshold, entering a tunnel we never knew existed until now.

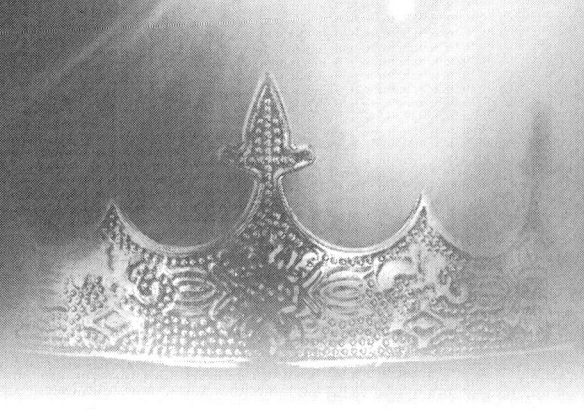

CHAPTER 38

Maelyn

"Wakey, wakey, pretty bird." Gideon rattles my cage, and I try to pretend to be asleep. His fake pleasantness drops. "Either you come out on your own or I'll drag you by your hair."

That gets me moving. Uncurling myself from a ball, I push up on stiff arms. My joints ache as I crawl out of the confines of the cage and stand. Gideon doesn't give me time to stretch before he's pulling me toward the canvas flap.

Stopping by the torches, his eyes do a quick assessment of me in the light. "Your hair's a mess. Your dress is wrinkled, but it's luxurious. I think I'll let you keep it for your costume. When we get to the stage, you're going to sing your heart out, understand?"

"Yes," I whisper, not wanting to piss him off. "I need to go to the bathroom, though."

"There's no time."

And then we're speed walking in a dark tunnel.

Panic makes my heart race. This is really happening.

I'd hoped to be rescued by now, but my optimism is dwindling.

Stalling is a tricky option. It's obvious Gideon is in a hurry, but for once, my nervous rambling comes in handy.

"This is quite the place you've got here," I say. "So many tunnels. Are they natural or manmade?"

He cuts me a suspicious look, like he doesn't expect me to be chatty in this situation. "Manmade. Thousands of years ago, this place was carved out by a clan of wizards who wanted to live in secrecy. Because if the king gets wind of a wizard, you can bet he'll force the man into his employ. And do you know what happens then?"

"What?"

"The king kills the wizard once he's not useful anymore."

"I'm really sorry about what happened to your father." It's not difficult to sound sincere, because I mean it.

"Don't do that."

"Do what?"

"Try to appeal to my compassion. I have none."

"What I said isn't about your compassion. It's about mine. There are some things you can't take away from someone, and you'll never rob me of my heart."

His footsteps falter, and for a second I think he's going to stop to yell at me. I'd welcome it. Anything to delay the inevitable.

But he keeps dragging me along.

"Business has been slow since we moved locations," he says conversationally, as if he's talking about opening a café in a new part of town. "I only have two customers this morning, but I'll get a hefty sum for you. Most men around here hate Zander and will pay a high price for his royal pussy, but Orin has his own grudge against your husband. He's going to enjoy taking it out on you."

I almost gag. "Why? What grudge?"

"There was a raid on my distillery several days ago. Orin escaped through one of my portals, but two other workers died. One was his brother."

That shuts me up.

Guess I know what happened to the third employee we couldn't find, and now he's here, wanting his revenge.

Gideon takes me through more twists and turns. There are so many tunnels, and I see what Sloan meant now. I'll never find my way out of here.

All too soon, we come to another dome-like room. This one is nicer. Colorful tapestries cover the rock walls, with candle sconces between each one. A few tables are scattered in front of a stage-like platform. I can't tell if the rock is naturally flat there, or if it was chiseled out, but red curtains frame the space and light glows dimly overhead from a few lanterns.

There's a long table off to one side, with several jugs and bottles spread out. Like a bar, only shitty.

A really shitty club is what Gideon has created here. I suppose no one cares about the ambiance as long as they get what they came for.

Two men occupy separate tables, and they're both looking at me. Leering.

And I immediately know which one is Orin. Half of his face is scabby from being burnt, and his right arm is in a sling. There's a crutch leaning against his chair, and the lower part of his leg is wrapped tightly.

Marek's work, I'm guessing.

Well, it could work in my favor if Orin buys me. Since he's injured, I might have a chance at fighting him off.

Bringing me over to a ladder at one side of the makeshift stage, Gideon lets go of my arm. "Sing your heart out. Give us a good show. You have no idea how boring life gets after thousands of years."

Unable to control my anger, I sneer, "If you're looking for a way to end your miserable life sooner, I'm sure Zander would be happy to oblige."

Rage contorts his features, and he shoves me. "Go."

I have no other choice but to do what he says, and I put my hands on the knobby wood.

On my way up, Gideon suddenly grabs my ankle. "Where's your shoe?"

"Left it in the cage, I guess," I lie, keeping my face forward so he can't see the fear on my features.

He lets go and mumbles, "Fine. You won't need shoes for what's happening after anyway."

Gross fucking asshole.

I shuffle across the stage, and the floor is cold beneath my bare foot.

Once I'm centerstage, Gideon turns to the two men occupying chairs in his messed-up mancave. "I give you, the queen of the Day Realm. She sings like a morning bird. I wonder how beautiful her voice will sound when you make her scream."

Shifting in their seats, the men lick their lips and clench their fists as their eyes violate every inch of exposed skin. Mainly in my chest area. Like most fae, they're good-looking on the outside. Blond mohawks. Built bodies. Even with a charred face, Orin would be considered model-worthy in my world.

The other guy looks a little older, comparable to a human in their forties, which means he's probably fifteen thousand years old or more. Has he been raping women his whole life? How many girls has he hurt in his lifetime?

Am I next?

Stall.

That's all I can do.

Coughing a little, I meekly ask, "Can I have some water?"

Looking annoyed, Gideon surprisingly agrees. He goes over to the bar, pours liquid from a pitcher into a cup made from an animal tusk, and hands it to me. I take several gulps, but then Gideon picks something up from the floor. A black riding crop. He slaps it against his palm. A clear warning.

I set the cup down and decide I need a long song. Or at least to sing it very, very slowly.

I start "She Used to Be Mine" from the musical *Waitress*.

As I sing, I measure my words and draw out notes. I lose myself in it, closing my eyes and imagining I'm with the Belting

Belles. When the end note comes, I sing it softly, prolonging it as I add some vibrato to keep it interesting. It goes on for so long that spots dance in front of my eyes from lack of oxygen.

When I finally stop, I suck in air as my small audience claps.

But just like I knew it would, the time for bidding has come.

The men shout out prices, desperation in their offers.

They don't even know they're buying a virgin. Bet the price would go up if they did but fuck that. I'm not earning any extra money for Gideon.

Tears I've been holding back finally barge their way through. My eyes burn and overflow. I feel an ugly cry coming on. Hot tracks trickle down my cheeks, and my chest is so tight I can barely breathe.

The auction is a blur. It's gotten heated now, both men standing, getting louder as they compete for me.

Just as Orin barks, "A thousand gold coins," something happens.

The ground trembles.

A loud crack resonates off the dome ceiling, and a fracture appears in the stone. Thinking the place is going to collapse on us, I crouch down, duck my head, and protect my neck and skull with my arms.

A second later, it sounds like a bomb goes off. Rocks and debris go flying, the biggest boulders hitting the floor like thunder.

I peek under my elbow, and I'm shocked when the griffin I've seen twice before is bursting through the small opening of the hallway. Chunks of the cave fall away to make room for his big body.

He just busted in here like the Kool-Aid Man.

The disturbance causes one of the tapestries to fall from its mount, and it lands on some of the candles. Fire spreads immediately. Smoke fills the room.

"No!" Orin shouts as Marek shows up. "Not him. Gideon, get me out of here. Get me away from him!"

Gideon just laughs, then he's disappearing through a portal. The opening vanishes as soon as he's gone, leaving Orin and the other guy to fend for themselves. They both run to the far wall, pounding on the unforgiving rock as if it'll do any good.

Marek does his thing, crippling them. Coins scatter as the would-be rapists crumple.

"Fuck!" Thayne exclaims roughly, gesturing to where Gideon escaped. "He was right there."

The griffin roars, seeming to share his sentiment, and the deafening sound shakes the already compromised structure around us.

I whimper with fear.

Then the animal's eyes sway toward me and clash with mine.

Haunted. Relieved. Loving.

Gold and glowing. I didn't notice how bright the griffin's eyes are before because we were in daylight, but in the darkness of the cave, they shine in my direction in the most familiar way.

"Zander?" I whisper, so quiet I'm not sure anyone heard me.

"We knew Gideon would probably escape us," Torius grumbles, quickly tearing down the burning tapestry to stomp out the flames. "He's a fucking wizard. The important part is rescuing the queen."

Marek must've been ordered to kill on sight, because the two men who were previously bidding for my body are unrecognizable. Their limbs are twisted at unnatural angles, their bloody faces are sunken, and some brains spill out from their skulls.

I'm not sure if it's dehydration, low blood sugar, or the gory scene on the floor, but my head gets woozy. I've never passed out before, but it's like my brain is shrinking. Everything around me seems unreal and far away.

I wobble a little as the griffin—no, Zander—reaches the stage.

My vision gets splotchy, and everything goes dark as I fall face-first from the platform. Just before I completely lose consciousness, my body is cradled on a net of soft feathers.

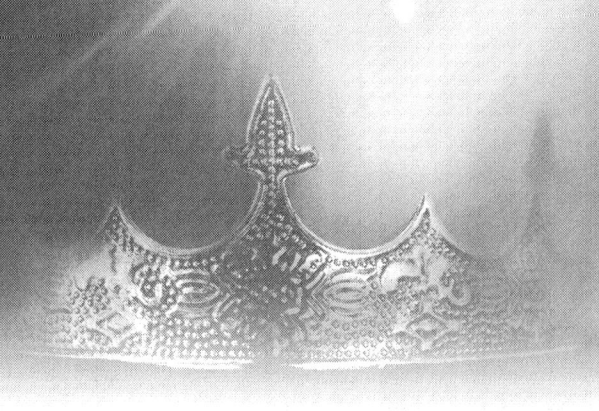

CHAPTER 39

Maelyn

I'M BEING CARRIED. THE GENTLE ROCKING MOTIONS TEMPT me to stay unconscious, but I feel a sense of urgency, like there's something I'm supposed to be doing. Morning birds twitter somewhere in the distance. Without opening my eyes, I soak in the good smells. Sandalwood and sunshine. The air is fresh and sweet. Clean.

Not dirty and dank like—

"The cave," I mutter, peeking up at Zander's serious face. His usual face, not the griffin one. "There were other girls. We have to go back for them."

I start to struggle in his arms, but he tightens his hold. "They've been found. Everyone will evacuate shortly, but I had to get you out of there."

"Did I pass out for long?"

"A few minutes. Were you—" His jaw clenches "—were you violated?"

"No." I cup his face. "You got there just in time. I knew you'd come. I knew it."

"You never should've been taken in the first place. I failed you, Mae. I'm so sorry."

"It's not your fault."

"Yes, it is."

Slowing, he comes to a stop and rests his back against a rock wall. Blue skies are above us. Bright yellow clouds reflect the sunlight, but we're in the shadows of a grassy valley. When I look up, tall mountains loom over us with mist floating around the peaks.

It's cool here, almost chilly, but Zander's body feels so nice against mine. It's warm. And safe. So safe. Did I mention warm? I just want to snuggle into him, close my eyes, and forget where we are.

But I can't.

I stare at Zander's stoic profile, trying to reconcile everything I've learned about him. About us.

Zander and the griffin have been two separate entities in my mind up until this morning. When he saved me from the quicksand, I gave credit to a mythical animal. And when he tore into that house to rescue Marek and Kai, it never occurred to me that the king and the creature were one in the same.

"Can you put me down?" I ask, wiggling.

"No." Zander doesn't relent. "We'll wait here for the others."

"I can stand."

"I know."

"We need to talk," I tell him seriously.

"Yes," he agrees.

"So, we're gonna have a serious conversation while I'm just flailing like this?" Kicking my legs, I notice my missing shoe has rejoined my foot. I'm so lucky the dang thing fell off when it did. My wonky foot came in handy for once.

"Your mouth works whether you're here or over there." Zander tips his head to a place next to us. "I'd rather have you as close as possible so you can't run."

"Zander." I sound disappointed, and maybe that's because I am. "After everything we've been through, why would you think I want to get away from you?"

"Because you know what I am. I saw the look on your face, the recognition in your eyes."

"You *saw*. So you're not blind when you're…"

"A griffin?" he finishes for me. "Yeah. For some reason, when I shift, I have my sight."

"That's how you knew what I look like."

He nods. "I'm sorry I lied to you."

The guy's so morose, I feel the need to lighten the moment, even though I'm the one who was just kidnapped and almost sexually assaulted.

"So you're a griffin." I shrug. "I've seen stranger things since I've come here."

"Griffin shifter," Zander elaborates.

"And Gideon's father made that possible? With a spell?"

Jolting with surprise, Zander almost drops me. "What did you just say? Gideon's father? Gideon is Alonius' son?"

"Yeah, I guess so. Gideon went all evil-monologue on me last night and said that's why he's after you. Or after me, in this instance. He was trying to use me to hurt you. He wants you to suffer because your dad killed his after the spell was done."

"Zarid murdered Alonius?"

I try to remember everything Gideon said. "Zarid was mad because the spell made you more powerful than him. So he spiked the wizard in front of Gideon and his mom. Then his mom died because her fated mate died. And that's another thing, dear husband." I poke Zander's shoulder. "You conveniently left out the fact that you and I will die if we're separated. Would've been nice to know that from the get-go. Anything else you want to tell me?"

Zander shakes his head. "You know all my secrets now."

"But I don't," I shoot back. There are so many questions to be asked, and I force myself to have some patience and ask one at a time. "How old were you when the spell happened?"

"Seven." After heaving out a sigh, Zander elaborates, recounting the wizard's abrupt arrival at the palace and the agonizing days that followed as he transformed for the first time.

"That's awful." I lightly rub his stubbled jaw.

"It's the other reason my father kept me hidden away. Only a handful of people were allowed to know about my shifting power. I couldn't be trusted to be out in public because strong emotions can force the shift against my will."

A puzzle piece falls into place. "Is that why you left so fast after we…?"

"Yes."

"Gotcha. I thought maybe you just didn't like to cuddle."

Zander's face screws up with anguish. "I wish I could be normal for you. I'd rather have no power at all than live as I am."

"But wasn't it a blessing in disguise?"

"No. It's a curse, Maelyn. It's painful. It's wrong. People despise what I am, and I do, too. I'm a monster."

"You're not a monster."

"How can you deny it? You've seen me."

"And what did I say in the stream that first day? You're magnificent, Zander."

Some of the tension leaves his bunched muscles. "You did say that."

"And I meant it."

"You should be scared of me."

"I'm not."

"Why?"

"Because." I swallow hard as my emotions threaten to boil over. "Because you would never hurt me. And I care about you. A lot."

Commotion comes from uphill in the valley as people start spewing from a portal.

First, the girls come out, clinging to each other like someone's going to rip their new freedom away at any second. Keeping a respectful distance, the men follow behind them.

Pushing away from the wall, Zander finally sets me on my feet and calls out, "Thayne, I need a portal."

The warrior jogs over, searching me from head to toe with his eyes. "My queen. You gave us a fright when you lost consciousness. Are you all right?"

"I'm okay, thanks to you guys."

Lifting the lid on his portal box, Thayne removes one of the little orbs and places it in Zander's palm. "Your majesty, I have three left after this. Not enough to send each woman home, if that's what they each choose."

Nodding, Zander pockets the portal. "We'll need to use one to get back to Hailene, and we'll make the females as comfortable as possible until we can reach a permanent solution for them. Wait for me here until I get back. Excuse us."

With that dismissal, Zander leads me away with an arm hooked around my waist as we proceed out of the valley. Although he keeps me close to his body, there's an emotional distance between us.

He's not doting on me like he usually does. His fingers don't constantly move around, seeking places to caress me. The walk is stiff and feels business-like.

A bad feeling comes over me. Like an ominous event is looming ahead.

"Zander? Where are we going?"

"I'm taking you home."

Oh. Twisting, I glance back at the crew. "Why aren't they coming with us? If we're low on portals, we should all use the same one."

He grunts. So we're back to that?

"That sound you just made—it's not an answer," I tease, trying to pull a smile from him.

"You'll see," he responds cryptically.

The mouth of the valley is up ahead, opening into a grassy meadow and some trees beyond. "Where are we?"

"Yelissa's Peak."

I'm so startled by his answer that I stumble. "What?"

Craning my neck, I look up behind us. Rocky points and cliffs surround the tallest mountain. Sunlight catches in the clouds, a mashup of pink and orange floating around the snow-capped heights.

It's beautiful. "You said this place is forbidden."

Zander nudges me along. "It is, but it would seem that the rumors about strange happenings might've been caused by Gideon and other wizards. From the looks of it inside, they've been occupying the mountain for quite some time."

"Yeah," I confirm. "Gideon did say that."

More questions sit on the tip of my tongue, but they disappear when we come across a large dirt patch in the grass. An inscription is chiseled into the stone above it.

From dawn 'til dusk, from dusk 'til dawn, I'll never love another.

Lowering my eyes, my gaze follows the shape of the place where the grass has died and never grown back. The outline is a perfect silhouette of two people curled up together, facing each other.

It actually looks like a heart, with a jagged line of green in the space between them.

Correction: A broken heart.

Fascinated, I kneel and place my hand on the dirt. As soon as I do, I get a rush of love, contentment, desperation, and need. It's so overwhelming, that I sway a little.

It's like I'm touching the very source of the mate bond.

This is the place where Yelissa and Conrad died, and they left behind some of their magic. Magic I can feel. This is where they made the vow, sacrificing their lives so others could have soul mates.

And Zander is most definitely mine.

I hadn't been able to feel the connection before, but here, now, I do.

Tears blur my vision as I look back at Zander.

No wonder the dude's been going crazy over me. This is some heavy stuff. I feel primal. Possessive. I yearn for his love, attention, and acceptance.

How awful it would feel to be rejected by him, and I put him through that. I rebuffed him over and over again, yet he stuck by my side, patiently waiting for me to love him back.

"I'm so sorry, Zander." A tear slips down my cheek.

"For what?"

"For not realizing how important and special you are right away."

"Come along, Mae," Zander says gently, helping me up to continue our trek out of the valley.

Maybe he's taking me somewhere private to complete the bond. After being apart, he must be desperate to have me in every way possible.

And I'm game.

So I'm surprised when he stops under the cover of some trees and puts the portal in my hand. "It's time for you to go home."

That's when his words register. Earlier, he'd told Thayne to wait for him until he gets back. He'd said *I*, not *we*.

"What?" I ask dumbly, denial refusing to let me accept reality.

Zander closes my fingers around the cool, wet-feeling portal. "You remember how to use it, right? Just picture Texas. Your home. Go to your family."

"No." Suddenly angry, I step back. "This is my home."

"You're too good for this world." Blinking, Zander's misty eyes become red-rimmed as he turns his head away. "You don't belong here."

"You are not doing this." I stomp my foot. "Not now. You made me look forward to a future in Valora, and you want to send me back?"

"It's for the best. You can't be here with Gideon on the loose."

"What makes you think he won't chase me down anyway?"

Zander still won't face me. "My men and I have already discussed it. We'll spread a rumor that you died when the cave crumbled. Gideon will think he's won. If he believes I'm too weak to fight back, he'll let his guard down, and then we can catch him."

Exasperated, I lift my arms in a violent shrug. "So, do that anyway, but keep me in the palace."

"I need to appear absolutely miserable for it to be convincing. I can't do that if you're still with me."

"What about me? What about my misery? We'll both die, Zander. Gideon said—"

"Not you."

"What?"

"You won't die. Our connection is complicated. My blindness curse was interrupted when some of the coven members died. That's why you can't feel it. As long as we haven't completed the bond, you'll be fine."

"Bond or not, I don't want to be without you." Deflating, I start to realize arguing with a king who has his mind made up won't work. Whimpering, I shake my head. "Back there at the spot under the promise, I felt it. Felt you. Us."

Zander's lips curve down so hard they tremble. It's the most severe frown I've ever seen on him. The frowniest frown to have ever frowned.

If I leave, I'll miss that face, scowls and all.

Placing his hands on my shoulders, Zander draws me to him until our foreheads touch. "A week ago, you couldn't wait to be rid of me."

"A week ago, I didn't love you."

His fingers spasm on my arms, affected by my declaration of love. "And you do now?"

"Yes."

"Do you mean that?"

"I've never been more positive of anything in my life." My feelings for Zander have been building during our time spent together, but today shoved me over a cliff and I can't come back from the fall.

Zander owns my heart.

My soul.

Linking my fingers behind his neck, I tug his face down and press my lips to his. I let my passionate kiss communicate everything I'm feeling.

Delving my tongue deep, I let him know I love and accept him. Every single part.

It's not until I taste salty tears that I pull back.

Not my tears.

His.

Zander's golden eyes glitter more than usual as wet drops spill over his lids and slide down his face. They drop onto the tan skin of his chest, rolling down his stomach, soaking into the waist of his pants.

"Say it again," he rasps.

I don't hesitate. "I love you."

"I love you, too, Mae. I always will."

"Please, don't send me away," I beg.

With hurried motions, he lifts his necklace off and deposits it over my head. "Take care of this for me."

"Zander, no."

Chest convulsing with a silent sob, he places one more kiss on my mouth before quickly backing way.

"Go. Now, Maelyn." His voice doesn't even sound like his own. Half animal, half man. Shaking, he drops to the ground. On all fours, his body violently twitches as he lifts his head. Oblong black slits peer up at me. "I'm serious. Go. I don't want you to see this."

But I can't move.

I won't.

I need Zander to watch me watch him shift. I want to show him I'm not afraid.

I can't help grimacing, though. It's a gruesome sight.

Groaning, Zander's chest splits apart. I get a peek of his internal organs as his exposed ribs turn into talons. He crumples when his arms snap in dozens of places. Shards of bone break through the skin, the limbs become longer and floppy as feathers start to form.

His head cracks.

Cracks apart.

A bloody bubble fills in the space where his skull separates, as if his brain is expanding to create more flesh.

The skin of his face seems to melt, then it elongates and re-hardens as his nose and lips disappear and a beak forms.

He'd said it's painful. I didn't realize the extent of it, and now I'm horrified.

Not horrified *by* him.

Horrified *for* him.

I don't know what I was expecting. Just a magical, *Poof! Now you're a griffin*, I guess. But that's silly. Of course it wouldn't be that easy.

This makes more sense. His body is rearranging itself, becoming something inhuman, something bigger.

Covering my mouth, I gape as Zander's pants rip off. His legs are getting the same excruciating treatment as his arms, and when his boots slip from his feet, I see his toes swelling and growing fur, the nails turning into claws.

Finally, it's done.

Stretching his wings a few times, Zander huffs as he acclimates to his new form. Tears still trickle down his beak, but I doubt it's because of the physical pain.

His heart is breaking.

So is mine.

A few seconds go by as we stare at each other.

We've been face-to-face before, but this time is so different. Because he's not a mythical creature. He's my husband, and he can see me. See my tears. See the love on my face.

Wanting to comfort and reassure him, I step forward, but I stop when he lets out a menacing growl.

That rumbling sound gets louder until it's a deafening roar. A cry of agony.

Covering my ears, I cower a little. Because, crap, that's loud.

Seeming satisfied by my fear, Zander chuffs and flies away.

Landing on a rock ledge on the lower part of the mountain, he sits to witness my retreat from a distance.

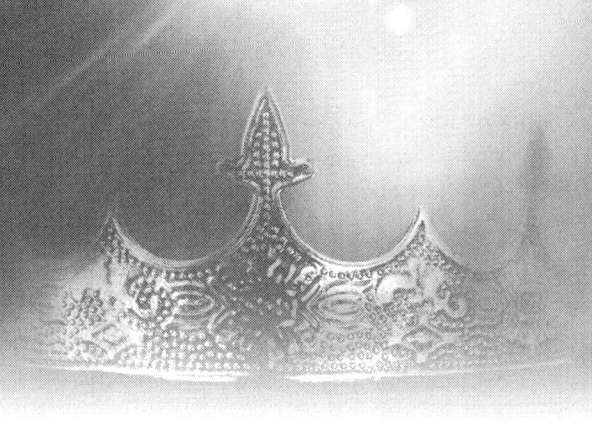

CHAPTER 40

Zander

I suppose one more secret remains. A lie by omission. I didn't tell Maelyn being separated from her would kill me. Because if I did, I know she'd have stayed by my side.

I wish I could've kissed her more. Given her a better goodbye. I tried mentally fending off the shift, but devastation pushed it to the foreground. To be honest, I'm surprised I lasted for as long as I did, and now I ache all over. Partly from shifting for the third time in less than an hour. Partly because the other half of my soul is about to be ripped from me.

It wasn't difficult to come up with a plausible way for Maelyn to die, because I could've very well killed her when the griffin took over inside the mountain. Losing control in those small tunnels was a dangerous mistake, but I couldn't help it. When I discovered the cages and the emaciated girls, knowing Maelyn had been kept there for any amount of time was more than I could bear.

I've been so selfish, so desperate to keep her, that I've been in denial about our future.

The truth is, I can't protect her here. Staying in Valora will destroy her. If Gideon doesn't get to her first, eventually someone else might.

I have too many enemies.

As long as my position as king isn't respected by all the citizens of the Day Realm, I'll be a magnet for danger.

So I'm sending Maelyn away, regardless of how destructive it will be to me and my soul.

Her heartbreak threatens to cripple my resolve as she glares at me through tear-filled eyes.

Under a tree filled with pink flowers, she's like an angel as the petals flitter down around her. An angry little angel. Fists balled tightly at her sides. Her mouth set into a frown that would rival my own.

Looking at her pain is like gazing into a mirror. My own misery is reflected back at me.

Still, I force myself to stay in place and watch her walk away from me.

A sob wracks her chest as she uncurls her fingers. The portal glows from her palm. Sparing me one more sorrowful glance, she drops it to the ground at her feet. Light shines through, illuminating her profile.

The one-way portal vanishes as soon as she steps through.

And then she's gone.

Minutes go by as I stare at the empty spot where my wife once stood. Where she begged me to keep her. Where she told me she loves me.

"Your majesty." Thayne approaches me slowly from below, as if I'm a wounded animal.

I guess I am. Out of all the pain I've experienced in my life, putting such distance between my mate and me is the worst.

"If I may have a word." Hooking his thumbs into his pockets, Thayne rocks back on his heels where he stands in the grass.

I shift back, barely feeling the pain, not even caring that I'm naked. There's no hiding how broken and vulnerable I am.

"What?" I ask, pushing myself up to a sitting position on the rock.

"Did you seriously just let Maelyn leave? You're not going after her?"

"Of course I'm going after her," I bark, revealing the part of my plan I hadn't told my men when I discussed Maelyn's departure. "As soon as I get affairs in order for the kingdom, that is."

"Yes, with your mother gone, you'll need to appoint someone to rule in your absence," Thayne states the obvious.

Kirian and Quinn might be holding down the fort right now, but they have their own kingdom of people who need their undivided attention.

What Thayne doesn't realize is, this isn't temporary.

"Arrange a tournament," I tell him, "immediately."

"W-what?" he sputters.

"I'm leaving. For good."

"You mean to tell me you're going to live in the human realm?"

"Yes."

"But—but—" My soldier is shaken. "Once your body acclimates to their world, you'll only live for seventy or so years, give or take a decade."

"I know."

"You're trading twenty-five-ish thousand years of life to go to Earth." Whether he's spelling it out for himself or me, I'm not sure, but I confirm it when I nod.

"Time is worth nothing without Maelyn. I'll go where she goes, even if it means dying sooner."

"Much sooner," Thayne emphasizes. "Damn. Maybe I don't want to find my mate after all. It makes you crazy."

Despite my grieving soul, I smile a little at how true it is. "You have no idea."

He sighs. "So that's it, then? You're really giving up the crown?"

"I was never cut out for this role."

"Yes, you are." My faithful warrior believes that with every ounce of his being, and I'm honored to have had such a man fight by my side.

"It means a lot to me that you think so. You've been a good soldier. I hope the next leader is kind to you. Hey, it could even be you."

Always humble, he chuckles. "I'm just a man with a few portals. So many others are more worthy than I."

I'm not going to argue with him because he's right. There are powerful people in this realm. It's been over a hundred thousand years since the throne was taken over by a non-royal. Since someone who wasn't born into the role was given a fair chance to win the position of king or queen.

People have probably been waiting for this day, and with so many citizens possessing fire-wielding abilities, I have a feeling the result could be interesting. According to history records, these things usually end in death for some of the contestants.

"As soon as you get back to Hailene, set up the tournament and spread the word far and wide," I order. "Any man or woman who wants to enter the challenge will be allowed to compete."

"Are you sure about this?" Thayne tries one more time, giving me an out.

I nod.

I'll stay long enough to make sure the new ruler is settled in. I'll help them hunt down Gideon. Then I'll go after my wife.

CHAPTER 41

Zander

I DECIDE TO FLY BACK TO HAILENE IN GRIFFIN FORM INSTEAD of taking the portal like all the others. I'm fiercer when I'm a monster. An exterior made of talons and claws gives me a sense of armor. Armor I need right now.

I soar for hours, high above my home so I don't frighten anyone. Weaving in and out of clouds, I survey the forests, rivers, and towns. I watch little fae children learning to fly for the first time. I see gnomes working their gardens. Wild horses run through unkempt fields.

I thought I'd feel relief at knowing the burden of kingship will no longer be my problem, but nostalgia sweeps in.

I wasn't given the chance to shine as king. I didn't have enough time to explore my own lands.

Now I never will.

Exhaustion weighs on me as I near the palace. Far below, soldiers and servants scurry about, most likely spreading the news and setting plans for the tournament.

I just want to sleep for a while, dream about being with Maelyn, and wake to a new reality where I'm no longer king and I'm free to be with my love.

As soon as my paws touch down on the stone balcony outside my room, I shift back.

I swear I can still feel Maelyn's nearness. When I enter my room, her scent hits me. My sheets smell like her. She's embedded herself here, marking every crevice and corner. My comb holds her hairs. My laundry basket is filled with her clothes. Even the quill pen elicits memories that make me hard.

Heat rushes to my cock.

My body fools me.

My veins betray my battered heart, fizzing and buzzing as if Maelyn's right next to me.

What a cruel trick.

I miss her. I miss her so much, I'm imagining things. Is the mate madness setting in already?

Heading over to the armoire, I'm about to get out some pants when I hear, "I hope you didn't let the whole kingdom see you in your birthday suit."

Slowly, I turn around, my heart thumping so hard my sternum hurts.

Yes, I've gone insane. I've heard stories of men and women who'd lost their mate, only to swear they still see them sometimes. In some cases, they've followed their hallucinations off cliffs and into the sea.

I hear the rustling of the bedsheet as Maelyn crosses her arms. "What took you so long to get here? I've been waiting for hours. Do you have any idea how difficult it is to sneak into this place? And I'm hungry, but no one knows I'm here, so no one's bringing me food. And another thing—I had to wrestle myself out of that dress on my own. Not easy to do, Zander."

Not even my crazy mind could come up with an original Maelyn ramble like that. She's actually here.

"You're not supposed to—you're supposed to—"

"Be in Texas? Uh huh. Well, you know how portals work, right? I tried to picture where I wanted to go, and you know what came up in my mind? This palace. The portal spit me out by some bushes next to the secret entrance. So it looks like you're stuck with me."

"Mae," I scold, rushing over to the door to make sure it's locked. No one can know she's here. "You defied me."

"You bet your muscular butt I did. You and I have more in common than you think. Because—like you—when I love someone, I love them with everything I have. I'm loyal. And this world? The abused trolls, the abducted women, and you... You have me. I'm in. For all of it. I don't abandon ship when things get tough." The mattress dips as she gets to her knees and lets the sheet fall away. "And now I'm in our bed, naked and horny. What are you going to do about it?"

I hear her hands move through the air before they land on her stomach. The quiet wisp of her soft fingertips trailing up her skin raises goose bumps on my own body. She palms her breasts, squeezing the flesh and plucking her nipples.

Teasing herself.

Tempting me.

Checkmate.

My cock is at attention, straining toward her. My erection throbs, sticking straight out as it bobs up and down in time with my pulse.

Happiness and anger mix with my desire. My infuriating mate. I'm at war with myself, unsure if I should fuck her, spank her, or both.

"Did anyone see you?" I grit out, resisting the urge to grab my cock and squeeze it to get some relief.

"No. I'm sure of it. You know how everyone's all, *Queen Maelyn this* and *Queen Maelyn that*? Well, like I said, they didn't bring me any food. There's no way they wouldn't feed me."

All right, I believe her. Everyone knows I'd have their head if they let my mate starve.

"You've made a very dangerous move, wife." I gave her a chance to leave, and she ran right back here. If she thinks I'll have the strength to spare her a second time, she's mistaken. "Cornering the king in a game is one thing. But in real life? You'll find yourself at my mercy."

"Good. Do your worst, husband."

Pivoting, she perches on her hands and knees, sticking her ass toward me. She wiggles her backside. She's toying with me, but she has no idea how serious this matter is.

Clenching my fists, I keep my hands at my sides as I go to the side of the bed. "You don't understand what you're asking. If we do this, the bond will solidify. You won't be able to be apart from me. You can *never leave me.*"

Her hair swishes across her back as she glances over her shoulder. "I already can't. I belong where you are."

Giving into her ploy, I grab her hips with both hands. I drag her backward until my cock pokes her ass cheek. She sucks in a breath at the feel of my hardness against her skin.

Trembling from the effort it takes to hold back, I swivel my pelvis until my tip is poised at her soaked pussy.

And it is soaked. Some of her juices collect at the underside of my cock head, and a rivulet slowly trails along my length.

"Beg," I command, my voice barely a husky whisper, because her greedy pussy lips are contracting around me, trying to suck me in. But I won't give her what she wants until she says the right words.

"Please," Maelyn whines.

"Please what?"

"I want you."

"And?" I need more than that.

"I want my husband to fuck my pretty pussy."

Good girl.

Notching myself at her entrance, I slowly push forward. Her hot flesh is silky. Pliant, yet tight. As the first couple inches of my cock are enveloped in wet warmth, I moan.

I hadn't planned on taking her like this our first time—rutting her from behind like a wild beast. Then again, Maelyn seems to enjoy my beastly ways.

Pumping gently, I encounter resistance.

Maelyn's virginity.

Mine.

Ours.

Together, we're experiencing something wonderful and new.

I drive in, pushing past the barrier, but pleasure quickly turns into pain.

Maelyn cries out and tenses.

Well, fuck. That hurts. I feel the sting of breaking through her virginity, a white-hot burn somewhere low in my belly.

"Sex doesn't normally hurt with fated mates," I grunt out, bending to cover my wife's back with my body. Wanting the closeness. Kissing between her shoulder blades.

"Of course we're the exception to that," she scoffs, strained.

It's probably the fucked-up bond, combined with the fact that she's completely human. But you know what? I'm glad.

"I'm not happy that you're hurting," I tell her, "but I'm with you. I'm sharing your pain."

"You feel it, too?"

"Yes."

"Good. Sorry," she amends. "I've just always thought it's unfair that women have to suffer when they have sex for the first time."

"I'll make it better," I reassure her, wrapping an arm around her front to find her clit.

Pleasure zings from her to me when I rub it in gentle circles, and Maelyn's inner muscles start to relax around my thickness. I'm only halfway in, but the worst part is over.

Drawing back, I gently thrust, repeating the motions several times. Inch by inch, my cock is sheathed by snug velvety walls. Once I'm all the way in, a shaky moan works its way out of Maelyn's quivering body.

The pain has faded to a dull ache, and as I toy with her clit and one of her nipples at the same time, wetness gushes onto my cock.

Pushing back against me, Maelyn whimpers, "You can move now."

"Ah, ah." I stay seated deep, earning a growl from her. She's a vicious little thing when she's horny. "What do you say?"

Rising up, Maelyn flattens her back against my front and turns her head. Cupping my jaw, she encourages a kiss, which I'm more than happy to give.

Her breath ghosts over my lips when she says, "From dawn 'til dusk, from dusk 'til dawn, I'll never love another."

The words reach into my heart and grab on. Hold tight.

Euphoria makes my head light, my stomach flutter. As if I'm free falling.

Any resentment I might've held against Maelyn for her disobedience melts away.

I've never been more grateful to someone for not listening to me. I'm still not sure how we're going to deal with her ongoing presence here—especially since she's supposed to have died in the cave—but we'll figure it out later.

Although we've already exchanged the promise once, this time it's important. This time, it counts. In a low whisper, I repeat the vow back to her.

"Now make love to me, husband. Take my soul."

There's a request I could never deny.

Putting a knee on the mattress, my cock lodged in Maelyn's pussy, I guide her forward until we both have enough room to lie down. With her stomach pressed into the mattress, I start to pump into her with slow strokes.

Moaning, she fists the pillow near her head, and I'm jealous of the fabric and fluff for having her hand. She should be holding onto me instead.

Sliding my palm under hers, I interlock our fingers.

I've waited so long for this. For love. For intimacy. Now that I've had a taste of it, I can't imagine going more than a day without it.

My sight will return soon, but for now, I rely on my other senses.

I listen to Maelyn's heady gasps every time I bottom out inside her.

Running my nose along her shoulder, I inhale her sweet scent mixed with mine.

I feel the silky glide of her pussy, igniting nerve endings from root to tip on my shaft. With her luscious ass squished beneath my pelvis, her supple tit filling my other hand, and my cock buried deep, it's like I'm dominating all her best parts.

Well, almost all of them. "Give me that pretty mouth."

As she turns her head to comply with my demand, I catch her lips in a breathless kiss.

We find a good rhythm, both with our bodies and our mouths.

We writhe together as one.

We breathe each other's air.

Cries and groans fill my room as I unintentionally speed up. The bond is urging me to fulfill its demands, and my hips start working harder. My cock goes impossibly deeper, stretching her pussy to the limit.

"Mae," I growl, unable to stop fucking her long enough to say, "you have to turn over."

"Why?" she rasps. "It feels so good like this. God, I could do this for hours."

"I'm happy to hear that, but I can't. At this point, I'd be lucky to last another five minutes. Plus, we need eye contact to break the curse."

"Okay." Maelyn wriggles against me, raising her ass and changing the angle of my thrusts. "If you want me to turn over—" she whimpers when I hit a new spot "—you're going to have to pull out of me for a second."

I groan huskily.

Easier said than done.

What she says is true, but my body has a mind of its own. While my brain tells me to slow down, the bond makes me go faster.

"On the count of three…" I drive into her with almost frantic urgency, and skin starts slapping on skin. "One."

"Two." Her hand grips mine tighter.

"Three." With all the self-control I possess, I force myself to slip out of Maelyn's tight heat long enough to flip her body over. Knocking her knees apart, I cover her body with mine and slam back into her pussy.

There's no pain this time.

Just need. The burning necessity to come.

And now her breasts are bouncing. I can feel the soft globes jiggling against the skin of my torso. I want to play with them. Squeeze them.

I will next time, when I can see the flesh bulge between my fingers.

Right now it's time to finish this.

I press a thumb to Maelyn's clit and rub it in time with my thrusts. Of course, that only doubles the sensations for me, and my balls draw up tight. My entire body tingles.

"Keep your eyes open." My lips land on hers and I speak through kisses. "You have to look into my eyes to complete the bond."

"Is it going to happen soon?"

"Yes." Flecks of light are already detonating in the ever-present darkness. "And a couple warnings." *Thrust, thrust, thrust.* "Sparks will go off in the air once our mate bond ignites. And…" Now for the part I'm dreading. "I'm going to shift after. I'm sorry, Mae."

"You're going to leave?" Her fingernails dig into my back as if she can keep me near her by holding on tight enough.

"I wish I didn't have to."

"Then don't. Just stay. Stay here with me."

"I could be shifted for hours," I warn. "Fae powers are amplified after the first coupling between fated pairs."

"I don't care," she pants. "Just want to be with you. I love you."

My wonderful mate. She doesn't realize what a gift her words are to me.

"I love you, wife." Kissing her deeply, I keep my eyes wide open while I pinch her nipple and her clit at the same time.

Several events happen in quick succession.

Light and colors appear, and when I blink down at Maelyn's face, I find her gorgeous eyes staring up at mine.

As soon as we connect, my vision is restored. Bright light and sharp lines make up flushed cheeks, swollen pink lips, and sweaty just-fucked blond hair.

I make a noise that sounds like a combination of a shout and a laugh.

Maelyn starts to smile, but her face suddenly contorts as her orgasm reaches a pinnacle. Her mouth turns into an O shape. A silent scream.

Absolute rapture floods us both as Maelyn's pussy spasms around my cock.

The tight contractions trigger my own orgasm, and a roar erupts from my throat as I spill my seed inside her. I keep pumping through it, jet after jet shooting from my cock, coating her snug walls with heat and slickness.

Finally finding her voice, Maelyn screams. Pinned under my weight, she arches and thrashes as her scream turns into sobs of pleasure.

Sparks detonate in the air around us as I rock over her a few more times, making sure she milks every drop from me.

Maelyn's eyes go wide as she watches our magical connection celebrate itself, but I barely spare it a glance. I'm too busy watching my beautiful mate.

Within seconds, the twinkling lights flicker out and die away, but I'll never forget the way they reflected in the hazel pools I love so much.

Then there's a change in my soul.

A sort of healing.

All the lies and broken promises that have darkened my insides over the years disappear.

My soul is renewed. I've been washed clean, and a child-like giddiness invades my heart. The kind of giddiness one experiences when they're unburdened by life.

Maelyn really did bring her light into my shadows.

Despite the happiness I feel, my chest begins to rattle, warning that the shift is coming. Sharp pain shoots through my sternum and I grunt, "Can you feel it?"

Maelyn's forehead wrinkles with confusion. "Feel what?"

"The shift. It might be painful for you now that we're bonded. I'm so sorry, Mae." My new eyes search her face for pinched features or distress, but I only see contentment.

Could it be? Will she escape the pain?

I send a silent plea up to the spirit of Alonius. I promise the wizard I'll never complain about my power ever again as long as it doesn't hurt Maelyn.

My wife smiles. "I don't feel anything but satisfied."

I smile back.

Thank the suns and Alonius for sparing my mate.

It must be because my power was given, not gained naturally.

And it really is a gift. One I'll never take for granted in the future.

Begging the shift to wait just a minute, I shower Maelyn's face with kisses as words of praise tumble from my lips. "You're everything to me. I love you. I'll never let you go."

She smiles and lightly scratches the stubble on my jaw as I allow my softening cock to slip from her body. "Never let me go."

It's a command I'll always obey.

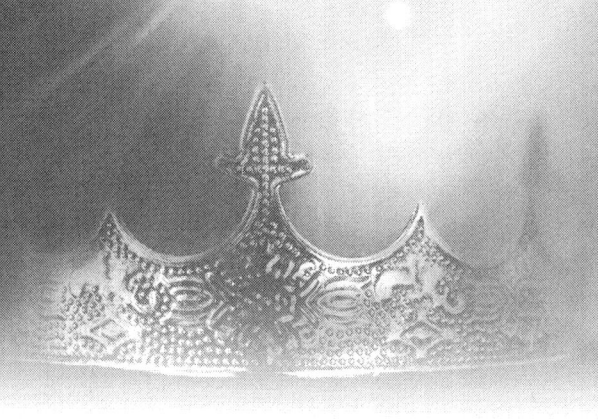

CHAPTER 42

Maelyn

Loud thuds interrupt my peaceful sleep. I burrow further under the blankets, seeking the warmth along my back. But then I feel the hard surface beneath the comforter digging into my hip bone, and for a second, I picture myself inside that cage.

My eyes pop open.

My immediate view is of Zander's bed. I relax, even though I'm looking at the footboard from the floor.

Why am I on the floor?

Oh, yeah.

After we had sex, Zander turned into a griffin. Watching the transformation the second time seemed just as painful as the first, and the poor guy must've been pooped, because as soon as the shift was complete, he collapsed in the middle of his room with a huff and started snoring. Refusing to spend time away from him, I'd grabbed the blankets and curled up next to him.

I roll over and softly touch the fur on his side. My head is cradled by his back leg and the lower half of my body is covered protectively by one of his wings.

The thudding starts up again, and I realize someone's knocking on the door.

"King Zander, we have an emergency." That sounds like Thayne.

I sit up, disturbing Zander's wing, and he instantly tenses as he wakes. Swinging his beak from left to right, he searches the room for a threat and finds none. His relieved eyes land on mine.

Wife. Love you. Love you so much.

"What?"

The words were clearly spoken, but not from Zander's mouth. I heard the thought in my head.

Cool air shocks my naked skin as I crawl over to his face. "Zander? Say something. I mean, *think* something."

He tilts his head in confusion.

Did I fuck her silly? What's she going on about?

Gasping, I cover my mouth and whisper, "Your thoughts. I understand them. You can communicate with me. Think something else."

His head swings from side to side. *That can't be.*

"It is."

More knocking. "I know you're in there, your majesty. Thaddeus witnessed you flying to your balcony and no one has seen you leave."

Sending a warning growl to our interrupter, Zander gives me a panicked look. *You can't be here.*

"Well, I am," I hiss. "Want me to hide?"

Thayne clears his throat. "Uh, if you're with a woman, I'm going to have to ask her to excuse herself while I brief you on the news."

I glare at Zander. "Can you read my thoughts, too?"

I let a string of expletives loose in my mind. Because I won't have anyone believing Zander took a random woman back to his room to nurse his heartache. No one gets to be his rebound but me.

Wait. That doesn't make sense. I can't be a rebound to myself. Whatever.

It takes me a second to realize Zander's shaking his head. *No, wife. Whatever rambling is going on in that pretty head of yours, I'm not privy to it.*

I sigh. "Can you shift back? Sounds like Thayne has something important to discuss with you."

I don't think so. I'm still riding the high from our mating.

A flood of sexy memories stains my cheeks red. "Well, then. There's only one thing to be done."

Quickly fashioning the sheet into an ill-fitting toga, I march to the door.

Maelyn, don't—

I ignore Zander as I flick the lock and turn the knob.

As soon as Thayne's eyes fall on my face, his jaw drops. "Queen Maelyn. You're supposed to be home."

"I am home," I state firmly.

Chastised, his gaze falls to a paper in his grasp. "Right. I was under the impression you were leaving Valora, but we're so glad to have you."

"We?" When I step back to let him in, I realize he's not alone. Kirian and Quinn shuffle in behind him.

In hindsight, I should've put on some clothes, but it's too late now.

Clutching the sheet tighter to my chest, I watch everyone's reactions to the griffin sitting in the middle of the room. I'm not sure what conclusions they're drawing, but they're all gaping like fish.

"He wasn't like this when we—" I cough awkwardly while waving a hand between us "When we—"

Kirian's face lights up and he looks to Zander. "You completed the bond?"

"Yes," I say at the same time Zander nods.

Letting out a triumphant shout, Kirian picks Quinn up by the waist and swings her around while laughing. An unstoppable smile spreads over my face at the sheer happiness Kirian has for Zander's success. He's a true ally.

His face sobers as he sets his wife down. "Zander, why did you give up your kingdom? You should've consulted with me first."

It's not like Zander can answer him, but this is news to me. "Give up your kingdom?" I ask him. "What's he talking about?"

In a silent exchange, Zander explains his decision to give up the crown in order to be with me. He describes the tournament, and how the wheels have already been set into motion.

I forgot about it as soon as I realized you were here. Besides, word was already spreading. It was too late. Will you still love me when I'm not a king and you're not a queen?

Touched, yet still sad at the same time, I walk over to him and press a hand to the side of his face. "I'll always love you no matter what. Are you sure this is what you want?"

He nuzzles my palm. *It's for the best. We don't have to go to the Earth realm if you don't want to. We can live in the Night Realm with Kirian and Quinn.*

If thoughts can sound sad, his do.

The Day Realm is his home and, despite what he thinks, he's an awesome king.

Noting the time stretching between us, Kirian's finger goes back and forth from Zander to me. "Are you two speaking to each other right now?"

Not knowing if this is a secret we should keep under wraps, I look to Zander and raise a questioning brow.

Tell them. I can trust these three.

"Apparently, Zander can talk to me, mentally, when he's in this form. I don't know if that will be the case once he shifts back. This is all new."

"Quite handy," Kirian remarks. "You can be our translator of sorts then. We've got urgent matters." He gestures to Thayne, and the warrior grimaces as his eyes fall to the paper again.

"The sprites we sent out this morning went far and wide to collect submissions for the challenge. There are three. First up, Marek."

A string of satisfied feelings come from Zander, and I'm a bit taken aback that I can sense his emotions. "You like that idea?"

Marek will be a great ruler, and he has a good chance of victory. His power will be hard to beat when he can cripple his opponent within seconds.

I nod and glance at Thayne. "Who else?"

"Nikita, a Pyro from Olphene."

Her power must have some oomph if she thinks she can win, Zander muses.

"The last entrant." Swallowing thickly, Thayne pauses. "Your majesty, we didn't anticipate this outcome. It's been so long since a tournament has happened, we forgot about a loophole—"

Out with it. Zander growls low, and the sound is enough to convey his message.

"Gideon, wizard from Azerdeen." Thayne blows out a defeated breath.

"Gideon's coming here?" The blood drains from my face as I stumble backward. Zander's big body is there to catch me, but I'm trembling. "Well, that's good, right? You can arrest him."

"No, Queen Maelyn," Thayne says regretfully. "He must be allowed to compete."

"Why?" I question passionately. "How can he be a part of this when he's a wanted fugitive?"

Thayne's expression is bleak, clearly just as troubled as I am, but Kirian speaks up, "Anyone with outstanding warrants or crimes has immunity once they've entered into a challenge for the crown."

"That's—that's bullshit!" I exclaim.

"I agree." Kirian rubs his temple. "Like Thayne said, it's been so long since an official tournament has been held, the rules and loopholes aren't well-known. If Gideon loses, he can be arrested or executed on the spot."

I'm still shaking. "And if he wins?"

All the faces around me darken.

Then he'll be the new king.

Horrified, I turn to my husband. "No, Zander."

Yes.

"We can't let that happen."

It's out of our hands.

"But he's going to win!" I'm in full-blown panic mode. "You've seen how powerful he is."

Then we won't stay. We'll go to Texas and live our lives where you're the happiest.

"I'm happiest where you are," I whisper. "And you love this world. You care about your people. How could you leave them with a sadistic asshole like Gideon?"

Brief shame blankets Zander's eyes. *I'm a selfish man. I would damn everything and everyone if it meant I could be with you.*

As flattering as that is, I can't accept this. Synda, Tabitha, and all the other trolls. The human girls who've made a life here. Zander's loyal soldiers.

They'll all be headed for a life of misery when Gideon is king.

Unless...

"Zander." I pat him excitedly. "Are you allowed to enter?"

He cocks his head, but Kirian answers before Zander can.

"Yes, he is." With a growing smile, Kirian paces around aimlessly. "Brilliant idea, Maelyn. Zander, you can take back your position as king. And since you just mated, you'll be stronger."

"When is this tournament?" I ask to no one in particular.

"Dusk." Gazing out the windows, Kirian seems to be judging the time when he elaborates, "In about two hours."

My worried eyes bounce to Zander.

"What do you think?" I don't give him time to respond because a thought comes to me. "When you're in griffin form, you're immune to magic, right?" Squeezing his beak in my hands, my words come out in a rush, "You're the only one who can beat Gideon. He can't touch you with his tricks and he'll be forced to fight you with physical combat. Plus, he isn't expecting you to be his opponent. You'll have the element of surprise."

Kirian chuckles as he rejoins Quinn's side. "I like the way you think, Maelyn. You're right about all of it."

Zander's eyes bore into mine. *You want this? For me to be king? You want to be my queen?*

I nod. "More than anything."

Zander's happiness leaks into me. *Then I'll do it. Tell them to add me to the roster.*

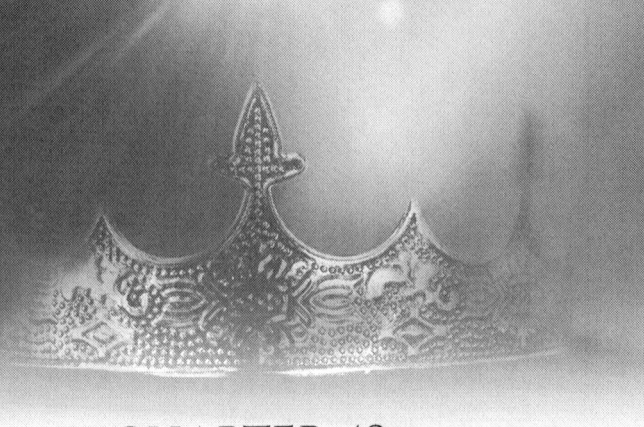

CHAPTER 43

Zander

MY IMPULSIVE DECISION TO LEAVE THIS WORLD HAS become one of my favorite mistakes. Because after tonight—after I win—my legitimacy as king won't be in question ever again. I won't be viewed as a weak leader. A half-human abomination.

I'll have respect. My power will be earned. Most importantly, my victory will ensure Maelyn's safety.

Gideon won't be shown any mercy when I'm up against him. He won't leave here alive. Tonight, he dies at my hand. Or, in this case, my talons, my claws, or my beak. I'll happily rip him to shreds.

As I stalk through one of the stone tunnels leading to the execution courtyard, I hear the cheers from the stands. People have flocked from all over to witness the epic showdown.

Still holding the position of current king, I'm one of the only people who've seen the tournament lineup. Luck of the draw put me against Marek first. I don't want to hurt him. I'm sure he doesn't wish me harm either, which will make for an interesting match.

Light from the end of the tunnel becomes almost blinding as I step out of the shadows. In the distance, someone announces me, and the noise from the crowd turns into a combination of deafening cheers, gasps, and a few boos.

No one expects me to enter my own challenge.

Especially not my opponents. They're already emerging from their own tunnels, and the shock on their faces would be funny if they weren't realizing their lives are in imminent danger.

Anger plays over Gideon's face. Flared nostrils. Bared teeth. Narrowed eyes in my direction.

I remember the words his father told mine the day he cast the spell—that I would be the most powerful man in the Day Realm. I never believed it. Thought it was an analogy or maybe the wizard was trying to sell my father on a lie.

But now I wonder if what he said is true. And if, at the time, he knew someday his son and I would go head-to-head.

The scent of fear wafts from the spectators. Most citizens aren't used to seeing me in griffin form. Not up close. They might get a fleeting glimpse of me when I'm flying, but now I'm in their faces—just a leaping distance away from severing their heads from their bodies, like I did to my father.

I spare a glance at the top row on my right where the special box for royalty sits. Maelyn's there with Quinn and Kirian at her side, the ruffly periwinkle canopy shading them from the suns.

My wife is beautiful in a light pink gown she borrowed from my mother's wardrobe. People keep casting glances her way, and it's not just because she's gorgeous. They're realizing the death rumor was false, and now they're wondering if she'll remain their new queen. Wondering if I'll win.

I love you. I can do this.

Maelyn gives me a subtle nod, and the pride on her face makes me feel invincible. I never knew someone could build me up with a single look. The confidence my mate displays fascinates me.

She believes in me.

If only my mother could see me now. I know she'd be wearing

the same expression of wonder and admiration. A tinge of melancholy twists my heart. I wish she were here to watch me take back what's always belonged to me, but she's choosing herself for the first time in her life. As much as I don't want to, I have to respect her decision.

The announcer blows a horn, signaling everyone to be quiet while he states the terms of the tournament.

Zero rules. Anything goes. No trick is considered too dirty, no weapon too dangerous, including magic. Mental and physical warfare knows no bounds in this arena. We're allowed to take the fight elsewhere—to the sky or the pastures around us—but only for one minute. If sixty seconds passes before one of us returns, it's considered a forfeit. The crowd can cheer and make noise, but they can't interfere by using their own powers.

On instruction, Marek and I meet in the middle. My claws scrape over the stone. Stone that's been soaked with blood over the years. I can tell someone tried to wash this place today, tried to scrub away the rust-colored stains. Still, red remains in all the cracks and crevices.

Warbling from the horn sounds again.

The first challenge begins.

Marek knows his power won't work on me while I'm shifted, so I'm curious to see what strategy he adopts instead.

Weapons are strapped to him in various places. An ax on his belt. A dagger in his boot.

He removes the long sword from his back. Grabbing the hilt, he raises it up above his white-blond mohawk before lowering it. Slowly, he holds the blade horizontally across his chest, cradled in his palms.

Dipping his head, he drops to a knee and lays the sword down. "I will not fight against my one true king. I forfeit. King Zander forever, until the suns no longer burn!"

Cries of outrage and whoops of joy erupt from the crowd. Some are probably upset that there won't be bloodshed between us. Others are relieved because they actually want me to win, which is astonishing to me.

Maybe I've got more supporters than I thought.

I nod at Marek, and the announcer has no other choice than to declare me the victor of this round.

I wouldn't have blamed Marek for challenging me, for wanting to better his life, for wanting to gain power.

But I'm beyond grateful for his loyalty.

Someone's getting a promotion.

Nikita and Gideon are next.

As Marek climbs the steps to take his seat on the first row, I sit somewhere off to the side in the arena. I'm not about to try to sit my big ass on the stone benches lining the circular stadium. My weight would likely crack it.

Opening with a strong foot forward, Nikita tries to set Gideon on fire with her eyes.

Tries being the operative word. The stones at his feet start to smolder, yet he remains untouched by the heat.

He must have a protection spell in place.

Displaying the true extent of her power, she erects a wall of fire around Gideon, caging him in with fifteen-foot flames.

He smiles, throws down a portal, and walks right out.

Next, Nikita hurls a giant fireball. Instead of simply ducking or stepping out of the way, Gideon vanishes through another portal and comes out behind her. With a twist of his hands, he changes the direction of the flaming orb. It gets sucked backward before Nikita even realizes where Gideon is.

Since she can't be harmed by her own power, the fire doesn't burn her when it hits her square in the face, but it does disorient her for a second. Long enough for Gideon to cast a spell.

Shouting with alarm, Nikita starts frantically scraping at her bare arms. The rest of her is covered in cream-colored canvas pants and a vest, but she slaps at her exposed skin and swats at her blond hair.

It dawns on me. An illusion. Gideon's distracting her with something she fears—something that's not really there—while he brandishes a long, serrated knife.

He comes up behind her, clearly intending to slash her throat. Maybe take off her entire head.

Nikita twirls out of the way, avoiding a blade to the neck. Instead, the sharp tip slices over her upper chest, and blood immediately soaks her clothing.

Snarling, she removes a sword from her belt. She and Gideon begin slowly circling each other. Getting a few good swipes, Nikita causes some deep gashes on Gideon's arms and one on his torso.

Why is he letting her get so close?

He's planning something, using himself as bait. There's a glazed look in his eyes as he drags his boots with measured footsteps in a perfect ring.

Suddenly, he portals himself to one end of the arena and, with a snap of his fingers, an electrical forcefield appears around Nikita.

Her screams of pain are loud and echoing as she crumples to the ground under the dome. Not giving up, she flails while trying to shoot some more fire from her hands. Every flame she lets loose dies as soon as it touches the torturous forcefield around her.

Between screams, she manages to yell, "I'm done! Forfeit!"

The announcer has now become the referee as well. When he calls the fight, naming Gideon as the winner, the forcefield stays up way longer than it should.

"Turn it off." The man blows the horn like a warning bell. "I'm serious, Gideon. You'll be disqualified if you don't stop."

My eyes go to Gideon's face. He's not even paying attention to what's being said. With a sadistic grin on his face, he revels in his opponent's pain. Watches the way she writhes and cries.

The horn sounds again. "Disqualifying Gideon, Wizard of Azerdeen in three, two—"

"All right." The forcefield drops, along with Nikita's hair-raising screams, and Gideon lifts his hands in surrender. "I stopped."

Bastard.

The crowd is quieter now. Exchanging worried glances and whispered words, they look at Gideon with concern and fear.

Most Day Realm citizens like to stay oblivious to political conflict—it's natural for faeries to be self-absorbed—but they're not dumb.

They recognize danger when they see it. In this moment, they're realizing what it could be like living under Gideon's iron fist, so to speak. He'll crush anyone who gets in his way, and he'll enjoy doing it.

Guess I'm not looking so bad now, am I?

Marek takes it upon himself to jump down and help Nikita make it to the stands. Thanks to Gideon's house of horrors, he knows what it feels like to be trapped in that particular hell.

Now it's my turn to face off with Gideon.

Time to end this once and for all.

I barely hear the speaker say our names to officiate our round. Gideon's a dead man walking, and all my focus is on him. Tuning out Maelyn's ramped-up nerves is difficult, but I manage.

Gideon must not have the power of healing, because his cuts are still bleeding. I watch the way the red soaks his white tank top and how the dark rivers drip from the hands hanging casually at his sides.

He's still holding his knife, and his eyes dart around my body, likely assessing my weak points.

I can't let him get to my wings or my hind legs. With my feathers already damaged from the fire, losing delicate bone structures would definitely hinder my ability to fly for quite some time.

Just for intimidation, I snap my beak forward and roar. Gideon's hair blows back from the force of it. Leaping at me, his blade arcs through the air. I avoid it by ducking and swiping one of my talons across the back of his calf. The sharp claw rips through his pants and makes a deep cut in his muscle.

Rolling, Gideon gets out of my reach and disappears into another portal.

Assuming he's going to come out behind me, I swiftly turn.

Like I guessed, he appears about fifteen feet away. What I didn't expect, though, is for him to come back with a spear, and a bow and arrow. He must've had the weapons stashed somewhere.

I have to admit it's not a bad play. Smart and fair. He thought ahead, and he's not breaking any rules.

Obviously, he can't get close enough to use a knife or sword without the risk of losing a limb or his head. Shooting me might be his only chance.

With a battle cry, he throws the spear. I dodge to the left, and it narrowly misses my wing, ruffling the feathers as it skims by.

I don't have time to recover from the close call before Gideon nocks an arrow and sends it my way. He's good with the weapon, fast and aiming well.

I jump out of the way of the first two, but the third gets me in the shoulder.

It hurts.

And I'm livid. Not because he injured me, but because I heard Maelyn's faint cry when the arrow pierced my skin and embedded into muscle. We're bonded now. I'm thankful she doesn't hurt when I shift, but I know she felt that because the pain echoed back at me.

Gideon unloads his arsenal. The last arrow slices my side, but it's a shallow cut.

He rolls backward into another portal.

That fucker. When he reappears at my side, he's wielding a leather-wrapped handle with a spiked ball dangling from a long chain. Whipping it around in the air a few times, he launches it at me.

I duck and catch the chain with my beak. Giving it a hard yank, I pull Gideon toward me.

Adrenaline forces his wings out, and he releases his hold on the weapon as he stumbles back.

Coming at him hard, I tuck my wings close to my body while charging forward. When he realizes he's in danger of being cornered, he takes flight.

I follow.

Jumping to the sky, I snap at his feet and get his boot. I spit the rubber and leather out, letting it fall to the arena below.

Raucous laughter spreads through the crowd.

I'm making a fool of Gideon. He yells with outrage and embarrassment.

A chase ensues in the sky. We're getting nowhere with the fight—just tiring each other out—but that's fine.

I can tell Gideon's trying to use his magic on me. I feel the mystical waves coming at me and bouncing off my body. Shouting out his frustration, he flies through another portal among the clouds.

Flapping my wings, I hover in place as I wait for him to reappear. When he does, he wears a sinister smile as he holds up two glass bottles.

Blaze and stardust.

He glances at the arena full of people below, and his intent hits me with a bolt of terror as he loosens his hold on the containers.

If he drops them together, it'll destroy the amphitheater while killing many.

Maelyn certainly wouldn't survive it.

The bastard laughs as the bottles slip from his fingers.

Diving, I head for the ground and catch the Blaze with my beak just ten feet from the stone floor of the arena. Snatching the stardust with a talon, I pull up at the last second, swooping low to the ground while planning to take the dangerous substances somewhere else. Somewhere far away from each other.

They can be recovered later.

Landing in a field, I start digging with my back paws. Large chunks of dirt kick up, and I spit the Blaze there before covering it. I sprint to another field to bury the stardust in the same way.

By the time I'm flying back to the arena, I hear the announcer counting down my absence.

Fuck.

Gideon's a coward for trying to get me disqualified.

With five seconds to spare, I free-fall.

I go straight for his smug face, planning to crush him, even if it means being impaled by his knife. His smirk drops when he realizes my intent, and his weapon clatters to the ground while he fumbles in his pocket for another portal.

Just as I take a bite out of his shoulder, he vanishes.

I spit his blood and flesh to the stone.

When he rejoins the fight twenty feet away, his quiver has been refilled, but his grip on the bow is shaky. His aim is poor, and the arrow doesn't travel more than fifty feet before skidding to the ground. The chunk of muscle I removed from his arm makes it difficult to hold up any weapon.

The ache in my own injury is increasing with every movement. I want to reach over and rip the arrow out, but that would mean looking away from Gideon. I can't afford to do that.

"You can do it, Zander!" Maelyn shouts. "Beat him."

With the unique setting of my bird eyes, I can see her standing up, her knuckles white from clenching her fists, her face etched with worry.

It'll be all right, I tell her. *I've got this.*

"Don't you worry, pretty bird," Gideon taunts. "You can be my queen after this is done. You'll sing for me every morning."

Instead of rage, his taunt has the opposite effect.

A sense of peace infiltrates my body.

His words are wishful thinking.

Maelyn is my queen, and she'll sing for me, but only if she wants to. I've never requested a performance from her, and there's a reason for that. I don't want to remind her of the day she was on the auction block. Her infinite value is the sum of all her parts, not just her body and her voice.

Limping toward me, Gideon swipes his knife through the air, missing me each time I jump back.

The crowd is silent now. They know their own future is on the line, and they watch with bated breath.

The next time Gideon slashes his knife through the air, I lean into it. He doesn't expect that. Catching the blade in my beak, I rip it from his hands and fling it away.

He shouts with agony, and I realize I took off his thumb in the process.

Good.

Next, I snap at his abdomen. His shirt rips while blood drips from the new wound I inflicted. The slash is deep, and I see layers of muscle exposed.

I come at him a few more times, ripping his clothing to shreds while making new cuts.

I'm toying with him. Like the animal I am, I'm basically playing with my food. I could end him now, but I'd rather continue humiliating him instead.

He jumps through another portal, but when he comes through the opening twenty feet away, he lands on his hands and knees. Weakened. Broken.

For the first time, I see real fear and defeat in Gideon's eyes.

"Okay." Finally admitting he's fighting a losing battle, he holds one of his hands out while pressing the other to the worst injury across his middle. "I'm done. Forfeit."

Gideon doesn't even see the men coming up behind him with the iron net. I'd ordered Thayne and Torius to make sure Gideon doesn't leave after my triumph.

A cheerful victory tune toots from the horn before the announcer says, "Ladies and gentlemen, I give you King Zander, ruler of the Day Realm."

The stadium erupts with cheers, and I don't hear one boo among my people.

My people.

I've earned my place as king.

Wrapped in iron from head to toe, Gideon grimaces as he's shoved down, face smashed against the stone.

"You can't kill me," he claims, seeming oblivious to the fact that I absolutely can.

"Why's that?" Thayne asks while digging a boot between his shoulder blades.

"Because I'm part of the tournament."

"*Were*," my soldier emphasizes. "You *were* part of it. You're not anymore because it's over. Your immunity ended the second you lost, and now you have to answer for your crimes against the Day Realm." Unrolling a scroll, Thayne quiets the audience with a sharp look. "Gideon of Azerdeen is hereby charged with human trafficking, fae female trafficking, and illegal Glow and Blaze production and distribution. How do you plead?"

"Not guilty." Pain from the lie causes his eyes to narrow, but otherwise he shows no sign of deceit.

"He's lying," Quinn pipes up from the stands. "Like, majorly lying."

No one questions her word, and hundreds of accusing eyes damn the man at our feet with quiet, seething judgement.

Now that my energy is spent, I feel the urge to shift back, but I'm not sure if I should.

I'd imagined when I defeated Gideon, it would be done the same way I killed my father. The monster in me wants to taste his blood when I rip his head from his body.

It's not exactly a standard execution around here, but it would send a clear message—don't fuck with me, my kingdom, or my wife.

Maelyn must be able to read my conflicted thoughts, because she starts climbing down through the stands. "Excuse me. Coming through. Zander!"

People part for her, some graciously offering their hands as she makes her way to the half-wall at the bottom.

I come over to her, and she immediately places her palms on either side of my beak while resting her forehead between my eyes. "You did it. I knew you would."

What should I do now?

She pulls back to look at me with seriousness. "Kill him."

How? There are many ways to get the job done. This is your justice, my queen.

"And this is your victory. Do what you want."

Will you fear me after?

"I might've been scared of you at one time, but not anymore. Not ever again."

In my peripheral vision, I can see people gaping at us. They're shocked by the picture in front of them. Me, a beast covered in my opponent's blood. And Maelyn, a petite, beautiful woman touching me as if she loves me.

Because she does.

Tell them to clear the net away from Gideon's head, I communicate to Maelyn, and she reiterates my wishes to Thayne.

Wire cutters snap through the netting while Gideon pleads for his life, but all his blubbering falls on deaf ears.

Did he listen to all the women he's brutalized? When they cried, did he show mercy?

No.

So he'll get the same treatment from me.

Although he doesn't deserve a quick death, I want this done with. Without pause, I prowl over to him. I open my beak wide, turn my head to the side, and let his neck slide into my mouth.

He screams.

Then I bite down, silencing him once and for all.

The crowd goes wild.

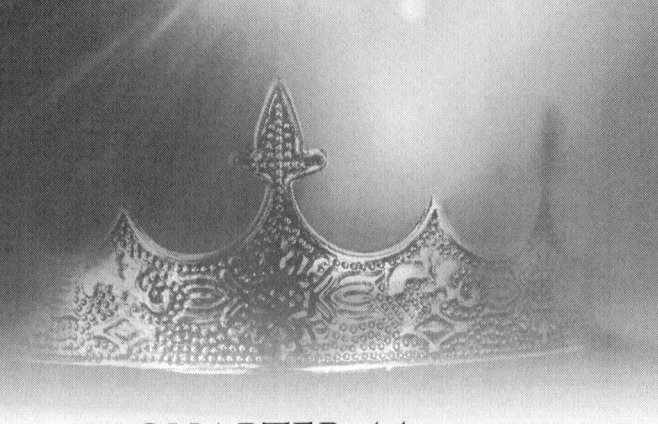

CHAPTER 44

Maelyn

I MOAN AS ZANDER FILLS ME UP FROM BEHIND, PEPPERING my shoulder with slow kisses to match the leisurely pace he's set with his cock.

The morning birds have stopped singing. Our breakfast has gotten cold on Zander's desk.

Which means I need to take a shower, find a dress, and tame my hair.

"We have to hurry." With my side pressed to the mattress, I wiggle my hips and try to force Zander to speed up.

"No." He runs a hand down my thigh as he continues his torturously slow thrusts.

"Let me come," I request breathlessly.

"Not yet."

Frustrated, I whimper.

I suspect Zander's prolonging it because he doesn't want to shift afterward, but I'm burning from the inside out. We're sweaty. My flyaway hairs are plastered to my forehead and neck, and Zander's slick skin is sticking to my back.

Every time he slowly pulls out of me, I can feel every ridge of his smooth cock dragging over my sensitive walls. My inner thighs are soaked, and I'm pretty sure there's a wet spot on the bed.

We've been going at it for at least an hour.

Turns out, I can't read Zander's mind when he's not in griffin form. While I'm kind of glad about that—because I don't want to be aware of his every thought—I am curious about why he's okay with being late for a very important meeting.

After the tournament last night, Zander shifted back, and Marek healed his injuries. Then, while he had the attention of so many citizens, the honored king gave a speech about unity and loyalty, tacking on a promise to do right by his people in return for their cooperation. Everyone needs to work together if we want to repair the kingdom. He told them about my plans to set up hospitals and wellness centers in other cities of the realm, and when one man suggested law enforcement being implemented as well, Zander was open to the idea and invited him to lunch at the palace to discuss details.

Before we knew it, people were coming forward, offering to be part of a royal counsel. With Ro gone, a spot needed to be filled, and I had ideas for new roles to add.

After all, Zander can't police an entire kingdom by himself.

With the help of Quinn's internal lie detector, we were able to gather a group of ten people from different areas of the realm who have truly good intentions. Since Carielle is still indisposed in the dungeon, Zephina took on the temporary job of planning the official luncheon where we'll nail down definite plans.

That is, if we actually make it there.

My hand snakes down to touch my clit.

Zander catches my wrist. "That's my job."

"Then do it," I hiss before begging, "Please, husband. Please, please."

That does the trick.

With a groan, Zander cups my mound and circles my throbbing bud while thrusting faster. I spread wider for him, hooking my leg over his.

His lips latch onto the side of my neck, and the coil of need winding in my lower belly finally breaks.

I cry out, having been denied my orgasm for far too long. My pussy clenches around Zander's cock so hard it almost forces him from my body, but he won't let our connection end until it absolutely has to. Gripping my hips, he slams into me, rooting his cock deep as it jerks and fills me with warmth.

Grunting, Zander's harsh breaths puff against my skin as he covers my shoulder with more kisses.

A desperate apology.

I know he feels bad that he has to put distance between us after sex to allow the shift.

So when his dick stays planted inside me for at least a minute, I glance at him over my shoulder. "Zander?"

His eyes roam my face as a huge smile appears on his. "I'm not going to shift."

"What?" I try to turn over, but that would cause Zander to slip out of me, and apparently, he doesn't want that.

He pins an arm across my middle, holding me in place. "I can tell when it's going to happen. It's not," he says, punctuating his statement with another thrust.

"How? Why?"

"Maybe it's because we fulfilled the bond. Maybe it's because my soul is content. You make me settled. Stable. I feel more in control since we've become one," he says, gazing down at me with love. "Whatever the reason, we can continue, my beautiful mate."

"No, we can't." I try to scramble away, but Zander won't let me go.

My body lights up again when he pulls my hips down while pumping his up. With his release coating my insides, I'm extra slippery down there, and it feels amazing.

He grabs my breast and plucks my nipple.

Arching, I surrender. Plans will have to wait.

I love watching Zander's face now that he can see. After a fifteen-second visual inspection of his bread roll—as if knowing what it looks like will make it taste different somehow—he takes a hefty bite. His cheeks puff out as he chews, and he pokes the inner texture of the bread.

It's adorable.

Since we completed the bond, his smiles come more easily. When he catches me watching him, his lips curl up and love shines from his eyes.

For the counsel meeting, we opted for the dining room instead of the tactics room. Nothing we're going to say is top secret. Soon, the newly assigned roles for Zander's team will be publicly announced.

Trays of mini-sandwiches and other finger foods are spread out around us on the long table. A delicious squash soup was served first, then the staff brought out a spread of savory and sweet appetizers.

"With Maelyn's assistance in the dorms, I think I'll have time to plan all the palace events," Zephina offers, waving her hand around. "I enjoyed putting this together, and it's not like you have many parties anyway."

Zander looks to me for my opinion, and I nod enthusiastically. "I bet if you asked the human girls to volunteer for a party committee, they'd be thrilled."

The beautiful blonde beams at me. "That's a wonderful idea. Yes, we should include them."

"And now that you're officially the event coordinator, I have your first assignment." I smile shyly. "That is, if you're up for it."

"What is it?" Zephina curiously tilts her head as she glances down at a calendar. "It says we're open until the winter solstice."

"A wedding." I look to Zander and hold his glittering eyes. "Our wedding. The sooner the better."

He grins as Zephina starts marking down possible days.

Yes, Zander and I are already married. But I want a real

wedding this time. One with a beautiful dress, flowers, friends… and the knowledge that it's actually happening. That last part is sort of important.

Pippin raises a hand. "I can be the queen's official bodyguard. It'd be a good idea for her to have someone with her when she leaves the palace."

Zander narrows his eyes. "Are you sure that's not just a ploy to get back into the ladies' dorms?"

Innocence blankets Pippin's face while he presses his palm to his chest as if he's wounded by the accusation. "Your majesty, my concern for the queen trumps all else. Besides, you haven't lifted my celibacy order." He pauses. "Are you going to lift it?"

"No."

The young soldier's hopeful expression falls so quickly it's almost comical.

"Next," Zander moves on, "Thayne and Marek will both be the head of my guard now. Marek, that means you'll get a room in the palace instead of staying in the barracks."

"Thank you, your majesty." The man grins proudly.

"Then there's the matter of Queen Ro," Zander says solemnly. "I need someone to go to the Earth realm to make sure she's all right. I don't want her brought back against her will. I just need to know she's okay."

Torius stands. "I'll do it."

Zander spears him with a serious look. "You realize you'll likely be gone for many years. It could take you two weeks to find my mother. That's fourteen years. By the time you get back, so much will have changed."

"I'm aware." From his quick response and twitchy fingers, I'd almost say Torius can't wait to get away from here. His shoulders sag with relief when Zander grants his request, confirming what I already suspect—he doesn't want to be in Valora anymore.

Maybe the turmoil has been too much for the warrior. He might seem tough on the outside with his tattoos and long dark hair, but all Zander's soldiers have seen unimaginable tragedies in this kingdom.

Kai didn't even want to come to the meeting. The rough-looking man is an enigma. He seems to truly enjoy his role as a soldier, but he refuses to step foot inside the castle. In fact, palace grounds seem to be a place he avoids regularly. He always requests to be stationed outside of the walls. Zander told me when he was a child, his father punished Kai for something. Punished him brutally before banishing him from the Day Realm all together. And I wonder if that's where all the scars came from.

"I'd like to discuss the prisoners." Thaddeus, the new warden-slash-executioner, sets his sandwich aside. "The dungeon is mighty crowded these days."

"Yes." Zander frowns, and I'm glad he hasn't lost all his surliness because if I'm being honest, he's hot when he's broody. "You and I will meet tomorrow morning to decide their fates."

"I assume the snatchers and anyone charged with treason will be executed. Should we make it a public event?"

"I think it would be wise. We need everyone to know those crimes won't be tolerated."

Public executions. I don't think I have the stomach for it. I know Zander's right, but that doesn't mean I want to see it happen.

Swallowing my food too soon, the bread goes down like a rock in my esophagus. "Is Carielle included in that group?"

My husband puts his hand over mine. "She tried to poison you and my mother."

"I know, but—"

"If we show her mercy, it will invite others to do the same."

"She was victimized, Zander."

"I won't excuse her behavior."

"I won't either. I'm just saying, she didn't choose to be here. If her life hadn't been taken from her, she'd never even know about this place. I believe she did what she had to do to survive, and it made her into the person she is today."

Heads swing back and forth as everyone observes our exchange. From the wide eyes and slack-jaws, I'd say no one argues with Zander. Ever.

I won't always interfere with Zander's decisions, but I can't let Carielle be killed. It wouldn't be right.

"Send her back to the Earth realm," I propose. "That will be punishment enough, and she won't be a threat anymore."

"Banishment from Valora." Slowly, Zander nods. "All right, my queen. If that's what you want."

"It is." A little heaviness leaves my chest. "I just want her gone, not dead."

The discussion moves along to the new sheriffs of Olphene and Azerdeen. They've each got a second in command to switch shifts with—one of whom is Nikita—and they sound excited about being part of the Day Realm crime control. They'll be the eyes and ears in those parts for any distilleries or auctions that pop up, which means Zander can be here more.

As the Day Realm citizens would say, thank the suns.

I'll go anywhere with Zander, but I don't want to be out on the road all the time, especially once we start a family. My hand slips to my lower belly, cupping the place where I'll grow our children someday.

Not too long ago, kids were the last thing on my mind.

But I want them.

I want babies with Zander.

He's told me it could take a while—years—to conceive. Knowing how rare pregnancy is here just makes me want it more, but I have to be patient and trust fate.

"Counsel meetings will be once a month," Zander says as he wraps up the meeting. "The sheriffs can alternate turns coming here, and I'll have suites ready for your stay."

With words of respect and pledges of loyalty, our guests file out. Zephina engulfs me in a hug, and we make plans to visit the dorms in two days. I thank the staff for a great meal as they clear away the dishes, and then it's just my husband and me.

"What now?" I ask him as we stand by a window facing the garden.

He runs a seductive finger down my throat. "I'd like to play a game with my wife."

I idly toy with the king on my necklace. "Chess?"

His head rocks back and forth as he mulls it over. "I was thinking hide-and-seek."

I almost shiver from the thrill of being chased by him. "Inside or outside the palace?"

"Inside. I'm not quite ready to send you into the maze just yet, even if it is safe."

Poor Zander. I think he's more traumatized by my abduction than I am. He loves me so fiercely.

I start backing away. A smile lifts my lips, and Zander gives an answering grin as I say, "Cover your eyes and count to sixty."

"One, two, three…" The numbers are definitely coming out way faster than they should, cutting my time in half.

Holding in a squeal, I dart for an entrance to a hidden passage behind a tapestry. I'm a hundred percent certain Zander hears the panel sliding back. In fact, I'm counting on it.

When he finds me, he's *so* getting laid.

CHAPTER 45

Six Months Later
Zander

"Hey, Mom," Maelyn says into the device we picked up from a place with headache-inducing lights and electronic frequencies.

A cell phone store, she'd called it.

She already talked to her dad, and now we're standing outside a three-story apartment complex. The exterior is a combination of red brick and white plastic. Colorful automobiles line the parking lot. Heat from the early evening summer Texas sun rivals that of the Day Realm, but I study the air conditioning contraptions set into the windows of each apartment. According to Maelyn, the second one from the bottom is hers.

"Yeah," she says. "I'm fine. I just felt like calling. I guess I miss you."

Her mom laughs, and I can hear her words clearly when she says, "I just saw you yesterday at dinner."

"Right. Well, it feels like longer than that. I've had one heck of a day."

"Are you all right?" Her mom's jovial tone turns to one of concern.

"I'm great," Maelyn responds honestly while she absentmindedly rubs the roundness of her belly.

Yeah, we didn't need to worry about her getting pregnant for long. A few weeks after the first time we had sex, Maelyn realized she'd missed her monthly cycle. She'd laughed and said I knocked her up on the first try.

Fuck yes, I did. I'm anxious for her to have the baby just so I can do it again. I don't know how many children we'll have, but I think our chances are better while she's still fully human.

Even after six months in Valora, Maelyn's ears haven't sprouted yet. She's a little self-conscious about that, but we expected her to take longer to turn fae. Besides, she's perfect just the way she is.

And Valora loves her. Our people have dubbed her the Queen of Kindness, and she takes pride in that. She's worked hard for it.

Thanks to her, our kingdom is healing faster. The broken human women respond well to her, and the wellness centers have been a success. Many of the women and trolls who were former victims have moved to the hospitals as workers. Helping gives them a sense of purpose.

We've only had to break up one auction and two distilleries since I regained power over my kingdom. Seems beating Gideon was an effective warning.

"Dinner on Friday?" Maelyn parrots, looking to me for confirmation, and I give her a nod.

Technically, it's still the same day she was kidnapped here in the Earth realm. It's Saturday, so it'll be six years before we have that dinner with her mom, but it'll be something we can both look forward to.

Maelyn's happy smile nearly knocks the breath from my lungs as she continues speaking into the black rectangle. "Yeah, of course. And I have someone I want you to meet. Yeah, I finally met someone and he's great. It is serious." Her mom squeals excitedly, and Maelyn winces from how loud it is. Then she laughs. "I'm going to let you go. Paige is probably awake by now, and I want to see what she's up to tonight. Okay. I love you, too. Bye."

As Maelyn lowers the phone, I give her a smile. "You ready to do this?"

"Yep."

"How do you think Paige is going to take it?"

"I have no idea. This is the weirdest, wackiest, off-the-wall thing I've ever done. She'll be surprised, that's for sure."

Taking my hand, my wife leads me over to an entrance on the ground floor and hits a square button next to the number 208.

"Who is it?" A tinny female voice comes from a speaker.

"It's me," Maelyn replies. "I lost my keys."

"Is that why your car was still at the Slippery Pole this morning?"

"Something like that."

"I'm so sorry if you tried to come home earlier. I was asleep and you know nothing wakes me."

"I didn't, and it's fine. Just let me up."

There's a buzz and a click, then we're inside a hallway lined with doors on the right, and a narrow staircase to the left. We ascend the stairs and walk until we come to Maelyn's door.

As soon as we step inside, my eyes scan the plain walls, the shabby gray couches, and the kitchen with a small square dining table with two chairs.

"I figured that junker you call a car finally gave out on you," a blonde on the couch says, her face turned toward the television flashing bright colors and loud music. She doesn't look this way as she continues shoveling wet-looking chunks into her mouth from a bowl with a spoon. "I tried to call your cell like a dozen times, but it went straight to voice mail."

"Lost my phone, too." Maelyn sets the new device onto the table. "Paige, I have someone I want you to meet."

Finally glancing our way, Paige drops the spoon into her bowl with a splash when she sees me. "And who do we have here?"

I don't miss the appraising tone or the way her eyes linger on all the parts of my body. I sense Maelyn's jealousy for a split-second before she tightens her hold on my arm. The arm that's shielding her pregnant belly.

"This is Zander." With a nudge to my back, Maelyn pushes us farther into the apartment until we're standing behind one of the couches.

Paige squints. "What happened to your glasses?"

"Lost those, too. A lot has happened." Maelyn takes a deep breath. "Listen, I'm going to start off by telling you that everything I'm about to say is going to sound crazy."

With a disbelieving smirk, Paige goes back to eating her meal while talking at the same time. "Your definition of crazy is different than mine." A few wet bits fall to the black leggings on her lap, but she doesn't bother to pick them up.

"What kind of soup is that?" I interject, both fascinated and repulsed by Paige's poor manners.

"It's Cheerios," Maelyn tells me with an amused smile. "Cereal. Breakfast food."

"It's five p.m. here."

"Judge-y." Insulted, Paige gapes at me, and some milk dribbles down her chin. "Maelyn, seriously, who is this guy?"

Maelyn gazes up at me with absolute love. "Zander is my husband."

Coughing, Paige wipes at her mouth with the back of her hand before grappling with the remote control. She doesn't take her eyes off us as she scrambles to turn off the racket coming from the television. "I'm sorry, what? I thought you just said your husband."

Maelyn nods. "I did."

"You're kidding."

"I'm really not."

"Do your parents know? Where did you meet him?" Now Paige is studying me with scrutiny, like I'm her enemy. "Does that mean you're moving out? Or is he moving in? I can't believe you got married without telling me first. I was supposed to be your maid of honor, bitch!"

Odd. She flings the insult, but her tone suggests it's a term of endearment. Unsure if I need to defend Maelyn's honor, I glance at her.

She doesn't look upset at all. "Paige, I told you I'm going to sound nuts, but what I need you to keep in mind is that I'm happy. So happy."

Paige's face softens, and I can tell she cares a great deal for Maelyn. "This is just so unlike you."

"There are things you don't know," Maelyn says softly, breaking away from me to move around the couch.

As soon as Paige gets a full view of Maelyn's stomach, she sets her half-full bowl down onto the table in front of her with a clatter. "Are you wearing a prego suit?"

"No."

Maelyn moves to sit next to her friend, and she starts filling her in on everything that's happened. The abduction. The marriage she didn't know she was agreeing to. Falling in love with me anyway. The curse.

The fated mate stuff is difficult for Paige to grasp. As a self-proclaimed cynic, she's never believed in soul mates or love at first sight.

But Maelyn's proof it's real.

I stand in place as she talks and talks, telling Paige about the kingdom, the palace, all our people, and how much time has passed.

"This can't be happening," Paige states, rubbing her temples. "You're pulling my leg. Are you getting me back for the time I tried to set you up with that bouncer from my work? Enzo wasn't so bad, okay? I had no idea he had a fiancée, and I thought you two might be a good match."

Unable to help myself, I growl at the thought of Maelyn

being with anyone else, and Paige's eyes go wide as saucers as she shrinks away from me.

"You believe in aliens, Paige." Maelyn tosses her hands up. "How is this all that different?"

"Because he's hot, and aliens aren't supposed to be hot."

A smile plays on my wife's lips. "He's not an alien. He's a faerie. Here…"

Picking up Paige's hand, Maelyn presses it to the curve of her stomach. Our child is already responsive to touch. Usually, if I poke around enough, I'll get a kick in return.

Apparently, so does Paige, because she shrieks and pulls her hand away. "There's something in there."

Maelyn laughs. "Right. It's called a baby. I'm telling you the truth. I just saw you this morning." She gestures to herself. "How would this be possible otherwise?"

Still as a statue and quiet as a mouse, Paige takes a full minute to let everything sink in.

Then her blue eyes glisten with unshed tears as she blinks at Maelyn. "So you're moving away? You're leaving, not just me, but this whole world entirely?"

Patting her friend's shoulder, Maelyn gives her a reassuring squeeze. "I was hoping I could convince you to come with me."

Several seconds pass. "To the faerie world?"

"To Valora, yes."

"You want me to leave all this behind?" Paige glances around the drab apartment, and I can't help chuckling. She glares at me. "What's so funny?"

"If you saw the room you'd have at the palace, you'd understand why I'm laughing." I come around the loveseat adjacent to the girls and sink to the creaky cushion. "You could be Maelyn's lady in waiting. It's a very prestigious position."

"Like her servant?"

"It's not like it sounds," Maelyn corrects. "You wouldn't be my maid or anything. More like my companion. My best friend."

"I am your best friend."

"Exactly. Only you'd be getting paid for it." Switching to a different tactic, Maelyn lays a protective palm over our unborn baby. "Loyalty is constantly in question in our kingdom. With you around, that's one less person I'd have to worry about. You'll always be on my side, and it would be an honor to have you on my team."

Paige is crying now, and I'm not sure if it's because she's touched by Maelyn's complimentary words or because she's not coming with us.

Then she looks to the bedroom that must be hers. "What am I supposed to do with all my stuff? Do I have time to pack?"

"Take some of your favorite things," Maelyn answers, "but everything will be provided for you. Zander and I already discussed it, and it would be a good idea to keep the apartment. We can come back once a year—remember, only a day will have passed here—and it'll be good to have a place to come to. Regardless of what you decide, Zander already paid up the rent for our lease."

Paige wears a shocked and grateful expression as she looks my way, and I just shrug because it's not a big deal. Apparently, pawn shops in the human world will pay a good sum for jewels the size of my thumbnail.

"Are all the guys there as hot as him?" Paige jerks her chin toward me, and Maelyn laughs.

"I think you'll be quite pleased with the male variety."

"But you said there's no Netflix?"

"No electronics at all."

"What about cars? How am I supposed to get around?"

"Well, portals, horses, or there might be men who'd be willing to fly you somewhere."

"Fly?" Paige squeaks.

"Come on." Maelyn uses her best convincing tone. "You're my missing piece. My life won't be the same without you."

Hence, the reason we're here. I know I'm enough to make Maelyn happy. But Paige is like a sister to my wife. She fills a role I can't.

It's like how I feel with my mother gone—something's missing.

I wish she were present for all my victories and milestones. I haven't heard back from Torius on her whereabouts or well-being, but I never expected to this soon.

"I can't believe you're having a baby." Paige can't stop staring at Maelyn's stomach. "That kid needs Auntie Paige."

"I know. I need you, too."

"Okay," Paige relents. "Well, then. I guess this is it. I'll go with you."

"Yes!" Maelyn cheers, engulfing Paige in a hug. "Now, call The Slippery Pole and tell them you quit. Then pack a bag."

♛

Paige packs four bags. Despite Maelyn telling her we'd provide clothes and toiletries, she wants to bring almost everything she has. I never knew a woman could have so many cosmetic products. I draw the line at perfume and hairspray. I'm not sure what the vapors would do to the sprites, so those items can't come with us.

"How are we getting there?" Paige asks behind me, her arms empty because I insisted on carrying all her belongings.

When did I go from king to concierge?

Add in Maelyn's luggage, and I've got three trash bags slung over my shoulder, a duffle on my elbow, and a rolling suitcase at my side.

"There's a portal in the alley," Maelyn tells her.

"I'm still skeptical. I don't think I'll believe it until I see it. This could be just a big prank."

"It's not. Remember the baby?"

"Right." Glancing over her shoulder, Paige gives me a look before muttering, "He doesn't talk much, does he?"

I smile as Maelyn says, "He's the strong, silent type."

"Ohh, you gotta look out for those," Paige responds, hushed. "They're the dirtiest talkers in the bedroom."

I can feel the heat from my wife's full-body blush.

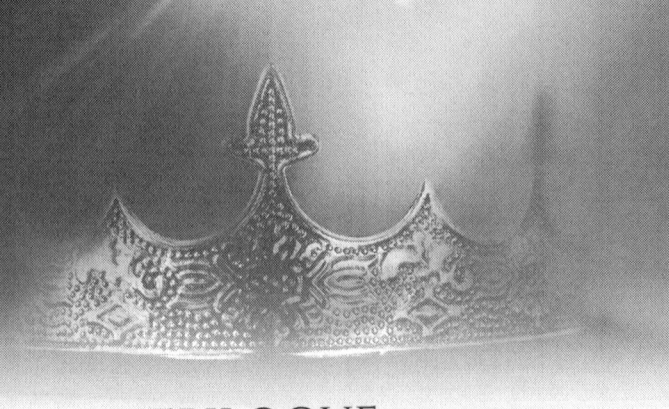

EPILOGUE

Ten Years Later
Maelyn

"Checkmate," my handsome husband says from the life-size chess board we built out in the yard.

Zaylee gapes at her father. "You cheated."

"I never cheat. You know that."

"You never let me win either," Zaylee grumbles.

"Now what would be the fun in that?"

"Um, victory?"

Zander just laughs.

"It's my turn!" Maverick jumps up from the bench beside me to help put the pieces back where they belong.

"Good luck." Zaylee pats her little brother on the shoulder as he passes her.

Although he's younger, he's not smaller. The siblings are just over twelve months apart, and they're the same height.

Zander and I had no idea I'd get pregnant again so fast after Zaylee's birth, but it happened. At that rate, we thought we'd have a soccer team of kids by now, but it wasn't meant to be. Despite our vigorous efforts, Maverick is probably our last baby. I've accepted that, and I'm truly satisfied with our family.

Both the kids are the spitting image of their father. Jet-black strands. Golden eyes. Their skin is paler, like mine, but the contrast with their hair only makes them more striking.

Zander had been terrified that his shifting ability would get passed down, but it didn't.

Lucky for the kids, some fae power filtered through their genes. Both of them have Pyro power, likely inherited from Zarid and Zella in the family line. Though they're not intensely strong, it's better than nothing.

Aside from my ability to communicate with Zander when he's in griffin form, I never developed a power. It's fine. We knew it was a good possibility that I wouldn't. However, I did grow wings. A few years ago, the iridescent flaps finally got big enough for me to get into the air. I can't go long distances, but if we need to fly somewhere, Zander's always happy to shift into the griffin and let me ride on his back.

Zaylee's yellow dress swishes around her legs as she makes her way to me. Morose, she sits with a huff.

"Someday you'll beat him," I tell her, "and when you do, it'll be the sweetest triumph because you'll know you earned it."

"Like you did with Grandma?"

Giving her a bittersweet smile, I nod. The kids have been told all about Grandma Ro. If she comes back someday, we want them to feel like they've known her all along. I understand why she had to leave—she has a family out there. A life she was ripped from without closure.

Of course, we hope she'll return to us after she finds whatever it is she's looking for. I just wish that day would come sooner rather than later. For Zander's sake.

He can't wait to show her how successful the kingdom is. The Day Realm is thriving. It's been a long road, but crime has been almost completely eliminated.

Peace and prosperity like Valora's never known has spread across the lands.

The three kings—once united in their curses—are now

allies with their strength. More than that, they're friends. Family.

Speaking of friends and family, I spot Paige, Thayne, and Pippin coming out of the front entrance of the palace.

Paige flirtatiously bumps Thayne's shoulder, but I know it's nothing serious. They had a short fling when she first arrived, but the romance quickly fizzled out before she moved onto her next conquest. I can't fault her for dating. She's been having the time of her life here, living with me, swimming in luxury, and acquiring an endless string of boyfriends.

Zaylee perks up and waves at Pippin. "Hide-and-seek! Start counting, and don't even think about using your power to find me." She backs away toward the maze, but Paige stops her with a shake of her head.

"It's time to go or we'll be late."

Having Auntie Paige around has been quite handy when it comes to the kids. She's always up for babysitting, and no one can manage a schedule like her.

Zander and Maverick put their chess game on pause, and I meet them in the open area where Thayne likes to use his portals. In the few seconds it takes for him to open the portal box and choose the correct one, Zander and I come together like magnets.

Sweeping me into his arms, my husband gives me a kiss. My fingers weave through his hair, careful not to disturb his crown—a new crown we had designed for him soon after we got married. It's a simple band with no jewels, and it matches my rose gold tiara.

During our years together, my craving for him has gotten out of control. I want him all the time. It's like each day together strengthens our tether, sewing our souls together until I don't know the difference between mine and his.

As his tongue plunges into my mouth, I think about skipping the Dream Realm festival. We could send everyone else along while staying home to get lost in each other for a few uninterrupted hours.

Although the kids are used to our affectionate ways, they groan with disgust.

"Get a room," they both say at the same time, then bust out laughing.

Snickering, Paige ruffles Maverick's hair. "Just wait until you find your lady. Then you'll understand."

"I don't want a mate," he shoots back. "Thayne says it makes people crazy."

"That it does." Zander laughs, and I love the sound.

My broody man still frowns, but his laughs are more common than his scowls these days.

"Hey, princess." Pippin turns his back toward Zaylee and crouches a little. "Your piggy-back ride awaits, milady."

Entering the Dream Realm is always a bit disorienting. The adjustment from bright sunlight to dark star-filled skies makes all of us blink as we look toward the glowing castle in Cassia. The temperature drop is always shocking, too. In an instant, we've gone from sweating in the heat to crisp air with snow flurries tumbling from the sky. It feels good.

Thayne placed the portal around the back of the palace, and the outdoor party is already underway. With a carnival-like set up, there are tents with games and vendors selling handmade goods.

The kids cheer when they spot Danyetta, Kirian and Quinn's daughter, by a dunk tank with a jester inside. At fourteen, she's a beautiful young lady, with long light-brown hair and lavender eyes.

Aeryn and Micah, Damon and Whitley's daughter and youngest son, capture my kids in a group hug. Soon after, Kirian and Quinn's twin boys, Caspian and Cassidy, join in. The six of them are so close in age, it makes me wonder if the older ones ever feel like they're herding cattle when all the kids get together.

Kallum, Damon and Whitley's first child, is twelve, so he has more in common with Dani. I watch them exchange an amused look before Dani asks the kids what they want to do first.

"Stick together," Zander calls out, "and be back here in four hours."

Pippin sends us a wink as he discreetly follows after them from an unnoticeable distance. He's been a great bodyguard to me and I'm glad to be able to call him a friend. Sadly for him, Zander never lifted the celibacy order. My husband says it keeps the soldier focused and more responsible.

"What would you like to do?" Zander nuzzles a spot behind my ear. "I can buy you some new dresses."

Fighting off a shiver, I scan the crowd. "We should probably greet the other kings and queens."

A show of unity is always important.

Zander hums low. "Or we could take part in a game."

Even after a decade, my husband still loves to play. I glance around at the different booths. "What did you have in mind?"

His eyes dart to the enchanted forest in the distance. "I bet there are lots of places to hide in there."

Oh, I know what that means. Our games of hide-and-seek aren't so innocent. They always end with orgasms.

"The sprites would see," I hiss at him, scandalized at his suggestion.

"Let them."

"They'll talk."

"Good. I want everyone in Valora to know how well I ravaged my wife."

"If you get this dress dirty..." I let the half-hearted threat hang in the air.

Tabitha spent a week on all these cotton-candy pink layers, and I won't let them get smudged up.

"There are ways to get to your pussy while keeping your gown in pristine condition, Mae."

My heart flutters and flips. I still remember how annoyed I

was when he'd first called me Mae. How presumptuous it seemed. Now I can't imagine him calling me anything else, unless it's *wife*.

Zander's thumbs brush the underside of my breasts while he whispers, "You have a ten-second head start."

"Ten? That's not enough."

"It's not supposed to be."

As I turn to run, I lift my skirt and glance over my shoulder at Zander's devilish smirk. Heart hammering, I dash toward the trees. I've just passed the enchanted barrier when I hear Zander laugh behind me.

He's too close.

There's no way he waited the full ten seconds.

Refusing to look back, I slip behind a large bush and wait. I listen for footsteps or twigs snapping.

Nothing.

My pulse pounds faster.

I peer in the direction I came, expecting Zander to jump out any moment now.

Instead, arms wrap around me from behind, and more wicked snickering tickles my ear.

"I've captured you. What are you going to do now?" He places a kiss on the side of my neck.

I turn my head over my shoulder and cup his jaw. Tenderly stroking his face, I kiss his lips. "Stay with you. Forever."

THE END

A note to the reader: Thanks for reading Zander and Maelyn's story! If this is your first introduction to the world of Valora, you can read the other kings' books in *The Fae King's Curse* (Kirian and Quinn) and *The Fae King's Dream* (Damon and Whitley). Also, you can get the prequel *Between Dawn and Dusk* (Keryth and Zella) for FREE by signing up for my newsletter.

If you're on Facebook and you'd like to interact with me and other readers who love my books, you should join my group Jamie Schlosser's Significant Otters!
www.facebook.com/groups/1738944743038479

OTHER BOOKS BY JAMIE SCHLOSSER

The Good Guys Series:
TRUCKER
A Trucker Christmas (Short Story)
DANCER
DROPOUT
OUTCAST
MAGIC MAN

The Good Guys Box Set

The Night Time Television Series:
Untamable
Untrainable
Unattainable

The Night Time Television Box Set

Standalone Novellas:
His Mimosa
Sweet Dreams

Between Dawn and Dusk Series:
Between Dawn and Dusk
The Fae King's Curse
The Fae King's Dream
The Fae King's Prize

ABOUT THE AUTHOR

Jamie Schlosser writes steamy new adult romance, romantic comedy, and fantasy romance. When she isn't creating perfect book boyfriends, she's a stay-at-home mom to her two wonderful kids. She believes reading is a great escape, otters are the best animal, and nothing is more satisfying than a happily-ever-after ending. You can find out more about Jamie and her books by visiting these links:

Facebook: www.facebook.com/authorjamieschlosser

Amazon: amzn.to/2mzCQkQ

Instamgram: www.instagram.com/jschlosserauthor

Bookbub: www.bookbub.com/authors/jamie-schlosser

Newsletter: eepurl.com/cANmI9

Website: www.jamieschlosser.com

Printed in Great Britain
by Amazon